Not Quite Out

Louise Willingham

SRL Publishing Ltd

SRL Publishing Ltd
Office 47396
PO Box 6945
London, W1A 6US

First published worldwide by SRL Publishing in 2021

ISBN: 978-191633736-7

This book is for everyone who ever felt like they weren't quite enough.

One

I meet Dan on a Monday afternoon, when the cold September weather cuts across campus and catches fallen leaves in little tornadoes. My first lecture of the year starts in an hour, and the notes I've spent all morning trying to revise slip from my mind as soon as I reach the Students' Union.

The doors slide open to let me in and I shake some of the cold from my hands. It's busy so I join the queue for food, counting coins into my palm. My stomach rumbles at the smell of hot food and I'm looking down, hoping no one heard, when the door opens again.

A gust of wind comes through with the next group of people, and everyone around me looks up. A few leaves have skipped across the mat and I'm caught watching them for a second, letting a gap open up in the queue.

I look up, a moment late, and see Lilley for the first time in months. She's remarkably close, like she's considering joining the queue, and freezes when she sees me. I regret smiling at her almost before the movement's finished because the guy she's with notices and frowns between us.

'Who's this, Lil?'

'Just Will,' she says, sighing and doing a great job of looking anywhere but at me. Nice. It's too late to ignore each other now and she presses her lips together. 'Have you seen Cassie yet?'

'No.' I'm amazed I manage to make a sound.

I'd love to be able to ask Lilley how she is, but she shrugs and turns to face the guy she's with. I haven't given him a second glance. Lilley's dark hair is a little bit tangled at the back, messed by the wind, and it's cut differently to the last time I saw her. Between staring at her and imagining teasing out those knots with my fingers, I've almost worked out how to speak again when she starts to walk away.

'Fine. See you around.' She catches the guy's arm in hers without looking back at me.

I don't even say *bye*. I just watch her go, feeling like I've missed a step, and try to process that incredibly awkward exchange with my ex-girlfriend.

A gap has opened ahead of me in the queue, so I shuffle forward with my eyes back on my shoes.

I haven't spoken to Lilley since I dumped her before summer exams and I definitely hadn't even considered that she'd be the first person I have a conversation with this semester.

I don't think I recognise the guy she was with, so I guess he must be someone from her course. Maybe I should have paid him more attention. The only one of Lilley's friends I ever got on with was Cassie because, like this year, some of her biology modules were shared with my medicine course. Cassie's easy to spend an evening with. Lilley's… difficult.

It's not like we didn't get on while we were dating. It simply became clear after a few months that we just expected opposite things from a partner: I wanted to spend every moment with her, and two hours a week with me were enough for Lilley. Officially, I ended the relationship. It saved her feeling like she'd made me cry.

I'm slow to look up when I reach the food counter, still thinking I should have said something pleasant to her, and make a highly unattractive 'hmm?' when the guy serving asks me what I want.

He's very tall. I have to tip my head back to make eye contact with him and, once again, I've forgotten how to speak.

He's smirking at me.

I clear my throat, shuffle the coins in my suddenly sweaty hand, and drop one. Shit. I force a laugh as I bend to pick it up and stand again with a face like a tomato, thinking I'm quite lucky to have not hit my head on the way.

'Hi—sorry, lost in thought.' Terrible laugh.

He's still smirking, waiting for me to pull myself together like he has all the time in the world.

'Jacket potato, please.'

'It happens to us all,' he says, giving me a bright grin and turning around to grab a polystyrene box. Where's that accent from? He stretches his neck to look back at me and I blink a few times. 'What do you want on it?'

'Just cheese, please,' I manage, cringing at the rhyme.

'Here you go. Don't drop it.' He winks, flashing the blue of his irises.

Something in my chest shatters, like a hammer to ice.

A pin-badge on his shirt tells me his name is Daniel and I'm a moment away from introducing myself, as if he's asked for *my* name. But he hands me the box, the dark ink of a tattoo showing under his sleeve, and moves seamlessly to the next customer and my chance has gone. I haven't even said *thanks*. Burning bright red, I shuffle towards the till and pay with my coins.

I walk away, moving blindly through the busy room, and forget to collect a plastic fork.

I'm through the door and back outside before I realise my mistake and there is no way I'm going back in there to make a fool out of myself. No, thanks. Instead, I make the only slightly less uncomfortable walk into one of the other food outlets and grab one of their forks.

I perch against a soggy brick wall, facing away from the SU, and spend a minute just staring into empty space. As lunch times go, that couldn't have gone much worse. Well, it could—

I could have dropped the food.

God, I can't get that teasing wink out of my head. I start eating, trying to distract myself, but it's not going well. I feel a bit sick. Every breath is uncomfortable, like the shards of ice are cutting my lungs. Daniel's accent is unlike anything I've ever heard and I'm certain I'm still blushing.

There's one real reason I chose Keele University above all others: the LGBT society. Specifically, the male co-president. After slipping away from my parents at the open day three summers ago, I made a beeline for the society stands and stumbled to a stop in front of a rainbow flag personalised with black sharpie names. The co-president grinned at me, stunned

3

me with his blonde and cherry hair, and told me very confidently that *everyone* was welcome at their society. The society meets every Monday, and I've been going as a semi-regular ally for a whole year next week.

Ally, because I still haven't quite worked out how people pronounce the words *'I'm bisexual'*.

Anyway, my failed relationship with Lilley taught me something: I don't even *want* a relationship at the moment. I was overly clingy and desperate to make everything perfect, but I can't say I've missed putting kisses on the end of texts and spending the night in her room. My degree work fills the evenings and I have placements this year, so I'm not going to have time to live across two bedrooms.

Daniel's voice and that sneak-peek of a tattoo are almost enough to convince me otherwise.

I hadn't realised tattoos were a *thing* for me until about ten minutes ago. Maybe it wasn't the ink so much as the tone of the muscle beneath the illustrations—maybe it was his voice, or his white teeth, or the knowing grin when my cheeks burned red.

I crush my mostly empty polystyrene box into the nearest bin and turn, ready to leave lunch behind and get to my first lecture of second year.

Daniel walks straight into me and I make a noise a bit like a startled hen.

'Sorry,' he mutters, head down and blue eyes reluctant to look up.

Where's that smirk gone? I can feel my pulse in my throat and swallow quickly.

'It's fine, it's me. I'm not with it.' I duck my head, trying to see his face. 'You okay?'

He finally glances up and, recognising me, turns pale. Like the sort of face you make when you realise the deadline you thought was tomorrow is in fact *today*.

'Yeah,' he breathes, right before shaking his head. 'Sorry.'

And he's gone.

I watch him march up the hill to the library, hands stuffed

in his pockets and ears hidden in his shoulders. Has he just been sacked? Why else would he be leaving work at lunch time? I stare at him for far too long, until he's disappeared up the steps and through the sliding doors. I almost follow him.

Hey, is on my tongue. *What's wrong? I'm not going to hurt you.*

Because, I realise, walking again to my lecture, he looked like he was anticipating pain. And it's unnerving, but not so upsetting I forget to grin when I see Cassie across the square in the middle of campus.

*

By the time I get to my room, all thoughts of Daniel have been replaced with work. My first assignment of the year is due in three weeks, and I should probably start working on that this evening. My first year of studying medicine was exhausting, but I like to think I know what to expect now. Even so, I'm somehow already behind on reading and I really don't have time to daydream about cute café workers.

I chuck my bag on the floor, kick off my shoes and sit on the edge of my bed. I'll take my jacket off in a moment, once I've warmed up, and I pull out my phone.

No messages.

I twist so I can sit back against the headboard and open Facebook, instead. My sister, Kirst, has clogged my timeline by sharing tragic post after tragic post about lost cats, so I refresh the screen and check the Freshers' page, instead. Here, the lost and found posts are less heart-wrenching: missing notebooks, student cards, and memory sticks.

I stop scrolling, a lump in my throat.

I haven't thought about last year's revision notes since I left the library. Even worse, I haven't thought about the memory stick they're saved on since I plugged it into the library computer.

I sit up sharply and grab my bag to shake its pitiful contents onto the floor. Pens. Tissues. Spare change. More pens. A battered box of plasters.

No memory stick.

I swear and check my pockets.

Nope. I start typing into the *write something* box.

William Anson: *Hey, I'm an idiot and left my memory stick in the library. Near the door in computer lab 3. Anyone seen it? need it back desperately!*

And I wait.

But not for long. Notifications fly in—Cassie likes it. People from my course like it. People I've never spoken to like it.

Daniel Taylor: *One like this?*

It's my memory stick and the profile picture is someone I can't believe I recognise. I click on it before trying to word a response and hit a brick wall: his profile is locked. Privacy is sky-high. I can't even send him a friend request, let alone see his date of birth or relationship status.

It's Daniel.

William Anson: *THAT'S IT oh my gosh thank you! Are you still on campus?*

Daniel Taylor: *Yes. Can you meet me downstairs in the SU?*

I reply with a thumbs-up emoji and drag my shoes back on, hands slipping from the backs. I hit my wrist against the metal underside of the bed and swear and I'm totally expecting to fall over on my way across campus.

Of all the people here at Keele, he had to be the one who found my notes. Haven't I embarrassed myself in front of him enough already?

The evening air hits me in a blast as soon as I step out of my building and I shiver. Summer is definitely over and I'm glad I kept my jacket on. I reach the SU in record time, powered forward by the wind licking at my neck and ears, and scan for him. It's still busy, full of people who are excited to reunite with friends after the summer break, so I *excuse me* my way through the crowds.

There he is. Looking at the floor, leaning against a table and spinning my memory stick between his finger and thumb.

'I believe you have something of mine,' I say, and some god must be watching over me because my voice doesn't wobble. It doesn't crack and I don't sound like a startled chicken.

He looks up at me without lifting his head. 'I can't be long.' Disappointment settles in my stomach. 'I think I used the computer after you.'

'Yeah, probably.' Someone should turn down the heating. 'What were you in the library for?'

What a stupid, personal question. He hesitates, like he can't work out why on Earth I asked. I don't know, either.

'Printing an ingredients list.' He drops the stick very softly into my hand. 'I left it, but it was still there after my shift.'

I can't even blink. 'Thanks for going back for it. Did you have a look through?'

'Should I have?'

'Well, I guess it would be a way of me proving it's mine.'

He forces a little laugh and puts his hands in his pockets, looking everywhere but at me. The disappointment trembles.

'I believe you. Maybe you should attach it to your keys.'

'Then I'd just lose my keys,' I point out. He doesn't try another laugh. 'Hey, thanks, though. I mean it.'

'Not a problem.'

'Would have been for me if you hadn't found it.' There's an almost awkward silence, but I jabber forward and tell him something he already knows. 'I'm William, by the way.'

'Daniel,' he sighs, as if it were a secret he was trying to keep hidden.

Maybe we should shake hands. His are firmly in his pockets now he doesn't have my memory stick to play with, and I can't quite equate this bowed head and hunched shoulders with the guy who served me a jacket potato and a beaming smile a few hours ago. He's twitchy, forehead and cheeks shining under a thin layer of sweat. I can't help but wonder if he's ill and I'm trying to get a decent look at his face but we haven't made eye contact even once.

I'm still spilling words. 'Do you live on campus?'

He nods. 'Z sheds.'

'Oh, that's near me!' I sound far too pleased about this and clear my throat. 'I'm in K. Are you going there now?'

'No, I have somewhere else to be,' he mutters, eyes on the ground again as he pushes away from the table. He towers over me, even when he's so clearly trying to make himself look smaller and turns away. 'Take care.'

'You too. Thanks again!'

Something is wrong. I can taste it around him, like smoke after you blow out a candle.

Two

Cassie and I are in the SU on Friday night. It's the first Friday of the semester, so the bars are hot with crowds of sweaty students and the walls are slick with condensation. If it weren't for alcohol, I don't think I'd enjoy it even slightly.

'Something happened this week you're not telling me,' Cassie shouts. My vision is a little hazy and the bass of the music pulses through my chest, making it difficult to hear her.

I pull a face.

'Spill.'

I haven't seen Dan since Monday.

I blow raspberries and finish the room-temperature dregs of cider left in my cup. 'Nothing happened.'

'Will, you are the *worst* liar.'

'I met someone,' I snap. 'A new friend, maybe. And he's—I dunno. I'm worried about him.'

'Worried? Why?'

I don't really believe she cares. I tell her, anyway, tapping my fingers against the clear plastic of my cup and failing to make eye contact.

'He seemed really—I dunno. Twitchy? One moment he was lovely and smiley, the next he looked like he wanted to run into the woods and never be seen again.'

Cassie laughs. 'Sounds mad.'

I don't like that. 'He was nice. Found my memory stick.'

'Oh!' Cassie pulls her phone out of her bra with fumbling hands and makes a great show out of tapping the screen with her index finger. 'Daniel!'

She finds the post and shows me the screen, as if I need to be reminded what he looks like.

'Oh, he's cute,' she says, zooming in on the picture. 'He works downstairs now, right?

Throat tight, I nod.

'He's Russian, I think. I know him. Well, his boyfriend lived upstairs in my block last year, so close enough.'

The cider I just finished drinking threatens to come back up. Even in the dim lighting of the SU, Cassie can see something's wrong.

'You look sweaty. Want to step out?'

I nod, pretty sure if I open my mouth I'm going to be sick and follow her to the outdoors stairs. We slip and slide down them, through the cold night and into the smoking area. It's much easier to talk out here, and I could do with the air. Even if I must share it with cigarette smoke.

Boyfriend.

I *bet* he noticed the way I gawked at him. I've got used to not letting myself hope the gorgeous boys on campus are also queer but, for once, I might be in luck. Maybe this is how I finally come out to my friends. My heart's racing, caught up in some ridiculous daydream where I'm brave enough to tell a *guy* I'm attracted to him, and I'm glad my hands are free. I push them into my hair, trying to look like I'm enjoying the cool breeze.

Cassie is still talking.

'I forgot all about him over the summer, but I recognised him the other day.' She pauses to squint at me. 'What's up with you?'

'I—nothing,' I say, hands slipping behind my head. 'It was warm.'

'Yeah, it was.'

'Something about a boyfriend?'

I must have spoken too quickly because she gives me a funny look. 'Yeah. I guess they're still together, but they argued *loads* last year. Like, shouting most nights. I dunno, though. He always seemed quite sweet. He's got a cute little smile, you know? I hope he's alright. I think he was studying politics.'

Boyfriend.

I'm thinking of about five things at once, imagining a beautiful fantasy where I stretch up and kiss him while also boiling under jealousy that Cassie knows him better than I do and trying to not get my hopes up too high—he has a *boyfriend*—and wondering what sort of small-talk you can make with a politics student from Russia. One thought cuts through the rest and I turn grey.

'What did they shout about?' I ask, remembering fidgety hands and reluctant eyes.

'I dunno. Just relationship stuff. I don't see why people bother getting into serious relationships at our age—it's just asking for extra stress. Especially dating guys—sorry, Will, but your whole species is a headache.'

I just about roll my eyes. 'What's his boyfriend like?'

'Oh, he's horrible,' Cassie shudders, which turns into a genuine shiver, and looks up and down me. 'Why?'

My mouth opens and closes a couple of times. I can't exactly say *because I think I could treat him better*, can I?

'I think there's more to their relationship than you've seen,' I manage, thoughts whirring. 'You said they shout.'

Her lips purse. 'Yeah. Dan can definitely do better.'

Is she hinting?

'I'm not sure it's a *good* relationship, if you know what I mean.' Cassie shivers again, and I wish she'd wear something warmer. 'They were always going out and getting drunk, but Dan just seemed miserable all the time.'

My heart lurches. 'No one should be in a relationship that makes them miserable.'

'No, I know.' She squints at me, like she's only just catching up. 'What are you thinking?'

I'm jittering. Maybe the cold's getting to me, too. 'I think I know why Dan was so apologetic, and why he wouldn't look me in the eye, and why he practically ran away when I asked where he lives.'

Cassie opens her mouth to say something, but the curse of a tiny campus strikes again. Daniel could be anywhere, doing anything, but right now he's walking down the steps to the smoking shelter and we make eye contact.

His eyes—

I skip past Cassie and head straight towards him, certain he'll try to turn and run without letting me have this

11

conversation.

I'm quick enough that he doesn't have time to react and I speak without thinking.

'Hey—hey,' I skid to a stop at the foot of the steps and stretch my neck to look up at him. 'How are you?'

He blinks and looks away from me. I think I can see the pulse in his neck.

'I wondered if you wanted to spend time with us.' It's so weak I cringe. 'I'd like to spend more time with you. I'd like to be your friend.'

Dan takes a slow, measured breath and shakes his head. 'No, thank you.'

He's purposefully hiding his face from me, but I'm sure his eyes are swollen and red like he's been crying. I can't blame him for wanting to come outside, and now I've got in the way and made him uncomfortable.

Dammit. 'Well,' I say slowly, 'I guess I'll see you around. You can talk to me whenever, alright? I could give you my—'

He shakes his head again but, this time, his lips twitch in a small smile. It looks sad. 'Please don't.'

I'm right.

I'm right, and he's trying to tell me. If he didn't want me to keep an eye out for him, if he really wanted me to leave him alone, he could just turn and run. But of course he doesn't want another guy's number in his phone.

'See you on Monday?' I try instead, because I know just how important it is for someone in Dan's situation to know they've got someone thinking about them.

He hesitates. Nods. Turns on the step and leaves.

I watch him go and just about convince myself to not chase after him.

'I see your point,' Cassie says from right behind me.

I turn, feeling grey, and pull a face at her.

'You gonna talk to Kirst?'

I rub my forehead. I wish I'd had slightly less alcohol—or slightly more. 'I don't—maybe. But her experience isn't a resource for me, y'know?'

'I know, but it might help to know what she'd have found useful in a situation like—like this,' Cassie waves vaguely at the stairs. 'He looked high.'

I recoil. 'You think?'

'Don't tell me you didn't see.'

Ah. Maybe I got it wrong. Maybe he was hiding his face because his eyes were red for a different reason. I feel this possibility add to an ever-growing stack of problems and groan.

'Shit, Cas.'

'Can't help him right now,' she says, slipping her arm through mine and walking past me to start climbing the stairs. 'Come on. Talk to Kirst tomorrow.'

*

My sister is six years older than me. When she's not sharing posts about lost pets, she's working as a lab technician using her master's degree in organic chemistry. I think she's half the reason I wanted to study medicine.

I don't think I'm going to forgive myself for being so slow to notice something was wrong.

Kirst had been dating her boyfriend for about two years before our parents grew suspicious. While she was at university, we didn't worry about hearing from her every day, or even every week. We didn't think we needed to.

Everything fell apart last Christmas, while I was home after being away for nearly four months. Kirst and her boyfriend visited, but something was off and hung around us, like the smell of mouldy bread in a kitchen cupboard and we just didn't mention it. It wasn't our business if they'd been arguing.

When they came over again for New Year's Eve, she had a bruise across her cheekbone and angry red marks around her wrists.

I've never seen Mum move so fast. She grabbed Kirst, snatched her from the boyfriend's arms, and dragged her into the house. I spent the following argument sat in the bathroom with her, wiping tears from her cheeks and brushing away her endless apologies. It wasn't the *happy new year* we'd been expecting, but at least Kirst never had to see that guy again.

She moved back home for a couple of months but, by the time I'd come home for the summer between first and second year, she'd moved into her own flat. My parents and sister navigated the fall-out following New Year without involving me in the details, but I'm certain it wasn't the first time he'd hurt her.

And I'm fairly sure Daniel's relationship is hurting him.

Three

The next time I see Daniel, my heart sinks right through the floor.

It's Monday lunch time, and I'm so nervous I'm not even hungry. I've been rehearsing what I'm going to say to him all weekend. I jitter through the door into the SU as soon as it's open wide enough, hands trying to keep warm in my coat pockets. My eyes flash to the counter and he's there, heartbreakingly gorgeous and looking for all the world like nothing's wrong. Everyone he serves is getting a beautiful, polite smile, and I stand still to watch him for a moment, like how you might catch yourself gazing at a sculpture.

I chew my cheeks and join the back of the queue, hoping he hasn't seen me and hoping he doesn't ask someone to cover for him for the next couple of minutes.

I adopt his hunched, identity-concealing stance and shuffle until I'm at the counter. It gets harder to breathe with each step.

'Oh.'

At the sound of his voice I look up, feeling like I've been punched in the stomach. Did I actually hear him say that?

His expression is flat. 'What can I get you?'

I'm about to ask for my usual, but something awful catches my eye. 'Could—what have you done to your hand?'

He snatches his left hand from the counter and hides it behind his back. 'Nothing. What can I get you?'

Oh, shit.

I gag for a moment on my words before managing to say, 'jacket potato, please'.

He doesn't smile, and that pushes something sharp between my ribs. Swollen black and blue knuckles were the last thing I'd expected to see. He's punched someone—or something. Was it self-defence? Retaliation? Something worse?

15

I'm not fully paying attention when he asks his next question.

'Cheese?'

A slow puncture develops in my lungs and I stand there, mouth open. Maybe he doesn't want to be as distant from me as I thought.

'I—' Anything I'd planned on saying has slipped from my mind and I'm lucky to manage a syllable. 'Yeah. Yeah, please.'

He adds the cheese, gives me a tiny smile like he couldn't help it, and hands me the box with his good hand. 'You're welcome.'

Shit. 'Thank you.'

We've made eye-contact. I'm useless. Maybe it's the electric of the SU lights, but his eyes are the brightest things I've ever seen, and I'm hypnotised like a moth. The soft skin beneath them is a little bit dark and it looks too delicate, like he's never felt fully refreshed. And I know. God, I know.

He blinks and we look away and I am pissed with myself. A massive gap has opened in front of me and there's a line of people waiting to be served and I wish I thought he was going to trust me.

'Speak soon,' I blurt, because he's just about still smiling.

The smile drops but he nods, practically giving me palpitations.

Unable to help myself, I glance at his damaged hand as I shuffle towards the till. I pay for my food. Remember a fork. Glance back again as I walk away to see him smiling at the next customer.

There's even more competition for space in the SU today, and the colder weather is entirely to blame, so I spend a moment trying to find somewhere indoors to sit. The single space I find is facing away from the counter, so I can't stare at Daniel, and this is probably a good thing.

Oh, God, he's done something awful. Something horrible has happened and I bet it's not the first time and I would bet my degree that it's to do with his boyfriend.

Four

Only having time to go to the SU for lunch once a week never irritated me before. I'm desperate to see Daniel, but every spare moment is spent researching or revising, and Monday can't come soon enough. I rush out of the library at twelve, slip and slide down the rain-washed path to the SU, and scan for him like I'm already so used to doing.

He isn't there.

Instead, there's a stupid little lump in my throat that tastes of disappointment.

I tell myself he might be in the back of the kitchen and I still have a bubble of hope in my chest, even when I'm asking someone else for my jacket potato. Cheese. Even when I pay.

It bursts from me, like air from a punctured balloon.

'Where's Dan?' I try to make it sound like I'm friends with him.

It works because the guy taking my money falters and his expression drops.

'You haven't heard?'

I try to control my imagination and shake my head, palm sweating between us.

'Shit. Are you his friend?'

I'm picturing the very worst. 'I mean, we talk.' I sound like I'm not breathing. 'We've talked quite a bit. I thought—'

'Shit.' He glances down at the queue and leans over the till to whisper to me. 'He doesn't want loads of people to know, but he was taken to hospital Friday night.'

Vomit rises in my throat.

'He fell down some stairs and broke his ribs.'

That's code.

I know that code.

What happened to your wrist, Kirst?

Oh, I fell over on some ice...

I swallow and nod. 'Thanks for letting me know. If you talk to him and he wants to know tell him you told me—I'm William.' The world sways, like I'm trying to stay balanced on a floating piece of foam. 'He—yeah. Shit.'

The guy frowns. 'He's okay. Promise. I'm Owen, by the way.'

I realise far too late that I should have shaken his hand. I just nod and pick up my food, which I really don't want now, and step away. 'William. Speak soon.'

Owen watches me as I go and, of course, I march straight past the plastic forks. This time, I don't care about being embarrassed and double back, snatch one up in a sweaty hand, and sit in the first empty seat I see.

I hold my box, lid closed, for a long time.

I'm struck, as I sit there between strangers, that I don't know *who* Dan's boyfriend is. It could be Owen, but I doubt it. He wouldn't have been so willing to tell me what's happened, would he? It could be any of the guys around me, and I'm scrutinising them now as if one is going to do an evil villain laugh and give me a side-eye. They all look completely normal.

But, of course, this is how this works.

Anyone could be the person who pushed Dan down the stairs, or kicked him hard enough to break his ribs, and I'm sliding into a pit of despair when Peter stands in front of me, blocking the SU from view.

I'm sure he's been sent here by some greater power to look out for me. He has the round baby face of a cherub but that's not all: Peter has an uncanny ability to find me whenever I feel like the world's ending, and I'm terrible at returning the favour. Today, I see him and almost cry.

'You look shit,' he says brightly, and it's the first thing we've said to each other this semester. 'Coming to the social tonight?'

I pull a face. 'As your wing man?'

'Please, dear.' He plonks himself down on the chair opposite me and looks at my chilling food. 'The freshers will all be there and I'm only going to be one year older than them max.'

I roll my eyes.

'Some might be older than us and it's an excellent opportunity to meet other people—'

'You want me to help you talk to cute boys?'

'Yep.'

Peter is gay. We became instant friends last year and he's the main reason I keep going to the LGBT socials. I can't bear to play *Cards Against Humanity* with anyone else, and he's genuinely interested in my medicine course.

Why haven't I told him I'm bi? I haven't got a clue. Every time I think about it, he calls me *dear* or gives me a hug and it feels ill-timed. It looks like I'm hinting for something. He's adorable, and the best friend I could ask for, but I don't have a crush on him. That's one thing I know for certain.

'I'll come.' I kick his shin softly. 'But I do feel shit.'

'Tell me.'

'Just discovered a friend broke his ribs this weekend.'

Peter takes one of my hands from the box and gives it a squeeze, waiting for more details. I'm not going to give him any.

'But—but hey. He's gonna be alright.' I don't sound convinced.

'You're sure?'

'Yeah.'

'You heard from him?'

'From a mutual friend.' I guess Owen could be a friend. 'But it's fine. He's with people who can help, I've got a busy afternoon of academia lined up, and then I get to take you out on the pull.'

'That's damn right,' Peter says, grinning at me but still holding my hand. 'Eat your lunch, stupid.'

*

Cassie comes and finds me before Peter leaves, and I'm grateful for the company. I'm irritable and twitchy, bouncing my leg, and having someone there makes it more difficult for

19

me to descend into a complete panic.

'So, you're distracted,' Cassie says, arm through mine as we walk across campus together. It's a ten-minute walk from the SU to today's lecture room, and most of that is uphill. Everything at Keele is uphill. 'What's up?'

'Nothing,' I mutter. 'I just feel a bit off.'

Why don't I just tell her about Daniel?

Last week, when it was just a bruised hand, I managed to bite down the worry. I manged to greet Cassie with a smile like every other week and pretend I wasn't spending every second thought thinking about Daniel. But this week it's different. It's harder. I don't think I'm breathing properly because I'm imagining shattered ribs and punctured lungs—

'You look it.'

'Thanks.'

'You gonna sulk all the way through micro?'

'I'm not sulking,' I snap, and she pulls her chin back to hit me with a glare. 'I'm just stressed. How was your morning?'

I love her for how easily she accepts the change of subject.

'Shit,' she says. 'I overslept, so I haven't washed my hair and I realised there's a fact sheet I'm meant to submit by midnight which is currently just a list of bullet points.'

'Oh, Cas.'

'I know. But it's fine, because I have a seminar after this but then I'm just gonna sit in the library until it's all done. It's on my memory stick,' she says, and I hold my breath, sure I know what's coming. 'How is he?'

There you go.

'I don't know.' I could tell her. 'Why would I?'

'I dunno.'

'Me neither.'

'Let me know if you do talk to him, though.'

I can't help but be annoyed. My lips purse and I pick up speed. 'Why? Why does it matter?'

'Jesus, Will. I'm a bit worried about him too. He wasn't at work today, right?'

I glare at her. 'How do you know?'

'I have eyes, William.'

I chew my lip. 'Sorry.' *Maybe* I'm being a bit of an arse. 'He's just—yeah. I'm worried about him too.'

'Maybe he's on holiday,' she suggests, and I try to smile. Oh, I wish I could believe he was on holiday.

'Yeah, maybe.'

Five

Peter and I grab a pint of cider each before heading to the social. It's upstairs in one of the SU bars, where a heavy door and covered windows do a decent job of providing some sort of privacy. Not everyone is comfortable letting people know they spend their Monday evenings at an LGBT social. I let him lead the way, clutching my glass and keeping my eyes on the floor. No matter how many times I come here, nervousness makes my feet heavy and I forget how to use my words.

'Peter!' A girl I've not met before squeaks, throwing her chair backwards in excitement as soon as we walk through the door. Peter laughs, holding his arms open, and catches her when she launches herself at him. A splash of cider spills to the floor.

I stare, for a moment, at the reflection of the lights.

'Will, this is Annie,' he explains, kissing her curly hair and lowering her gently back to her feet. I don't think I'd feel more out of place if I'd walked in with a bucket on my head. 'She's first year and in my block.'

I smile and hold my hand up in a tiny wave. 'Hey.'

'What are you?' she asks, and the confidence I always have coming here as *Peter's friend* is smothered under a heavy blanket. My face drops and all the blood rushes to my heart and cheeks.

'He's my ally.' Peter slips an arm around me. I barely feel it. 'He's straight, but he's cute so I keep him around.' Oh, God. 'You gonna let us in?'

She grins and steps back, leading us to where she was sitting with a group of people I don't recognise, and I want to leave. I want to say *actually, I'm not fucking straight* but the words don't come because I've never been good at making a scene and I don't want people to look at me. I don't want their sympathy, or their attention, or their gentle frowns.

Why didn't you say?

Christ, does it matter? Is it law that you have to announce your sexuality to every room you walk into? It's not that I'm embarrassed to be bi—I just can't *say* it. Does that make me a terrible person?

Peter introduces me to more people, but it's instantly obvious why we're here. A guy with warm, tawny skin like Peter's is listening to the conversation with a quiet smile and massive, soft brown eyes. I'm sure it's the hair Peter likes. His own is limp and a bit boring; this guy's is thick and waves through its medium length to just past his ears. Spanish prince. It frames his face beautifully.

I nudge Peter's leg after a few minutes, trying to catch his attention. He doesn't notice, too caught up in conversation with Annie and this guy, whose name I completely missed, and I'm left clutching my glass for a while.

'You look tense,' a voice whispers.

I grin without thinking and look up and, shit, nearly fall off my chair. 'You should be in hospital.'

'I'm fine. I wanted to see some friendly faces,' Daniel says, grabbing a chair and dragging it over to sit beside me. It looks like it hurts him, and I realise far too late that I should have offered to help, because he's sat next to me now with his hands pressed between his knees. 'I didn't know you're part of this society.'

'I'm not really,' I say, and I hate myself for it. His head is still bowed when he talks but we're close together, and neither of us are drunk, so I can see the dark outline to his powder blue irises. Well, of one. He's facing dead ahead. But it's like someone thought the blue in the middle was too soft and worried people would accidentally fall into them if they weren't highlighted somehow, so the blue is circled by a thin line of indigo. My pulse in my throat might suffocate me. Oh, crap. 'I'm here with—with Peter.'

'With?'

'As his friend.' Shit. 'Are you—are you alone?'

'Yes.' He looks up at the ceiling and lets out a slow breath.

'I'm sorry I missed you today.'

I'm choking on something. Or maybe I've already choked, and this is heaven. Or maybe it's not quite heaven—maybe it's purgatory. He does look pretty ill. He's still doing that not-quite-looking-at-me thing, waiting for me to respond, and I've forgotten how to move my lips.

'Is that a bruise?' I blurt, eyes on the corner of his jaw.

He clears his throat and looks down again, shoulders rolling forward.

'It's okay. I just—it looks sore.'

He nods once and I'm fairly sure I've ruined it. There's an unbearable silence between us and I'm crushing my glass with my hands, waiting for it to shatter.

'How did you know where I was?' he asks, talking to something between us. His head is tilted towards me, like he's expecting me to whisper the answer, so I do. I owe him a whisper.

'I asked Owen, the guy you work with downstairs. And he sort of panicked, thinking I was your friend—like, thinking we're proper friends instead of whatever.' Oh, God. 'I told him we talk, which I guess isn't a lie, is it?'

He shakes his head, and I think I can see the promise of a smile.

'He said that you—you fell.'

If there was a smile blooming, it's wilted pretty quickly. 'Yes.'

I think that's it. I think he's had enough of talking to me because he sits up, like he's been pulled towards the ceiling by a piece of string, and looks around the room.

If Peter's noticed I'm talking to someone, he doesn't show it. The guy with the hair is talking to him and I wonder what the point of bringing me along was.

Maybe I should just leave.

'Would you come outside with me?' Daniel asks, and I'm on my feet before answering. He looks startled and I need to control myself; I can't be bouncy with him. I've got to tread carefully, like I would around an injured dog.

'Yeah, good idea. It's warm in here.' It's almost true. Peter has pushed up his sleeves, but I haven't. Dan hasn't.

The tiniest smile comes back and it's more in his eyes than his lips. They've softened and he looks straight at me for the first time.

Oh. Never mind the bruise on his left jaw. His right eye is bloodshot in the most spectacular way, flooded red from corner to corner and shadowed by a black crescent. Pointing it out will help exactly no one so I smile, force myself to look at the other eye, and wait.

'Thank you,' he whispers, and I stagger back to let him up, putting my glass down on a table. It's more of an effort than I'd like to admit keeping my eyes somewhere appropriate when Dan stretches, taking a deep breath and wincing.

'What did they say about your ribs?' I ask as soon as we're even potentially out of earshot of the others. He doesn't answer, and only part of me thinks he genuinely didn't hear.

He leads me outside and down the stairs to the smoking area and I wonder if he remembers Friday night. Was he really high?

'What course are you doing?' He reaches into his pocket without looking at me. He's actually facing a fence. Am I really that bad to look at? Maybe I should stop asking so many questions.

'I'm—medicine,' I say, and my heart drops. He's lighting a cigarette. He smokes. Why else would he want to go outside? 'That's bad for you,' I say, because I can't help it, and because I'm already worried enough about this guy.

But he actually smiles. This is a proper smile, lips and all, and I think he's laughing at me. 'This makes sense,' he says. 'It explains your curiosity.'

'I just care about people.' I feel like I'm grasping onto this conversation with the tips of my fingers. At least it's not raining anymore. 'And I—' *I like you.* Stupid, because we don't know each other. 'I'd like to be your friend, I guess.'

It's just us. There are only two ways in and out of this courtyard and he's facing them both now, so he will know if we're about to be interrupted. So, he's relaxed—more relaxed than I've ever seen him—and he leans awkwardly against the wooden fence. It makes his sleeve damp, but I don't think he cares about that.

'You guess?' He's teasing me.

'I'd like to be your friend.' The night air is cold against my teeth, but I grin, way more excited about this than I should be.

'Why?'

'I think you're nice,' I say, carefully leaving out the bit where I'm worried about him. And religiously leaving out how gorgeous he is. 'And you *did* rescue my memory stick.'

He looks really happy. Like someone just handed him ten thousand pounds, because a scratch-card he nearly threw away was actually a winner.

I'm not ten thousand pounds.

'Okay.' He keeps his eyes on mine, cigarette burning between us. I'm glued to the spot. 'I could try this.'

Six

Peter's moved onto my abandoned glass and looks up at us as we walk back in.

'Alright?' he asks, one eyebrow raised as if he's suggesting something's happened.

I pull a face. 'Alright.'

Daniel sits beside me again.

I twist in my chair to look at him. Now we're indoors, he's back to facing the floor with his hands pressed tight between his knees.

'Do you mind being called Dan?'

He just shakes his head.

'Cool. Basically everyone calls me Will.'

He nods and the contrast to outside, where he laughed at me, is painful. I'd think I've upset him if I weren't so aware of the reason for his nervousness. I'm still not sure how to talk about that.

Someone from the committee comes over to talk to us and Dan's remarkably pleasant with them. He gives actual answers, using whole sentences, but doesn't make eye contact with them either and I'm oddly relieved.

This person laughs about Daniel being clumsy and he smiles but I bristle. *You don't get it*, I think, and the words are between my teeth before I stop myself. My silence beside him is the best support I can give without making him uncomfortable and I hate it but it's enough.

It must be enough because he almost looks at me at about half ten.

'I'm going to leave,' he whispers, and I panic very slightly.

'Where are you going?'

He frowns, almost facing me, and I realise I wouldn't have asked anyone else that question. I'm blushing when he says, 'my room' and I'm almost too slow to offer to walk with him.

'Actually, yeah.' I hit Peter's knee a bit sharply and stand up. 'I'm gonna go too. It's getting late.'

'You alright?' Peter asks, catching my hand and locking me in place for a moment. He's rosy-cheeked and frowning, staring up at me like he doesn't trust whatever I'm about to say.

I grin. 'I'm fine. Have a good rest of your night and text me when you get home, alright?'

He nods and I turn to go. Dan's standing by the door with his head bowed again, clearly not sure if we're walking together.

'Thanks for waiting for me,' I say, dodging puddles of spilled liquid. 'I just thought it makes sense. We're basically neighbours.'

He nods and we walk in silence until we're out of the building. This doesn't surprise me anymore.

What does surprise me is how harsh he sounds when he stops, hands on his pockets, and swears.

'You okay?'

'I left my keys—'

'Want to go and get them?'

'No. I haven't had them all day.' He looks desperate, like he needs me to understand something he can't physically say. He's pale in the dim lamplight and I can't look away. 'I'll go to security.'

'I'll come with you.'

'No, it's—'

'Hey, I'm your friend.' I try to smile at him, but it's interrupted when he takes another deep breath and winces. 'Have you taken any painkillers?'

'What?'

'For your ribs.'

His nostrils flare and he looks away into the distance, like he's considering running. Which would be a terrible idea.

I step towards him. 'I bet they hurt.'

28

'They hurt,' he agrees, turning back to the SU.
'Goodnight, William.'

I can't watch him go.

Instead, I chase him back into the building, catching the door before it shuts behind him. It makes him jump.

'It's alright, okay?' I have to trot to keep up with him and his long strides. 'I just want to make sure you get let into your room.'

'I'm—ah,' he hisses, hands flying to his face.

I panic and squeak if there's anything I can do, but he shakes his head. I stand there as useless as a concrete pillow until he explains.

'I can't go to my room if I've left my keys,' he whispers, and I think I understand.

We're alone. No one can hear us, and we haven't reached security yet, so no one can see us. I just ask.

'You left them at his?'

As bad decisions go, this one is golden.

His hands drop from his face and I think, for a moment, that he's going to answer me. Instead, he gives me a look that turns me to stone. I'm trying to work out how to apologise when he takes a sharp, rib-cutting breath, looks up at the ceiling, and shoots away from me.

I want to explain that I don't know who his boyfriend is, and I wouldn't tell anyone anyway, but he's gone. The door to the SU toilets slams shut behind him, and I don't even consider he might not want to be near me. I follow him, not at all sure what I'm going to do, and see him disappear into a cubicle.

'Dan,' I breathe after a moment, trying to be soft. I hear him jump and slip anyway. 'It's okay.'

'You have no idea,' he snaps, voice so much sharper than I've heard before. I frown at the door between us. 'You don't know anything.'

Oh, God. I edge forward. 'I know. You don't have to explain. But I'm gonna wait here for you because I'm not leaving you on your own. I'm not letting you get hurt any more by this.'

He coughs, like he's trying to cover up a sob, but then

something worse happens. I hear the unmistakable sound of him throwing up and some tight, invisible force in my chest drags me closer to the door.

'Are you okay?'

No response.

'Dan? You don't have to hide anything from me, alright? I'm your friend. I want to help you.'

He takes a few horrible rasping breaths. 'You can't help.'

My hands are on the door. They're sweating, steaming up the plastic. 'You can stay at mine tonight. We'll sort something out about your key tomorrow, so don't worry about that.'

'What?'

'You can stay with me if you—if you'd like.' I clear my throat. 'It's a ground-floor room, so no more stairs.'

I can picture the little almost-smile and close my eyes. I feel like I'm guarding him, fighting off bad energy from entering the little cubicle.

'You don't want me,' he mutters. 'You have better things—'

'Well, I'm not leaving you here all night,' I snap. 'Anything could happen to you. My room's a couple of minutes away and it's safe. No one will know you're there so you can relax.'

The toilet flushes but he coughs again, and I hold my breath, waiting.

The door swings away from me very suddenly and I fall forwards. My eyes flutter open just as I catch myself on his chest and he hisses, in pain or in shock or in both, and I leap back like I've been burned. My face must look like it's been burned.

'Sorry,' I choke, heart running a thousand miles an hour. Daniel is *warm*. 'Sorry, I wasn't expecting you to open the door.'

He's clearly been crying, and he's a horrible colour, but he smiles at me. It's another proper smile and it catches me by surprise, stealing the breath from my lungs.

'You are tenacious. Thank you.'

30

My lungs will never inflate again. I'm stunned, scrambled, and so scattered I can't even find the muscle memory to smile. I gawk at him, wondering if I've ever heard someone say *tenacious* before, and I'm useless until he glances passed me at the door.

'You're—' *incredible*— 'welcome,' I gasp. 'It's fine—it's nothing. What do you want to do?'

His lips press together, and he swallows, still looking past me. He doesn't want to ask for this.

'Want your own space? Or do you think you might be sick again?' I'm surprised he can't hear my pulse. 'It's okay.'

'Can—' he sighs sharply and his face twists. 'Can I stay with you?'

'Of course you can.' Would it be weird to take his hand? 'You okay to walk?'

He nods and lets me lead him from the toilet. I glance back at him every couple of steps, until there's enough space for us to walk beside each other, and the silence between us is heavy.

Seven

I'm incredibly nervous about having Daniel in my room for the whole night. Why did I suggest it? We stand outside my block for a moment, letting him finish the latest cigarette, and he looks like he's about to collapse by the time we reach my room.

I open my door, muttering something about being sorry for the mess, and my lack of en suite is concerning. What if he's sick again? I don't think my washbasin is cut out for it, somehow. Maybe this was a bad idea.

'Sit anywhere,' I say, even though there's only really the option of the bed or desk chair. 'I'm gonna get a drink. Do you want anything?'

He shakes his head, eyes on the floor, and I rethink leaving the room. Instead, I drop my keys to the desk with an obnoxious *clink* and talk to him.

'I have lectures in the morning, but I want you to stay here for as long as you like. Do you have anything tomorrow?'

He could lie to me. He could say he has a nine AM, which would give him a great excuse to leave without speaking to me in the morning, but he half shrugs and takes a breath that seems to exhaust him. 'At two.'

'Okay, awesome.' My eyes are restless trying to catch a glimpse of his face. 'We could meet up for lunch. I mean, if you want. I'm not sure if I snore or not, so you might end up hating me for keeping you awake all night.'

He looks up enough to show me his slight smile. 'I would like that.'

'Awesome. Sure I can't get you a drink?'

He hesitates.

'Water?'

'Thank you.'

I pull my gaze back over to the slightly less damaged half of his face. 'You're welcome. Get yourself comfortable.' I point to the bed. If he thinks I'm letting him sleep on the floor he's in for an education. 'Do you want any painkillers?'

He's looking down again. Maybe I've been too firm because all he does is shake his head.

'You sure?'

'No, thank you.'

I don't push him, for now. Instead, I walk in silence and very hurriedly fill two of my glasses with water from the kitchen tap.

He's still standing there when I get back.

'Water.' I hold the glass up for him to take. He smiles, like he wants to thank me but can't find his voice, and I reach back to turn off the light. 'Is this better? I know it's a bit awkward but we're literally just sharing some air while we catch some sleep.'

There's a gentle laugh, and I think I've startled him. When my eyes refocus through the gloom, he's facing me, but I can see the way his eyes bounce around us.

'Thank you, William.'

Oh, he said my name.

'It's completely fine.' I sound far more confident than I feel. 'I'm serious about the painkillers. Do you want something? I have paracetamol and ibuprofen.'

He hesitates again—that micro moment of doubt—so I fumble through the darkness to open the right drawer. The first thing my hand lands on is a packet of condoms.

Blushing, because now I'm thinking about sex and I really don't want to be, I grab the half-used boxes of painkillers.

'They're right here,' I say, standing them on-end on the desk, 'and you can help yourself whenever. I recommend you take something sooner rather than later, to give it chance to start working before you fall asleep.'

He's really smiling at me. I think he's happy. I think he must actually like me, and my heart skips when he speaks again.

'Whatever you say, Doctor.'

I swear to God, I have to cough to cover up a whimper.

33

'I'm not a doctor yet,' I point out, finally taking my jacket off. I fold it up and drop it to the floor, leaving the back of the chair for whatever Dan wants to take off. Jesus. I shouldn't think about that. 'Not even close. Four more years of this place.'

'And then what?'

I explain the placements looming over the next few months, and the endless exams, and the rotations I'll do as a junior doctor before I specialise. He absorbs every word, head tilted towards me while I speak, and we're both sat on my bed by the time we realise it's after midnight.

'We should sleep,' I say.

He nods and stands up so I have to be quick.

'You sleep in the bed. It's clean, and you've got to look after your ribs.'

'It's not so bad.'

'Daniel.' I stand and push one hand into my hair. 'You broke them.'

He shrugs and I can see him curling back into himself, trying to shrink.

'How many?'

'Only three,' he whispers, and I want to scream. *Only.*

'Sleep in the bed.' It comes out too harsh. And now I feel awful, because he's twisted away from me and I don't think he's breathing.

Even in the dark, I can see his eyes are closed.

'Dan, I'm sorry.'

I see a lift and drop of his shoulders.

'I'm sorry. I'm just so worried about you,' I say, hands in my pockets because they nearly reached for him. 'I know you don't want to take my bed, because you want to be polite, but you'll damage yourself if you sleep on the floor. So please just don't worry about it.'

Dan sighs. He takes something from his pocket and reaches over the bed to put it on the desk, beside the painkillers. 'Thank you.' He's still not quite looking at me. 'Do you lock your door?'

'Oh, yeah.' I dance around the bed to lock it. The thud

of metal on metal is reassuring. 'Thanks. Goodnight, I guess.' I grab my spare blanket from where it's stuffed into the bottom of my wardrobe and wrap myself up in it, like it's a really chunky cape. 'Wake me if you need anything.'

He nods and sits down, and I realise I shouldn't watch this. He might want to get undressed, and this definitely isn't the right time to gawk at his chest. Especially because I'm fairly sure I can still feel him against his palms.

Oh, God.

I sit on the floor, realising a moment too late that I haven't got anything for a pillow, and reach for my jacket. It's not exactly the softest material, but it's dry—it will do.

'William?'

I spin around and the relief I feel when I make out the shape of him lying in my bed is incredible.

'Thank you.'

I grin. 'No problem, Dan.'

'Goodnight.'

'Night. See you in the morning?' It's a question, because I'm not convinced he's going to stick around. But I see a smile peeking over my duvet and fall asleep dreaming of it.

'Yeah. Thank you.'

Eight

Dan's still asleep when my alarm goes off at eight. I haven't slept well, but I didn't expect to. My neck creaks as I sit up and his name is on my lips when I catch myself, the word frozen somewhere in a breath in my chest.

Some people become less beautiful when they sleep. Their faces drop and fold and it's peaceful, but you could never call it beautiful. Some people are *cute* when they sleep, like Peter. Picture a baby wrapped up in a warm swaddle.

Daniel looks like a painting.

He's lying on his front with his face tucked under his arm, so I almost can't see him. Even in sleep, he's hiding from the world. The tug of despair in my chest when I realise this is nothing compared to the fluttering rush to my head when I stretch enough to see his face—bruised side up—and the way his dry lips have parted. The gentle blush of his cheek glows pink over the bruise on his jaw, like a sunset reaching over a low cloud, and it's impossible to blink.

Maybe it's the light coming through my maroon blinds. Maybe it's how his sandy hair contrasts against my dark bedsheets, but he looks like he's glowing.

Someone has hurt him.

Someone he trusts, or maybe even loves. And they put that bruise across his jaw, which has darkened even since last night. And they burst the vessels in his eye, and bruised the soft skin above his cheek, making this perfect moment that bit painful to swallow.

He is no less beautiful for his injuries. I would almost say that they add a heroism to him, but I've grown well past idolising pain.

I grab some clothes from my wardrobe, opening and closing the doors as quietly as possible, and slink out of the room to the showers. He's fast asleep and I doubt he's going to wake up but I rush, an anxious knot in my stomach.

I'm gone for less than ten minutes and he's exactly the same.

Just like when a cat falls asleep on your lap, it's impossible to wake him. I just can't do it. I know I should, because he'll be embarrassed to have slept while I've gone to lectures, but I *can't*. He's too relaxed. Too perfect.

And I'm too aware of how frightened he is each time he draws a conscious breath. There's none of that fear, now. He's hiding himself, sure, but he's smiling. It's a small smile, and I might not have noticed it on anyone else, but it's significant for him.

I don't even know how old he is.

He's older than me, that's for certain. He looks more like an adult; his face is sharp around the edges and, while the stubble on my jaw comes in patches, his has formed an even shade over his skin. There are a couple of lines on his forehead, like he's spent a lot of time being surprised, and I really hope the letter I'm scribbling out for him is a *good* surprise.

Daniel,

I've gone to my lecture. There was no way I was waking you up—me having an early start is no need for you to miss out on sleep. Stay in my room for as long as you want.
I'm free from 12-2 so I'll head back to my room and we mentioned getting lunch together. I'd like that. If you still want. If you need to go somewhere though don't worry—but also don't worry about still being in my room.
Okay?
Help yourself to anything.
See you later?
William x
(Here's my number just in case)

And now I only have fifteen minutes to get to my lecture because I *might* have spent a while just watching him.

Not in a creepy way. In a *holy crap, he's right there* way. I'm hyper aware of his ribs. How could I not be? I fell into them.

I grab my bag, whisper an incredibly soft *see you later*, and sneak out of my room. I know I'm being ridiculous. I should have just woken him up.

Out of the question.

Nine

I'm prepared to explain to my lecturer why I'm spending more time looking down at my phone than taking notes, but I don't have to. No message. No phone call. I don't know what this means. Is he still in my room? Is he still asleep? Has he gone, but he's too embarrassed to tell me?

Maybe I'll get back and there'll be a reply to my note.

I wonder what his handwriting's like.

As soon as I'm free, I throw a quick excuse at a classmate who's been generous enough to sit beside me and run across campus. It's not far, but there's a stitch in my side and I take a moment to catch my breath when I see my building.

I don't know what I'm expecting to find, but the blinds in my room are still down. I'm not sure Dan would dare touch them, but it does mean I can't see in, so I have no idea if he's still there. The butterflies in my stomach are doing somersaults.

Standing outside my room door, I strain my ears for any sign of movement. There's nothing, so I tell myself to be disappointed when I put the key into the lock. It scrapes a bit.

The sound of him jumping to his feet is hidden by the *whoosh* of the door over the carpet and I'm clearly not thinking so I yelp in surprise when I see him. Which is *not* the reaction I was hoping to give.

He's bright red, which is an improvement from last night, and one of my books is closed on my pillow, far from the shelf where it had been this morning.

'Hello,' I say, cheeks burning and voice tight. I swallow, pulse pounding in my throat, and he looks like he might cry. Actually, the red of his eyes makes me sure he *has* been crying. 'I thought you'd have gone—I'm happy you haven't, but I thought—I didn't expect you'd want to stay.'

His fingers ball into fists beside his legs. The bruise across his jaw is almost purple and I have to keep looking away from the damaged, bloodshot eye. And he doesn't speak.

'How was your morning?' I move into the room just enough to lean against the wall. The door clicks softly shut behind me.

'It was okay. Thank you for letting me stay.'

'You're welcome, it's fine.'

'I'll find somewhere to go tonight.'

I smile at him, trying to be soft, and shrug. 'You're welcome here whenever. Want to go and have a word with security about maybe changing the lock on your room?'

The fists by his sides relax and some tension leaves his lips. 'You think they could?'

'I dunno. They might just move you, actually. But anything would help, right?'

He nods and glances down at the book. I can't imagine he was enjoying *An Introduction to Medicinal Chemistry*, but, of the other reading material in my room, I guess it was the least technical.

I squint up at him, certain, now, he's been crying. His eyelids are swollen.

'I'm so glad you stayed,' I say.

For the first time since I walked into the room, he looks straight at me. 'Why?'

'Because it means you were safe.'

Once again, I've overestimated him.

Any of the lightness he'd felt at the idea of security helping him has been washed away. He presses his lips together and looks at the floor, tilting his head so I can mostly see the side of his neck.

'I mean—you know what I mean.' I chew each word in my mouth before I say them. 'You were somewhere you felt safe, right?'

He nods.

'And no one knows you were here.'

'They don't?'

'No, Dan. Of course not.'

He looks like he doesn't understand why I haven't told

everyone on campus he's staying in my room and I sigh. I've got to be patient with him, but I want so badly to jump over there and hug him that I've had to wrap my arms around my chest.

'It's okay. You can trust me, alright? I don't want to see you getting hurt.'

'Does it fucking matter?' Holy shit. His eyes catch me, piercing right through my skin like scalpels, and this fury looks unnatural in his soft blue. 'People get hurt.'

'Not like this!' I hear myself and I cringe.

Daniel looks away, building up to his next argument. I should not be shouting at him, and I hate it. God, I feel sick.

'Dan, getting hurt like this *isn't*—'

'I don't expect you to understand,' he says, voice clipped and cool after that initial burst of anger. I'm terrified, but I can't tell if it's *for* him or *of* him. 'It doesn't matter.'

'It does.'

'It doesn't.' He steps towards me like he's going to leave the room. 'You need to concentrate on your work.'

I reach back to lock the door. It upsets him, but I can't let him leave and I can't run the risk of anyone coming in. The metal scrapes, sealing us together, and his eyes flash up to look at me.

'Why don't you think it matters?'

He looks like he might throw something.

'Dan, no matter what you think, I haven't learned *anything* about you that means you aren't important.'

'Really?'

'Really.'

His chest swells and he does well to hide how much his ribs hurt, but his eyelids flicker. 'I smoke.'

I roll my eyes. 'I know.'

'I skip lectures.' He isn't blinking. It's like he's preparing himself for a fight.

'Everyone skips lectures.'

'You don't.'

'No, but that's because I'm a giant nerd.' I try to smile.

'So there. You haven't convinced me.'

He considers for a long time. I almost think I've won, but he pulls a face—wrinkles his nose, twists his lips—and takes a deep breath. It's another one that must hurt him.

'I take drugs.'

I miss a beat. 'Shit,' I breathe, and I can't tell if he's satisfied with my reaction. I think he's going to cry. I think *I* might cry, and my eyes are flashing all over him like I'm about to find a needle dangling from his skin. 'Well, okay. I'll help you.'

'What?'

'I'll—'

'You're not going to help!'

I raise an eyebrow. The rest of me is frozen. 'Try to stop me, Dan.'

His nostrils flicker with each sharp breath. 'You shouldn't waste your time like that.'

'Why not?'

'It's my own fault!'

I hold back a groan and defrost enough to walk away from the door. He flinches, anticipating pain like I've seen before, and the argument I've thought up fades to nothing. His eyes are closed tight, chin drawn to his chest, and I'm sure he's holding his breath again. It's heart-breaking.

'Hey.' My voice cracks.

He shivers, and I can't help it. I take his hand, trying to reassure him by being gentle, but he rips it away. I could have predicted that, but it still hurts. My fingers are burning where they touched his.

'It's okay. I want to help.'

He doesn't respond. I'm not surprised.

'Is it—is this why he hurts you?'

I'm expecting him to run away again at the mention of *him*, but he looks crushed. Instead of trying to push past me to get to the door, he covers his face. His sleeve slips, showing the tattoo on his left forearm, and now really isn't the time to ask about the Cyrillic lettering and grey feathers which climb towards his elbow.

'I don't care that you smoke.' I take his right hand again and fight with him for a painful moment. But then he relaxes, like he's given up, and he grasps my fingers. *Good.* 'I don't care that you take drugs. I want you to be safe.'

He takes a deep breath which ends in a cough and I want to scream. His left hand is still covering his eyes but the other is holding onto me so tightly he might leave a bruise.

'Trust me. Give me chance to be your friend, okay?'

Eventually, he nods. I want to keep him here in my room forever, where he's safe. Instead, I breathe his name like a prayer and put my free arm around his chest, being so very gentle.

He's warm again.

The most surprising thing, though, is he lets me hold him. I'm uncomfortable, because I haven't got my feet right and he's stopped at a sad angle and I'm really trying to not put any pressure through him, but we stand there for a while. He smells a little bit like bed, but I don't care. I can feel his pulse where my cheek is against his neck and, for the moment, I'm just grateful he's here.

My stomach rumbles and he starts to pull away.

'Don't go.' I sound far too desperate and try again. 'I mean, we should go and get food, but I've wanted to hug you for weeks.'

Exactly *who* do I think I am?

Dan sounds as confused as I feel. 'Why?'

Not the time to admit to my massive crush. 'You look like you could do with a hug,' I say, and it's true.

He pulls back anyway, cheeks a lovely sunburned red, and smiles at me. The smile catches me by surprise.

'You want to help me?'

'Promise.' I'm still holding his hand.

The smile grows. 'Even though I'm addicted to heroin?'

The detail is a shock, but I answer without hesitation. 'Even though.'

He licks his dry lips and I realise he thought he was going to make me stumble. No chance.

43

'I've been okay since Friday,' he whispers.

I'm not sure what he means. I nod and give his hand a squeeze, waiting for the right words to come. There's no easy response to *I'm a heroin addict.*

'The hospital helped. You don't—you don't need to do anything.'

I squeeze his fingers again. 'That's cool. But I can support you and tell you you're doing incredibly well, right?'

He barks a little laugh and looks at the door, cheeks red again. 'Yeah. Thank you.'

'Not a problem.' As I say it, I think of one very real, very serious problem and catch my face before he can see the fear. I slide our fingers together. 'Dan, you know Friday…'

I trail off. He's going to freak out. There's no way of asking this without upsetting him. I reach up to put my free hand on the side of his neck, like I'm protecting his pulse, and he just waits.

'Are you still in a relationship with him?'

The relief drops from his face, but he doesn't try to hide. He shakes his head and I almost break out in dance.

'Good—oh, man, that's *good*.' I drop my hand from his neck because I can feel his heartbeat. It's thundering. So is mine. 'Well done. Do you want to go and speak to security?'

Back to business. He frees his fingers from mine. I suppose I can't complain.

'You don't have to go with me.' He pulls a face like he knows I'm going to argue. 'I can speak to them.'

'Yeah, you can, but I want to be sure they listen.'

I haven't actually put my bag down so we can just walk straight from the room. I lock the door behind us.

'You're always welcome here,' I say, glancing up at him as we walk. 'I mean it.'

He manages a little smirk and I'd forgotten how good they look on his face. For a moment, he looks like I imagine he looks when he's relaxed.

'Always?'

'Even without warning.'

44

He laughs. 'Except if you bring a girl home. You do not want me interrupting.'

It's a perfect opportunity, and I almost do it. I almost laugh, take his hand, look him straight in the eye, and say *I'm not straight*. It's like he's fed that line to me, but I can't use it because I *might* bring a girl home, so I just do the laughing bit.

'Well, I guess.' I sound far away. 'But I don't think that's going to happen.'

'Why not?'

Is he asking me to say I'm gay? I'd love to be able to give such a simple answer, but I stick to the truth, instead. His curiosity in my personal life is an amazingly obvious way to stop us from talking about him, but I indulge in telling him about Lilley. I explain how stressful I find relationships, and how I just can't be bothered to go through all that again, and lead him gently to security.

*

He hits me with an absolute curveball while we're there. Security agree to take him to his room and help him clear it out, and we're talking about finding a different room on campus when he shakes his head and makes a decision.

'I'm going to rent somewhere privately,' he says, and the disappointment hurts my stomach. 'I'm going to take a few months off.'

So he can get clean.

Pride swells and I just about don't drag him into another hug. I satisfy myself by smiling at him, instead, and I hope he knows I realise how important this is. I'm not sure many people look this pleased with themselves when they have to take an intermission from uni, but he looks happy. And happy suits him.

The lady we're talking with leaves us for a moment to find someone from student support to explain how this is going to work. I take this very brief opportunity to whisper.

'Will you be able to afford all this?' I ask, even though it feels rude.

He nods.

'You're sure?'

'I'm sure.'

They manage to set up a call with Dan's tutor while we're sitting there and, between them, they discuss giving him medical leave. They agree he can return at the start of semester two, which means he'll have to re-sit the semester one exams, and I feel like I should be taking notes.

When we're eventually released, it's quarter to two and we haven't eaten. Dan apologises constantly from the security room to the door to the SU.

'Stop—stop apologising,' I laugh. 'It's fine.' I catch his arm in my hand and he doesn't pull away like he might have done a few hours ago. 'What are you gonna do?'

He shrugs and looks almost like a new person. He still looks inclined to throw up at any moment, but he's standing properly, reminding me how short I am compared to him, and there's a steady smile on his lips.

'I have a lot of work to do for my VISA. I will have to re-apply before studying again.'

I don't like this. 'But that will take time, right?'

He nods.

'So what else today?'

A gust of wind whistles through us and I shiver. Dan takes a sharp breath and a lot of the strength leaves his shoulders as he folds in on himself, cowering from the cool air. He hasn't even got a coat.

'Heroin is a strictly night-time thing,' he teases, looking at me sideways, and I'm blushing like there's no tomorrow.

'I didn't mean—'

He winks at me. I bite hard on my lower lip, stopping anything stupid from slipping out, and stare into his eyes like they're holding me to the ground.

'Don't worry,' he laughs. 'I don't want it.'

I wonder who he's trying to reassure.

'I'll spend some time in the library,' he says, glancing up the hill.

46

I want to tell him to go to my room, but he's probably had enough of it by now. Security are going to sort his room tomorrow, so he needs to look for somewhere to live. Or, at least, to store all of his things. The library is a good idea, so I nod.

'Be careful.' As if he needs reminding. 'Phone me or text me whenever.'

'Thank you, William'

Oh. It feels like the end, and there's a strong chance I won't see him again. I chew my cheek and half start to walk away, heading to the path to take me to my lecture just as the sun comes out from behind a cloud. I double back.

'Do you want to stay at mine again?'

He loses some of that precious confidence and shrinks into himself.

'I said you can and I mean it. We'll talk later, okay? But you—you can stay.'

He licks his lips. They glisten a little in the early afternoon sun and, for a moment, they don't look quite so cracked.

'You will argue and worry if I don't, won't you?' There's the hint of a smile on his wet lips. Oh, God. I'm grinning. 'Meet me here at six.'

'If you're not here, I'm going to think something *really bad* has happened to you,' I warn, fully aware that I'm overreacting. And I'm walking backwards because I can't look away from him.

But he smirks, having to squint against the sun to keep his eyes on me. 'Something bad *will* have happened if I am not here.'

Ten

The rest of the day crawls by. I'm starving and dash out of the lab as soon as the words 'ten-minute break' are mentioned and walk back eating a sandwich, checking my phone for the first time in hours. And there it is: the unknown number I've been wanting to see for far longer than I'd like to admit.

> 15:29 William, it's Daniel. Thank you for everything. I'll see you this evening.

I nearly scream.
Instead, I tremble as I type out a reply.

> 16:09 **William**: Hi! You're always entirely welcome. I'm looking forward to it!

It doesn't feel like enough to show him how much it means to me that he actually sent a text. This must mean he's no longer worried about someone looking through his phone. This must mean he likes me enough to want to spend more time with me.

There's another text. From Peter. Somewhat less exciting.

> 15:46 **Peter**: What happened last night? You and that guy walked home together???

> 16:10 **William**: That guy is the friend I was worried about. Broke his ribs?

> 16:11 **Peter:** Ooh. So you didn't bang

48

It's almost impossible to walk back into the building. My stomach tightens and I stumble, but I can't leave him hanging without an answer. He'll think he's onto something.

> 16:12 **William**: No. No, Peter, I did not bang my friend with the broken ribs. No.

16:13 **Peter**: Pffft I believe you. So what happened??

> 16:13 **William**: Walked him home. He lives in the sheds.

16:15 **Peter**: that's convenient. Was he alright?

> 16:15 **William**: Yes. Why?

16:16 **Peter**: looked peaky

> 16:16 **William**: Ribs, Peter.

16:17 **Peter**: yeah, I know

It hurts.

I stumble back into the lab and everyone else is full of energy. Something must be happening tomorrow, because they're all chatting about some sports game half the university seems to be going to watch, but I couldn't care less. I sweep my notes out of the way and sit down, sinking to put my forehead against the plastic laminate desk.

It's like buying someone an amazing present but you've got to keep it secret because their birthday isn't for another eight months. Only it's not eight months: it's already been *years* and there's no guarantee there's even going to be a birthday. And it's not an amazing present: it's just a handwritten note that says *I'm bi*.

Four letters. That's all it would take. That's fewer than saying *I'm gay* or *I'm queer* and it should be so easy.

Peter is gay. Daniel is gay—I think. Neither of them would care that I'm bi.

But why should I have to say it so explicitly? I didn't tell Lilley before we started dating—she didn't need to know who I was attracted to, beyond that I liked her.

I lift my head and try to put my mind back on the problem I've been given, rather than the one I've created, but don't get very far. The first time I realised I had more than a neutral appreciation for men was when my English class watched the Leonardo DiCaprio *Romeo and Juliet*. At the time, I told myself it was just the drama of the film—but I've learned. I've been on the edge of coming out for five years, now, and I keep thinking I'll just say it. I can't. I can't and I *don't*.

16:26 Peter: BTW Cas sends her love. We wanna go to the cinema tonight. You in?

Oh, Peter. Any other time.

Eleven

I stay behind after the lab to get more work done. If Daniel does stay with me again, I know I'm not going to be doing anything productive. And I need to finish writing up a report, so I give myself until quarter to six.

It's great. No one's around, because they'd rather work in the library or in their rooms, so I get the report finished off. I save it, submit it, and close my laptop.

Relief mixes with nervousness when I realise I'm about to see Daniel.

He hasn't sent me any more messages so I guess that means we're still on. Because he'd tell me if he wanted to cancel. Right?

Is this the sort of thing someone *would* cancel?

What am I even walking to? I rush, because I want to see him, but I don't know what he's expecting from this. I don't know what *I'm* expecting from this. I just—

He is exactly where we left each other. A little bit away from the SU door, one hand in his pocket and a burning cigarette in the other. I can't be angry at him for the smoke.

What I'm feeling is the polar opposite of anger, actually.

He smirks, seeing me, and I glance down. I couldn't be more obviously excited if I tried. I slow my pace, take a deep breath, and smile at him.

'How was it?' he asks, moving to kill the cigarette as I get closer. I appreciate it.

'Good. I finished a report.' I have a huge grin on my face. The air is cool and tastes of rain, so I must have missed some while I was working. He looks like maybe he wasn't so lucky and caught a bit of drizzle. It's not a bad look. 'How was your afternoon?'

'Very good,' he says. We start walking to nowhere in

particular and I almost reach for his hand, which is just ridiculous. 'I found an apartment.'

'Oh, cool. Think you'll take it?'

'I have.'

I burst out in laughter. 'What?'

'I sent a deposit.' He looks like he wants to join me in laughing. *Do.* 'And it's empty, so I can move in tomorrow.'

'Holy crap.'

He makes a noise like he doesn't understand so I explain my massive eyes and gaping mouth.

'You're organised. If I ever need help to move, I know who I'm asking.'

He stops walking. For a moment, I think I've upset him. 'I owe you,' he whispers, 'but could I stay again tonight?'

Something erupts in my chest and fills me with warmth.

I want to hug him. I nearly do. We're facing each other, and there's absolutely no rule that says I can't hug him. There are hardly any people around us. There's no reason for me to be nervous about a hug, but I don't do it.

I grin, instead. 'Of course you can. What do you want to eat?'

We eventually decide to go to the SU, and I'm surprised that he suggests it. Hasn't he seen enough of the place? But he leads the way, and this is so unlike the guy I took to my room last night that I have to keep squinting at him.

Maybe I need new glasses and I've met up with the wrong six-foot, sandy-haired, blue-eyed Russian with a bruise on his jaw and cigarette smoke on his breath. But I don't think so, somehow.

He glances back as I follow him through the door and goes straight up to the counter. His confidence, compared to the way he flinched away from me this morning, is enough to make my sinuses heavy with tears. I've lost my appetite.

Owen's serving us. I'm bright red. So red, I have to unzip my jacket.

Daniel notices and glances at me before turning back to Owen and asking for a sandwich. I default to a jacket potato and nearly collapse at the knees when Dan says 'cheese?' like he's known me my whole life.

I nod. Owen gives me cheese. We grab drinks, I grab a fork, and we sit together at a four-person table.

*

It's quiet in the SU on a Tuesday evening. Most people have gone to their rooms or off-campus to eat and I'm conscious that Owen is watching us. I keep catching him looking in our direction. Dan's talking almost constantly, practically ignoring his food, and it feels like I've achieved something by getting him to say more than one sentence at a time.

It's raining again, and the sky is dark and heavy.

'I will be able to go on a bus to most places,' Dan says. I really try to concentrate on what he's saying, rather than just his voice. 'And I'm already starting to feel better.'

It feels like a dangerous moment. 'What did they say at the hospital?'

He shrugs. 'I have a daily phone call. An appointment with the campus doctor in the morning. And—and these,' he says, taking a small box out of his jacket pocket. I haven't seen this before and hold my hand out, expectant. He hesitates before letting me take it. 'They're reducing the pain of it.'

It being heroin withdrawal. I nod and turn the box over in my hands, reading the name and trying to become familiar with it. And then, because I'm not convinced I trust Dan to look after himself properly, I throw him a glance and pop one end open. Three tablets have been pressed out of the foil, so I guess I have to assume he took them. Eyes on his, I put the box back into his waiting hand.

'Did you take it last night?'

'Yes. You were asleep.'

I nod, telling myself to believe him. 'Are they helping?'

'Yes,' he sighs. 'And no. I was very sick yesterday and today.'

I chew my lip and try to sound like I'm *not* absolutely terrified of whatever else he isn't telling me. 'You didn't say.'

Something tightens in my chest and I have to take a deep breath. 'What happened?'

He pulls a face and casts a very obvious glance down at the food I'm meant to be eating. I take his point and laugh, ending it in a shrug.

'Well, you can tell me whenever. Medicine student, remember?'

His timid little smile tells me *yes*.

'You've got an appointment here?'

He nods.

'Want me to go with you?'

'You have lectures.'

'What time?'

'Ten thirty.'

I grin because I've won. 'I'm in from twelve to five. I can come and sit with you in the waiting room if you'd like. I don't have to go in, but I can if you want.'

He considers for a while. I try to not be obviously waiting for him to answer and pick at my food, ears listening to every raindrop and every time Owen moves something.

'Wait with me,' he says. 'I think I will be fine in there.'

I push my hand into my hair because it almost reached for him. 'That's cool. We'll do breakfast and go—you can use the shower, by the way,' I say, reminding us that he's staying the night with me again. 'I have spare towels and stuff.'

'Thank you.'

'It's nothing, don't worry.'

We're looking at each other. Really looking. What's left of our food has been abandoned and we're side-by-side, my bag occupying the seat to my left and his body warming my right. I hadn't realised, when we sat down, how close we are.

One of us needs to do something.

But we don't, and we just stare at each other until the sound of crashing plates makes us both jump. Daniel ducks forward, like he thinks some of those broken shards are going to fly towards him, and my hand is on his arm without either of us knowing how it got there.

'Just Owen being an idiot,' I whisper, shooting the guy in

question a *horrible* glare. He sees it and frowns but I do not care. 'We're alright. Want to go?'

Maybe Daniel feels safer now he's split up from his boyfriend. Maybe he doesn't. I actually wonder, as we scrape our chairs back and brace ourselves to step out into the rain, if he's more terrified than ever before.

Twelve

We don't say much on the dash back to my room. It's chucking it down, now, and Dan hasn't got a hood. I'd rip mine off and give it to him if it would help.

'Think a *warm* shower is a good idea after that,' I mutter, opening the door to the building and holding it so he can duck in. 'You can sit and be cold and wet if you really want.'

His laugh echoes down the corridor.

'Thank you.' He pushes his hand through his hair, lifting it away from his eyes. The rain has made it darker and he laughs again, showing me the water on his hand. 'I might take the offer of a towel.'

I hold the bedroom door open and follow him through. 'Good shout. I—uh.' There is no way of saying this which isn't embarrassing. 'Do you want to borrow a t-shirt or something to sleep in?'

Last night, we didn't think about it. We fell asleep in our clothes and, now I see the wet of his shirt where his jacket failed, I realise he can't do the same again. He must feel gross, actually; he's been wearing the same thing for days.

He doesn't want to accept it. 'I don't—won't I be too tall?'

It's a feeble excuse. I raise an eyebrow and open my wardrobe, throwing a faded t-shirt at him. And then I grab a pair of pyjama trousers and he looks, for a moment, like he doesn't know what to do with them.

'I'd offer you boxers, but I don't think you could take the embarrassment.' My cheeks blush enough *anyway*. 'Neither could I.'

He smiles and holds his hand out for the trousers. 'I will look ridiculous.'

'*Excuse me*,' I sniff, holding my chin up as I grab the last pair for myself, 'these are *gorgeous*.'

'I believe you.'

If he were Peter, I'd thump his arm.

I laugh at Dan, instead, and turn back to the wardrobe to find my clean towel. I'm pleased to find it still smells of detergent.

'I think we'll have to take it in turns.' I glance over at where my in-use towel is draped over the radiator. 'One bottle of shampoo.'

'You have doubles and triples of everything else.' Dan holds the trousers out for emphasis.

I pull a face and it's childish, but it makes him laugh even more and my stomach jumps.

'No more soap?'

'Unfortunately not,' I mutter. 'But you go first— shampoo and stuff is here.' I pass my wash bag to him. Another thought hits me. 'Crap. I don't have a spare toothbrush.'

He does look embarrassed about this. 'I could just steal some toothpaste and improvise.'

I want to tell him to steal anything he likes but, fortunately for us both, I satisfy myself with a smile. 'Good idea. Do you know where the showers are?'

He bundles up the collection I've given him—towel, shirt, trousers, wash bag—and nods. 'I think I can work it out. I won't be long.'

'Take your time.'

'Thank you, William.' His whisper fills the room. I want him to keep whispering to me.

He doesn't. He leaves without another word and I'm left there on my own, staring at the door.

Another night with Dan.

When I met him three weeks ago, I didn't dare think we'd be doing this. I sort my bag out and check my laptop's survived its journey through the rain, drifting passively through thoughts of memory sticks and bruises. I need to research heroin withdrawal. I need to research Russia.

I'm lost in thought when the door opens again and he's

back.

'Thank you, William,' he says, voice still in that warm whisper. It hums through me, like the purring of a distant motorbike.

'You're welcome,' I say, after a little delay. I have so many questions to ask and all of them feel like they might upset him. 'Get yourself comfy. I won't be long.'

'Thank you for letting me stay again.' It comes out suddenly, like he didn't think he'd have the courage to say it.

'You're welcome.' I grin and take the washbag, adding it to my bundle. 'See you in a minute.'

*

When I get back, he's quietly sitting on the edge of my bed, and I realise I failed to appreciate how fucking *cute* he looks in my clothes. The shirt drowns him, but it drowns me, and the trousers don't even hit his ankles but that really doesn't matter. No one ever expects pyjamas to fit perfectly—least of all borrowed ones.

'Nice PJs,' I say throwing my towel over the radiator again and draping his more gently over the wardrobe door. 'Very stylish.'

He laughs. 'A dear friend let me borrow them.'

Dear friend. That's me, now—a *dear friend.* Jesus.

'Dan, how old are you?' It slips from me and I don't dare to look at him while I wait for an answer. Instead, I put my washbag back by the basin. I hold my breath.

'Does it matter?'

Ah, shit. 'I'm just curious,' I say. 'Because I'm a baby. Nineteen.'

Thank God, he laughs. 'You *are* a baby,' he agrees. 'Twenty-five.'

'What?' I spin to look at him. Okay, I thought he looked older than me—but not six years. 'Five?' Good job he's blushing because I feel like I'm about to faint. 'You're twenty-five?'

'Is that bad?'

58

'No! No, I'm just—I'm just surprised.' Shit. 'You don't look that old.'

He raises an eyebrow. 'I didn't try university until I was twenty-three. I couldn't.'

'I don't mean it in a bad way.'

'No, I know. But it is strange to be older than everyone in my lectures and, next year, I will be another year older and still surrounded by twenty-one-year-olds."

I almost sink to my knees. I want to apologise. I want to kiss his hands.

'Does it upset you?'

I swallow. 'Why would it?'

'You sounded upset.'

'I'm just surprised.' I could kick myself for reacting so loudly. 'You don't—you don't seem twenty-five.'

'No?'

'No.'

He tilts his head. 'When is your birthday?'

'Ten—' my voice breaks, so I try again. 'Tenth of August."

He groans and sinks back onto the bed, elbows taking his weight. Unease twists my stomach.

'How am I so old?' he mutters, neck stretched, and face tipped to the ceiling. 'November seventeenth.'

My heart stops. There are more like seven years between us, and that's not a problem—that's not a problem, because we're friends—but I feel bad about being so obsessed with his smile.

'That's soon,' I say, unhelpfully.

He groans again and pushes to sit up. I bet leaning like that hurt his ribs. 'I suppose it is, yes.'

We should stop talking about birthdays. We should stop thinking about how much older than me he is, and we should do more than stare at each other while our hair's still dripping wet.

I grab the book from where he abandoned it earlier and flick through a couple of pages.

'Tell me about your degree,' I say, being careful to sit on the desk chair and not the bed. 'Politics, right?'

He nods and seems grateful for this change of topic. We talk for hours until I admit defeat to the night and grab my blanket again, remembering to bring a cushion down to sleep on. I want it to smell of him, but it doesn't, and I struggle to stop myself being disappointed.

Thirteen

The floor's uncomfortable, so I've been waking on and off for the last couple of hours, but that doesn't mean I'm any more prepared for the shrill scream of the fire alarm than Dan is.

The room is a blur as I leap to my feet and hit the desk light, flooding us in a low, warm glow. Dan is sitting bolt upright, eyes huge and shaded.

'We're okay,' I say over the ringing, stuffing my shoes onto my feet and snatching my glasses from the desk. 'Ground floor—we're okay.'

I realise far too slowly that it isn't the thought of fire that's upset him: it's being snatched so cruelly from the peaceful arms of sleep.

So, I grab his hand because I'm not convinced he can walk and tug him to the door. He lets me hold him just until I unlock it, when his fingers slip from mine and brush against my waist, instead.

Oh, God, I wish I'd slept in jeans.

We break contact as soon as we're out of the building and it is freezing. I'm not sure I've ever been so cold in my life. We stand a little way from everyone else, in our own bubble, and I whisper to him as if it's going to help.

'You okay?' I ask, and he just nods. What would he do if I touched his hand? 'You won't have to worry about this when you're in your flat, at least.'

Another little dip of his head.

'And it's still really early so we'll be able to get back to sleep.'

This time, his head shakes from side to side. 'I can't.'

'Why not?'

Stupid question. He doesn't answer, but his nostrils flicker

61

a little bit and his arms crush his chest. I want to get in the way, so he has to crush me, not himself, but I settle with putting my hand on his elbow, instead.

'You know you can tell me anything, right?' I'm relieved to see him nod. Accommodation support are starting to call us to order. 'Whenever you're ready.'

He doesn't say anything because they start reading our names from the register.

And my name is right at the top of the list.

'William Anson?'

We both jump, and he jumps even more when I shout out a 'yeah' in response. Fine—I don't have to concentrate any more. Instead, I stand as close to him as I can, so his arm is touching my chest, and I try to tell him I want to help. I try to show him, through standing that bit too close, that I care.

Security turn the alarm off. Someone admits to trying to cook bacon—at half two in the morning!—on a filthy grill pan and are kept back for a talk. We file back into the building, groggy and cold from our unexpected few minutes outside.

I'm jittering when we reach my room, but Daniel looks awful.

Where it wasn't already bruised, the delicate skin under his eyes is grey, tinged blue over the tiny blood vessels. The bleeding in his right eye has started to go down, so it's more concentrated around the iris, and I want to say it's an improvement but it's still alarming. It's the same for his jaw: it's browner now, than purple, but it still looks painful.

I realise it must be and point sharply to the boxes of painkillers which are still there from Monday night.

'Take something,' I say. He almost looks at me. 'You look like you're in agony.'

The light from my desk isn't the most flattering, but he's wincing. It takes me this long to remember his ribs, and the way he crushed his own chest, and I think I deserve a slap.

'Dan, breathe.' I take his glass and refill it in the washbasin. 'You're okay.'

'They will wonder why I am here,' he croaks.

This wasn't quite what I was expecting. I take his hand

62

and wrap it around the glass, forcing him to at least hold it, and it works; he takes a sip and smiles.

'They will ask you.'

'Yeah? You're my friend who's just staying here while their room gets sorted.' It's true, but my voice cracks. 'I don't care if they're nosy.'

'They might speculate.' He stretches his neck and looks away from me. 'I'm so sorry.'

The familiar urge to out myself drops through me. It should be so easy.

'It's fine,' I say, without much conviction. 'I don't care what they think. I don't care if they think I'm—I'm—' Shit. I hesitate, choking on the words, and now it looks like I'm not okay with the idea of someone thinking I'm gay. Oh, God. 'I don't care what they think I am—it doesn't matter.'

Until this moment, I've been sure Dan's noticed the way I stare at him. Isn't it obvious? I can't find the words to say *hey, I'm queer, too* and he doesn't even look like he's trying to read between the lines. He doesn't ask me to confirm anything one way or the other. He doesn't even hint that he doesn't know for certain what my sexuality is, and it hurts.

I want him to care.

I'm rambling, trying to hide the way my fingers are twisting together. 'Because it's—they don't matter. Not that sexuality matters—but you—Dan, you know what I'm trying to say.'

Except he doesn't.

He smiles without looking at me, takes another sip of the water, and sits down. Good idea. I join him, leaving not quite enough space between our legs.

'I think so,' he says eventually. 'I appreciate it.'

Silence fills the room while I'm trying to work out how to physically say the word *bisexual* and he's thinking about something equally uncomfortable.

'Do you mind?'

I frown. 'What?'

'That I'm gay.'

He says it with less confidence than when he told me he's

been taking heroin, and I can appreciate that. You can pretty much guarantee how someone's going to react to hearing you take drugs. Actually vocalising that you're queer, on the other hand, is downright terrifying.

I would know.

I over-do it, but I've decided I physically can't shower Dan with too much love. He needs every hug and every smile he can get.

I take his hand and give it a squeeze, fingers sliding between his. 'I really don't mind,' I whisper. 'It's a bit like saying I don't mind you have blue eyes.'

In my head, I just told him he's perfect.

A minute passes before he speaks again. Time flies when I'm with Daniel, and silences are remarkably comfortable.

'Thank you.'

We're still holding hands. If I tilt my head, I can see white satin scars reaching across his forearm. I'm desperate to ask about them but it couldn't be worse timing if I tried, so I bite my cheek and save my questions.

Dan shrugs. 'You understand why I was nervous.'

I laugh, and it sounds hysterical. It is. 'I totally understand,' I say, accidentally rubbing my thumb into the back of his. My head's rushing with the thought of saying *I like you*, so I take a deep breath, eyes closing before I speak again.

'Don't worry. I don't mind—at all. But you should take painkillers.'

He lets out a gentle sigh and I think I'm going to win, but he twists to look at me. 'My ribs are the least of my problems at the moment,' he whispers. 'This is the longest I have gone without heroin in weeks.'

Ah.

God, I'm stupid.

I frown up at him, concerned. 'Is there anything I can do?'

I'm beginning to expect the way he shakes his head. 'Sure?'

'Sure. But thank you.' He takes another sip of water

64

before reaching behind us to put the glass down. 'I am better than I was. And I have not used it for many months.' The world sways around us. 'I will be okay. But I do not think I could give up smoking—I would like to, but I can't.'

I stare at the little smudge of water still on his lips. 'Even with all the quitting aids around?'

'Even with.'

I try to not look too disappointed and close my eyes, like I'm scared of seeing how he's looking at me. 'Maybe that will change one day. Can we stay in touch?"

He wasn't expecting that. 'Of course,' he says, voice higher than before. Surprised. Off-guard. 'I will not be far away. And I'm finishing my degree.'

My eyes snap open. 'You'll have to re-sit the exams, right?'

He nods once. Thinking about our sexuality is a dangerous path and I'm glad we've drifted away from that. I flounder for something else to talk about and almost blurt about his scars.

'I like your tattoo,' I say instead. The words come out in a jumble and I'm impressed he hears enough to laugh. 'What is it?'

'A collection,' he says, holding his left arm out in front of us. The bruising on his knuckles has gone down since last week, and the dull light makes the ink stand out against his pale skin. 'Nothing important to me. I stopped adding to it when I moved.'

Did he purposely leave me with so many questions? *When* did he move? *Why* did he move? *Where* did he move from? *What do the words mean?*

'Well, it suits you,' I say, eyes fixed on the feather that seems to follow his radius. 'I never considered getting one.'

He laughs again and shrugs, dropping his hand to rest on his lap. 'No, I am not surprised. You would not risk the infection.'

I laugh, but he's right. He asks me about the book he borrowed from my shelf, inviting me to jabber about my degree for a few minutes, and I'd keep talking all night if it

65

wasn't for yawning.

'Go to sleep,' he whispers. 'Do you want the bed?'

'No, because if you do feel like you can get a few minutes you have to be comfortable.' I stand slowly, reluctant to put any distance between us. It's only now that our hands separate and the air feels cold after the heat of his skin. 'I'm fine down there.'

He hums, not approving but not arguing, and shuffles round to lean against the headboard. 'Thank you. I'll see you in the morning.'

I put too much thought into how I walk around the end of the bed and to my patch of carpet. I take my glasses off slowly, worried I'll drop them, and fold them back onto the desk. 'Technically,' I mutter, when all that's left to do is to lie down under my blanket, 'it *is* morning.'

His laugh is like heaven. 'I'll see you when the sun is up.'

I don't respond. I would definitely embarrass one of us. Instead, I curl up on my side—facing away from him—and beg my heart to slow down. I feel like I've been plugged into a socket and no one's thought to check what voltage I can handle.

*

The next thing I know, the sun is burning through the gap in the blinds and Daniel is swearing.

I sit up, dragging the blanket with me, and squint at him. I grab my glasses and try again. 'You okay?'

He coughs and nods, bleary eyed and tangled in the duvet. 'I slept on the wrong side of my face,' he explains, smiling a little ruefully, and I'm sat on the edge of the bed without thinking about it.

Who do I think I am?

I put my fingers very delicately over the bruise, using the tiniest bit of pressure to find his jaw. He's lovely and warm from sleeping.

'Did they x-ray it?' I follow the line of bone up to his ear and back down to his chin.

66

He stays perfectly still, like he knows one wrong movement will ruin us.

'Your hand is very cold,' he whispers, instead of answering.

I shrug and snatch it away from his skin, only just realising what I'm doing.

'Were you cold?'

'I'm always cold.' It's a lie and he sees through it.

Dan purses his lips. 'You should have said.'

I shrug again and plaster a smile over my face. 'I thought you weren't getting back to sleep.'

He raises an eyebrow and moves so quickly I don't have chance to react. He's obviously not as tangled in the duvet as I thought, because he manages to drape it around my shoulders without jostling me. And he's grinning.

He's really, really grinning.

'Do not change the subject.' He's alarmingly close to my ear and my cheeks are red hot. 'You have helped me more than enough this week. You shouldn't have made yourself cold for me.'

I would make myself *anything* for him.

'Changing the subject worked for you,' I point out. 'Did they x-ray your jaw?'

'Yes.'

'And?'

'And? Nothing.'

'No fractures?'

'No, just bruises.'

I grunt and feel myself sinking into the duvet. Bundled up in it and my blanket, I could fall straight back asleep.

Just when I think I'm the most comfortable I've ever been, Daniel moves. I twist to watch him lean against the headboard, looking nicely bedraggled in my borrowed clothes.

He's staring at me, eyes soft with sleep. 'It is only half seven,' he says. 'Do you want to get up?'

'May as well. Do you want breakfast?'

His expression hardly changes. It's a well-rehearsed mask,

but I think I'm beginning to understand it.

'We should eat something before going to your appointment,' I whisper.

The mask slips, revealing a frown between his eyebrows. 'You will come with me?'

'Told you I would, didn't I?' I rest my head on a mound of duvet that's bunched up over my shoulder and grin, because he's surprised I want to go with him. 'But we have hours.'

Fourteen

Remember what I said about time flying with Daniel? The morning rushes past us like a cross-country train. We make breakfast, we eat breakfast, we go to his appointment in the medical centre. He tells me very quietly, while we're alone in the waiting room, about taking heroin. Apparently, it hasn't featured in his life for more than three months, and I guess that's a good thing. I suppose I'm relieved, but I just feel like I've been tipped over the side of a barrier and I'm holding on by my feet.

I have plenty of time to think about this while he's in his appointment.

Thinking about his relationship scares me. Thinking about his drug use *terrifies* me—what else isn't he telling me? How long will it take for him to get clean again? This is what he's talking to the doctor about, and I wish he'd asked me to come into the room with him. I wish I knew what I could do.

But then he re-joins me, grinning from ear to ear. It's such a new expression for him that it takes me a moment to get to my feet, and a moment to catch up with what he's telling me. He's doing well, his prescription seems to be doing its job, and they've agreed he doesn't need to be admitted to any rehab centres. Honestly, I'd been worrying about that.

We're walking out into the sunlight when his phone buzzes with a text from his new landlord confirming he can collect the keys this afternoon.

While I'm in lectures.

It feels significant when we part outside the SU. Dan's going to meet with security and a member of staff from student support, so they can clear out his room. They've arranged to pack everything into one of the SU minibuses and are going to drive him to his new flat—as if they feel bad about what's happened.

They should. I'm not convinced they're planning on doing anything about his ex—even though the guy put him in hospital—and I'm quietly fuming. Dan doesn't mention it, though, so I don't dare ask.

For now, I'm going home after my lectures to an empty room.

'I'll text you when I'm settled,' he says.

A text. After the couple of days we've had, a text could *never* be enough. So much can hide in a text.

'Thank you for everything.'

It feels like I'm never going to see him again.

'You're completely welcome, Dan.' My voice is embarrassingly heavy over tears. Crap. I think Dan's about to experience how easy it is to make me cry. 'If you—if you ever need anything, or just want to chat, you know where I am.'

He looks at me for a moment like he knows how upset I am. Like he understands why. *I* don't even understand why.

'I'll talk to you later.' He glances at the time on his phone. 'Have a good afternoon.'

I swallow something down and smile, waiting for him to take the first step away. He doesn't. I wish he would.

Instead, he steps forward and puts his arms around me, like I've been desperate for him to do for days. He's warm again, and I think now that he must just be a very warm person. I duck my head into his shoulder and hide from the world, eyes closed and heart hammering. Doing this every day would be heaven.

'Visit me soon,' he whispers, like he's read my mind. 'I'll be at the social on Monday.'

'You will?'

He laughs, shaking me. 'I like seeing people. Let me know if you will be there.'

I don't want to ever let go, for a hundred different reasons, but I take a deep breath and let my arms return to my sides. His hands slip from my back.

'I will do. Right, I'm going to be late.'

'Go, William.' He takes that first step away from me, like

70

he knows I need help. I feel his foot hitting the concrete like a shockwave passing through me. 'I'm fine. I'm okay. And we'll talk soon.'

I nod, chew my lip, and turn. I glance over my shoulder as I walk away and he's smiling after me, watching as I leave. He has the expression of a man who has been granted permission to go anywhere he likes. I guess he has.

I do have to rush to my lecture.

Time flies with Daniel.

Fifteen

13:37 **Peter**: You missed the best film last night

13:40 **William**: Did I?

I'm grateful for Peter's predictably well-timed text, but I can't pretend to be enthusiastic. I reply between lectures, only half paying attention to the world around me. I'm only quarter paying attention to Peter.

In the back of my mind is a constant ticking, like the second hand of a clock.

14:02 **Peter**: Yes, you did. What are you doing this evening? Work?

14:03 **William**: Work, but I could see you for a bit if that's what you're asking

14:16 **Peter**: YEEES ok you me and Cas in the pub for drinks??

His enthusiasm does lift me a bit. So does the thought of spending an hour or two with my best friends. I agree to be there, warn them I'm bringing my laptop, and do my best to be a brilliant student through the next four hours.

My eyelids are heavy after the last lecture and I stumble out into the cool evening air, not entirely convinced I'm not going straight to bed. When my phone buzzes again, I almost ignore it.

17:05 **Daniel**: My apartment is big compared to your room. One bedroom, but there is space. I hope you've had a good day and have a good evening.

Daniel.

My hand shakes as I reply and then my thoughts are so scrambled I start walking back to my block, rather than to meet Peter and Cassie.

> 17:07 **William**: Do you like it? Thanks! It's been a good day. I'm meeting with Peter and Cas for a catch-up in a few minutes

17:10 **Daniel**: I like it. I hope you have a great time with them. See you soon?

> 17:12 **William**: I will do. Definitely, please. What are you doing this evening?

17:16 **Daniel**: Getting used to freedom and sleeping, I think

> 17:17 **William**: Excellent plan. Text or call me whenever you want—you know I'm here

17:20 **Daniel**: I know. Thank you.

> 17:21 **William**: You're always welcome

Freedom.

I want to celebrate this. But with Dan, because it's Dan's achievement—even if it did take being knocked about within an inch of his life. I still haven't found the courage to ask about his wrist, or the bruises on his face, and at this point I don't think I ever will. What's the point in upsetting him further?

Thinking about this makes me lose sight of where I'm putting my feet, so I concentrate on the positives, instead.

Dan's free, and he's got his own place to live, and he's my friend. And I can still feel the ghost of him in my arms if I think about that hug.

I realise, as I walk up the hill towards our preferred pub, that I can't tell Cassie and Peter everything. Dan was terrified someone might find out he was staying in my room and, as I don't know *who* he's just broken up with, I don't want to accidentally give anything away.

I feel just as protective of him now, when I know he's in control of his life again, as I did on Monday night.

The pub we're meeting at is at the western end of campus, just within the village, and past a field of cows. Once, I heard someone describe Keele University as being '*like a farm*'. It's an exaggeration, but we *are* right in the heart of countryside and I guess if you've spent your whole life in a city the rolling glacial hills dotted with livestock are a bit overwhelming.

It doesn't take me long to get to the pub. It's on the bus route, so it's convenient for Peter and Cassie, and most of the journey home for me is downhill. As soon as I walk through the heavy door I'm hit by the smell of spilled alcohol and old carpet, which I'm always surprised to find I don't actually mind. It's familiar, like summer holidays with my family, and I weave past the scattered tables and chairs, thinking I can treat myself to something other than water.

I see them, sat together at a table tucked away in the corner of the room. Cassie launches into the air, hand raised, and I trot over to them, squeezing past some lecturers I recognise who have clearly decided they can afford to have a hangover tomorrow.

'You look depressed,' Peter says, instead of *hello*.

I raise an eyebrow. I thought I was doing a fairly good job of keeping myself together.

'What's happened?'

'Nothing bad,' I hear myself say, dropping my bag down on the empty bench. They haven't got glasses in front of them, so I gesture broadly at the table. 'Is this you saying you want me to buy drinks?'

The absolute outrage at such a suggestion is hilarious and

I roll my eyes, take their order, and go up to the bar.

I wonder if Daniel drinks.

I manage to carry all three glasses back to the table at once and they both congratulate me, so I find myself grinning.

'So,' Peter starts, folding his arms on the table and leaning towards me as soon as I've sat down. Facing them both, I feel like I'm being interviewed. 'What's happened?'

I roll my eyes again but my grin falls. 'Daniel and I have talked a bit. He's moved off-campus today and he's split up with his boyfriend, which is good.'

I very purposefully avoid mentioning my room, or drugs.

Peter wrinkles his nose and looks over at Cassie to gauge her reaction. 'I've missed something.'

'Daniel's the guy who rescued Will's memory stick the other week,' Cassie explains. 'We were a bit worried about him.'

'Why?'

Cassie hesitates and looks at me before answering 'He just seemed down,' she says. 'But you said he's okay, now.'

I shrug, holding my breath. 'Seems better.'

Peter pulls his phone out and spends a moment tapping icons to open Facebook. 'He's the friend you were worried about on Monday, right?' He doesn't look up to see me nod. 'The guy who found us at the social.'

'That's the one.'

'Him?' Peter brandishes his phone at me, screen full of Daniel's profile picture. I should have expected it this time, but my words get stuck in my throat for a moment. 'Will?'

'Yeah.' I lick my dry lips and tap my fingernails against my glass. 'His profile is useless, though.'

Peter spends a moment trying various buttons before giving up and agreeing with me. While we wait, Cassie and I share a long look where I try to thank her for not blurting *he's being abused*, and she tries to do something like reassure me.

'So I guess we're happy, right?' Peter continues, phone finally back down on the table.

I nod and sip my cider.

'So why don't you look it?'

75

'Rude.' I sit up, shoulders back, and kick him under the table. 'I'm exhausted. But, yeah. I'm happy. Dan's happy. It's all good.'

They look at each other for a moment, and I'm expecting more questions, but Cassie presses her lips together. *Drop it*. She moves the conversation away from me, and I take the opportunity to let my shoulders relax.

'Lilley's new boyfriend is weird,' Cassie says, and I feel my heart sink. 'I don't think I like him.'

'What's he done?' I hide behind my glass and share a look with Peter, this time. He keeps squinting at me.

'Well,' Peter says, 'when you were being boring last night, we invited her, instead.' I can take the dig. There is no world in which I'd admit I was spending the night with Dan. 'And she just said no.'

'Just no?'

'Literally just no. Look,' he says, waking up his phone again and showing me a conversation with Lilley.

There it is: a brief *no*.

'Is this all we're basing this opinion on?' I point at the screen and glance between them. 'Because even I'm not convinced.'

Peter hits me with a glare which is so out of place on his soft face that I burst into laughter.

'No,' he sniffs. 'How judgy do you think we are? This is just one example of her being weird.'

'I thought the guy was the weird one.'

'Don't be a smart-ass,' Peter mutters, folding his hands beneath his chin.

'I haven't seen her all semester,' Cassie says, tucking her bright hair back behind her ears. 'We talked a couple of times and said we'd meet up, but she never committed and we just… haven't.'

I cringe. 'That's not cool.'

'No, it isn't.'

'Have you upset her?' Peter asks me, nudging me under the table.

I glare at him. 'Me?'

'Have you seen her?'

'I've seen her *once*—like three weeks ago.' I remember it vividly. 'She didn't seem pleased to see me, but it wasn't like we argued or anything. We barely talked.'

'Maybe she thinks I've chosen you over her,' Cassie whispers, as if she's ashamed to think it.

'Definitely not—she knows you love her,' I say quickly. 'And she wouldn't suggest meeting up if she didn't mean it, would she?'

'I suggested it.'

'Oh.'

We spend a moment looking between each other. The table between us feels like a storm cloud and I hold onto my glass, as if I'm expecting the wood to vaporise.

'Give her a couple more weeks,' I suggest. 'We know she doesn't like being crowded.'

Peter laughs at me. 'Yeah, but this isn't a needy boyfriend —this is Cassie.'

My skin feels cold. 'The same still applies. Sometimes you just need space and you don't want people poking into your business.'

'Are you getting at something, Will?'

'No—why do you think I am?'

Peter shrugs and looks into his glass. 'You didn't tell me about Dan.'

I purse my lips. 'You think me not telling you about Dan *means* something?'

'Yep.'

'What?'

'Means you don't trust me, or whatever,' he mutters. 'You know you can, don't you?'

I can't say I do.

'There's nothing to say about Dan,' I lie, purposefully not looking at Cassie. 'We're friends, but that's it. So why don't you like Lil's boyfriend, Cas?'

My attempt at changing the topic is pathetic but she takes it.

'I haven't met him, and I don't think she wants me to,'

she sighs. 'I just feel abandoned. Like *I've* been dumped, y'know?'

'Yeah,' Peter says, bumping her with his elbow. 'Don't worry. You always have us.'

Cassie rolls her eyes. 'Thanks, guys. You're not—Lilley!'

I cower, hiding against the back of the bench, and hold my breath. I have a bad feeling about this.

Cassie waves, her desperateness to contact her friend oozing out in a bright grin and erratic movements, and I'm relieved to see Lilley walk towards us in the corner of my eye.

She doesn't stop—she bends down and gives Cassie a hug.

'Hey,' Lilley says, sounding so much warmer than the last time I saw her. Something flutters in my chest and I find myself grinning at her. 'How are you both?'

Ouch. She leans against the end of the table, back to me, and only looks at Peter and Cassie. I don't mind much because Cassie looks like a celebrity just told her she looks nice.

'Good, thanks,' Cassie says, cheeks a little bit red. 'Who are you here with?'

Lilley shrugs. 'Course friends. I keep meaning to get back to you about meeting up, but things happen—can you do Monday evening?'

A bulb just lit inside of Cassie and she's beaming. 'That would be great.'

'Awesome.' From here, I can just about guess that Lilley's grinning. 'I'll message you over the weekend and phone me if I forget, alright? I miss you.'

I'm pretty sure Cassie is going to cry. 'Will do. I miss you too.'

Lilley hesitates before pushing away from the table. 'Nice to see you, Peter,' she calls, walking away with a cheerful wave.

Cassie is too happy to notice what Peter and I can't escape.

'That was rude,' Peter mutters, eyes wide on me. 'You okay?'

'Yep.'

'She completely—'

'I dumped her,' I remind them, fingernails rapid against my glass. 'It's fine.'

'Do you think she means it about Monday?' Cassie asks, gazing after her friend. 'She's not just gonna cancel again?'

'I don't think she would,' I say, wishing I'd just got water for myself. The cider is too sweet. 'She probably said no about yesterday because she thought I'd be there.'

'Probably,' Peter says. '*Why* didn't you come?'

I thought it had been accepted I was just *busy*. 'Working,' I say, glancing between them. 'Why?'

'Working in the SU?'

My stomach tenses and I hear, in the background of my thoughts, something like guilt.

Peter shrugs and looks at Cassie for back-up. 'Saw you with Dan.'

'So?'

'Looked pretty cosy.'

We definitely shouldn't have sat so closely together.

'When were you going to tell us?' Cassie asks, smiling softly like she's telling me it's all okay. 'We don't mind.'

'Tell you what?' I can feel my pulse picking up speed every other beat. If Peter saw us, who else did?

'Are you two dating?' Peter asks, smiling like he's getting a toddler to confess to stealing the last chocolate.

I nearly erupt.

'No,' I say, voice clipped, 'and I'd tell you if we were. I don't—we're friends. We're friends, and he—Cassie, you know what he's been through.'

She holds her hands up as Peter glares at her. 'Don't drag me into this—all I know is he was high the other week and we decided he'd probably be better off not dating his boyfriend.'

'Yeah—and he isn't dating him anymore so that's all we need to say about it,' I snap. 'I'm his friend.'

Peter purses his lips and looks across the pub, towards where Lilley disappeared into the crowds. 'Sure.'

'What's that supposed to mean?'

'Means I don't believe for a moment that you left the *gay* social with a hot *gay* guy and had dinner practically *sat on his lap* and nothing—'

'Nothing happened.' I sound like iron.

'Will—'

'Why do you want me to say it did? Is this why you asked me out with you this evening—to interrogate me?'

Cassie sighs dramatically and rubs her forehead. 'Why don't you both just calm down?' she suggests. 'Pete, you can't make him tell you something just because you want to hear it. Will, we'd appreciate a bit more transparency with your new friendship. That's all.'

I grab a spare beermat and dog-ear the corners. 'Fine. I walked Dan home because his ribs are broken, Peter, and he was getting out of breath. He told me about dumping his boyfriend and we agreed to meet up the next day because he wanted someone with him while he sorted out moving off campus—and then we had dinner together, because he hasn't had a friend in forever and it was just nice to get to know someone new. Is that okay? Am I allowed to do that?'

Peter rolls his eyes. 'I didn't mean like—'

'Felt like it.'

'I don't want you feeling like you have to hide things from me, Jesus,' he mutters. 'I want you to know it's okay if you're gay. Of course it is. If that's why you dumped Lil—'

'I'm not—and it isn't.' I sigh and stretch my neck. My back is tight, ready for impact. 'I'm not gay, Peter.'

It's as true as saying *I'm not straight* and I'm hoping one of them will smile and ask me if I'm bi. Then I can just blush and shrug, say *yeah*, and that'll be the end of it.

'Alright. Keep an eye out, though,' Peter mutters. 'Dan looked like he was into you.'

My skin burns. 'You think?'

'Don't be leading him on.'

'You only glimpsed him. He's not—he's not after a relationship. He's got enough going on as it is,' I mutter, trying to convince myself as much as them. 'Thanks for the concern, though. I'm not interested in anyone. I don't want a relationship.'

Peter seems to relax. 'Fine,' he says, sipping at his drink.

'Fine, okay.'

The conversation falls flat and Cassie sighs again. 'What are you both doing this weekend?'

I cringe and say *work*, expecting them to doubt me, but I'm saved. Peter grins and says, cheeks rosy, that he has a date.

My eyebrows leap up my forehead. 'A date? Who's being secretive now, huh?'

He laughs and shrugs. 'Didn't want to take anything away from your news if you had any,' he mutters. It's fair enough, and I nudge him with my foot. 'But, yeah. Anthony plays football and he has a game on Sunday against Staffs so I'm going to watch.'

I hum and wink at Cassie. 'A field full of sweaty footballers—what's not to love?'

Peter snorts, embarrassed, and cradles his glass. 'You don't know what you're missing, dear.'

Sixteen

The earliest I can justify seeing Dan again is Sunday afternoon. It's a bright, cold day, and the taxi pulls up in front of a block of flats along the bus route to the hospital. I can't justify how happy it makes me to know he lives in such a convenient place. I'm grinning, despite slight travel sickness, and reach forward to pay.

I'm expecting to have to text him once I'm standing on the pavement but the door to the building swings open and he's there. I forget what I'm doing, fail to take the change from the driver, and stumble out of the car. Some part of my brain is still functioning because I manage to step back and shut the door.

'Hello.' Dan sounds nervous.

God, I feel nervous. I think it's a good nervous, though, like going to see your favourite band for the first time. I just stand there, staring at him, as the taxi drives off.

'Hey.' Brilliant. I managed a syllable.

'I'm upstairs,' he says, holding the door open for me. He looks bright. Happy. The relief of seeing him look like he's had a decent night's sleep is enough to choke my sinuses with tears and all I can manage as I walk towards him is a little smile. 'How are you?'

'I'm okay, thanks.' I follow him up narrow, twisting stairs to the next floor. 'How are you?'

It feels so formal. Like maybe I'm coming over to do some university work.

'I'm okay,' he breathes, unlocking and pushing open a door. I guess this is his apartment, and make sure he can see me smiling as I step past him. 'What do you think?'

It's a lovely flat. It's clean, which is enough to make anywhere feel nicer than student halls, and the air still smells of fresh paint. We walk straight onto the tiled floor of his little kitchen, which has just enough space to cook food for one. The rest of the room is open, and it's a just a couple of steps before we're standing in the middle of his living room. There are two doors to the right: one which is ajar, showing me more tiles, and the other which I guess is his bedroom.

'This is really nice.' I'm a moment too late, trying to take it all in. 'Cute settee.'

Dan laughs and walks towards it, like he's going to sit down. 'Thank you.'

A ridiculously small part of me is beginning to think this might not have been a brilliantly thought out idea. We barely know each other.

He turns and looks at the kitchen, rather than at me. 'Do you want a drink?'

'I—yeah, please.' I stand there, hands in my pockets, and try to not look like an idiot. 'Am I allowed to have a nose around?'

I can't believe I just asked that.

He laughs again, shrugs, and walks past me to the sink. 'Of course. There is not much to see. What would you like?'

I would like to look less terrified. 'Just water, please.' Chewing the inside of my cheek, I walk around the living room, taking in the little collection of books he has piled up at one end of the settee, and the stack of DVDs beneath the TV.

He doesn't say anything, so I drift to the doors. I peek into the bathroom, smile at the toothbrush and razor sat on the sink, and glance back at the kitchen. He's running water, his back to me, so I open his bedroom door. It feels like I'm crossing a boundary.

Part of me is expecting to find something awful—some sign of his ex-boyfriend, or of drug use—but I get nothing like that.

His bedroom is gorgeous.

The walls are cream, except for the one facing the bed, which is covered by an inky blue wallpaper. The carpet is soft, like it's not long been put down, and I kick my shoes off as soon as the niceness of it all registers.

His bed is huge. It must be king-sized, and it's fairly tall, and I'm almost tempted to leap onto it.

'Did you get lost?'

I jump so sharply I almost elbow him and catch my arms against my chest, so it doesn't happen again. I'm red, and my pulse is sky-high.

'This is beautiful,' I say. My shoes are right in the way. 'Is the carpet new?'

'It is all new,' he admits, stepping past me to look out the window. 'Redecorated after the last tenant filled it with smoke.'

'Ah.'

'I go outside,' he clarifies, glancing over his shoulder at me. 'To smoke.'

'I'd expect nothing less.' I pick my shoes up to move them to somewhere less in the way before I join him. The view out of his window is across a supermarket carpark, which falls away to a maze of streets and houses that roll into the distance.

I don't look at him when I ask my next question, because I know it's going to be uncomfortable for both of us.

'How's everything else?' It's been just over a week. He must be struggling.

'Difficult.' He leans through his shoulder, against the wall, and almost faces me. I carefully keep my eyes on the view. 'I spoke to Matthew.'

I have an awfully bad feeling.

'Who?' I ask, even though I can work it out. Dan slumps, like he might collapse, and I hold my breath.

'My ex.'

I look up to face him, dreading whatever's coming next. He doesn't seem to notice I've turned and his eyes, neither of them bloodshot, now, are hard and unseeing. For a moment, he looks his age.

And I feel so, so young.

Who am I to think I can help this man? He's so much older than me. He's seen so much more of the world—he's had so much more pain—

'What happened?'

I watch the way his eyelids twitch, like he's concentrating on something he can't quite see, but he answers without hesitating.

'He phoned me,' he says. 'We spoke for some hours.'

'What about?'

'What I'm doing next. I told him I've moved but I didn't say where to.'

I nod, but I don't think he sees.

'He apologised for Friday.'

'Do you believe him?'

His eyelids twitch again. 'Yes.'

'Dan—'

'I believe he was sorry,' he whispers. 'I don't believe he would ever change. Don't worry.'

'Good, because—'

'I'm not going back. No matter how much I miss him.'

Oh, God. I don't know what to say to that. It's early afternoon, but it feels like something past midnight, and any wrong word might ruin everything he's built in the last week.

I frown as I speak. 'You don't miss him. You miss the company.'

His eyes flash down to me. 'I think it might be more than that.' The space between us is impossibly large. 'I miss being allowed to feel weak.'

'You're not—you're not weak.'

A little smile, which I don't quite believe. 'Thank you.'

It sounds like he wants to leave the conversation there. I'm not sure I physically can.

'Are you going to talk again?' I ask.

He sighs. 'Probably. Yes.'

The pessimism in my voice makes me cringe. 'Let me know when you do.'

He moves his eyebrow just enough to ask *why*.

'I want to be able to help you.'

Once again, I feel incredibly young. He finds another smile and relaxes his shoulders, the breath of a sigh just about reaching me before he speaks.

'Maybe I will tell you next time. Thank you for caring.'

'You *know* I care,' I mutter, crossing my arms. 'That's why I'm here.'

'Not just because you could not think of anything better to do this afternoon?'

I think something just ruptured in my chest. Dan's teasing me. After the things he just said, I'm struggling to process this cheeky smile. He's joking. He's messing around. Most importantly, he's happy.

We're caught smiling at each other. I'm stuck there, staring up at him, and time has stopped. It's only been four days since I last saw him, and the bleeding in his right eye has almost completely gone. It looks like he's just had a reaction to something, but there's still a smudge of red around the iris and a harsh black shadow beneath his orbit. His jaw looks less damaged: more brown and yellow, now, than the black and purple of last week.

I could stand here and look at him forever.

'Our drinks are in the kitchen,' he says eventually, unblinking. 'We should sit down.'

I nod, not trusting my voice, and follow him out of his bedroom. I think he glances down at my hand before he leads the way out. I think I see him consider touching me, and that is incredible. He wants contact.

So I follow him a little too closely and hover right beside him while he finishes making his drink. Coffee. Black.

'Just water?' He checks, handing me the glass.

I nod.

'You drink water even at the SU.'

'I didn't at the social,' I point out, taking the glass. 'And I had a drink with Peter and Cassie on Wednesday night.'

He nods and asks me about them as we sit down. We share the settee and it *is* cute; it's meant for two, but it isn't spacious, and it would be so easy to lean into him. I'm having to consciously stay sitting up straight.

I tell him about my friends, leaving out the details about Peter seeing us on Tuesday evening. I don't think he needs to worry about that. The TV is on, just as background noise, and gravity wins: I sink towards him, drawn to the warmth of his body over the rough cushion covers. Who can blame me? I keep expecting him to get up and say he's going outside for a cigarette, but he doesn't, and we sit there for hours.

Seventeen

I wake up suddenly. Shit.

I whisper his name without thinking about it and he groans, sitting up away from the arm of the settee.

Remembering his broken ribs, I realise he must be in agony and slip from the settee to kneel on the floor beside our abandoned dinner plates, hands fluttering up to his shoulders to support him. The TV's turned itself off, which might be why I woke up, but the rest of the room is still bright with electric light.

We fell asleep.

He winces, squinting through his eyelashes at me, and I shake my head before he speaks.

'Go to bed,' I croak. We're both blinking at each other like moles coming to the surface at midday. 'I'll stay here.'

'What time is it?' He stretches, doing a great job of hiding how much it hurts. I find my phone, which mercifully still has some battery, and sigh.

'Three,' I say. We both groan. 'Should you take some painkillers?'

It appears I have a compulsion to suggest he takes paracetamol at every single opportunity.

He ignores my suggestion and stays sitting there, one hand clutching the arm of the settee like he thinks he's going to fall. I'm still kneeling in front of him and, now the haze of sleep is waring off, I'm beginning to think maybe it wasn't a good move.

It's a while before he speaks. 'I can't make my guest sleep out here. Take the bed.'

'There is no way I'm letting you sleep on this.' I gesture to the settee. 'Come on, Dan. You're hurting. Go to bed. Be comfortable.'

He braces himself against the back of the settee and stretches again and I can almost hear how he creaks. 'I'm not taking the bed.'

His stubbornness is infuriating, and I get to my feet. 'Don't make me drag you,' I say, holding out my hand for him to take. In theory, it's just to help him up. 'You're in pain. There's no point in making it worse. Have you had your prescription? What time are you meant to take it?'

He's pissed off, not quite looking at me. His face is shining with sweat and I almost mention painkillers again when I wonder whether the pain is related to heroin withdrawal, and I falter. Researching heroin addiction wasn't pleasant bedtime reading, but I think I understand the green tinge around his mouth.

'Let me help,' I whisper, trying to be soft. 'Come with me.'

Eventually, he takes my hand. His is warm and I grasp it too tightly, fingers wrapping around his. It looks like it's a huge effort for him to get to his feet and he stumbles a little, pulling a face as his legs take his weight. I suppose that, if he was pushed downstairs, his hips must have taken a bruising, too. Did I lean against him? Did I press against his ribs and hurt him? I wish I knew which ones are broken.

I expect him to just release my hand and sulk in his room, but he doesn't. Instead, he holds onto me for a moment longer before shooting through the other door, to the bathroom. The lock clicks behind him.

And I'm left in no man's land, between the settee and the bedroom.

I stretch my neck, pushing my fingertips down either side of my spine. Sleeping on the settee was a terrible idea. The side of my nose hurts, where my glasses were pressing, and I can't begin to imagine how much pain Dan must be in.

The far too familiar sound of him being sick brings me back to the present and I step right up to the door, as if this weren't something that went wrong last time. If anything, it sounds worse than Monday night, and I cringe.

'Dan? Let me in.'

No response. I can't say I'm surprised.

'Do you want some water? Let me help.'

The toilet flushes and I step back, anticipating what comes next. There's a silence, broken by the running tap, and then the door swings open.

Ah, shit.

He looks like he's been fighting a flu for weeks. His perpetually dry lips are bleeding, adding a splash of colour to his otherwise grey face, and he's shaking.

'Go to bed,' I whisper.

He leans heavily into the door and looks down, hiding his face.

'You need your prescription, right?'

He nods, right hand reaching out to grip the doorframe. I take his other hand and I am not surprised to find its trembling.

'You look awful.' I tug softly on his arm, trying to coax him to the bedroom. 'Come on. Are the tablets in your room?'

He groans and, for a moment, I think he's going to double back into the bathroom. Instead, he stands up and catches my shoulder with his free hand, making me look at him and using me as support.

'Thank you. Stay with me.'

I couldn't ever resist that. Not in a month of Sundays.

So I nod, give his hand a squeeze, and guide him to the bedroom. 'Sounds good to me. Do you think you should take some painkillers, too?'

He closes the bedroom door and gives me a look I was almost asking for.

'Perhaps,' he whispers, finally dropping my hand. The air burns my skin. 'Thank you.'

'For what?'

Instead of answering, he throws me another *look* and tugs open the drawer beside his bed. I hear the familiar crackling of foiled plastic as he pops out a tablet and swallows it dry, keeping his back to me.

'Goodnight, then,' he breathes, sitting down on the side

of the bed closest to the door. I can't feel my legs, and wobble across the room to perch on the side near the window. Should I say something? I take my glasses off, but it feels wrong to lie down in his bed—especially with him there—when the air between us feels so sharp.

'Dan?' Through the gloom, I see him turn to face me. 'Are you oaky?'

'Yeah.' It barely reaches me. 'Go to sleep.'

'Were you sick?'

'Yes.'

I'm not sure why I asked. I *know* he was sick—I just wanted him to tell me what's going on. But maybe three AM isn't the best time for this conversation.

'I'll see you in the morning, yeah?'

A tiny nod. 'I have work. I think we should travel to campus together.'

I flash a grin. 'Great idea. Thanks for letting me stay.'

He laughs, and it's such a relief to hear. I feel myself melting into the mattress. 'Thanks for reminding me to take my prescription.'

I shrug, and I think he can see the way my shoulders jump.

'You are a very good friend.'

I fully expect a *but*, but it doesn't come. Instead, I can see him smiling. 'You know you're welcome. Goodnight, Dan.'

He moves so he's face down, chest against the mattress, and I don't think he's noticed how close I am to him. There's no way I can move now, though, and I just get comfortable and… watch him.

I watch him for far too long.

He's scared. Not as scared as Monday night, and I dread to think what he was like for those couple of nights he spent in hospital, but he's hidden away under his arm again, face turned away from me. It's defensive. His shoulders relax while I'm watching and then, when I'm starting to realise I really should go to sleep, his breathing changes. It's regular and smooth, now, instead of tight and just when he feels up to inflating his lungs.

    I close my eyes, vaguely wondering what the time is, and fall asleep almost straight away. The bed is very nice.

Eighteen

I wake up first again. This time, it's not the absence of noise from the TV, or my alarm telling me to get going to lectures. It's unfamiliar groaning and whimpering.

It takes me about five seconds to work out Dan's hurting, and another few to realise he's *dreaming*. Mercifully, the streetlights are still glowing through the curtains.

His name falls from my lips without me thinking about it. I've propped myself up against the pillow and I don't even think about the fact I'm in *his bed*. This might be overstepping some boundary, but I reach over the expanse of mattress and duvet to touch his tousled hair.

My voice gets through to him and he doesn't gently wake, like I hoped. He twists into a tight ball, trying to shrink away from everything, and shudders.

'Dan? It's me.' As if *me* means anything. 'It's Will. You're okay. You're safe.'

He's panting, now, and I don't know if it's from pain or fear. And my fingers are knotted in his hair. And I've managed to move right next to him, like I'm going to cuddle him.

'Breathe, Dan.' I touch the side of his face incredibly lightly with the back of my thumb. His lips part and I catch some of his breath on my skin. 'It's okay. You're okay.'

He opens his eyes and looks straight at me, bringing a prickling blush to my cheeks. He looks like someone's drained him of all his blood, but his eyes are red—that right one looks bad again—and a vein thunders under his jaw.

'You okay?' I keep my hand in his hair because I can't move it. I just can't. He's still staring at me, like he can't decide if I'm really there, so I smile. 'You worried me, Dan.'

'Sorry,' he breathes, and it comes out shaky and weak. My smile slips to a frown and my hand slides further into his hair.

93

'I—' he drops his breath and closes his eyes, a little bit of colour filling his cheeks. Good. 'Sorry.'

'Does this happen lots?' I am very aware he's pushed his head into my hand. It was a little movement, when he closed his eyes, but it means the world.

He nods, pushing more hair between my fingers and making it harder to breathe.

'Want to tell me about it?'

I think I've pushed him too far again. I expect him to shake his head, apologise, and roll over. I don't expect the way his eyes catch me, mismatched twins of red, white, and blue.

'I don't sleep much.'

I've already worked that out for myself, so I nod and wait.

'I get a lot of bad dreams.'

I should take my hands out of his hair, but I *can't*. 'What happens in them?'

'I think he's here.' He closes his eyes and sits up. Okay. My hand drops to the pillow and I sit, too. 'And I miss it.' He says the last bit so quickly I have to ask him what he means. 'Heroin.'

'Ah.'

'It is worse at night.'

I'm not thinking. 'Does anything help?'

He's awake enough, now, to give me one of those precious little looks that tells me I've been a bit of an idiot. 'Cigarettes. Heroin. I imagine alcohol would do something, too.'

'Well, obviously I'm not letting you have any of that,' I mutter.

He flashes a cheeky grin and I feel it happen. Something blossoms in my chest and I reach for him, my hand crawling across the duvet again.

He tilts his head to one side. 'Not even a cigarette?'

I give up instantly. 'I suppose that's allowed. I'll come with you.'

He gets up, shaking his head. 'It's cold. Stay here.'

'I don't—'

'I'm okay,' he whispers, giving me a look that fixes me

where I am. 'I'll be a couple of minutes.'

I give him a smile and watch him leave, twisting a handful of duvet to keep myself where I am. I'm being careful to not let myself think he wants time away from me. I'm being careful to give him space, and respect his boundaries, but, shit, I am in his bed.

I doubt he'd mind if I got up and grabbed myself another glass of water.

I slide out of bed and tiptoe across the room, footsteps cushioned by the new carpet. Compared to student accommodation, this flat is a palace. It must have had a good impact on Daniel. Living here must be a good change.

I'm standing in the dark, sipping from a new glass of water, when the door to the flat opens.

He hears me jump, laughs, and I've never been more pleased to be surprised.

'Are you okay?' he asks, flicking the light on.

My smile falters and I squint at him, the bright light and lack of glasses making the room hazy.

'It is only five,' he says.

I groan and rub my eyes. 'Back to bed, then. Do you think you can get more sleep?'

He laughs again and the contrast to the last time he was awake is blinding. Even so, I'm not surprised he shakes his head.

'Almost definitely not. But it is worth trying.' He kicks off his shoes and leads the way back to his room.

I switch the light off behind us and follow him, glass of water in my hand.

'What time are your lectures tomorrow?'

I groan. 'Not until one.'

'That's a shame,' he mutters and, for a second, I'm frozen. 'I start work at half nine.'

'You're still working?' I ask, finally managing to put my glass down on the bedside table. 'Even though—'

'Even though he's still there? Even though I'm only one week into therapy? Yes.'

Louise Willingham

I'm staring at him, and he softens.

'I'm volunteering,' he explains. 'I want to keep some sort of purpose.'

'That makes sense.' I sit back on my side of the bed. 'Is it working?'

'Tomorrow is my first day back,' he points out, and I'm an idiot for not realising. I pull a face and he laughs again. It's a beautiful sound. 'Don't worry. I'll let you know how it goes.'

'Really?' I sound too excited. 'Thanks.'

He smirks at me. 'It's fine. Thanks for not being angry at me for smoking.'

That thing which flowered in my chest comes into full bloom, choking me.

Somehow, I manage to speak around the petals. 'I don't mind. I think you're doing amazingly with everything else.'

A tiny chuckle. He has one last stretch before lying face-down, arms folded under his pillow. 'Thank you, William.'

This is definitely the moment I should say *okay, goodnight* but I don't. I'm wide awake.

'Are they broken at the back?'

He turns his head to look at me, frowning.

'Your ribs.'

He nods, moving his arm so he can see me better. I can't believe I'm about to say this, but it spills out.

'Do you—can you show me?'

'Curious?' he asks, smirking through the orange light.

I press my lips together and nod.

'You will be a good doctor.'

'I don't know. I should have asked earlier.'

I pull my knees up to my chest as he sits up. My breath catches because he pushes the duvet away and pulls his shirt up and, fuck, I'm never going to get this out of my head.

'You don't—you don't have to,' I stutter.

He throws me a look—a sideways, *but I already am* look which twists my stomach—and stands up. I don't know where to put my eyes. I'm burning with embarrassment, and I should

96

definitely be focussing on the sprawling bruises on the lower left side of his back, but the scars—

I must have sworn out loud. He sighs and starts explaining, as if he owes it to me.

'The bruises are where the ribs broke.'

I'm shaking and shuffle closer, so I can see.

'This,' he points to a patch of shining skin over his right shoulder that reaches down towards his waist, 'is from fire.'

'Fuck.'

'Do you see the round ones?' he whispers.

I definitely do. They're scattered down his spine and I've worked out what they are before he explains.

'Cigarette burns.'

'Dan, shit.'

'It wasn't the first time,' he says, and my hands are on his bare back. He jumps a tiny bit but keeps talking and I'm going to think about this moment for the rest of my life. 'He broke my wrist last summer. And I think—I think you know why I took drugs.'

I shake my head, but he doesn't see. Obviously. So I have to find the strength to say something other than a curse and my hands slide to his shoulders like I'm supporting him. I think I'm supporting myself.

'Tell me.'

He takes a deep breath that stretches the bruises and rattles through the room. 'He had more fun if we were both high.'

It's too much. For both of us. I wonder if he's ever explained this to someone. He'll have mentioned the drugs, of course, but he's been riding on this lie that he *fell* down the stairs. I close my eyes and slip my arms around him and, after a moment where he's frozen and I think I've broken something between us, he sits down and leans into me. Where my arms are touching him, they feel like they're resting against a radiator.

We're on a roll and I don't think I'll ever get him to talk about this again. I don't think I want to.

97

'When did you leave him?'

His hand moves to take one of mine from his waist. 'Friday evening.'

I have to catch myself, lips moments from his shoulder. But would that be a bad thing?

It would be a very bad thing.

What I'm doing right now is a *bad thing*. I shouldn't be sharing a bed with him. I shouldn't be holding him like this when I'm so helplessly attracted to him, but he thinks I'm straight. He doesn't have a clue.

In my crisis, I've forgotten to respond. The pause has gone on for too long, stretching between us and pushing us to opposite sides of the room, and I should just let go of him.

I've never *said* I'm straight.

Even Peter and Cassie have noticed how nuts I am for him, and they've barely seen us together. Dan's been there each time my mouth has dropped open and I've stared at his hands. His eyes. His lips.

My lips press against his shoulder and he doesn't react.

'I'm so sorry you had to go through this,' I whisper, holding him like this is okay. 'I wish I'd done something.'

'What?' He twists to look at me and I drop my arms, like the heat from the radiator finally got too much, and look up at him. He's smiling. 'You did *everything*.'

'I knew straight away, though.' My lips are buzzing. 'I knew from basically the first time I met you.'

He shakes his head. 'You did everything. Look at us,' he says, and I'd really rather not. I think if I stood up now, I'd just keel over. 'Thank you.'

Oh, shit.

I don't quite manage to smile, and he turns to fully face me, still perched on the edge of his bed. We should be asleep. I should be letting him recover from his nightmare but, instead, there's a horrible lump in my throat.

'Don't—don't *cry*—'

Excellent. Just like that, hot tears are zipping down my cheeks and I have no excuse. Except I'm tired. And I'm scared of what's going to happen when I'm not next to him.

He whispers my name and reaches towards me, like he's going to wipe my tears, but I beat him to it.

'Sorry,' I sniff, looking anywhere but at Dan. 'I'm just—yeah.'

'It's a lot to take in, I know. But I'm okay.'

'You're not, though.' I sound like such a dick. 'You're hurt.'

He sighs, and I feel the breath flutter against my skin.

'You can't get upset like this every time you see an injury.'

I appreciate it. I really do. It's exactly what I'm trying to tell myself, but in Dan's voice which makes everything so much better.

'I'm okay,' he repeats. 'I'm much better than I was this time last week.'

I splutter a nervous laugh and he does it—he closes the gap between us and touches my face with his fingertips.

'We're okay.' His thumb wipes across my cheek and my breathing stops.

'Sorry,' I mumble. 'I'm just worried.'

'I know.' He drops his hand from my face, leaving my skin burning. 'Talk to me when you're ready.'

Now I'm not actually crying, the room feels brighter. We shuffle so we're both sitting with our backs to the headboard and I know we should just go back to sleep but he's right there, bare chested, with a very gentle smile on his perfect face. I blurt *everything*.

I tell him, for the first time, about Kirst. I tell him how suddenly everything changed, and how helpless I felt during the whole of last year. I tell him about Christmas, and New Year, and how terrifying it was to see someone I love trapped like that. We're too close together and I tell him about the last few weeks, and how convinced I was that I was going to lose him, and he pulls me under his arm.

'Breathe,' he says, when it becomes clear I haven't been doing enough of that lately. 'I'm better. I'm getting help and it's going well, I think.'

Despite the night we've had, I'm inclined to agree.

'Kirst is okay?' Her name sounds strange in his voice, and I'm smiling.

'She's okay. I'll see her over Christmas.'

'Good.'

We sit there for a moment, letting morning crawl towards us. Dan smells of cigarettes and I can't quite hate it.

'You should go back to sleep,' he says eventually.

'So should you.'

'I don't think it will work,' he warns, stretching his neck and taking his arm away from my shoulders. 'But I will try.'

I shiver, glad I'm still wearing my t-shirt, and glance up at him. 'Wake me up if you need me, alright?' I say. 'I'm serious.'

He sinks back under the duvet and smiles at me. I've never been more transfixed by a smile.

'I will. Goodnight, William,' he whispers, twisting to face away from me. 'Thank you.'

'You're welcome.'

Now he's not looking at me, my voice sounds small and lonely in the darkness. I take a slow breath and close my eyes. I need to sleep. I need to stop worrying about kissing his shoulder, because he doesn't seem to have even noticed, and I need to calm my fluttering heart.

Movement on the other side of the bed makes me open my eyes and I'm sure—I'm *certain*—he's inched closer to the middle of the bed. I'm dangerously close to touching him as it is, so I tuck my arm under my chest and do my absolute best to breathe lightly.

What did Peter say about Dan looking like he was *into* me?

Nineteen

Waking up to his alarm isn't much better than waking up because of the TV, or because of a nightmare. Actually, I think this is worse.

We're tangled together.

I'm sprawled across his back, and he's found my left hand and he's holding it, keeping my arm tight around his chest. I've hooked my leg between his during the night, and it's as if we're lovers. Every breath tastes of him.

We don't speak. We're both awake but something has shifted in the room, and I'm embarrassed enough to die.

'Good morning.'

He doesn't sound upset. He doesn't sound like he's trying to hide from me, so I scoot backwards to let him up. Safely back on *my* side, I lean against the headboard and clutch my knees to my chest.

'Morning.' *I* sound upset.

He pushes up onto his knees and looks over at me and *that's it*. I'm gone. It's the moment I'll think about over and over, again and again, for the rest of my life. He's smiling, happy to see me, and his eyes are soft. Hazy. If I didn't know better, I'd think he's high.

He sits beside me, putting weight through his shoulder and into the headboard.

'I'm sorry about upsetting you last night,' he says.

My stomach is spinning. He shouldn't be apologising, but I can't speak.

'But thank you for being my friend.'

Friend.

It cuts me and I'm bleeding. I can feel blood pouring from my chest, soaking my t-shirt before spilling onto his lovely sheets and ruining them.

I should tell him.

He knows I'm struggling with something. He must have worked it out last night when I kissed his shoulder, and now I'm dying at the sound of just one word. I can't even smile.

Making everything worse, he reaches over to touch my chin.

'You look like you need coffee,' he breathes. 'Do you take sugar?'

I shake my head, but I don't know. I don't drink coffee, and I'm hurt he doesn't know. But why would he? I've never mentioned it.

'We have time,' he whispers, and I'm not sure if it's for me or him. I don't respond and he slips away, promising that he won't be long.

I shouldn't have stayed in the bed with him. I shouldn't have asked to see the bruises, because I think it tripped me over the edge. I *definitely* shouldn't have kissed his shoulder because I can still feel his skin against my lips. I shouldn't have slept so close to him.

I feel sick.

And I've got to go through the rest of the day without him. That's the worst bit. He'll be working, smiling at strangers, and giving them tasteless, defrosted jacket potatoes, and I'll be in lectures. I'm going to be in lectures and seminars and placements for the next *four* years and he has one year of university left. He can't put that off indefinitely. He'll have to graduate next year.

And then what?

I growl and shake my head, hands over my eyes, trying to get away from this. It doesn't matter *what*. We're *friends* and we'll stay in touch—probably. He'll be happy, find some lovely guy his age, and send me sickeningly perfect Christmas cards.

I'm getting way ahead of myself.

He comes back in, being sure to make a noise as he pushes the door open, so I don't jump too much, and hands me a mug. He's given me milk, and that's probably right. But I don't know and I'm glaring at the handle of the mug like it's all its fault I'm in a mess.

Am I in a mess?

Does he ever have to know how I feel? This could all blow over. He doesn't even have to know I like guys—I've survived this long without telling anyone. I'm sure I could just never mention it.

'Talk,' he says, sitting on his side of the bed and almost destroying me. He's slept in his jeans, obviously way too embarrassed to do anything else and I am *grateful*, but he's still shirtless. 'William?'

I'm getting a really good look at his tattoo and it climbs up his arm, thinning out towards his shoulder. I guess he started at the wrist, where something in Cyrillic crosses his radial artery, and added in stages. It's a good distraction.

'I'm trying to get my head around this,' I say.

'This?'

A spike of frustration hits me and I struggle to control it. I swap my mug into my left hand, so I can gesture with my right at the bed. 'Being so close to you.'

Oh.

Oh, shit.

There is no way he doesn't understand.

I may as well have produced a pink, purple and blue flag from my trousers.

If anything, he makes it worse. I know he's trying to show me *he doesn't care* but it's awful and I want to cry when he reaches over and touches my cheek with the back of his finger, trying to make me look up.

'I'll see you this evening,' he says, voice soft. 'Are you okay to come to the social?'

'Of course—of course I am.' I'm sharp, and I hate myself for it.

He pulls his hand back.

'Sorry. I think—I'm just being an arse. Sorry.'

'It's okay.' He shouldn't be so soft with me. He's still leaning towards me, twisted, and resting on his hands and I want to tell him to *sit up*. 'I haven't seen you like this.'

I laugh and it's cold and humourless. 'Yeah, me neither,' I mutter, tipping my head against the headboard and cradling the mug to my chest. 'Sorry. I think you're right; I need

103

coffee.'

He smiles and he should stop smiling at me. Doesn't he realise how difficult he's making things? His eyes are still soft and he should be frowning, angry. He should stand up and walk out, telling me to talk to him when I've calmed down.

'Drink up,' he says, taking a sip from his own mug. 'We have over an hour before I have to be on campus. You have a quiet morning, yes?'

I nod, not trusting myself to speak.

'We can get a taxi whenever we're ready.'

I smile, hoping he realises I'm not annoyed with *him*, and make the foolish mistake of letting us make eye-contact. I don't need to breathe when he's looking at me like this.

Something needs to happen.

I have no idea what the coffee's going to taste like, so I lift it to my lips just so we have to stop staring at each other.

It's hot. It's bitter. It tastes of rust, and I don't like it.

I burn my tongue but hide my pain in another little smile. I don't know how many minutes have passed since we spoke about a taxi. I've missed a few breaths and now I'm lightheaded, ears ringing

'Thank you for this. I don't drink coffee much.'

'Really?' He sounds surprised. 'I cannot survive a day without at least three cups.'

'That's bad for you,' I say, and it's hilarious. For some reason, a caffeine addiction is the funniest joke either of us can think of and we're laughing so much I have to put my mug down beside my glasses.

'I think it's a risk I'm willing to take.' He looks down at his bare arms. The scratches on his right wrist are facing me and I don't want to think about them. 'It's been ten days.'

My smile falters and I almost reach for him. 'I'm very proud of you.' I don't think anything has ever been truer. 'When's your next appointment?'

He groans and tips his head back, facing the ceiling. 'Call with my counsellor this afternoon. Doctor on Wednesday morning.'

I find a smile. 'Hope it goes well.' Will he ask me to go

104

with him again? I hope so.

'Thank you.' He rubs his thumb across the rim of his mug, thinking. 'I don't want it.'

My mind is full of static, so I don't think. 'Not at the moment.'

I expect him to be upset with me. Instead, he nods.

'It comes and goes.'

'Will you tell me?'

'If I search for more? Yes. I think so.' He looks across at me and catches my eyes with his again. I believe him. He's impossible to not believe because the corners of his lips are in a light smile and his eyes—

His eyes look like they're in love.

What did Peter say? *Dan looked like he was into you.*

Before I can let my heart gallop away with blind optimism, I look away from him and consider the room we're sat in. He's dropped out of university and moved into a private apartment because of his most recent relationship. He doesn't need me swooning over him, now—he needs a friend. Over the last week, he's gone from cowering away from me to trusting me enough to let me stay in his bed. I can't risk breaking that.

The smell of coffee reaches me, and it is *strong*. It pulls me out of this haze and I pick my mug back up. 'Thanks. I—uh. What time do you finish work?'

'Three.' He shuffles, putting some distance between us, and I want to reach out and catch him. I tighten my hold on my mug, instead. 'When do you finish?'

I sigh. 'Not until five.'

'I might come home before the social,' he says. 'I will be back on campus by seven.'

I nod, refusing to be sad about two quiet hours without him. 'Good plan. I guess I'll see you later, then.'

'We don't have to leave yet.' He says it too quickly, like he's nervous. 'I'm glad you were here this morning.'

'Really?' I can't help but think I've been awful company.

He shrugs and hides in his mug.

'I like you,' he says, and I feel like throwing myself from

the bed to lie face-down on the carpet. 'You're nice to be
around.'

Before I can do anything, like blurt how much I adore
him, he glances at me and grins.

'Don't forget your coffee.'

Twenty

I do not have a great day.

There's a knot in my heart—a throbbing ache in my shoulder—and if I didn't know I'm just being emotional I'd think I'm having a heart attack. I can still smell Dan's cigarettes and, if I cross my arm over my chest, I can trick myself into thinking I can still feel him from this morning.

I stumble across campus after leaving him by the SU, feeling like I have a hangover and no doubt looking like it. My room feels like a distant, unfamiliar place now and I have a sneaky feeling everything I'd planned to do this morning is going to be put on hold. I unlock doors without thinking about them and make it to my room, where I collapse face-down onto my bed.

I should do something else—like shower—but that would mean standing up. Instead, I lie on my back and send a text to Peter, confirming I'm going to the social, and I think of Dan.

If I could walk with Dan into the social, with our hands together like I imagine every time I close my eyes, I'd be excited. As it is, I'm mostly dreading it.

Last night changed something. I'm not sure what I'm in the middle of now, but it's making me feel sick. I want to phone him. I want to hear him laughing at me again, and, importantly, I want to hear him tell me he's okay.

12:35 **Cassie**: So, uh, do you remember me?

12:39 **William**: Of course

12:41 **Cassie**: Come and meet me?? It's 20 to, dummy

I have to wipe a couple of tears from my glasses as I stand

up. I shove my laptop and some paper into my uni bag, grab my keys, and put my phone in my pocket. Feeling pretty grimy and still in my clothes from yesterday, I go to meet Cassie.

'You alright?' she asks, eyes flashing all over me as soon as we're close enough.

'Yeah, tired. Barely slept last night.'

'Oh?'

I get something like a stitch in my chest and frown at the floor. 'Just didn't sleep. How was your weekend?'

'It was fine.'

We start to walk and she sticks her hands in her coat pockets. I forgot to grab my jacket and tuck my elbows into my sides, trying to keep in some heat.

'Did loads of work on this report,' Cassie continues. 'Spoke to Lilley.'

I don't want to think about Lilley.

'Hope she's okay.' I concentrate on taking a breath. It catches in my throat.

'I think so. We're still on for this evening.' There's a lightness in Cassie's voice which almost makes me smile. 'Are you doing anything?'

I shrug. 'Hope you have fun. I'm going to the social again with Peter.'

'You don't seem thrilled about that.'

I overdo it, and make sure she can see me smiling. 'I am. I'm just tired, I told you.'

'Right. How's Dan?'

She doesn't know I spent the night with him. She doesn't know I went to see him. She doesn't know his nightmares are the reason I'm tired.

'He's okay,' I say, jaw tight. 'Think he's better now he's moved off-campus.'

'I saw him working.'

'When?'

'This morning.' She laughs at my twitchiness. 'Why?'

'I'm nervous about his ex seeing him,' I explain. 'He wants to keep busy while he's not studying but I don't like it—

he's too easy to find.'

Cassie bumps me mid-step. 'He can't hide from the guy forever, though.'

'No, you're right.' I let out a long sigh and my breath crystallises around us. 'I just worry about him.'

'Peter thinks he fancies you.'

'Peter needs to mind his own business,' I grumble.

The thought of Daniel *fancying* me—being as consumed by me as I am by him—is dizzying. I can't afford to think like this, not when we're steps away from our microscopy lab.

'He just wants you to be happy,' Cassie says. 'If you two are—'

'We aren't,' I snap. 'We aren't—and I don't want a relationship *anyway*. We're friends.'

'Friends?'

'Jesus, Cas—'

She laughs and nudges me again. 'Okay, okay. Grumpy. I'll tell Peter to drop it.'

I give her a side-eye and hold the door for her. 'Good.'

*

I realise, as I turn past the library towards my room, I haven't actually eaten anything today. We didn't do breakfast. I was definitely supposed to do something when I reached my room other than lie across the bed.

It's too late, now. I'll ask Peter if we can grab food together before going to the social, like we did last week.

Did I suggest to Dan that we meet up before the social? I can't remember. I take my phone out, considering sending a text to ask him, and get bumped sideways by an adult-sized cherub.

'You're deaf,' Peter laughs, steadying us and keeping his arms around me. I haven't snapped out of my thoughts, yet, and just grin. 'You're done for the day, yeah?'

'Yeah, but I need to spend half an hour finishing something off,' I say, and he *winks*. '*Peter*.'

'What?'

'You can't sit with me if you're going to be rude.' I free myself of his arms and put my phone reluctantly back into my pocket. 'I'm guessing that's what you wanted.'

'Oh, yeah. I've actually been waiting here for the last twenty minutes, ready to ambush you.'

I can't tell if he's joking and just roll my eyes.

'How are you?'

'I'm—' not *good*. That's an overstatement. 'I'm okay. How are you?'

'Buzzing that I get to take you to the social *without* having to beg you,' he says, bouncing along beside me as we start walking again. 'Did Dan beg?'

Ah, Jesus.

I shoot him with a glare and shake my head. 'No, Peter.'

'Wow. So, your *new* friend just *gets* to spend time with you—'

'Peter—'

'And *I* have to practically bargain away my life for just three hours with you!' I'm trying to ignore this, because he's being a dick on purpose, but *wow*. I can taste tears in my throat but he isn't looking at me. 'Fine. I know where I stand.'

'Don't be an arse.' I sound *awful*.

He catches my hand and we stumble to a stop. 'You okay?'

All the teasing has gone, now. I should tell him how it felt to wake up beside Dan this morning, but I *don't*. Instead, I stand there as useless as a landed fish and he has to pull me into a hug—a proper, rib-cracking hug.

'I know you aren't. Something's upset you, hasn't it? You don't have to tell me what's going on, but I fucking love you. Okay?'

I can't make a scene. Not here, outside the SU where people are rushing past us on their way to their rooms or out to get food. It's not exactly a private place to have a breakdown. Besides, I have work to do.

I feel my last conversation with Dan weighing me down, blocking my throat like a boulder. This morning feels like forever ago.

'I love you, too. Thanks. Sorry. I'm just a mess at the moment.'

'Yeah.' Very slowly, he releases me. 'I've noticed.'

'Sorry.' The boulder makes my voice heavy.

'Stop apologising.' He gives me a little smile, shoving his hand softly against my arm. 'Is this anything to do with Dan?'

I just look at him, the expression of complete devastation, and he talks quickly.

'Is he okay? Has something happened?'

'No—I think he's okay,' I say. Thank you, Peter, for not asking again if we've fucked. Because I know that's what he's thinking. 'Come on. I do need to get some work done.'

'Okay. Am I alright to sit on your bed?'

'Absolutely.'

Twenty-One

Peter and I sat together like this lots through first year. I was always working, terrified of falling behind and being kicked off this course I'd tried so hard to get a place on, and he was *sometimes* working. More often than not, he just sat near me and gave me random thoughts that floated through his head.

'Is he meeting us there?' he asks, some forty minutes after we reach my room. It feels so much longer, and I keep waking up my phone screen to check the time.

'Who?'

'*William*.'

I jump and almost scrawl across my sheet of paper. Probably for the best—I put my pen down, and there's nothing more to add. Not at this point. I swallow. 'Dan?'

'Well, yeah.'

'I don't—I don't know.' It's a good excuse to look at my phone. I spin on my chair so I'm facing Peter and shrug. 'Haven't organised that far.'

He's lying with his hands behind his head on my pillow and his legs tangled up. It does not look comfortable. 'You should message him. Ask if he wants to eat with us.'

It bursts out of me. 'You're not going to be rude to him, are you?'

'Me?'

'Yeah, you.'

'Nope,' he smiles at me, all dimples. 'Why would I be?'

'I dunno. I think he'll probably say no.' My leg is bouncing enough to make the chair squeak.

'Why?' Peter stretches his neck, making it crunch, and I cringe. 'Because I'm here?'

I don't want to say yes, but I shrug. And it's close enough.

Peter's other eyebrow rises. 'I'm not sure what to say to that. Are you two really that intense?'

'Peter.'

'Or is he really that shy?'

'He's that shy.' I open our conversation on my phone. 'And if you mention his injuries, or his relationship, or his nationality—'

'Oh, I forget he's Russian.' Peter's facing me, hand in his hair. I feel like I'm about to scream and he rolls his eyes at me. 'I'm not going to mention it.'

'You better not.'

'Or what?'

'Do you want to upset him?'

'No,' he sits up, 'but I seem to be doing a great job of upsetting you.'

I look away, down at my phone, and let out a sigh.

'Talk to me.'

'I'm just tired.' It feels like a good excuse. It explains my short temper, and the far, far away look in my eyes. 'Didn't sleep much last night.'

'Why not?'

I almost tell him. 'Just a bit stressed, I think. I kept waking up thinking of this exam Cas and I have got to do.'

I don't think I've convinced him, because he's still looking at me with both of his eyebrows in his hair.

'And I tried coffee this morning, thinking it would help.'

I've broken through that expression and he laughs. 'I can't imagine you drinking coffee.'

'No, I don't think it will be happening again.'

'Didn't get a buzz?'

'I've just felt like I'm crashing all day. What's the point in drinking caffeine if it just leaves you like this?'

He's grinning at me, like he wants to give me a hug. That would be very welcome. 'Not everyone's as delicate as you are, dear.'

I blow raspberries and think, for a moment, that I've escaped explaining why I feel so crap.

I can still feel Dan against my chest and waist and legs.

'Text him,' Peter says, stretching his arms. This time, his elbow pops and we both grimace. His legs are knotted together, ankles disappearing beneath calves. 'If he *is* freaked out by me being there, I'll just meet you at the social.'

'That's not fair on you.' It's obvious I'm grateful. Time alone with Daniel before the social would be excellent. 'He might be okay with it.'

'He might be. I don't care either way, though.'

I struggle to believe that as I write out a text for Dan.

> 17:45 **William**: Hey! Are you still going to the social tonight?

His reply is almost instant, like he was about to message me. The happiness this makes me feel is obvious and I can feel Peter rolling his eyes.

17:46 **Daniel**: If you are.

> 17:48 **William**: I am. Peter and I are going to grab something to eat—do you want to join us? He says he can leave us to it and catch us at the social if you'd rather it's just us

There was no way of making that sound better.

17:51 **Daniel**: On campus?

> 17:52 **William**: Yeah :)

17:54 **Daniel**: May I join you both?

> 17:55 **William**: You absolutely can. Where are you?

17:56 **Daniel**: Sitting in the SU.

> 17:57 **William**: Oh, I thought you were

going home for a bit

17:58 Daniel: I did.

Oh. Peter sees the way my expression drops, and I know he thinks Dan's changed his mind, so I speak quickly.

'He'll meet us both,' I force a smile.

'Then what's wrong?'

For once, I wish he were less in-tune with me. 'He's been sitting on his own.'

'So?'

'So?' I flash a glare at him. 'So he's been alone, on campus, where his fucking *ex* could find him at any moment.'

'Oh.'

I think I'm making this into more of an issue than it is, but my mind is cycling through a short scene where Dan's sat on his own and Matthew—a mysterious, blurry shape in my imagination—walks up to him. Takes his hand. Drags him away to do something horrible.

18:01 William: You should have said you were back! We'll come and meet you now

'Time to go.' I leap to my feet and grab my wallet from my desk. Peter groans as he stands up and I hear the familiar pop of his hip as he stretches. 'You shouldn't cross your legs like that.'

'Fight me, Will.'

18:03 Daniel: There's no rush.

18:04 William: There is. I wanna see you

18:05 Daniel: I want to see you, too. But I can survive on my own for a few hours ;)

I bite my lip. Can Peter hear my heart beating? I didn't

expect to lose my breath over a semi-colon and a parenthesis but here I am, feeling like one gust of wind could bowl me over.

'What did he say?' Peter asks, being very patient while I blindly grab for my keys. He holds the door but catches me before I leave the room. 'You'll want a jacket.'

You want to bet? I'm sweating, cheeks burning, and I feel like I've been sat in a sauna all afternoon. My mouth keeps filling with saliva, and I swallow again.

'He's just being him.' I'm not sure how to explain why I've lost control of my body at his last text. What's the worst bit? Knowing he wants to see me? The blatant teasing?

18:07 **William**: Leaving my room now

I make myself put my phone back in my pocket. Peter was right about the jacket and he just walks beside me for a moment, while I catch up with my thoughts.

'I'm surprised it isn't raining.'

He laughs. 'Being deprived of some pathetic fallacy?'

I elbow him mid-step.

'You *are* sulking. It's fine, but I think if you're going to be an arse, I'm allowed to tease you about it.'

I accept that one. 'Fine. It should be chucking it down with how I'm feeling.'

'Let me know if this doesn't pass in the next day or two.' Serious again, he lets his elbow hit against mine. 'I'm a little bit worried about you.'

'I'm just being grumpy.' It's time for another stunning topic change, and I groan. 'But I do have a nine AM tomorrow.'

'That's disgusting.'

Twenty-Two

It's a short walk from my room to the SU, but it feels like it takes at least twenty minutes. My feet rise and fall in slow motion. Peter chatters to me and it's light, requiring exactly no input from me, so he could be talking for hours.

We step through the sliding doors into the SU and I finally look up, scanning the tables.

Dan isn't here.

'Earth to William.'

I yelp in surprise and spin to glare up at him. Peter's waiting a little to one side, laughing at me.

Dan looks perfect. 'You missed me.'

'I thought you were in here,' I grumble. Fortunately for me, I don't sound as frightened or relieved as I feel.

'I went out to smoke.' I can smell it on him. 'I thought you would have seen me on your walk.'

I pull a face and narrowly resist poking him. It's not a good idea for us to touch—I think we've proved that. 'You shouldn't smoke. Or scare people.'

He flashes a grin and turns to our audience of one, letting me catch my breath.

'I don't think we've ever spoken,' he says, offering his hand to Peter. 'I'm Daniel.'

'Peter.' He shakes Dan's hand and raises an eyebrow at me, reminding me to calm myself down. I think I look angry. I'm not—I'm just struggling to catch up.

'William said you were going to get dinner,' Dan says, and I haven't heard him like this. He's confident. He's bright.

'Yeah.' Peter puts his hand back in his pocket. 'Want to join us?'

'If you do not mind.'

'Not at all.'

Why are they being so polite? Why are they being so

117

formal?

'Will?'

I grunt and fix a smile onto my face, but I'm too slow. Dan's smirking, like he understands, and Peter's beginning to look annoyed.

'Sorry,' I say. 'Tired.'

Dan's hand moves, like he's going to touch me. 'You should have let me sleep on the settee.'

I don't know why this is such a bad thing. I don't know why I'm suddenly ice cold, feeling like I could spit venom.

Peter looks like someone just bit him. 'You spent the night together?'

Dan blushes a tiny bit. 'William stayed with me. I think I woke him up.'

'You *did* wake me up.' It comes out far sharper than I wanted. 'But it's fine—I'll always wake up for you.'

Weak.

Dan stands almost too close and whispers to me, like he's ignoring Peter. 'My sleeping habits shouldn't interrupt yours. Are you okay?'

The *yeah* doesn't come out properly.

Peter's ability to read me shines through at the perfect time. He's already backing away from us, towards the door. 'I'll see you outside,' he calls, not giving us chance to protest.

I want to tell him not to be stupid, because I'm fine, but Dan puts his hand on my arm to hold me still.

'Thank you,' I manage, and I'm not sure who it's to.

Peter gives me what I think is supposed to be a reassuring smile and scampers off out the door we just came through. I want to scream. I want to hit something.

Instead, I find myself being pulled very firmly into Dan's arms.

Today has been a shit day for my emotions.

'Talk to me.' He holds me close, supporting me against him, and moves his hand down my back. Oh my god. I shiver. 'Why are you upset?'

I start with the most logical reason—the one that doesn't include how desperately I wish I could stretch up and kiss him.

118

'I didn't think you wanted anyone to know we've spent time together. Like, you were terrified on Tuesday that someone would find out you'd stayed in my room. And Wednesday. So I haven't told them.'

He smells of cigarettes and food and my stomach rumbles before he responds.

'I realise I am not very good at communicating.' He bows his head so his lips are by my ear. I could be dead. I honestly could have died and I don't think I'd know any different. 'I was worried someone in your block would know Matthew. It is highly likely. But now I know I can cope without heroin, and now I know I don't need him, I'm not as scared.'

I swallow and nod. It brushes our hair together.

'And I trust Peter.'

'Why?'

'You clearly love him,' he says. 'If you trust him, so do I.'

I don't really know what to say to that.

I find myself taking handfuls of his shirt over his back and we stand there, as if it's just us left in the whole world.

Eventually, I sigh. 'Dan, I've had a crap day.'

He chuckles, but it sounds sad. And I think one of his hands is trying to slip up beneath my jacket. 'I'm so sorry.'

'It's not your fault.'

'I think it is.'

I shake my head and press my forehead into his shoulder. The combination of cigarette smoke and deodorant has never smelled so sexy. I can't get enough of it.

'I shouldn't have made you stay in my bed with me,' he murmurs. 'That was weak.'

I'm going to tell him.

It's the perfect moment, really. We're wrapped around each other, like we're both scared the other is going to fall apart, and I would barely have to whisper. We're about to go to an LGBT social, for Christ's sake. I could not be surrounded by more support, even if I'd planned this.

I'm going to tell him.

119

Dan, I'm bi.

My lips part.

'Oh, are you two a *thing*?'

I shudder and slip away, arms falling from around Dan. I can't look at him. I really need an early night. I need to eat something. The world has been snatched from underneath my feet and I'm floating, falling through space.

'No,' Dan laughs, speaking over my head with his hands by his side again. 'No, we're friends. Goodnight, Owen.'

I think I hate Owen.

I don't look up as he sweeps past us.

Daniel catches me again between gentle hands. 'Are you okay?'

I nod but lying to him hurts like a broken rib. I shake my head.

'Should you go home? Do you want me to—?'

'I haven't actually eaten today.'

There—a perfect excuse. It's so much easier to tackle physical problems rather than emotional ones, and, when I'm brave enough to look up at him, I see how relieved he is to think this is something he can help fix.

'I knew I should have made you eat something this morning,' he groans, giving my shoulders a light squeeze. 'Do you want to eat now?'

'I'm bloody ravenous.'

He laughs once and stands away from me, finding my eyes immediately with his.

'I'm going to make sure you eat but, if I think you still look terrible, I'm taking you home,' he warns.

'I'm alright,' I say, even though it's another big fat lie. His thumb finds my jaw and I close my eyes. *Tell him.* 'Dan—'

My breath stops. It's like I've been cursed to never tell anyone, and I choke on something like tears.

'Are you sure you want to stay out this evening?'

No.

'Yeah.' The moment has passed. It's floated away downstream, caught up in a current. Swept up in rapids. I'm stuck in the same place as I was four weeks ago, wedged between boulders and branches. 'I'm alright. I'm just being a bit of a dick to everyone and myself, today.'

He smiles at me and rubs his thumbs, one after the other, across my cheeks. Drying my face.

'I cry a *lot*.'

'I've noticed,' he whispers, dropping his hands again. 'Is it because of me?'

'No!' I'm careful to smile. 'No, it's just my usual response to being tired. It's fine.'

He raises an eyebrow, not convinced.

'And you—you took my coffee virginity.'

Could that possibly be the worst choice of words ever?

It works; he laughs. 'What?'

'Never drank coffee before.'

'Why didn't you say?'

'I was trying to impress you,' I laugh. There. I can be honest with him.

His hands jump, like they thought about coming up to my face again, and find his pockets instead.

'I don't think caffeine agrees with me.'

'No, apparently not,' he laughs, shaking his head. 'You should have told me.'

I hum and we start walking towards the doors. 'Do you drink tea, too?' I ask.

He likes this topic and we keep it going while we walk with Peter. Dan stays very close to me, arm bumping mine with every other step, and I'm grinning. It's such a change from five minutes ago that I *know* Peter notices but, honestly, I don't care.

Twenty-Three

I convince them, while we're eating, that I'm okay to go to the social but I have conditions. I have to leave when Daniel does, because they both agree I need sleep.

'And you have an early morning tomorrow.' I should have expected that Dan would remember this, but it catches me by surprise and sends my heart skipping. 'You need an early night.'

'Oh, definitely,' Peter agrees. 'He's never this grumpy.'

I glare across the table at him. Dan and I are sitting side by side, facing him, and it feels risky. Are we too close? I can smell him in every breath.

They talk about their courses, and Dan explains the situation with his VISA. I have no idea how he's managed to stay on top of it all. The process is an endless assault-course of hoops and narrow doorways to slide through *and* none of it's in his first language. I freely admit to being lost.

Peter doesn't seem to struggle to keep up and grins across the table at him. 'Does this mean you'll be sticking around over the summer for re-sits? Poor William will be deep into placements then, right?'

I'm impressed he remembers and nod, lifting my glass of water. 'I'm looking forward to it.'

'God, you're such a nerd,' Peter teases, grinning at me. 'You know, Dan, he was doing work before we came out to meet you.'

Came out.

I put my glass down and pull my elbows into my ribs, like those words are going to conjure some horrible Stephen King monster. Is this what it's like to have a trigger word? It must be. My mouth tastes of blood, so I stop chewing my cheek. It's such a harmless phrase, and they're talking about me and my degree as if they haven't noticed the way I've been punched in the chest.

Am I going to react like this every time someone says *bye*, too?

I lift my head and they're both still talking, oblivious to my crisis. It's nice to see Dan looking comfortable, and I indulge in watching him. He's leaning into the table, supported on his crossed arms, and he's making eye-contact. His constant smile is like a spot of sunlight.

A warning bell screams between my ears and I clutch my glass, stopping myself from crying out loud. They're talking really well, so caught up in their conversation I don't think they realise I'm in agony.

They're both out. They're both gay. They're both enjoying this conversation, inclined towards each other like sides of a triangle, and I am going to be sick right here at the table.

Peter glances at me, then does a double take. 'You alright?' he asks, some minutes after my skin has faded to a chalky grey.

I shrug.

It's enough. Dan sweeps his arms around me, pulling my broken head into his chest, and Peter leaps up from his seat like he's been burned. In the corner of my eye, I see him walk away. Giving us a moment.

'Breathe, William.'

I can't. I'm so helpless and Dan's being so patient with me. Right now, when I'm being pathetic and getting myself upset over something that doesn't even matter—not really— he's cradling me like I'm made of fractured china.

The sound of terrible breathing reaches me. Is that me?

Dan holds me tighter. 'What happened? You know we both love you.'

Oh, no. I'm out.

I'm so out of here.

I strain against him for half a moment, like I think I'm going to get up from the table and run away, but Dan is strong. I don't think he realises how hard I'm trying.

'Dan—' Oh, shit. I sound miles away. 'Dan, let go.'

'I need you to breathe, first,' he murmurs. 'You are

panicking, and I will not let you do that alone.'

I have to be honest. It spills from me, and I've been holding so much in that I'm surprised other things haven't been leaking out all day.

'Do you like him?'

'Peter?' He takes my hand in his, lacing our fingers together. 'Yes, he is nice.'

Part of my brain understands he's terrified because his accent is filling the room. It's like how Kirst says I go posh when I'm uncomfortable. I guess he goes back to his roots, too.

'But do you *like* him?'

It takes him a moment.

'Oh.'

I can't help but mock it in my head. Oh. *Oh.*

'Not like that, no.'

'Are you sure?'

'I think I know who I am attracted to.' His voice is like butter, smooth and warm. 'Why? Did you think I was going to abandon you for him?'

Hammer, meet nail.

I nod and he swears down my ear, which is quite a thing to experience.

'Peter is a friend. You are a friend.' He moves and something rubs against my hair—I think it's his cheek. 'I could—' he sighs. 'I could not have a relationship yet. I could not trust anyone like that again—not for a while. Peter is nice, but even if I were attracted to him, I would not—I could not do anything. Do you understand?'

I look up at him and blink, not sure I do.

'I could not have sex with someone. Not after everything.'

I didn't expect that. And I don't know why.

I nod, wanting him to know his message has been received and understood, and twist enough to put my free arm around him. My chin is on his shoulder and, if I open my eyes, I can see across the room. I keep them closed.

Annoyingly, I feel much better.

'You shouldn't have to tell me that to calm me down.'

I feel a laugh against my shoulder.

'I'm sorry, Dan.'

'Don't apologise.'

'You need to follow that rule too, then.' I sound better, at least. 'Shit. Obviously, it's none of my fucking business who you fancy.'

'William.'

'I'm just being ridiculously protective over you.' It's a good excuse. 'It's not that I don't trust Peter, but I think I'd be worried if you did get into a relationship right now, even without you explaining.'

He laughs again and it's such a lovely, warm sound. 'It makes sense. Do not worry. It would make sense to be jealous if your two friends got into a relationship.'

'Really?'

'Yes. You have been my world for the last week so it would be difficult to see me loving other people—especially when you have seen me so ill.' He's still holding me and I'm wonderfully comfortable. I could fall asleep. 'Don't fight it. Just let me know if I surprise you, and we can talk about it. Like we did earlier.'

I nod and catch myself before I can twist and kiss his shoulder. It would be very easy to do. 'You're an incredible person,' I say, sitting up very slowly. 'Shit. Thank you.'

He keeps hold of my hand, even when I start to self-consciously tug it away. 'We can both look after each other,' he says. 'You are not a doctor yet.'

I grin up at him, and something has broken. One of the ropes around my chest snaps.

*

Peter comes back to us without warning, so I'm sure he was watching. This makes my cheeks burn red and I do my best to not react when they talk about the social, and when Peter asks about last week.

'I was a little bit drunk and didn't notice much,' Peter

admits, 'but I saw you two leaving together.'

Will he ever let this go?

I speak quickly. 'We walked each other home, like I told you.'

I think Dan understands; *we're lying about this one.*

Peter nods and, amazingly, doesn't ask me anything else. 'You've moved off-campus, right?'

Dan nods.

'Is it a nice place you've got?'

They talk about his flat in town and the difference I feel between now and before Dan reassured me he didn't fancy my friend is *stupid.* I'm listening, watching their conversation bounce across the table, and when Dan looks at me to check I'm okay I give him an easy smile. He relaxes.

But we're still holding hands.

This only becomes a problem when we move to stand up and when we both hesitate a bit too long. Peter raises an eyebrow at us, like he's about to ask what's going on, and I decide it's my turn to be strong.

I pull my fingers from Dan's and push to my feet without breathing.

I have a small argument in my head about platonic love as we walk, but I can't even convince myself. The way I feel when I look at Dan is *far* from platonic. The relief I feel when he smiles at me is a thousand miles away from a *friend.*

I am in a mess.

Part of me is trying to say that this will fade with time. Maybe his smoking will get *really* annoying, and all of this hazy softness I'm feeling will solidify to stone. I think this would be a good thing for all of us.

Remind me to never enter a debating contest, because I couldn't fight for these arguments even if I were paid.

We walk into the social as a group and I realise I'd completely forgotten about Anthony, the guy with beautiful hair. The footballer. The guy Peter went on a date with just yesterday. There's no way Peter's swooning over Daniel—he launches himself straight towards Anthony and they're laughing and talking in loud, excited voices. It's like they've been friends for years but haven't seen each other in months.

I stop still and Daniel smirks at me, like he knows. 'Okay?'

'I'm an idiot,' I say. 'I completely forgot about Anthony.'

'Anthony?'

'The guy Peter's been obsessing about all week.'

Daniel laughs, flashing his teeth as he glances around the room. 'What is better, knowing I do not fancy him or he does not fancy me?'

I grin, bright red, and answer him completely honestly. 'Oh, knowing you don't like him.'

'Jealous?'

'Hell yes.'

Another laugh. I join in, because it is *awful* that I've been so concerned about this, and he offers to buy me a drink. He isn't surprised when I just ask for water, and he isn't surprised when I go with him to the bar.

Twenty-Four

I don't think it will ever get easier to say goodbye to Dan. We leave together and Peter comes with us, kissing Anthony on the cheek and whispering that he'll see him tomorrow.

I can't help but be jealous and wish I were seeing Daniel tomorrow.

Even though he's had a bit to drink, Peter is thoughtful enough to give us some space when we step outside the SU. I'm trying to tell myself to be brave, because this goodbye definitely isn't forever, but my sinuses prickle with tears when Dan hugs me.

'Take care of yourself tonight.' His cheek is pressed against my hair. 'I'll text you in the morning. If you need to talk between now and then just phone me, okay?'

'Same goes to you.' I haven't forgotten how ill he was last night, and I shiver. 'If you think—if you think there's a chance you'll—'

'I will phone you,' he promises. We're just standing there, crushed in each other's arms. 'Are you okay?'

'I feel a lot better than I did this afternoon, yeah.'

'Good.'

'Are you?'

'I feel fine. Relaxed.'

I think I believe him. 'When are you on campus next?'

He hums and shuffles, moving his feet so he's more comfortable. It's difficult, because neither of us want to drop our arms. 'Wednesday, for my appointment.'

I nod. 'When can I see you?'

He hesitates. 'Maybe we should not do the same as this week.'

I'm glad he can't see the disappointment on my face. 'Maybe not.'

'You could come over Sunday morning, instead.'

'Is that okay?'

'Definitely.'

I close my eyes and take a huge breath, hoping to absorb his scent so it lingers on me, even when he's gone. Even when I'm in bed.

'Thank you. Have a good night, Dan.'

'You, too.'

I can almost hear us counting in our heads. *One, two, three—*

We release each other and I stagger back. I'd been leaning on him. He gives me a smile which I want tattooed into my memories and I do my best to give him an equally warm, reassuring one.

We both turn and walk away.

Shit.

I glance back and he's watching me, phone held loosely by his side.

*

'So,' Peter says, walking fairly slowly. I'm prepared for this, and comfort myself by remembering how tightly Daniel just held me. 'You stayed at his house.'

'Yeah.'

'In his bed?'

'Yes.'

'With him?'

'Yes.'

'Did you fuck?'

'No.'

'Did you want to?'

I sigh and shake my head. 'No.' I think it's true. If we *had* had sex, things would be really weird now. 'No, it was just nice.'

'Nice?'

'Nice.'

'But he woke you up.'

'He has nightmares,' I explain. 'He woke me up and we talked for a while.'

'He's very protective of you.'

I snort. 'I guess.'

'You guess? When you had your minor breakdowns—which were terrifying, by the way—he looked like he was going to sweep you up and kill anyone else who touched you.'

I shrug, being careful to not look at him.

'He likes you.'

'Well, that's nice to know,' I mutter. 'I like him.'

'Are you okay? I kinda left him to it because, well, I didn't want to get murdered.'

'I'm okay.'

'You're going to be okay tonight?'

I turn a glare onto him. I appreciate the concern—really, I do. But I'm okay. 'I'm going to be fine. I've just been stroppy today but he—I know I don't need to be an arse, and I'm sorry.'

He pouts and stops us. I can see my window, so I wonder who can see us. 'Did he help?'

'Yeah.'

'You feel better?'

'Loads better.'

He gives me a hug, and it's not as nice as the hug from Dan. Which is an awful thing to think about my friend. But it's true—Peter isn't as warm, or as gentle, and doesn't have the right combination of cigarettes and deodorant.

'Talk to me whenever you want.' He lets go of me and steps away, frowning. 'I'll message you in the morning.'

It sounds like I'm going to have a lot of texts tomorrow. 'Thanks, Peter.'

He walks backwards, smiling. 'Promise me you'll talk to me if you feel shit again.'

I sigh dramatically and throw a mock salute at him. 'I promise.'

Twenty-Five

I keep nicely busy all week but, honestly, my mind is *fixed* on Sunday morning, when I can go and see Daniel.

Once again, he's downstairs as soon as the taxi pulls up.

'Were you watching for me?' I hop out onto the pavement and grin up at him. God, he looks nice. Even though he hasn't shaved for a couple of days. Maybe *because* he hasn't shaved for a couple of days.

Oh, crap. My stomach flips.

'Yes.' He freely admits it, holding the door for me. 'You look better than you did on Monday.'

I laugh and walk beside him as we climb the stairs. 'Thanks. So do you.'

He chuckles and opens the door for us. 'Yeah?' It does not sound like he believes me. 'I have a confession.'

I'm ready to glare at him. I'm just scared of seeing a guilty look on his face, so keep my eyes on the floor as I walk into his living room. 'Tell me quickly before my imagination goes wild.'

He shuts the door before speaking. 'Please do not be angry with me.'

'Dan, I'm fucking terrified.'

He turns to look at me and, damnit, my eyes go straight to his beautiful arms. I'm anticipating bruises. 'I saw Matthew.'

I didn't expect that. I'm not sure why.

'What happened?' I sit down on the settee like my legs forgot how to support me. He joins me, not quite close enough to touch.

'He phoned me on Friday and asked to see each other.' Friday? Why didn't he tell me sooner? 'I went to his.'

I'm tight, like someone just pointed out that the chicken I'm eating is raw. 'What happened, Dan?'

He shakes his head, and the panic doubles. Triples.

131

'Did you take drugs?'

'No!' He says it too quickly, doing nothing to calm me down. 'No. But I miss him.'

I could very easily throw up. 'But he *hurt* you.'

'I know,' he hisses, palms pressed together between his knees. 'I know. I thought you should know.'

'I wish you'd told me straight away.'

He takes a deep breath but holds it, and I think about his ribs. I think about his wrists, and the history of scars I can't bring myself to ask about. I think about his eye, and the bruise on his jaw which has almost completely faded.

'He knows what he did he was bad.' Dan says, and I can taste vomit on the back of my tongue. 'He knows he made a mistake.'

'Dan, *no.*'

He flashes a glance up at me and we're close on this tiny settee, but he feels miles away. It's like someone's hooked him and they're dragging him out to sea far faster than I can swim.

'I'm going to see him on Tuesday.'

I shake my head, and he's getting irritated.

'William—'

'There is no *way* you can go back to him.'

'He's going to be better—'

'You don't know that!' I twist to face him, pulse flying. 'Dan, he *hurt* you. Don't you remember?'

'Of course I—'

'He *hasn't* changed. He's still the guy who gave you drugs and pushed you down the fucking stairs.' I really don't mean to swear, but I think I'm going to have to do something drastic. Dan's frozen, skin pale and eyes too wet, so I keep talking. 'He hurt you. He will hurt you again.'

His jaw jumps, like he caught himself from saying something.

'He just wants you back because he knows you're better than he would ever deserve. He misses you, and I can't blame him.'

He's still staring at me. The silence between us is awful and I have another round of arguments lined up, but he whispers, breaking me.

'I know it's stupid and he was bad, but he was *mine*. I miss him.'

I shake my head sharply. 'You don't miss him. You miss the idea of him. And you're scared—you're scared everyone you meet will just remind you of him so you think you should just give up but you *shouldn't*.'

He closes his eyes.

'Have you told your therapist?'

'No.'

'You should. You should phone them right now.'

A little shake of his head.

'Dan, I'm not going anywhere. But you need to talk to them about this because it is *not* okay.'

His eyes are still closed, and I'm fully expecting him to cry. Maybe I'm expecting him to sink towards me, and whisper about how confused he is.

I am not expecting the way he pushes up from the settee with a little grunt, taking handfuls of his own hair and drawing in a deep, sharp breath.

'I hate him,' he says. The relief is squashed somewhat by the way he's marching around the flat, every muscle tight. 'I hate him, William, but I loved him so much. I don't know what to do.'

'Talk to your therapist. Talk to me. Talk to—Christ, talk to Owen.'

He barks a laugh and I twist to keep my eyes on him.

'I can't let you go back to Matthew.'

I hate how his name sounds coming from me. Dan looks like he does, too, and he wrings his hands together in front of his chest.

'I can't say no to him.' It barely makes it across the room to me, and I hold my breath. 'If I cancel, he will ask why.'

'Don't cancel.' Isn't it obvious? I get to my feet. 'Just don't go.'

Dan leans against the kitchen work surface, energy seeping from him at an alarming rate. He laughs again, covering his face, but it's cold and doesn't reassure me at all.

I step towards him, amazed he hasn't left the room, and take his hands. 'Block his number.' Is it that easy? 'Block his number and don't go. Don't give him any explanation—'

'He'll worry.'

'*Dan.*' I squeeze his fingers. 'Let him worry. Fucking hell, he *broke your ribs*—'

'I know.' Something in the air has caught fire and he looks like he's ready to snap something. 'I know. I just can't do this to him.'

'You can.'

He stares at me, like he wants to believe me. We're about to have a break-through, but my phone buzzes in my back pocket and it makes us both jump. And, because I'm tense enough to snap, I jump into his arms, sweeping our hands out of the way and crushing myself to his chest.

I can hear his breathing and it feels very, very important.

How am I supposed to ever let go of him after what he's told me?

His hands find my hips and I swear I could fly. I don't think he's pushing me away. I think he's holding me right where I am. I think I might just have to hold onto him for the rest of my life.

'I will speak to my therapist.' His breath hits my hair. 'Please do not leave.'

'I'm going to be right here.' I manage to pull myself away from him, and the space between us aches like a stretched muscle. 'Promise.'

He gives me a tiny smile, drops his hands, and looks over at his bedroom. 'I don't know how long I will be.'

'That is *fine.*'

Twenty-Six

I won't tell him this, but I can hear him speaking through the door. He's on the phone for over an hour, and there's a solid ten minutes before and after his voice where I guess he takes time to compose himself.

Unsurprisingly, it was Peter who messaged me. I sit very quietly on the settee and send the odd message to him, not daring to mention I'm at Dan's. There is no way I'm ever going to tell Peter about this.

The bedroom door opens and Dan edges back into the living room, looking thoroughly exhausted. I jump to my feet, about to ask him about it, but he beats me to it.

'Do you want a drink?' He goes straight to the kettle. Nervous, I creep towards him.

'Maybe not coffee.'

He snorts a laugh that sounds like it surprised him and I can't believe it. I made him laugh. In the middle of all this, whatever *this* is, I made him laugh. I'm glowing.

'Good point.' He pours me a glass of water, instead. He hasn't looked at me yet. 'I'm going outside for a moment. Could you come with me?'

'Absolutely.'

'Thank you.'

I want to say it's fine, but our eyes lock. And, like a couple of weeks ago, I'm speechless. I feel my breath leave my chest and stare at him, not sure what to do.

He's been crying.

His eyes look sore and swollen and there are patches of red on both of his cheeks. I don't need to comment, and the silence stretches between us.

'Let's go.' I put my glass down and lead the way to the door. He snatches his keys from the hook, pats his pocket to check for cigarettes, and opens the door.

I follow him in silence, so close I almost touch him with every step.

*

It's a difficult day. Dan's shaken, left fragile and vulnerable by admitting what's going on, and I'm on edge. I'm on high alert, waiting for his phone to ring or waiting for him to say something else I really wish he wouldn't think about.

Something like *I'm going to talk to him.*

We spend most of the time sat together on the settee, chatting or in silence, and it feels like a refuge. Here, we are safe. Here, it doesn't matter I'm seven years younger than him. It doesn't even matter that I think he's gorgeous, because he hooks his arm around my shoulders and pulls me into his chest while we're sitting there. It doesn't matter that I think I'm going to love him more than the world, because he seems perfectly happy to have me beside him—as a friend.

'William,' he whispers, when it's six PM and we've definitely spent too long cuddled together. 'Do you need to go?'

I curl up, tugging my feet onto the settee. 'Probably. Yeah.'

Silence fills the room for a few minutes.

'Do you want to stay?'

'Yes, please.'

'Is that a good idea?'

'Probably not, but I don't want to leave you. Not tonight.'

I feel his head move against mine, like he's turned his neck to push his face into my hair. 'You didn't bring anything.'

'No, because I was supposed to be sensible.' I close my eyes. 'Or whatever I thought *sensible* was when we arranged this. I *don't* think it's sensible to leave you after—after.'

He hums. 'I think I agree. Thank you.'

Okay, I'd sort of hoped he was going to tell me there's no need to be worried. Never mind. I stay where I am, breathing in the mixed scent of cigarettes and his now familiar deodorant.

'You're welcome. I like being with you, Dan.'

Maybe that was a bit too honest. He's quiet for a moment, letting that sink in, and I can feel his breath in my hair. I wonder what we look like. I wonder if he's thinking the same as me, because we're too close and too comfortable for just friends.

He sits up. 'We should eat.'

Okay. I sit, too, and I realise how much weight I'd been putting through him. I mustn't forget his ribs are still broken.

'Do you actually want to stay?'

I give him a smile, trying to ignore the way my pulse is making a vein in my neck twitch. I can still feel him against my side. 'I actually do.'

'Even though it upset you last week?'

He's quite justified to be cautious about that, I guess. My smile flickers but stays and I nod, doing my best to not stare at him. 'I know what to expect this time.'

He shrugs, like maybe that wasn't a good enough answer, so I try again.

'Dan, I want to stay with you.'

Twenty-Seven

Something has happened to me. Everything I say to Dan is a little bit too close to the truth, and I can feel the words *I'm bi'* in every breath I take. Maybe this is it. Maybe this is the moment where I take that first step out of this box I'm hiding in.

Maybe not.

We don't mention sleeping arrangements until well into the night when we're both yawning. We talk about Monday, and last Monday, and he speaks with his eyes on my jaw.

'I wish we had been better.'

'We'll be better this week.' I think I've said this six or seven times now. 'I know what to expect. I'm not going to be as surprised when you wake me up with a nightmare.'

He lets that wash over him for a minute. 'So you aren't going to let me exile myself to the couch?'

'There is *absolutely no way* I am letting you sleep out here.' I don't realise, immediately, that he's joking. And now he's grinning at me, eyes dangerously soft again. Shit. 'Shut up.'

'Are you tired?' he asks suddenly, and I shrug. I don't particularly want to leave the settee, but he must be drained. I bet he hasn't been sleeping very well.

'You are.' I take his hand. Who do I think I am? 'Come on. Let's—let's go to bed.'

I want to say that to him every night.

It takes him a moment to respond and I wonder again if our thoughts are somewhere similar.

'I would offer you pyjamas, but I don't have any.' He pushes slowly to his feet, fingers tight between mine. 'Sorry.'

I snort a laugh and stand with him. 'I think only about three people in my entire block wear pyjamas. Don't worry.'

We turn off the TV, turn off the light, and go to his

beautiful bedroom. All while holding hands. I can't let go.

He doesn't speak. His hand slips from mine, leaving my fingers feeling bruised, and I drift across the room. There's the reassuring crackle of tablets being pushed out of their foil, and then, in the corner of my eye, I see his shirt drop to the floor.

Well, he was shirtless last week. I guess we could both do that.

It feels like a big step. Like a *really* big step. But I guess it won't hurt. It actually means I won't feel as gross tomorrow, and I'm standing there in nothing but my jeans without really thinking about what I'm doing.

I definitely shouldn't be doing this. But I take my glasses off and get into bed with him, sliding under the duvet. We're facing each other.

It feels surprisingly normal. We have our own sides already. He whispers to me about the morning, promising to bring me a glass of water—*not coffee*—and I touch his cheek. Bad idea.

'Go to sleep,' I whisper, fingertips finding his hair.

He closes his eyes.

'Settle down, Dan. I'm going to be right here.'

'Thank you.'

'Thank you for letting me stay.'

He manages a laugh, and it sounds sleepy. Oh, God. I follow him as he rolls over onto his front, moving closer together under the duvet.

I haven't told him.

I'm not going to tell him.

Louise Willingham

Twenty-Eight

This time, when we wake up on Monday morning, everything feels better. I'm a bit embarrassed, and my hand is dangerously close to his waist, like my arm spent the night draped around him, but I don't feel like death. Which is a *major* improvement.

He sits up just as I wriggle away, backing against the headboard. I'm not panicking like last week, but he studies me for a moment.

'Morning.' I smile, chin on my knees. He's still not sure. 'Sleep okay?'

'Yes, thank you.' He moves towards me, like he's checking I'm really there. I tip my head to one side and grin at him. 'Would you like a drink?'

'Not coffee.'

He mock salutes and gets to his feet, stretching. I'm almost caught staring at his waist, his lower back, his shoulders—

'Do you really not even drink tea?'

'Really.'

'You must be the only Englishman I know who doesn't drink tea.' He leans in the doorway, one arm reaching back behind his head. Good heavens. 'Water?'

I grin at him, being overly enthusiastic to hide how warm I am, and he leaves.

Oh, God. I think I've accepted I can't tell him I'm bi. If it were going to happen, it would have been last night. But I've tried so many times, now, and in so many different places. I've survived this long in the closet. Another few decades won't hurt.

Much.

I'm quietly contemplating the rest of my life under a mask when he walks back in, glass of water in one hand, steaming

140

coffee mug in the other. My reaction, for once, doesn't embarrass me. I just smile like anyone would at a gorgeous host and take the glass.

We sit in silence. It's comfortable. It's gentle.

'What are your plans for this evening?' He sits beside me, and I think back to last week. What a disaster.

'I don't know,' I say, quite honestly. 'If you're still around campus after five I'd like to see you again.'

He throws a grin at me. 'I can still be there after five. Will Peter be dragging you to the social again?'

'I think, actually, it was *you* who dragged me to the social last week.'

'I think it was good for you.'

'I think it was, too.' I sigh and shuffle in the duvet, making it cover more of my legs. 'Thank you.'

'You're welcome.'

'Will you want to go?'

He shrugs and watches me very carefully as he answers. 'I have nothing else to do, but no particular desperation to go. If you go with Peter, I will go.'

'What if I make Peter fend for himself tonight?'

He laughs and I think he's still trying to reassure me that he doesn't prefer Peter. Which is stupid. Because that shouldn't *matter*. 'If you do not go, I will not go.'

I pull a face at him and rest my chin on my knees again. 'Well, now all the responsibility is on me.'

'Just wait and see if Peter asks you. If he doesn't…'

He trails off and I do not know what we're both suggesting. Am I going to suggest we spend *another* night together?

Quite possibly.

We leave our evening's plans on a cliff for now, perfectly happy to just let the wind take us in any direction. To the sea or to the grass—I don't care.

Twenty-Nine

Instead of lying face down on my bed once I reach my room, I do some work. And, for the first time in a couple of weeks, I enjoy it. So I'm bouncing on my way to meet Cassie before the lecture, grinning to myself and not minding the bit of drizzle in the air. It's refreshing.

'What's got into you?' she asks, squinting a little at me.

'*Not* coffee.'

She pokes me in the ribs. We chatted on Friday night and had a catch up, which mostly featured me explaining some of the reasons I'd been miserable on Monday and Cassie telling me about her meal with Lilley.

'You should talk to her,' Cassie says while we're walking. I groan. 'She'd like to hear from you.'

'I *don't*—Cas, the last time I saw her, she totally blanked me. You were there.'

'Maybe she was nervous.'

'Maybe she just didn't want to speak to the guy who dumped her—honestly, I think you and Peter forget I didn't want to be in a relationship with her.' I lead the way to the row of seats we usually sit on. 'Why would she want to talk to me?'

'Because you're a nice guy.' Cassie elbows me as we sit down. 'And you were good for each other. I think you should talk to her.'

'I think you should mind your own business.'

I am not going to text Lilley. Mostly because the lecture's about to start, and I want to concentrate, but also because I *don't want to*. Does that make me a bad person? Lilley has a new boyfriend, now—okay so Cassie doesn't like him—and I broke up with her for a reason. We didn't work. Cassie knows this. I know this.

The lecture ends and Cassie blocks my escape from the room, catching me with a glare. We haven't interacted at all

142

since sitting down, and I should probably apologise.

'We're going to talk about this later,' she warns. 'I've had enough of you being weird.'

'Cas, I'm not—'

'I'll catch you about five.' She moves out of the way and joins the little flood of people leaving our lecture room. Great. I have a seminar, then a two-hour pharmaceutical workshop, and I *know* Cassie will be there at the door waiting for me. I don't know what this means for my evening with Dan.

*

She's right there as I leave my workshop. I groan, make some shady comment about her having too much time on her hands, and she just laughs at me.

'I want to talk about you,' she says, slipping her arm through mine and leading me across campus to nowhere in particular. It's not raining anymore, and I'm a bit disappointed. It would be a great excuse to run back to my block. I haven't had chance to speak to Dan and I'm searching for him, as if he would just be lurking around.

'I've already told you everything.' I let her drag me forward. 'What did you want to ask?'

'Why don't you want to talk to Lilley?'

I don't like getting angry with Cassie, but she *never* pushes me this far. So I snap. 'Because we were only dating for *six months*, Cas. I broke up with her—we didn't just stop talking. I broke up with her—'

'But *why*?'

I free my arm a little viciously and stand still. 'Because I don't love her! Because being with her didn't make me feel excellent so why should I stick around?'

She just groans, rubbing her forehead and making it look like it's her who is being nagged. 'I think she misses you. This guy she's with is a rebound and you two should give it another shot.'

I am *furious*.

143

'Cassie, I love you'—my voice is shaking—'but I don't think you've paid *any* attention to me over the last month.'

'What?'

'I don't want a fucking relationship with Lilley!'

'Why not?'

'She's with that Kieran guy, and that's none of my business. And I'm—I'm—'

'With Dan?'

Dust particles freeze in the air. Birds fall silent.

'No,' I say, but it sounds weak. 'No, and it's not like that.'

'What *is* it like?'

'He's—he's—' He's all I care about. 'He's important to me, Cas. But we're not dating.'

She pulls a face, not at all believing me, and doesn't let it go. 'Are we sad about that?'

'No—no, we're not.' I am lying through my teeth. I'd love to hold Dan's hand and introduce him as my boyfriend. 'It's just—it's difficult thinking about relationships in—in relation to him.' I almost smile at the stupidity of the sentence. She isn't convinced. 'He was so hurt, Cas.'

I think I might have just about reached her. Cassie softens, tucking her long hair behind her ear and tilting her head. 'Tell me about it.'

I don't really want to. Still, I find myself saying, 'you know he had that horrible boyfriend.'

'Yeah. And he left him—'

'He's still talking to him,' I blurt. Ah, shit.

'That's not good.'

'Nope.' I sound tired. 'So I'm a bit worried about him. And you know Kirst had a bad time last year.'

Suddenly, she understands. Or she understands enough. 'I knew it was bad,' she says slowly, 'but I don't know *how* bad. You haven't said.'

I shrug. 'Really bad. And it's worse with Dan.'

'How so?'

I shrug and say far too much. My sinuses are prickling with tears again. Brilliant. 'Broke his wrist, broke his ribs.'

'Oh, shit.'

'Yeah.'

She hums and looks around us. 'I get it,' she says. 'I think I get why you're a bit occupied with him.'

'Just a bit.'

'But don't abandon the rest of us for him, alright?'

I press my lips together.

'I know you care about him, but you've got to be careful.'

I don't like that and take a deep breath.

'Does he care this much back?'

I roll my eyes, trying to spread the tears around. 'I think so. Didn't Peter tell you what he was like on Monday?'

'He did, which is why we thought you were hiding a relationship from us.'

I shake my head sharply.

'Because you know we both love you, right? I don't care who you fall in love with, but I want you to be happy. And is—*are* you happy?'

I clear my throat. 'It's not related. I'm not—I'm not in love.' Big lie. Huge. It's swallowing me whole. 'And I'm not the *happiest* I've ever been but I'm not *bad*. I'm just stressed.'

She hums. 'You terrified Peter last week.'

'Yeah, I know.'

'Do you think you'll get like that again?'

'I dunno, Cas—'

'Because if it's Dan—'

'If it's Dan *what*?'

Her eyes narrow. 'Is Dan looking after you?'

'That's not what you were going to ask.'

She puts her hand on her hip and glares at me, sparking another little flame.

'He—I don't know why you've decided to hate him—'

'Because he's making you feel crap!'

'He is *not*!' I step away from her, heart thundering. 'You don't have a *clue*.'

'Tell us, then!' She steps to follow me. 'You haven't told us *anything*—'

'The guy broke his ribs, Cas. I told you *everything*—everything I can!'

145

'What *can't* you tell us?' She tucks her hair back again. 'I'm just worried about you.'

I can't help but believe her. 'You don't need to be. I'm fine. I'm just worried about Dan because he's been—he's been through so much shit and you and Peter going on about me for caring about him isn't going to help.'

The hand that was in her hair rubs her forehead. 'I'm trying to imagine what could have happened to him that you can't tell us.'

God, help me. I shove my hands through my hair and speak before I can think about it. 'Matthew gave him drugs.'

She blinks at me, dark hazel eyes swallowing her pale face.

'Bad ones. And he—he keeps talking to him and they met up last week so I'm really worried he's just going to relapse. Don't tell Peter.'

She blinks again. 'Do you feel safe with him?'

'More safe than I do anywhere else.' It's a little bit too honest. 'He's great.'

'Peter doesn't like him.'

'No, I didn't think so.'

'I'm not sure I like him.'

'*You* haven't really met him,' I point out. 'But whatever. Have you finished, now? Have I told you enough?'

She groans and shakes her head. For a moment, I think she's going to start arguing again—and I hate it. I'm ready to scream.

'I want you to be okay. You know you can talk to me whenever, alright?'

I nod, chewing down that scream.

'Please be careful.'

'I am careful.' I cross my arms over my chest and just about resist pulling out my phone to look at the time. 'I'm alright, Cas. Sorry for shouting.'

She hums and steps towards me, sweeping me into an awkward hug that pins my hands to my sides. 'Alright.'

'Trust me?'

'I guess.' She leans back and smiles at me. 'Are you seeing him tonight?'

Ah, crap. No point in lying. 'Yep.'

'Did you see him yesterday?'

'Yep.'

'Did you stay with him again?'

'*Yep.*'

She gives me a look, pats my cheek, and releases me. 'Be careful. Talk to me tonight, yeah?'

'Alright. Thanks for the interrogation, Cas.' I try to smile again. 'See you soon.'

And I escape.

Oh my God.

I do love Cassie. And I get it, I think. I'd have endless questions if she'd suddenly decided to spend all of her time with a guy who clearly has problems.

Oh, God, and I know she'd be fine with me being queer. That's not the reason I've barricaded myself in this dark closet with an ever-reducing supply of oxygen. I know she'd be fine with me falling in love with *anyone*, but I'm beginning to think she wouldn't want that *anyone* to be Dan. Especially if Peter's decided he doesn't like him. But that might just be because he's jealous, because I *have* spent a lot of time with Dan.

And that isn't going to change.

Thirty

I walk blindly past lecture buildings, my arms wrapped around my chest to try to keep some heat in. I need to start wearing a thicker coat.

17:05 Daniel: Have you had a good day?

Daniel. With the way my thoughts are whirring at the moment I'd expected a text from Peter, but I'm far from disappointed. I glance up as I walk, note I'm near the SU, and reply.

> **17:07 William**: Yes thanks! Are you on campus? I'd like to see you

17:07 Daniel: I'm here, yes.

> **17:08 William**: Where are you?

He doesn't reply. He doesn't have to because I see him and practically run at him.

I announce myself just before I crash into him. 'That's bad for you.'

He laughs and kills the cigarette on a bin, turning very slowly to face me. I'm buzzing.

'Are you okay?' He glances around us and then leans closer, squinting at me. 'Have you been crying?'

'Fuck off.' I rub my eyes again. I know I shouldn't swear at him, but he just smiles like he understands, and waits. 'Yeah, a bit. I was talking to Cassie.' Oh, God, I told her too much.

'Is she okay?'

'Yeah, yeah. We were talking a bit about Kirst. But she's

148

okay—it was just a difficult conversation. How was your day?'

He sighs, letting me know he noticed that abrupt change in topic, and puts his hands in his pockets. I can't help but think it's a shame.

'As long as you're okay. My day was good. Quiet. I didn't see him.' I hadn't even thought of that. 'We should eat something.'

I nod a little bit too enthusiastically, remembering only now that I missed lunch. Again. He realises and rolls his eyes, freeing one hand from his pockets to take hold of my arm and drag me forward a little bit.

'Where are we going?'

'To get you fed,' he mutters. 'I didn't think you were the sort of person to skip meals.'

'It's not on purpose.' I have to trot to keep up with him. We're going to the SU again and I can't help but smile. 'I just forgot today. And I felt too crap last week to do anything.'

'I know.' His voice sounds dark. Heavy. I bump his arm with mine as we join the short queue. 'I'm sorry.'

We're standing remarkably close together. 'Please don't apologise for it. This week has been a lot better.'

He hums, and I can hear the doubt in him. We buy food and it's someone I don't recognise serving us, but Daniel makes small talk with them. It's weird to see him talking like this, and I blurt my stupid thoughts as soon as we sit down.

'I've noticed something.' I've already dug a hole. 'Your—your accent changes.'

'Does it?' He looks genuinely interested, with one eyebrow raised, eyes bright. 'It is not intentional.'

I speak too quickly. 'No, I know.' *Breathe.* 'I thought it got stronger when you're tense, but it's there when you talk to me.'

He crosses his legs under the table and leans back, relaxed into the uncomfortable plastic chair. His head is tilted a little bit, but he's looking straight at me. Fortunately, I've had quite a lot of practice of making eye contact with him and not instantly falling to my knees.

Plus, I'm sitting down.

'I'll be listening to myself, now,' he says, after a moment.

I flash a smile.

'I forget about it. And no one mentions it.'

'Sorry.'

He rolls his eyes dramatically and his head tilts even more. 'You are allowed to mention it.'

I really wish I blushed less easily. 'Thanks, I think.'

He laughs and picks at his food. 'You're welcome.'

'I want to keep asking things,' I confess, and he just waits. I think that means it's okay. 'Do you ever speak in Russian?'

His answer is quick and much sharper than I'd expected. 'No. Matthew didn't like it, and I don't have anyone who would understand.'

I feel sick. 'I'm sorry—'

'It is not your fault.' His eye drops to the table for a moment. And then they come back to me, and he's smiling, but it looks tired. 'I heard myself.'

'For the record,' I say, several feet deep in my pit, now, 'you have a really nice voice.' He raises an eyebrow and I *keep digging*. 'It's just nice. Warm.'

'Would you say that if I didn't have such an obvious accent?'

'Yes.' I think he believes me, and he should—it's true. 'Sorry for being nosy.'

'It's fine.' He sits up again, back poker straight. I haven't actually touched my food yet, and he notices. 'Eat, William.'

I pull a face at him but do as I'm told. The smell of warm food is making me salivate and I don't need to make controlling my body any more difficult, thanks. We sit there, eating slowly and sometimes talking, until I become aware the SU has emptied.

'What time is it?' I fail to remember that I could simply look at my phone, like he's about to. Oops.

'Seven.'

'Oh, wow.'

'What?'

I laugh at him and look around us. 'Time flies. What do you want to do now?'

I know what I want him to say. I know what he *should* say.

150

Unfortunately, or fortunately, he's sensible enough to go for the latter option. 'I should go home. Will you be okay?'

He shouldn't have to ask me that. I smile at him and, somehow, our legs touch beneath the table. 'I'll be fine. Will you be okay?'

'I'll be fine.'

I really don't like saying goodbye to him. We hug again just before his taxi turns up and I almost ask him to come home with me—the words are in my mouth. They taste of a bad mistake.

'I'll talk to you later.' His hands are on my waist. He starts to pull his arms back, but we pause, frozen in an arguably *too intimate* position. I can feel his heart beating through his ribs and narrowly resist kissing his chest. 'See you Sunday?'

We've decided, somehow, that we're going to do this every week. So I nod and take a deep breath, catching him in my lungs, before I step back.

'Maybe even before then.'

His eyes are gentle and hazy again. My shirt falls away from where he pressed it against my waist and it feels cold—like stepping out of the sun and into an air-conditioned room. I check I'm still breathing and grin at him.

'See you soon, Dan.'

Thirty-One

I drag myself through the days where I don't see him. We text regularly, though, and it's just enough to keep the fear for what he might do at bay while I concentrate on coursework. He has his first group counselling session on Thursday and I know he's dreading it. I also know I should concentrate on my seminar. But I can't.

He fills every second thought.

So I phone him as soon as I'm done for the day.

He answers quickly. 'Hello. How are you?'

I grin at my feet and try to concentrate on walking. 'Hi. I'm good. How was it?'

'Awful. We sat in a circle and spoke about ourselves.'

'Gross.'

'Someone asked me where I'm from.'

I groan, being overly dramatic for him, and I'm rewarded with a little chuckle.

'How did you know?'

'Uh. Cassie told me.'

'How did *she* know?'

Oh, God. 'Good point.' I come to a stop. 'Lucky guess? Everyone just knows everyone here.'

'I don't think I have *ever* spoken to her.'

I frown at the pavement and tell him what I probably should have told him weeks ago. 'She lived in *his* block last year.' No need to ask who I mean. 'She recognised you at work and said she'd seen you with him.'

The silence feels swollen with something. I chew the inside of my cheek, wishing I could see his expression. Ahead of me, the orange lights of the SU spill out of the windows into the late afternoon sun, and I can almost smell the food.

'I am very afraid of Matthew finding out who you are.'

'Why would he?' Ah. I've just answered my own

question. 'I'm okay, Dan. He's not going to find me.'

'If he already knows Cassie—'

'He doesn't,' I say quickly, sounding too confident. 'She just recognised you. That's all.'

'He might recognise *her*—'

'But that doesn't mean he'll have any idea who I am—or that he'll make a link from me to you.'

'He will if he sees you with me.'

It's a punch to my throat and I stumble to a stop. 'What are you saying?'

'Maybe I shouldn't spend time with you on campus.'

I'm going to pretend this hurts less than it really does because, shit, I can feel myself caving in. 'He isn't going to find out who I am. And so what if he does notice us together? What's he gonna do?'

'He will hurt you—'

'He won't get chance,' I snap. 'I'm either with you, in my room, or doing work. I'm safe.'

Dan hesitates, nervous or angry. I can't tell.

'Do you want me to come over?'

'No, I'm—you have work to do.' He sounds faint, like he's not quite holding the phone properly.

'I can do it at yours.'

'I—'

'Dan, if you're worried about this, I want to be with you.' I walk again, heading straight to my room. So I can head straight back out. 'I'm coming over.'

'Thank you.'

I pick up speed, keeping my phone to my ear. 'You can always ask, silly. I'm just gonna sort my stuff out for the morning.'

'Thank you.'

'You're welcome. I'll text you when I'm getting in the taxi. You're at home, right?'

'Yeah. Thank you.'

The repetition is making me shiver, and I pull my keys out of my pocket. 'Okay. If you go outside to smoke, let me know. I'll be with you soon.'

'Thank you, William.'

He sounds awful. At the very least, I think he's holding back tears. I hesitate, wishing I had something better I could say to him, and hang up. The best thing I can do right now is get myself to his flat.

Thirty-Two

As always, Dan's there when I step onto the pavement. He's smoking, leaning against the wall, and doesn't even try to hide the cigarette. He just gives me a slightly guilty grin and steps forward.

'Thank you for coming.'

I roll my eyes and stare at the cigarette, trying to make a point.

'What?'

'You were meant to let me know if you were coming outside.' I glance around us, standing as close to him as I can. 'Something might have happened to you.'

He raises an eyebrow. 'Like what?'

'I dunno.' I cross my arms. '*Something.*'

'Nothing happened.' He breathes deeply on this cigarette and closes his eyes, face turned away from me. 'I'm okay.'

'Sure.'

'I am.' He blinks to look at me, hitting me with those blues. 'I just worry about you.'

I snort. 'Nowhere near as much as I worry about *you*.'

Good heavens, he winks at me. I'm stunned, stomach in knots, and watch him walk away from me to scrape the cigarette into a bin. God, I wish he wouldn't smoke.

He comes back and puts his hand on my arm, holding us close together to steer me to the door. 'I will probably be out again soon.'

'That's fine—hey.' I've largely recovered from that wink and, now the door's shut between us and the world, I pull him into my arms. It feels overdue. His hands find my waist, and I relax a little bit more. 'I'll always come over. Just ask.'

He breathes deeply, the exhale licking my skin. 'Thank you.'

'And you're allowed to worry.' I slip away very slowly.

It's as fast as I can bear. 'I brought my laptop.'

He laughs, takes my hand, and leads me up the stairs. It feels so *normal* to hold his hand, now—what would I do if one of us got into an actual romantic relationship? I don't think I'd be able to stop coming to spend Sunday nights with him—nor the odd Thursday night—and I don't think I would ever trust anyone to be gentle enough with him.

Plus, the jealousy would eat me alive.

We talk for hours, but it flies past us and feels like moments. He tells me about his appointment and I can see the stress evaporating from him, lightening his shoulders with each breath. And then he asks me about the report I'm doing for anatomy and I catch myself pointing to *his* abdomen, drawing an imaginary map of organs and arteries over his jumper without really thinking about it. Crap.

'I love hearing you talk about your work,' he says, when we're sat in one of those long silences.

I blink up at him, suddenly aware I was staring at his thighs with my hand on his waist. Oops.

'You are so enthusiastic about it.'

'You sort of have to be enthusiastic about medicine if you want to be a doctor.' My hand is burning. 'I want to help people, but it's tough.'

'It is. But you're smart.'

'Thanks.'

'You are. And you care—you care about it, and you care about people.'

One of my shoulders shrugs and I sink towards him.

'I'm very proud to be your friend.'

Oh, shoot me.

I hum and curl up on my half of the settee, pressing my glowing cheek into his arm. It takes the shortest moment for him to wrap his arm around my shoulders, pulling me closer.

'I'm proud to be your friend, too.' *Friend* doesn't feel enough.

He makes a disbelieving sound in the back of his throat and I have to resist kissing whatever skin I can find. It's difficult. My face is against his neck.

'You're smart. You know two languages—that's more than most people here, I bet—and you're *strong*. You've beaten a heroin addiction, Dan. That's incredible.'

I expect some sarcastic comment but he rubs his thumb into my arm, instead. I watch his hand, mind slipping from our conversation in the time it takes for him to reply.

'I have five languages.'

*

It turns out that Daniel is *clever*. I mean it. He speaks Russian, English, French, German, *and* Spanish. And I'm not talking GCSE level—he tells me quite confidently that he could have a natural conversation in any of those languages.

I'm still gawking at him, hours after finding out.

'What?'

'I want to ask you to say something in each language, but I realise that's rude.'

He laughs and sits up a bit. It's getting late. Really, we should go to bed. 'If anyone else asked, it would be.'

'You shouldn't—you don't have to.'

He gives me a *look* which knots my stomach and says, in each language, one after the other, that he is glad I am his friend. I want to cry.

I'm just staring at him, like I'm expecting more. I'm not —my brain just doesn't know how to keep piloting my body after being blown over by such a beautiful, *attractive* display of languages.

It takes me a moment. 'What's your favourite?'

He rolls his eyes and leans sideways into the back of the settee. We definitely should go to bed. I'm not letting him fall asleep out here again. 'English, because I can speak to you.'

I am melting. He's smirking, and I'm glad I'm sitting down.

He can see how ruined I am and winks, making it so much worse. 'But they are all good.'

'They—they are.'

'I would like to speak Russian more.'

I speak without thinking. Who can blame me? 'Then do.'

He frowns at me.

'What?'

'I can't talk to anyone using it.'

'But you could talk *at* me.'

He laughs—I was expecting him to be upset, but he laughs.

'What?'

'You are very generous,' he says, stretching his neck and sitting forward again. 'Maybe I will.'

'Do you think in Russian?'

It's a really stupid question, and I'm very embarrassed it came from *my* mouth. He's still being patient with me, though —I get the impression he likes talking about this—and shrugs. He's resting with his arms on his knees, back bent forward. Head turned to face me.

'I don't know. It all blurs together. Mostly, I think it's English.' He doesn't look pleased about this. 'It depends how I'm feeling.'

'What about the others?'

'I think if I was surrounded by people speaking the language, I would fall into it,' he explains, 'but it is difficult. I get them confused.'

'Really?'

'*Да.*'

Sweet Jesus.

It's just one little word but I'm staring at him with my mouth open and my eyes saucer wide.

'No more questions?' He's noticed my reaction—anyone even glancing through the window at us would notice my reaction—and he's teasing me and I *love* it. He's smirking again. My stomach feels warm.

'N—no.' I lick my lips and pray he can't hear my heartbeat. 'Should we go to bed?'

I love that this is something we can just do. I love that he and I can sit like this on the settee—sprawled across each other, arms around each other—and I love that sharing a bed has only been awkward once. Now, it's as natural as breathing.

Silence between us is as natural as breathing.

'Oh,' he says, when the lights are all off and we've closed the door between us and the world. 'I was going to tell you more about Matthew.'

A lump in my throat threatens to choke me. 'You don't have to.' I watch him through the gloom. He sits down on the edge of the bed—his side—and I catch myself wondering if he preserves *my* side even when I'm not here.

'I want to. Maybe not so close to sleeping.'

'Good shout.' I shuffle towards him.

'If I wake you tonight, I am sorry. The meeting was difficult today.'

As if it's something that *didn't* go horribly wrong last time, I'm hugging him. I kneel behind him and wrap my arms around his chest—his bare chest—and rest my chin on his shoulder. Cheek against his neck.

He touches my hand.

'Don't worry about it,' I say. 'Talk to me about it whenever. And I'm prepared for your nightmares, now. You won't scare me as much.'

He huffs a laugh and drops his hand from mine. This is a good thing, because we were being *far* too close and intimate, but I feel myself sigh. 'We will see.'

'You okay?'

'I'm okay. We should sleep.'

I slip away from him, suddenly aware of how *cold* the room is, and tuck myself under my half of the duvet. 'If you wake up,' I pause to yawn, 'you have to wake me.'

He doesn't comment for a moment, and I think he's doing that thing again where he ignores me but pretends to not hear. 'You have to, as well,' he says, voice muffled by the pillow. He still sleeps on his front. 'Goodnight, William.'

I'm staring at him, imagining how easy it would be to put my arm across his back, and respond *far* too late. If he notices it, he doesn't say.

'Goodnight, Dan.'

Thirty-Three

I'm back there on Sunday, and the Sunday after. Of course I am. It's become a *thing* now, and even Cas and Peter have stopped bothering to mention it. I just pretend it's normal for friends to share a bed every Sunday. I don't think I'm fooling anyone, least of all myself.

'So,' I say, when we've both settled in the bed at something past eleven, 'next week.'

His birthday.

He groans.

'What do you want to do?'

He tips his head back, face to the ceiling. 'Just come here. Just be *normal*.'

Normal. I find that very interesting but just about manage to not poke him about it. Instead, I stretch and get comfortable.

'Am I allowed to buy you a cake?'

He laughs and turns, so he's facing me. I don't think I'll ever get over seeing him like this, peering at me over his pillow with his lips lifted in a little smile. 'If you insist. But you realise it is just the two of us. Do not get over-excited.'

I roll my eyes and clasp my hands under my jaw, catching them before they reach for him. 'What if we went somewhere?'

He blinks quickly. 'What are you thinking?'

'I don't know—nothing, really. I just think we should do something.'

He groans and I feel the air move against my face. 'Fine. Maybe we could go onto campus. Have a drink or two. Would Peter be around?'

I just about manage to hide the way I pulled a face at Peter's name. I haven't told Dan about mine and Cassie's conversation, and I'm not going to. 'Possibly. We could ask him, if you'd like.'

'It might be nice. Come here. Just you. In the evening we will go onto campus, and maybe we'll find Peter.'

I'm chewing the inside of my mouth and he makes me wait. I think I know what he's going to say next—I know what I *want* him to say.

'Could I stay with you?'

'Definitely.' I speak too quickly, and I sound way too excited, but he doesn't seem to mind. I think he's getting used to me being overly enthusiastic about these things, and he just smiles at me through the darkness.

'Thank you.'

*

He hasn't even been to my room since that first week and, now I *know* he's coming over, I can prepare myself. I'm already making plans for tidying my room on Monday morning, while he's making coffee for himself and pouring water for me.

'I think I need to tell you something,' he says, snatching me out of my daydream and making me jump. I'm too embarrassed to worry about what's about to be said and just take my glass.

'Go for it.'

'You haven't asked what I did before university.'

My brain is slowly catching up. You can hear it coughing into life, like the engine of an old car. 'I kinda thought you would just tell me whenever you're ready.'

Despite my foggy thoughts, it looks like that was the right thing to say. He sits on the edge of his side of the bed and puts his mug down, not looking at me. I copy, putting my glass on the little table between me and the wall. And I wait.

'I moved to England when I was twenty-three,' he says, and I have to hide a smile. His accent is in the room with us, trying to shield him from something. 'After I was discharged.'

'From what?'

My mind has gone straight to hospital. I picture the painting of scars across his back and wonder if he was in some horrible, terrible accident.

But he's looking at me like I just asked something stupid. 'The military.'

Oh.

It's like the walls fall down around me and, suddenly, I'm sitting out in the open. I can feel the wind against my skin, cutting across my chest, and anyone passing by can look over and see me. They wonder how I can be so *stupid*.

Dan's waiting for me to react. So far, all I've managed to achieve is parted lips and a little sigh that sounded like a swear word.

'I—' Useless. I try again. 'Okay.'

'Okay?'

'I have no idea what to say,' I admit, and his expression softens. 'How long for?'

'Over three years.' He watches me very carefully. I'm acutely aware of the stubble across his jaw, and the area of burn scar tissue over his shoulder. Oh, no. I stare at it, wondering— 'It is only compulsory, now, for one year. But I stayed.'

'Why?'

'I had nothing else to do. I was able to make some money and I travelled well.' He is staring right at me. I don't think he's blinked, like he's challenging me. 'I was good at it.'

'What did you do?'

I don't think I actually want to know, and we both know the awful question I'm going to ask next. It's inevitable.

'I was based at home for the first year. Security. Checkpoints. That sort of thing. And then I joined Ground and I travelled more.' He closes his eyes—he finally closes his eyes and swallows, jaw twitching. 'I am a very different person to who I was then.'

My awful question has to wait for a moment longer. 'People change. It's okay—you don't have to be the same as you were.'

He squints at me, blue eyes swimming under too many tears. I hate seeing him cry, but it's going to happen. And he's waiting. 'Ask.'

My mouth is very dry. My water is just behind me—inches away—but I lick my lips and let myself suffer, instead. I don't want to say these words and I don't want to hear his answer.

But it happens.

'Did you kill anyone?'

'Yes.'

It hangs there, a spider on a single strand of silk, until one of us finds the strength to breathe. I'm numb. I think the shock of this is better than novocaine. Someone could drill a hole into the back of my head and I wouldn't notice.

He's tense, braced for impact. It must have been difficult for him to tell me this. It must have been difficult for him to be holding this secret for the last few weeks—especially with knowing my inclination for *saving* lives.

I'm the first one to disturb the air by breathing. It's a long, deep breath, which I suck in and try to stabilise myself with. I hold it, letting it bounce around my chest, and relax.

He hasn't moved.

'Okay.' It's a feeble way to follow his confessions. 'Okay.'

He shakes his head. A tiny, fatigued shake.

'How many?' Stupid.

'I don't know.' He sounds different—cracked and tired.

It was a stupid question. It upset him and I realise, now he's answered, that I *do not care*. It doesn't matter if he killed one person or one hundred people.

I force a little smile. 'Did you think I'd be upset?'

He closes his eyes again.

'Because I'm not.'

'You should be.'

'But I'm proud of you.'

'Proud?' He echoes, eyes snapping open to stare at me. A couple of tears fall but he ignores them. I freeze. 'You cannot be *proud* of this. *You* cannot be *proud*—'

'Dan, you did what you thought was right—you fought for your country—'

'A country that would never fight for me,' he spits. Oh

163

my God. My pulse throbs in my throat. 'I killed people for it and for *what*?'

I stick to my argument. 'You were young. Give yourself some context, Dan.'

At the sound of his name he turns away, and I think he's going to leave.

'I was older than you are now.'

'We've already established that neither of us match our ages.' Oh, here it is. My posh voice. My *absolutely terrified* voice. 'You were *twenty*. You had spent *twenty years* at home—being told that this was the right thing to do. You did not have an outsider's view—'

'I did, William—I knew I was not right for the place.'

This is not at all comfortable.

'You didn't know a way of being anything other than what you had been told to be.' Surprisingly, this seems to break through to him. 'I guess you—you joined, because you had to, and then you were told you were good at it—right?'

He shrugs, still facing away.

'We all like to be told we're doing well.'

'But you cannot be proud of me.' His arms wrap around his chest. 'Even justifying what I did cannot make you *proud* of me.'

'Well, I'm proud that you were brave enough to tell me,' I offer instead, and his shoulders drop. I'm shuffling over towards him, like I did on Thursday, and he doesn't expect to feel my hands.

He jolts, like he missed a step.

'Whatever you think of it, I'm proud that you did what you thought was right.'

He shakes his head. 'You should be upset.'

'Should I?'

'Yes—Yes, William, I killed—'

I do it—I kiss his shoulder. He definitely feels it this time because he shuts up, voice getting caught in his throat and choking him. I'm holding him too tightly, and I am definitely going to regret this when I get back to my room, but it doesn't matter. I've got to make sure he knows I care—or that I don't care. It depends how you look at it.

'It doesn't matter.' My lips are still against his shoulder. Oh, crap. I can't move away. 'It doesn't matter. It doesn't make me love you any less.'

Shit.

Fortunately, it's the sort of thing someone *would* say to their friend. It's the sort of thing you expect someone to say when they're trying to calm someone down. It doesn't mean I've just told him that I love him.

Even though, *news flash*, I totally do.

It's eating me alive, but slowly enough for me to ignore it. For now.

He leans into me. 'Thank you.' I give him a gentle squeeze. 'I understand if you change your mind.'

'Do I look like I'm going to change my mind?'

'Just do not be afraid of being honest with me. Okay?'

I want to kiss him again. I want to kiss his neck and taste his skin. I satisfy myself by pressing my face into his hair, instead.

'You have to be honest with me, too.'

Thirty-Four

By next Sunday morning, I'm beginning to get concerned about Dan. He hasn't really been talking to me. I mean, he's been texting me every morning, but it's his birthday and we haven't said more than 'good morning, have a good day, speak later' to each other all week.

So I'm extremely nervous when I turn up at his building, card and cake in hand, and wait for him.

For once, he isn't there waiting. He must have seen the taxi, though, because he throws the door open, windswept.

'Happy birthday!' I force my pathetic offerings into his hands. 'Did you run?'

He tries a smile and steps back, holding the front door for me. 'I lost track of time.' He's staring at the envelope, like he doesn't understand it. 'Thank you for this.'

'You're welcome.' I'm being purposefully bright and ignoring the bags under his eyes. 'Did you sleep okay?' Okay, I'm not ignoring them. I'm just trying to not stare.

'On and off.' He leads me to his flat and closes the door behind us, not looking at me. He takes my coat without speaking and hangs it on the hook. It's a little thing, but it makes his flat feel like home. But then he takes a deep breath and hands me his phone. 'He messaged me. Look.'

Oh, crap.

01:14 **Matthew**: Happy birthday, gorgeous. I hope you have a good day. I miss you

Gorgeous.

I hum and hand the heavy phone back, like it might hurt me. 'I thought you were going to block his number.'

'I meant to.' He walks away, to the kettle. He empties a mug, tipping the old contents down the drain. It looks like it was full. 'I don't know how.'

'Want me to try?' I'm trying to be gentle but, honestly, starting his birthday with a message from that horrible man has stressed me out. I can't even imagine how Dan must be feeling.

But he puts the phone down on the work surface next to me, nods, and goes back to the kettle.

It takes me very few taps of the screen to find the *Block Numbers* option. 'Dan?'

He looks up at the sound of my voice, looking lost. The new mug of coffee is cradled to his chest and, now we're facing each other, I'm not sure I believe he slept at all last night.

I find my voice again. 'I've worked it out. Do you want to block him?'

He nods, then steps towards me. 'I didn't try,' he admits, and I snort a laugh.

'Oh, I guessed. Don't worry. Here,' I show him the screen and let my finger hesitate over the button. 'Do it?'

'Do it.'

And, like that, I block Matthew's number from Daniel's phone. It feels important.

Especially when Dan puts his mug down and sweeps me into his arms in one beautifully gentle movement. I've stumbled and I'm holding onto his shirt, trying to balance myself.

He presses his face into my hair. 'Thank you. Thank you for everything you do for me.'

'It's nothing.' My voice is muffled by his chest. I take a deep breath, and it tastes of him. 'Have you—have you seen him again?'

'No, not since I last told you.'

I'm sure he can feel me relax. 'Good. Have you spoken to him?'

'Just last night and this morning.'

Ah, shit. A tight, high-pitched squeal comes from my throat and I hold him tighter, like he's about to be ripped from me. Oh, God. 'What happened?'

'He asked what I'm doing today.' He sounds like he's in a different room. 'I told him I'm busy.'

'How long did you talk for?'

'Some hours.'

Oh, God. I have no idea what to say.

Many minutes go past. 'I haven't taken any drugs.'

Any other time, I might have laughed. I just hum and slip my arms further around his chest, holding him like I'll never get another chance.

'Thank you for seeing me today.'

I groan. 'Thank you for letting me.' I move my head so my glasses are getting less crushed. If I thought I had the ability to let go of him, I'd just take them off. 'Have you heard from anyone else?'

'Like who?'

I find myself stumbling on my words before they even leave my mouth. 'I—your family?'

I can feel him holding his breath.

'I don't have any family.'

Oh. I can't believe I haven't asked about this before.

'My mother died, which was when I left the army. My father was older than her and I haven't seen him since I was sixteen. I think I should have told you this sooner.'

'No, there's no rush for this sort of thing,' I manage, concentrating on the thud of his heart through his shirt. It's a reassuringly familiar sound, after everything. 'I'm just glad you told me now.'

He sighs and moves his hands, one going up to my hair and the other one down to my hip. *Shit.* I move, too, dropping my hands from his shirt to his waist and lifting my cheek away from his chest. It's more difficult than I'd like to admit.

Oh, he looks tired. 'Let's sit down.' He looks past me at the mug of coffee he's abandoned. 'I didn't sleep last night.'

'Nope, I *knew* it.' I inch towards the settee, not quite daring to let go of him. He smiles a little ruefully at me and it's gorgeous. *Gorgeous.* Maybe I shouldn't use that word if it's something Matthew called him. 'You look shattered.'

He hums, cradling the mug to his chest and picking up his phone again. 'I'll be okay.'

'Did you forget you can call me?' I sit down on my usual

end of the settee. He sits right beside me and I don't even pretend to be polite, or *normal*—I kick off my shoes and curl my legs up onto the cushion so I can lean into him.

He laughs, hooking his arm over my shoulder, and I close my eyes. 'I forgot, yes. I forgot you think you would not mind being woken up.'

I huff, cheek against his shoulder. 'Always wake me up. Do you need to have a nap?'

'I have coffee,' he says, as if caffeine is ever a sensible substitute for sleep. But it's the perfect excuse for me to get some of the concern out of my chest by ranting about how much coffee he drinks, and I sit up while I'm talking to see the way he smirks at me over his mug. I know it's outrageous to lecture him about *caffeine*, of all things. He knows this, too.

We share the cake, even though it's ten in the morning and I don't think I'm going to be able to cope with so much sugar so early in the day. It's one of those small gift cakes—barely enough for four people—and we nibble through it while we sit there. When I ask what he wants to do for lunch, he just groans and pulls me closer.

Oh.

'My last birthday was nothing like this. Thank you.'

'All I've done is sit—'

'Yeah.' He never interrupts me. It sends shivers down my spine. 'That's my point—thank you for not forcing me to do anything.'

The shivers go from warm to ice cold and I wriggle, wanting to hold onto him. 'I never will,' I breathe, and that's enough for a while. I think he must fall asleep. I nearly do, and it's an hour before either of us think to speak again.

'We should find you something to eat.' He rubs his hand up and down my arm a few times. 'We should go out.'

I perk up at that idea and smile at him, neck a little stiff. 'You sure?'

He throws his eyes over me as he stands up, like he's checking I'm not too crumpled. 'I'm sure.'

I stretch, all too aware of how *snuggled* we were, and watch him move around the little living room. And I speak without really thinking about it. 'Have you been okay this week?'

'Why?'

'We haven't spoken much.'

He pauses with his hand out to turn off the TV and looks at me. 'I thought you wanted space.'

'Why would I want space?'

He straightens up and his eyes flash towards the bedroom. I know what he's thinking, but I sit there and make him say it anyway. 'What I told you about myself isn't easy to accept.'

I raise an eyebrow. 'I found it remarkably easy to accept. Dan, I don't care. And I'm still proud of you.' He throws me a *horrible* glare and I pull my chin back, like I'm flinching from him. 'Hey.'

'Be proud of me for other things,' he mutters, pulling on his shoes and very obviously not looking at me. 'Choose anything else.'

'I don't think it's the sort of thing I get to *choose*.' Still sitting down, I grab my shoes. 'Would you be like this if it was the other way around?'

'It would not *be* the other way around. You would not have *killed* people for a country where— where—' his hand is in his hair and he's looking at me, trying desperately to make me understand. I just feel flat. 'I could not be gay there. I know you can't understand that, but knowing I did *anything* for them hurts.'

I would like to place a bet.

The pain he feels for protecting a country which will not protect him is nothing—not even a fraction—on how much it hurts to hear him say this.

I know you can't understand.

Try me, Daniel.

I'm sitting there with a pale, drained face and he thinks he's won. He thinks he's explained why he doesn't want me to be *proud* of him and I get it—I'm not going to push that any more.

He still thinks I'm straight and I thought I was okay with this.

The back wall of my closet is bulging, threatening to push

me unforgivingly out through the doors. And it's tempting. I can see him out there, and he's glowing, and I am itching to feel the light on my skin.

'William?'

I should tell him.

For some reason, I'm smiling. And the words, 'okay, you win,' come out of my mouth, but it doesn't sound like me. It sounds like someone in a different room.

I don't think he's convinced.

He's still watching me, eyebrows pulled down in a gentle frown over his gorgeous, powdery eyes and he starts to walk to me. He's going to work it out.

'Did I upset you?'

'No, no—I'm okay.' I blink too quickly and look away from him. The room flashes around me and I can hear the hum of the lights. 'I'm okay. I'm sorry for being proud of you.'

He almost laughs. Instead, he's locked our eyes together, trying to read my thoughts. 'You can be proud of me,' he says, voice slow and full of his accent which, if I'm honest, makes everything ten times more difficult. 'But understand why I do not want praise for *that*.'

I swallow, and it tastes of blood. 'I understand.'

He looks like he wants to hug me. Please do.

'Do you want to go?'

I make a funny noise—somewhere between a hum and a cough—and look away from him again before I can do anything stupid. But I don't think he'd mind if I asked for a hug. It's the sort of thing we do, now.

I finish putting my shoes on, instead, and grab my wallet from the floor.

Thirty-Five

It turns out that I am not, in fact, okay with still not being out.

For a couple of weeks, I had myself convinced. I think I'd convinced everyone around me I'm okay but, shit, I am *not* okay.

Dan and I go onto campus in the evening, as planned. We find Peter and spend some hours sitting with drinks—I'm sticking to water, and I know Dan has noticed—and we're just chatting.

They're talking. I'm mostly sitting there in a miserable, self-pitying silence.

I could say it. At any time. Even if I interrupted them mid conversation, they wouldn't mind. They'd understand—Dan might understand too much—and they'd take me back to my room and sit with me until I felt okay again.

In my head, I've already told them a hundred times.

They notice something's wrong but, as I haven't actually started hyperventilating yet, neither of them really *do* anything. I can't blame them. I look like I'm lost in thought—and I am —and everything is *fine*.

'I don't know what to do about Anthony,' Peter says, looking directly at Daniel. I may as well not be here at this point. 'We fucked and I think he wants to meet up again, but I just don't know.'

'You don't know?' Dan echoes, leaning slightly towards me. I wonder if he felt me turn cold.

'It was fun, yeah. But I don't think this is a real *relationship*, y'know?'

'I think I am the wrong person for this,' Dan says, and I sort of smile. 'I have only had one *real relationship*, and it was not good.'

My tiny attempt at a smile fails.

'Oh, shit,' Peter mutters. I look up at him. 'Yeah, Will's mentioned.'

Oh, no. I think I'm going to be sick.

'What has he—what have you said?' Daniel turns to me. I must look *terrified*. For a moment, he looks upset—but now we're making eye contact he *must* be able to see the way I'm screaming. 'It's okay, it's okay. You can tell people—'

'Do you need a moment?' Peter's already getting to his feet. I need to catch myself. I need to wake up.

'I'm okay I'm just—I'm just lost in thought.' I swallow very tightly and try to smile at Daniel. He is not fooled. 'Sorry.'

'Happens to us all,' he whispers, unblinking. 'It's okay. What have you told Peter?'

'They know I was worried about you when we met.'

He's smiling very gently and I don't trust it.

'And I've explained I was so upset by everything because of Kirst.'

Dan nods and, under the table, touches the back of his hand to my leg. *Shit.*

'Okay. It was someone I met in my first year here.' He turns back to Peter, and I know this. He's told me this. I could stop listening again, but it feels dangerous. I might slip into something. 'I'm being very careful he does not find out how important William is to me.'

That is nice to hear. My chalky cheeks gain a little bit of a blush.

'Because you're worried what he'll think?' Peter asks, leaning into the table. Dan's left his hand very close to me, almost like he wants me to take it. 'But you know Will's straight, right? Everyone—'

I've done it.

I haven't actually outed myself, but I've leapt to my feet and walked away from the table before either of them can stop me. And they *must* know.

I have a handful of seconds to myself and I think I'm frightened and upset enough to say it. It's not like there are many people around us—it's Sunday evening, for heaven's sake, and—

Dan catches my hand.

'Don't run away.' He reaches around me with his free hand and successfully stops me in my tracks. My legs are shaking. 'Don't worry. Take your time. Just don't run away.'

Face pressed into his chest, I find it possible to breathe again.

'Do you want us to stop talking about relationships?'

Weak. Pathetic. I nod.

'Okay, okay. Take your time.' One of his hands is in my hair and I want to *scream*. I can hear his heart—if I stop breathing, I can hear each thud and each breath. 'Is Kirst okay?'

Oh, God. Bless him. I nod again and try to look at him but it's like I'm glued to his shirt.

'Good.' There's a pause, and I know we should go back to Peter. I should apologise. 'You know it's okay, don't you?'

I manage to make a small questioning noise in the back of my throat and, if possible, he holds me tighter.

'Whatever you're scared of. Whatever it is that keeps upsetting you. It's okay—I do not mind. Whatever it is. You do not have to tell me.'

Oh, but I do.

Just not right now. It would spoil the moment, because his heart would stutter and skip as he understood all the times I held him for a moment too long. He'd drop his hands from me and look away, so he didn't have to see my reaction when he muttered, 'sorry, I don't like you like that'.

I just nod, instead, and take a huge breath. 'Could we go outside for a moment? You can smoke and I can freshen up a bit.'

He doesn't question it, and I think I love him even more when he takes me back through the bar, pausing very briefly to explain to Peter where we're going.

*

Dan stands with one arm around me, carefully angled so he's between me and the door. He's smoking, giving us the perfect

174

reason to be here, and I am *out* of it.

I want to walk, just walk. Walk forever. Walk for hours, and days, and weeks. See if I really *can't* run away from my problems.

It's a clear, cold November night. The sky looks like it goes on forever, with stars shining here and there like they're marking the sides of an infinite mess of roads. I'm staring up at them, wondering how difficult it would be to actually follow them, and he nudges me softly.

'Something has been hurting you the whole time I have known you,' he whispers, leaning to kill the cigarette. No one else is around us, and he doesn't seem to care about keeping an eye on the door—not like the first time we did this, when he practically hid behind me. 'I don't know what I can do to help.'

I find a smile for him and shrug, letting out a little *huff* when he pulls me into his chest again. 'I dunno. I'll be alright.'

'You will, but don't *worry*. Whatever it is. You can tell me —or you can wait. It's okay.'

I am *convinced* he knows. He has to. He's smart. And I haven't exactly been subtle.

'Thanks.' I don't think I'll ever be able to say anything else on the subject.

We return to Peter. I'm working hard, now, to pay attention to the conversation—to smile, to react, to laugh at the right times—and it is *exhausting*.

I think I need a holiday.

My attempts at seeming normal must be working because we stay out until past midnight. At some point, I swap my water for cider. I think it's about the time Dan and I have a minor argument about who pays—which Peter slides straight through, brandishing a note.

We stare at each other for a moment too long.

Dan's drinking something with lemonade. His glass is fizzing beside mine and, when we reach to pick them up, our hands touch.

It's not exactly *unusual* for them to touch, now. It's not like we haven't spent hours holding onto each other. I should be used to this, but something shoots through my arm, like I've been stung by a bee, and I almost knock my glass over.

He notices.

God, he notices.

He's smirking at me, head dipped a little bit so we're closer together, and I can see the way his eyelashes have caught each other in the corners of his eyes. It's dangerous. It's tempting.

I sweep my glass up and scurry back over to Peter. We sit. We talk. We make it through the rest of Dan's birthday without any more breakdowns from me.

176

Thirty-Six

I am excessively relieved I had chance to tidy my room. I know Dan was considering asking if I wanted to go back to his—I could see it in his little frown when we said goodnight to Peter—but I'm okay. It's a small room, but I'm used to being so close to him I can feel his body warmth.

Sharing my room, when I know it's tidy, is close to perfect. When he takes my hand a moment before walking into my building, I nearly faint.

I open the door.

We're not expecting to see anyone, because it's after one in the morning and it's Monday tomorrow, but we're almost bowled over by someone I don't think I've spoken to before. He's on his way to the kitchen, or to the toilets; we're holding hands and clearly aiming for my bedroom.

My flatmate stumbles.

'Sorry—hey, I'm Simon,' he says, pushing up his glasses and failing to stop looking at our hands. I cannot let go of Dan. 'You live here?'

'I do.' Surprising me, my voice isn't tight. I sound shocked, sure, but I sound *okay*. 'Just at the end.'

'Oh, cool. Have you been here all year?'

I laugh and nod.

'Sorry, I've never said hi—'

'Neither have I.' I offer him my free hand. 'I'm William.'

'Nice to meet you,' he chuckles, smiling at me like we're already friends. He shakes my hand and shuffles past us, throwing us another grin. 'I'll see you around!'

Oh my God.

Daniel is silent until we're locked safely in my room and something gives way in him. We let go of each other.

'He thinks we're together.'

'It doesn't matter—I'll explain next time I see him,' I say, too shocked at how *calm* I was to share his anxiety.

'William, they might not be nice to you.'

'I don't care—they don't matter.'

'I care!' He cries, facing me with eyebrows pulled together and worry filling every part of him. I sigh. 'If you get hurt because of me—'

'Dan, no one's going to hurt me for holding your hand,' I say. He's very pale. 'They aren't. They just aren't.'

'You don't know—'

'I don't know what it's like?' Oh, God, of course I don't. Of course I don't know what it's like to have homophobia thrown at you from all angles—not like he knows. So I take a breath. 'I'll tell someone as soon as I feel uncomfortable.'

'Who?'

'Residence support, I guess.'

'He stared at us.'

'So?'

But he's still upset. I'm trying to not let myself think this means he doesn't want to be seen with me. I'm trying to not let myself get upset over how much he obviously doesn't like the idea of someone seeing us holding hands.

Because, when he touches me, I never want him to let go.

'I thought you would not like people to think we are together,' he whispers, voice heavy with the stress.

The words barely reach me, so I inch towards him.

'I don't mind. I *mind* because I don't want anyone linking you to Matthew, but I just thought—I thought you would be upset.'

My mouth is full of something and I just shake my head.

'I would be upset if someone thought I was with—with Cassie.'

I understand what he's trying to say. I really do. Even though it's not a fair comparison—he's never met her and I regularly *share a bed* with him. I manage a shrug—it's just a tiny lift and drop of my shoulders but it takes so much energy—and step towards him again. He's still wearing his coat.

178

'I don't care. I really don't care—I don't care what people think.'

He looks like he wants to smile. 'I hope you can always feel so comfortable.' He breaks through the air between us, resting his hand on the side of my face. Oh. *Oh*. 'The world is a dangerous place. I am glad you have not been hurt by it.'

I'm spiralling. 'I'm not scared of anyone.' It's a complete and utter *lie*. 'You wouldn't let anyone hurt me.'

Something flashes across his face. It looks like pain. It looks like desperation. 'No.' He lowers his hand. 'I would not. So tell me—tell me if anyone upsets you.'

I wink and *try* to lift the mood. 'Will do, Captain.'

This next expression is one I don't think I can get enough of. His eyebrows are up and he's smirking—lips pressed together but pulled to one side—and his eyes have swallowed me.

'I could have been Captain.'

*

He explains, as we get ready for bed, that if he had stayed with the army for another year he would have been promoted.

'But I told you why I left,' he whispers, looking at me like he wants me to help him.

So I nod. 'Your mum.'

'I was given leave and it was the perfect opportunity to get away,' he says, sitting on the edge of the small bed. Hmm. It's going to be cosy. 'I'm glad I did.'

'So am I.' I edge around the bed to turn the light off. In the darkness, I could almost forget how upset he was to be caught holding my hand. 'I'm still proud of you.'

He groans and laughs and it's the sexiest combination of sounds that I hesitate, lingering by the door for a moment longer. I pretend to check the lock.

'Don't start that again.'

I force myself away from the door, to what I suppose is my side of the bed, and make sure he can see me smiling. 'I'm not starting *anything*.' I tug the duvet back and consider the

Louise Willingham

space between us. It's barely there. 'I guess we should go to sleep.'

He sighs. 'Kick me out if I wake you up,' he mutters, and I love that this isn't even something we've questioned. We're sharing the bed. Because damned if I'm letting him sleep on the floor, and there's no way in hell he'd let me sleep down there again.

'Same to you,' I whisper, lying down in the crisp, clean sheets and catching myself grinning. The last thing he would ever do is kick me out of bed. The last thing *I* would ever do is kick *him* out of bed. And now we're lying together, as if it's completely fine that I can feel the duvet move when he breathes. As if we haven't just been caught holding hands. As if I didn't freak out an hour or two ago because Peter said that I'm straight.

I shiver a little bit, thoughts accidentally leading me back down that road. I suppose Peter has *some* justification for assuming I'm straight—I've never suggested to him I like guys—but I can't believe he hasn't worked it out. I can't believe he isn't sensitive enough to notice I'm a little bit in love with this guy who I spend every Sunday night with.

'Relax,' Dan whispers, making me jump. I squint at him and he's so close. 'You're very tense.'

'I don't want to take up all the space,' I mumble as an excuse. And, actually, it worked perfectly. Because he chuckles and moves, pushing one of his arms under my neck and resting the other one over the duvet—over me.

Suddenly, he is everything.

180

Thirty-Seven

I wake up to the sound of my alarm and my first reaction is to hide under the duvet. I am *exhausted*.

'William, I will have to go, soon,' Dan whispers, and I can't breathe. 'It is ten past nine.'

That doesn't make sense. I sit up way too fast and blink at the room. 'What?'

He's right there beside me, with his head on the other half of the pillow and his tattooed arm still on top of the duvet. The thought of being held by him all night is enough to make me lose my breath.

'You slept through a couple of alarms. It has gone onto snooze a few times.'

It's not quite the right moment to think about how he says *snooze*, but I file that thought away to pull out again once he's gone.

'I'm so sorry.'

He hushes me gently, twisted and propped up on his arm. We are *very* close together. I can smell his skin and his hair. 'Me having an early start is no reason for you to miss out on sleep.'

My mouth drops.

'I have a few minutes,' he whispers. 'How did you sleep?'

So I talk to him. I tell him I slept *fine* and I'm going to have a *fine* morning and the minutes flash past us like motorbikes on a motorway.

Time flies with Daniel.

He gets up at almost the last minute and pulls his shirt back on. Sticks his shoes on. I'm just sitting there, bundled up in the duvet that's still warm from him, and watch. I shouldn't be watching. I should get up and do something with my morning.

He's chatting to me, telling me about the people he's going to be on with, like he does every Monday, and I want this to be every morning. I want to fall asleep beside him anywhere and everywhere. I want to wake up with his arms around me, his lips in my hair.

'Have a good day, William.' He hesitates, waiting for me by the door.

I spring from the bed, about five minutes too late, and throw myself at him. If he doesn't want this, he's doing a brilliant job of pretending. He crushes me to him, crossing his arms over my back and letting out an incredibly soft, very gentle grunt when he presses his face into my hair, and I could stay there all day.

'Hope you have a good day, too.' I hold onto him like this is going to be the last time. Like I'm never going to see him again. 'Stay safe, alright?'

'Safe?' he repeats, one hand sliding down my back. 'I will be at work. Nothing will happen. But I will phone you if it does.'

I just about believe him and resist the urge to kiss his neck. I take a deep breath, instead, and fill myself with him.

'Speak later.'

I let go of him and, as always, it *hurts*. I'm cold. He's leaving, and I am going to go straight back to bed.

He throws me a smile, opens the door, and I stand there in the silence for just a moment after he's gone.

Thirty-Eight

I spend next Sunday with him (of course) and then, quite suddenly, it's December.

I'm not sure how that happened.

All of my outstanding work is due, and I am *stressed*.

'It's not just the coursework,' I say, for the hundredth time. Dan hands me my glass, refilled with water, and sits back beside me, cradling his mug. 'It's the exams.'

I have six which is *ridiculous*.

He hums. 'I will have four. And your degree is important.'

'But it doesn't have to be so *hard*.'

That was *not* supposed to sound sexual.

Fortunately, he laughs, reminds me I'm putting myself through this academic pain for a reason, and picks up my pile of flashcards. He's testing me and I'm pretty sure I'd be in with a *great* chance of memorising all of this if he just gave me a voice recording of him reading the cards.

We haven't talked about accents again but, right now, his voice is flowing. His accent is soft but covers every syllable, like a blanket.

I demand a respite at about half six, when I'm starving and my brain has started to feel like melted ice-cream.

Dinner has been ordered and paid for, and the flashcards are safely back on the floor when he rubs his hand through his hair and turns to me. 'I do have something to tell you.'

I hold my breath, expecting something to do with Matthew, and wait.

'It's not bad—stop looking at me like that.'

My face breaks into a giant grin. 'Like what?'

He just sighs and stares at me.

'Sorry. Continue.'

He looks *nervous*. 'I'm going away.'

I react far too quickly. I sit up sharply and I've grabbed his hand before he can get the next word out.

'Not—not forever,' he says around a laugh. 'Just for a couple of weeks over Christmas.'

My heart sinks, like a pebble in a lake. 'When are you going?'

His smile falters. 'Next Sunday.'

'*What?*'

'I didn't want to give you time to convince me to not go.' He locks his fingers between mine just as I start to pull my hand away. 'It is just for three weeks—'

'*Three?*'

'You will be at home!'

'Not until the twentieth!'

He gives me a look which tells me to *please, be reasonable*, and I want to cry. The thought of even one Sunday without him is horrible. 'I will be home by the time term starts in January.'

'That's next year—'

'You will be with your family!'

I bite down on my lip and he takes a sharp breath through his mouth.

'I don't have anyone to spend it with. I would rather go away—explore somewhere new, where I don't know anyone —and *not* be reminded it's my first Christmas alone.'

'But you have me.'

Something softens in his face. He traps my hand in both of his, cradling it between us, and lets out a sigh.

'Sorry.'

'It's okay. I knew you would be upset.'

I make a valiant attempt to calm myself down and smile at him. 'I shouldn't be, though.' Shit. He's going away. 'Where are you going?'

'New Zealand.'

'Holy shit.'

He laughs and explains why: how *far away* it is, how nice the weather will be, how friendly people are there. He reminds me, too, that he needs to reapply for his student VISA now the

184

university have agreed a return date. All being well, his therapist will give him a letter so he can come back for his semester two timetable.

I'm just gawking as he talks, desperately trying to accept that this has to happen, and I haven't paid enough attention to the plans he's outlining.

'You need to write all of this down for me,' I say, making him laugh. I think he was expecting me to start crying. Honestly, I'm impressed I haven't. 'And—shit. Will we be able to talk?'

He rolls his eyes and I realise, now, that he's rubbing his thumb into my hand. 'Yes, William. I will be able to phone you. But I don't think we should talk every day, it will defeat the point of going away.'

I manage a nod. Force a smile.

'Please do not be angry.'

'I'm not—I'm not angry.' I don't think I could ever be angry with him. A little bit pissed he didn't tell me earlier, but I completely understand. 'I'm going to miss you, though.'

Shit. He brings my hand up to his face and hides behind it, nose against my knuckles. 'I will miss you. But who knows? Maybe I will find a nice man in New Zealand to distract me.'

Well, fuck. Please *don't* do that.

'No one would be good enough for you.' Is that too honest? He deserves the world. No one could ever be soft enough with him, and I feel the thought of him in a relationship with someone else twisting through me.

'I think exactly the same for you.' He may as well have just stuck a knife in my chest. 'Will you let me know if anything happens while I'm away?'

It's an odd request. 'Anything?'

He shrugs. 'You might see Lilley.'

'I might *see* her, yeah—'

'I'm trying to say I want us to be able to talk about this sort of thing.' He's still speaking into my hand, voice muffled. 'Anything could happen.'

'It could, yeah.' I feel queasy, like I've been sat in a bus for too long. 'We can talk about it, of course we can. And you'll let me know too, right?'

'If I manage to find someone I trust like that? Yeah, sure.'

*

I'm still reeling a bit when we go to bed and I don't really think. I crawl straight over to him as soon as he's taken his prescription and put my arms around him, bare chest to bare chest, and speak.

'I'm going to be worried about you every day you're away. I'm going to be ridiculously excited whenever you *do* call so you're going to have to just bear with me while I calm myself down.'

He laughs, moving his thumb in gentle circles over my hipbone.

'I expect you to take lots of pictures.'

He laughs again and moves, so I'm pulled more convincingly onto him. My head is on his shoulder. My arm is tight around his waist. He's still wearing jeans, and I'm *very relieved.*

'When do you come back?'

'The twenty-ninth,' he whispers, and I know he's told me loads of times. I wasn't kidding when I said he'd have to write it down for me. 'Just in time to start a new year.'

'You're going to be *so* jet-lagged.'

It's the perfect thing to say and he keeps laughing, breath hitting through my hair. I make the mistake of closing my eyes.

'It will be worth it. Maybe if I like it, I will go again next year.'

I just about don't scream. 'Yeah, maybe.'

'Would you mind?'

'You're my friend, Dan. I don't think I have a right to mind. I might be jealous, but I don't *mind.*'

'Are you sure?'

'I'm sure. I want you to have a great time.'

He doesn't respond. Or, if he does, I completely miss it. Because I fall asleep.

I'm so warm and comfortable against him. It feels natural.

I'm almost on my front, with my face towards his pillow, and I can feel him against what feels like every side of me. I'm snuggled into his chest and I appear to have decided it's completely fine to cuddle him like this. He smells like heaven.

Sleep is peaceful. Sleep is safe. I don't feel the sharpness of the word *friend* when I'm asleep and I forget how awful it is of me to be so obsessed, so infatuated, so in love with this man.

He moves me at some point, and I half wake up. Not enough to understand I've been crushing him, but enough to feel a sort of sense of abandonment.

I turn and face away from him, curled up on my side with my arms crossed over my chest.

Probably for the best.

Thirty-Nine

He's already awake when I blink myself into consciousness. I'm facing him, and he's staring at me with his arm around my shoulders.

He doesn't even attempt to move it.

We just stare at each other.

One of us should do something.

I can only see one option for me and one option for him. Either he pulls his arm from around me and we carry on with our morning like we would any other week, or I—

I wriggle closer to him.

It's not a good idea, but it's the only thing I can think of. He's going to be away for *three weeks*. And I'm going to miss him, I'm going to worry about him, and I'm going to *dream* about him.

His hand slips further around my back as I make my way down to his chest. I hold onto his waist and listen to his breathing, like it's keeping me alive.

'You slept very lightly,' he whispers. I hum. 'I kept thinking you were going to wake up.'

'Does this mean *you* were awake?'

His face is in my hair. 'A few times.'

'I thought we promised to wake each other up.'

His laugh flutters through me and I shiver. 'I thought you would wake yourself up. I slept plenty, don't worry.'

For a few minutes, I can pretend this is going to be every morning. I can forget I *shouldn't* hold him like this, and I can forget he doesn't have a clue.

Except I'm fairly sure he's guessed.

There have been a few times where I think he's stopped himself saying 'it's okay that you're bi' and I *wish* he'd be brave enough to do it for me.

But, if he knows, he's definitely okay with it. He had his

188

arm around me while I was sleeping—this means he wants me to be this close to him, even though he knows there's a *chance* I like him more than a friend.

Maybe he just doesn't realise how wonderful he is. I wouldn't be surprised if everything with Matthew, the drugs, and his stint in the military has skewed his view of himself. It makes a lot of sense, and I think it actually makes it even worse that I'm pressed against him under the duvet in his bed.

'Thank you for being here for me this year,' he whispers. I turn cold and pull backwards slightly, but his arms trap me. 'Stay, it's okay. I just wanted to make sure you know how grateful I am.'

I press my nose into his chest and hold my breath. 'Well, you're welcome. I like you.'

A scream is burning my throat.

'I like you too.' He sounds bemused. His hand drifts up and down my back, leaving a trail of heat. 'I am so lucky.'

We're too close together. I grunt and make myself sit up because this is *ridiculous*. 'You're not the only lucky one.'

'I suppose.' His hand falls to cup my hip. Oh, God. His eyes are hazy, again. Out of focus. 'Thank you for being understanding.'

I laugh. 'Thank you for helping me with my revision.'

It worked—this weird, heavy mood that's settled between us, feeling like a honey trap, is beginning to melt. He smiles up at me, like he's only just noticed me, and I know how easy it would be to kiss him.

'Are you in lectures this afternoon?'

I groan. He laughs and pulls his hand very slowly from me, like it hurts him to break contact.

I shuffle, so I can lean against the headboard, and rub my eyes. 'Always. Are you at work?'

'Yeah.'

I don't know why we've asked each other. We've done exactly this for the last six weeks. He knows I've got another three weeks before the Christmas break and I realise, when I'm pulling my clean shirt on and he's making drinks, that he was trying to change the mood, just like I was.

Does that matter?

I've only just put my glasses on, and it always takes me a moment or two to appreciate his face, so I don't respond quickly enough when he walks back into the room.

'Come to the social tonight.' He hands me my glass, and, noticing my hesitation, starts to frown. 'Please?'

I laugh, because I don't think I could ever refuse him saying *please*, and roll my eyes. 'If you insist.'

'I would like to talk about New Zealand,' he admits, sitting on the edge of the bed and twisting to look at me. 'And I would like you to be there with me.'

I smile and sit back down. We're moving slower than usual and he's going to have to rush to get to work on time. 'It sounds good. I'll find you after my lectures.'

The smile he gives me is *blinding*, like he was expecting me to say I didn't want to go. I get it—our track record of going out in the evening with Peter leaves me looking pretty unstable —but I feel okay. I want to go with him.

Forty

I survive the social. We're close—I think too close—and we spend a lot of time just talking together. Peter's occupied with Anthony, so I don't talk to him. Dan speaks to a few people, and they make an attempt to talk to me, but it's sickeningly obvious why I'm here. Everyone can see the way I'm gazing at Dan.

I don't care.

For tonight, I don't care.

Dan's going away next week. He's going away and I'll go home for a couple of weeks and, maybe, things will be easier next year.

Next year.

Time really flies with Daniel.

I see him two more times. We meet up on Thursday, but he doesn't stay. He comes over on Saturday.

'But I have to go home tonight,' he says, when we're sat together on my bed. We're just talking, but it's already past eight in the evening. 'I leave early.'

'I know.' I'm trying to justify keeping him here, and it comes out too sharply. I need a loophole in time and space which will make the pain of being on the other side of the world from him for three *weeks* fade, even just a little.

'When will Kirst be home?'

I tell him—even though I'm sure we've already talked about my Christmas plans—and sink down on the bed, head on his shoulder.

'Will you see Peter over the holiday?'

'Nah, he's too far away.'

'That's a shame.'

'Is it?'

He hums and makes me sit up so he can push his arm around my back, like he's hiding into me. My heart can't take it, and I close my eyes.

'I think he is good for you.'

A laugh bubbles from me. 'Probably, yeah.' Except he still hasn't told me why he's so bitter towards Dan. 'He's always there whenever I need someone. I think he's psychic.'

Dan laughs and crosses his legs at the knees. His restlessness is making me nervous.

'I am glad you have him. Do you like him?'

My stomach flips like I just missed a step. 'What do you mean?'

'Would you ever date him?'

'No,' I manage. 'Why? He's cute, but he's my best friend. It would be weird.'

Dan tilts his head, so his cheek is against my hair, stopping me from twisting and looking up at him. I'm sure he can hear my heart.

How long has Dan wanted to ask me this? What does it mean? Does it mean he thinks Peter likes me? Or, worse—does it mean he *does* like Peter, after all? Maybe what he said all those weeks ago about not being ready for a relationship doesn't count now.

'I agree.'

I splutter a laugh and twist my hands together over my lap.

'Would you ever date a man?'

No point in lying.

Something presses against my throat and it's like trying to talk underwater. 'Yeah. I would.'

I think that's it. I think I just came out. I think I just told Dan I'm bisexual.

He must have been building up to this, saving it for the night before he flies away and puts a whole world between us.

I wait for a reaction which never quite comes. We're sitting exactly the same as we were ten seconds ago, before I bolted towards the edge of this cliff I've been living beside for months.

Silence. It soaks through the room, filling each space between each molecule, and I don't dare take a breath. I need him to tell me it's okay—he doesn't care. Or maybe that he *does* care—maybe I want him to say he's relieved. Maybe I want him to tell me he didn't know, or to tell me he guessed.

I'm standing right on the edge of this cliff, cutting my feet, and I don't have the strength to move until he speaks.

'I have been thinking about relationships,' he admits, 'and I still could not trust anyone like that. I think he ruined me.'

Excuse me?

I have to ignore how much it hurts to have such a non-reaction to coming out. I can deal with that later.

'You aren't *ruined*,' I grumble, fighting to be able to look up at him. '*He* has no influence on your value, Dan.'

He's pale, face in a flat mask to hide what he's really thinking, and this is an expression I recognise.

'He hasn't got any power over you.' I take his hand. 'He isn't here anymore. You absolutely *can't* let him ruin your life.'

'He already has,' Dan breathes, like he's explaining something to me. 'I don't need it—friendship is enough.'

Is he warning me?

Friendship is enough.

My head feels heavy, like all the blood just drained away, and I nod instead of screaming.

'Friendship is great,' I say from the other side of the room. 'But dating people can be fun. It doesn't have to be intense—sometimes it's nice to have someone thinking about you.'

Just before my vision fades to black, Dan's teeth flash in a smile. I think I have whiplash.

'I already have you worrying about me,' he says, voice slow and soft over *worrying*. 'I do not need anyone else.'

I'm hollow. Stick a needle in me and you'll draw out nothing but air.

'I don't mind sharing you,' I say, which is a complete *lie*. 'I'd never worry about you any less, though.'

His smile is still glowing and it's easy to believe that maybe he just didn't hear me say *yes, I'd date a guy*.

'Thank you. Chances of me finding someone I trust and like in just three weeks in New Zealand are low.'

'You trusted me in three weeks.'

He laughs, rubbing his thumb across the back of my hand like he doesn't know how it feels. His eyes haven't left mine since I sat up and I'm split; part of me is enjoying this conversation, but I'm mostly screaming. I just told him I'd date a man, and he doesn't seem to care. Does he really not know what I mean? Does he think I'd just be open to the idea?

'I did,' he says, 'but you did not give me a choice.'

A few millilitres of blood return to my head in the form of a blush. 'I guess not.'

His thumb rubs my hand again. 'Thank you for being here for me. I want to do the same for you, so phone me if you need to talk to someone while I'm away. I do not mind what time. You have a busy two weeks.'

My heart is audibly breaking. 'I will do—thanks,' I mutter. 'I'm fine, though. I can do this—I did it last year, and I didn't really know what I was getting myself into. I do, now.'

He asks me about the work I still have to submit, and that's it. That's the end of our conversation about relationships.

'I should go,' he mutters, after some minutes of comfortable silence. 'I do not want to.'

I close my eyes. 'You could stay.'

'I don't think I should.'

I need to be sensible about this. I try to not let myself think he wants to leave because of anything we've spoken about—he has to go. I know this. I also know I'm terrified of how he's going to treat me, now. Are we ever going to talk about dating again? I stare at something just to one side of us, feeling a now familiar glumness sinking through me, and he moves, like he's going to touch my jaw. I wish he would.

I speak quickly, before he can start worrying about me. 'Thank you for being such a brilliant friend. I'm going to miss you.'

He smiles and gives my hand one last squeeze. 'I will miss you, too. But we will talk. And it is not forever.'

'No, not forever—but it feels like it.'

He looks heartbroken. I've said too much.

'You—you need to go.' I push my glasses back up my nose.

He doesn't move.

For a moment, I'm convinced he's going to stay. He's going to lie down and drag me with him and we're just going to lie together—maybe sleeping, maybe not—until the sun comes up.

'Don't miss me too much.' His fingers slip from mine. 'Talk to your friends and have a good Christmas.'

I'm going to cry. Is that okay? He's seen me cry before and I guess this is an occasion where it's *okay* to cry.

He sees the tears and touches my cheek, just beneath my glasses, with the back of his index finger. 'Don't you dare.'

'Shut up.' I blink quickly and tip my face to the ceiling. 'Shut up.'

He takes a deep, shaking breath and drops his hand to take mine again, like he regrets letting go. This sustained contact is keeping me afloat.

'Don't make me cry. Not when I'm about to go.'

'You, cry?' I have to be very brave, now, and slip out of his arm. The only way I can do this—the only way I can *survive* this—is by trying to laugh, and I manage a smile. 'Want me to walk with you?'

'I think I know the way.' He stands up, moving into the space between me and the door. 'Stay here.'

This feels impossible. I'm trying to let him walk off with my heart while it's still beating and I'm stretched, ready to snap. I've got to let go of him—and the sooner the better. Before I beg him to stay.

It's far too late for that. He's spent a fortune on tickets.

We part at the door to my block. The night is cold and crisp, and my skin jumps into goose bumps as soon as the outside air hits it, making me shudder. Maybe it's a good job he doesn't want me to walk with him.

He steals my breath. Almost lifting me from the floor, he sweeps me into his chest and presses his face into my neck, breathing against my skin. I'm stretched up on the tip of my toes and the thought *does* cross my mind that he could probably lift me up.

'Have a great time, Dan.' I cling to him like the world is going to end. 'Don't forget me.'

God, how pathetic.

He laughs and I'm glad I'm holding him so tightly. I'm sure he presses his lips to my neck. I'm *sure* that was a kiss.

'Could I ever? Good luck with your coursework. I will phone you when I land.'

I have to let him go.

A breath staggers from my chest, a drunk leaving the pub, and I drop my arms. My heels hit the floor. I tear myself away from him and give him the biggest smile I can manage.

He doesn't say anything else. He stares at me for a moment, eyes wide and deep, and I already feel a thousand miles away from him.

He takes a step back. Grabs his cigarettes from his pockets and turns, lighting one as he disappears into the night. I can see the soft grey of the smoke against the gloom of the evening darkness and I think he looks back at me.

The path turns to the left, around a little patch of hedges, and he's gone.

Forty-One

For the first time in my life, I don't go to lectures. I send a text to Cassie early Monday morning, saying I've been sick in the night and don't feel like it's a good idea to be in a room full of people. She replies about an hour later, being overly sympathetic and promising to see me soon.

I don't want to see anyone. I'm curled up in my duvet, propped up against my desk, like I have been since four this morning.

I've moved a few times. Went and got a glass of water.

Dan's going to phone me at some point and it's all I've been able to think about since I woke up yesterday. Twenty-seven hours is a long time for Dan to be on a plane, and I think it's the longest we've gone without talking since that first Monday night.

I don't *think* it is. God, I *know* it is.

And I know this isn't good. I should be able to survive twenty-four hours without speaking to him, and I think I *could*, if our last conversation hadn't featured me being open to the idea of dating guys.

While I wait, I watch the world through my window. There's a rush of people going to lectures at about quarter to nine and then a calm, natural silence. I wish I could find the energy to sit outside—to go and do *something*.

My phone sings and dances across my desk.

For a moment, I don't trust it. I don't believe it.

But I snatch it up, just about manage to press the green button, and hold it to my ear.

'Hi—'

'How are you?' he asks, like he *knows*.

I close my eyes and lean back against the headboard, tugging the duvet to my chin. 'I'm okay.' It comes out in a croak. Why do I sound so bad? 'I'm not going to lectures

There's a pause. 'What?'

'I didn't sleep very well.'

'William—'

'I'm okay. I've just got a lot on my mind.' I can feel the mood sinking between us like a stretched piece of Blu-Tac. 'How are you? How was the flight?'

'I am fine—why aren't you going to lectures?' Oh, he sounds stressed. 'What's happened?'

He's on the other side of the world. I can be honest.

'I miss you.'

I can *feel* the way his chest falls with a little sigh.

'I'll be okay. I just needed to know you'd got there safely.'

He hums. 'I am safe,' he mutters, like he feels he has to say it. He doesn't want to talk about himself, and neither do I. 'Did I upset you?'

'What?'

'On Saturday.'

I sink, duvet up to my nose. 'No.'

'You do not sound confident.'

'You didn't—you didn't. I upset me a little bit.'

'How?'

Oh, God. The inevitability of this conversation wraps around my chest like ropes. 'It was talking about dating.'

His silence tells me plenty.

'I'm just—I hate that you think *he's* ruined it for you.' *Why, Will?* 'I hate that he hurt you so much and I can't do anything about it—just like with Kirst. And Cassie thinks something's dodgy with Lilley's new boyfriend, but I don't want to—I feel bad about it, but I don't want to get involved.'

There's a lot for him to take in, and the distance between us feels like it's growing.

'I will be okay,' he says slowly. 'You did everything you could, and I'm sure Kirst would agree. You can't save everyone, William. But I think you did—just by being here. Just by being you.' It's a very good job I decided not to go to lectures because I keep it together for *three, two, one—*

'William—'

'I'm okay,' I sob, wiping my eyes ferociously on the duvet. 'I'm okay. I just—thank you. I just want to be there for Lil, of course I do. But I don't—I don't have the energy, and I know that's really shit of me.'

'No. You have to look after yourself. You can be self-sacrificing once you've got your degree.'

I sniff and take a breath. Tight ropes around my chest start to relax. 'Thank you. I know this. I just find it so easy to worry, you know?'

'Oh, I know.' His voice rumbles like distant thunder. 'Look after yourself today. Will you go to your lectures tomorrow?'

I roll my eyes at the empty room. 'Yes, Captain.'

I hear his little release of breath—not annoyed but pretending to be—and *squirm*. Eyes closed, I can almost believe he's right there with me, in my bed, with his arms wrapped around me.

He tells me about the flight and the airports, how hot it is, and how nice his hotel room is. I imagine I'm there and ask him questions about his plans for the next week until he yawns.

'I need to sleep,' he admits, when my arm hurts from holding my phone up for so long. 'Call me if you need to talk. We can talk about anything, can't we?'

Oh, no. There's a little note of doubt in his voice and I *know* I should be comfortable enough with him to tell him anything—I should be able to say *you do realise I said I'd date a guy because I'm bisexual, don't you?*—but I can't. Not yet. It keeps choking me, a fist around my throat, and I feel incredibly shit about it.

But I say, 'of course we can' and we agree to talk again on Saturday night.

'And any time in between, if you want,' he says.

I hum.

'Okay?'

'Okay—and if you want to talk too. You know I worry about you, so try to make me forget you're all alone in a foreign country.'

What an idiot.

He barks a laugh and I wish I'd recorded it somehow. I wish I'd saved it, so I could always hear him feeling *happy*.

'Oh, William.'

I'd quite like *that* recorded, too.

'I am used to that.'

Forty-Two

I plan on wallowing in this misery all day, but my phone buzzes at about half twelve. I expect it to be Peter, so I keep reading and ignore it.

But it buzzes again. And, shit, it's Lilley.

12:32 **Lilley**: I want to see you

12:40 **Lilley**: Please talk to me. This is important.

I suppose there's nothing else for it. I phone her.
'Will—'
'What's wrong?' I ask, aware that this is the first time we've spoken since the first Monday of semester. 'Are you okay?'
'Not really.'
Oh my God. I sit up straight, heart in my throat. No matter what Dan said about looking after myself, I need to help her.
'Cas said you're not in lectures today, so I thought you'd have no excuse to say no.'
'Except the fact I've been throwing up.' I'm sticking to that lie like glue. 'What's wrong, Lil?'
'Can I come over?'
'I'm in bed.'
'I've seen you worse.'
'Wanna bet?' I'm pretty sure I've never felt this awful in all my life.
'I really need to see a friendly face.'
Well, I guess I can't say no. I sigh and rub my tired eyes, pulling my knees right up to my chest. 'Okay, come over. I'll make you a tea.'
She half laughs. 'You have teabags?'

'I'll nick one.'

I tell her my address, force myself to get out of bed, and spend a moment looking at myself in the mirror. I look rotten. And I wish I hadn't already spoken to Dan today, because now I have nothing to look forward to. When am I going to get an opportunity to tell him about whatever Lilley wants to tell me?

I pull on a hoodie, wish it were one of Dan's, and shuffle out into the corridor and into the kitchen.

Last year, Lilley and I spent every day together. We practically lived with each other, and I wouldn't have thought twice about her seeing me in such a mess. Now, though, it feels weird.

I make a cup of tea for her, glass of water for me, and take them back to my room before she phones to ask to be let in.

She's outside the front door looking even worse than I imagined.

'Wow,' I say, opening the door and making her smile. 'You look shit.'

'Thanks.' She marches straight past me, shivering from the cold. 'Where's your room?'

'Down there.' I point before realising I should probably lead the way. 'What's up?'

Unsurprisingly, she doesn't answer until we're in my room. She takes a moment to look around, probably trying to work out what she recognises and what's new, and sits on the edge of my bed.

I stay standing, looking at her and wondering why Cassie hasn't told me how *ill* she looks. Her eyes are dark, and her lips look like they've been bleeding. It's horribly similar to how Dan looked on our first Monday night.

'Have you had a cold?' I ask, not daring to think she's been taking drugs. That would just be one disaster too many.

She licks her dry lips and shakes her head. 'Grandma's died.'

I breathe a little *oh* and step towards her. I'd met her grandma a few times, and she'd bought me a present that one Christmas we'd had together.

'Last night. I was talking to Cas this morning and she mentioned you and I thought—I thought you'd want to know.'

'Of course I do.' I sit beside her and, because I'm an idiot, put my arm around her waist. She feels smaller than she used to, and I don't like it. 'Has—had she been ill?'

She shakes her head. 'She fell.'

I'm not sure what else to say. We sit there and I don't mind much when she leans into me. I don't mind that I find myself kissing her hair, pulling her further into my arms.

It feels very strange to hold someone who isn't Daniel.

'When's her funeral?'

'Not sure yet. Probably around the eighteenth.'

I nod. That's next Wednesday. 'Is your boyfriend going with you?'

She sits up to look at me through wet eyelashes. I feel my heart break a little bit and raise my hand to dry her cheeks.

'Kieran? How do you know about him?'

I roll my eyes. 'Cassie and I talk.'

'Oh, right. No. He didn't know her and he has work to do, anyway.'

I hum.

'I guess you have a really busy week that week, don't you?' Her eyes are on mine and I'm stuck. I haven't quite managed to lower my hand, yet. 'How's everything going?'

'Fine.' The lie brings me back to the present and I snatch my hand back. 'Busy, yeah.'

She smiles. 'Cassie said you've got a boyfriend.'

I *choke*.

'She—she what?' I sound pissed off, and I am.

Lilley grins. 'Well, not exactly. She said you've been hanging out with Daniel from the SU and Peter's jealous because he thinks you two have a *thing* and won't tell him.'

'I haven't—I don't have a boyfriend.' God, I wish I did. And I wish he weren't in *New Zealand*. 'I don't—Lil—'

'Breathe,' she says, one eyebrow raised. 'What's going on, then?'

'We're friends—just friends.' Breath isn't filling my lungs. 'Who else has she told?'

203

'What do you mean?'

'Who else knows we've been spending so much time together?'

Lilley raises her chin. 'Why? None of us care if you're bi.'

'That's not it.' Any other time, I'd have smiled. I'd have managed to be honest with Lilley, I think. 'His—his ex is still on campus and we've been so careful he doesn't find out I'm Dan's—Dan's friend.'

The eyebrow jumps again. 'Friend?'

'Jesus Christ, Lil—'

'Alright, alright, clam down,' she mutters, sweeping her dark hair back and squinting at me. 'This ex. An ex-boyfriend?'

I hesitate. Nod.

'What's his name?'

'Matthew—Cassie *knows* this because she lived with him last—'

'Cas definitely hasn't told anyone but me,' Lilley sighs. 'Why do you think she would?'

It's a good question. I shrug.

'She said you were both worried about Dan at the start of the year so why the hell would she put him in danger?'

My mouth is dry.

'See? Just chill out. None of your friends want Dan to get hurt,' Lilley says, sounding fed up. She has a point; that shouldn't need to be said. 'And it doesn't *matter* if you're dating —not to us.'

'Thanks, Lil.' I sound feeble.

'It's fine. Want to tell me about him?'

I sigh heavily but I don't think I've got it in me to keep all this to myself. I can tell Lilley anything, and move out of her arm to lean against the headboard. She follows me, and something about the way we're moving together makes my skin prickle with heat.

'Matthew broke his ribs,' I whisper, picking at the sleeve of my hoodie. 'Gave him drugs. Put him in hospital. And Dan —I think Dan used to hurt himself, but we haven't talked about it.' I could probably sketch the scars on his wrist from memory. 'Matthew keeps trying to talk to him and Dan—Dan isn't okay, I don't think. He's on holiday right now.'

'Where?'

'New Zealand.'

'Jesus Christ.'

I laugh. 'Yeah, I know. But he said before he left that he feels *ruined* by Matthew and I know what he means but it's not true—it's not fair.'

Lilley hums and takes my hand. Her skin is soft, like petals, and her gentleness surprises me.

'It's not fair,' she agrees. 'But he'll get there. He'll recover. He trusts you, right?'

I nod.

'Give him time. As long as he keeps his distance from his ex, I'm sure he'll be fine. Those sorts of scars don't go away overnight, and you need to be patient with him.'

'I am patient,' I mutter. 'It's just difficult when everyone keeps asking about him.'

Lilley rests her head on my shoulder. 'I get that. But why does Cas think you fancy him? She and Peter know you better than you do. Is it because you *do*?'

I hesitate for just a moment too long. What's my excuse —I'm cuddled on my bed with my ex-girlfriend? I'm sad about Lilley's grandma? I'm pining for Dan, even though it's only really been a day?

I shrug. That's all I can do, and she wriggles closer. She's being unusually tender, trying to let me catch my breath, but I don't think I'm ever going to be able to breathe again.

'Does he like you like that?'

Am I going to pretend it's okay that I basically just told Lilley I'm queer? I think I am.

This is one thing I know I can answer. 'He doesn't.' My voice is thick, like I've got something heavy stuck in my throat. 'He basically said he doesn't. And even if he did, it would be weird. We're friends—he made it very clear that he wants to be *friends*.'

She hums and slides her arm right around my back. I think she'd probably understand if I started screaming.

She kisses my shoulder. 'I get it. I've missed you so

much. Sorry for being icy this year—I didn't know what to do around you.'

Despite everything, I smile. 'It's okay. I get it.'

'Thanks for letting me come over.'

It sounds like she wants to leave, so I sit up, putting some valuable space between us. 'It's fine.' I glance away from her, out the window. The sky has darkened over the last few minutes, like it might snow. 'Don't tell Cassie.'

'Tell her what?' She sits up and winks at me. 'Nah. Will. Don't worry. And don't worry about this Matthew—he doesn't know anything. Are you alright?'

I nod. 'I'm alright. How about you?'

She snorts a laugh and shrugs, twisting to face me. 'Bit heartbroken still,' she says, reminding us of the reason for her coming over.

I give her an entirely sad smile.

'But I'm glad I spoke to you.'

I nod. 'Yeah, I missed you too.'

'Maybe we could meet up for drinks.'

It's not a bad idea. I agree, she stays for another few minutes while she drinks the tea I made for her, and I catch myself almost kissing her when we say goodbye. Which is weird. And not at all okay.

Forty-Three

Lilley and I go out on Friday night. I haven't spoken to Dan since Monday morning and it hurts like a throbbing bruise in my chest which just gets worse each time I take a breath so it's no surprise, really, that I accept the invitation to go for drinks.

Just Lilley. Peter is spending the evening with Anthony and Cassie cancels an hour before we're meant to meet, saying she's been feeling sick all day and doesn't want to risk it.

We go to the SU. It's hot and dark and we drink sour shots at one of the upstairs bars, which is a terrible idea. I have a headache already from music so loud it rattles me to my core, but I don't think to say no when she buys me something with vodka.

I don't drink vodka.

But, tonight, I do. Tonight, I look like I've forgotten how much the emptiness left by Dan aches and I dance with Lilley. We sing together, voices horrendously out of tune, and catch each other from slipping on the wet floor. Too many times, my hands slip around her back and get stuck. They catch her hips, bringing her closer when she's danced too far away, and they don't seem to be able to let go of her. And neither of us stop to think it's a bad idea.

Tonight, I almost forget she has a boyfriend. And I kiss her in the middle of the dancefloor.

She tastes like sticky alcohol and I don't like it. She feels much smaller than she did last year, but her waist is so familiar between my hands that I don't quite think about it. Instead, it takes me several minutes longer than it should to remember Kieran.

'Oh, shit.' I push her away from me, catching her shoulders so she can't fall. My lips are wet and I can't see.

Her hands slip from my neck, leaving my skin burning,

and she stumbles away like I just slapped her.

'Lilley, you have a *boyfriend*.'

'He's an arse,' she snaps, ripping my hands from her shoulders and pushing them away. Okay. 'He's *my* responsibility to remember, not yours.'

'We should leave.' I have to shout over the music, and she looks pissed off. 'Lil—'

'I saw some people from my course.' She starts to walk away from me, into the crowd of drunk students. 'I'll stay with them. See you—'

'Lil—'

'Just *go*, Will!'

'Where are these people?' I catch up with her, hands finding her waist from behind. It's not my best idea. I blame the vodka. 'I'm not leaving you here on your own.'

She grabs my hands a bit too roughly, pinching my skin, and drags me back over to the bar. The lights are brighter, here, and I can see how red her lips are. Shit. She leads me to a group of people who definitely recognise her, because they've turned to grin at us and I think one waved.

'This is Will,' she says, dropping my hands like they stung her. 'He's going home so can I stay with you?'

There's a resounding *yes* from everyone in the little group, and I have little choice but to trust them. One or two try to beg me to stay but, honestly, I need to sleep. I need to think about what the fuck I thought I was doing when I agreed to come out with Lilley.

I call a goodnight, which she barely acknowledges. Which is fine. She's probably embarrassed and annoyed with me, just like I am.

Oh, God. It's a good job my room isn't far away. I stumble across campus in the dark, arms wrapped tight around my chest against the cold air, and I feel sick. I'm not sure it's because of the alcohol. Actually, I'm pretty certain the two AM chill has sobered me right up.

No. I don't feel even slightly drunk anymore. But I can taste Lilley, and if I close my eyes tight enough I can almost remember how Dan's arms feel around my back when we're sitting together. I can feel his breath in my hair.

My room is a mess. I trip over the mounds of paper, and clothes, and plates, and crash onto my bed, leaving the door unlocked. Who's going to come in? I think enough to kick my shoes off and fumble for my phone charger but that's it.

*

I wake to the sound of my phone vibrating across my desk and I think, for a moment, it's my alarm. So I consider ignoring it.

But it's *Saturday* and Dan said he'd phone me today. My eyes snap open like I've been pushed, and I grab for my phone, hitting my arm off the edge of the desk and hissing in pain.

'Dan,' I croak, bringing the phone to my ear. 'Dan, hey.'

My head is spinning. I might throw up.

'Good morning, William. How are you?'

His voice does something to me and I twitch, curling up as tight as I can around the duvet.

'A bit hazy,' I admit. 'I went out last night.'

'Oh?' He laughs and I can almost see his teeth. 'With Peter?'

Oh, right. I haven't spoken to him.

'I—nah. I saw Lilley.'

He doesn't say anything.

'She came over Monday, after we talked. Her—her gran died,' I explain, and he makes a sympathetic little sound. 'I'd met her a few times, so she wanted me to know.'

'How is she?' He sounds like he actually cares.

'Alright, I think. She's going to the funeral next week.' I rub my eyes. 'But we went out for drinks last night and—and—' I can't tell him. Does he need to know? 'I guess I had too much.'

He laughs, but it's gentle, and I press my face into the duvet.

'Have you been sick?'

'No, it's not that bad. But I'm glad it's Saturday.' Largely, if I'm honest, because it means it's already been almost a week since he went away. Two more to go.

'This time next week, you will be home,' he says. 'Will you go out next Friday, too?'

Why does he care? Does he *care*?

'Maybe,' I say. 'Depends how I feel. I have three things to hand in this week.'

He hums. 'I remember. Have you nearly finished them?'

And then we're talking about my work, as if he's at all interested in pre-clinical reports and reviews. He updates me on his VISA application, and it sounds like he's on-track to come back like nothing happened when we start the second semester. This is clearly more of a relief to him than he let me see before he went away, so I let him talk about the process as much as he needs before turning the conversation back to his holiday. I ask about the things he's seen and done and I'm surprised and jealous to hear he's been making friends.

'There is a nice couple from Scotland,' he says. 'I sit with them most mornings.'

I don't respond quickly enough, and he notices.

'William?'

The words fall from me. 'I can't believe how much I miss you. And I'm jealous of everyone who's spent time with you this week.'

He laughs, and it's a laugh I'm beginning to understand. *You've embarrassed me, but I'm glad you did.* 'Two more weeks. And you have Lilley, now. You don't need me.'

He's teasing me, but I can't help but grumble. 'It's not the same, and you know it,' I hiss. More laughter. It's so beautiful. He's so beautiful. He's so far away. 'And I'm not going to *see* you when you come home.'

'We'll see.'

The excitement twists my stomach. 'Don't do that to me.'

'Do what?'

'Get my hopes up like that.'

'Just don't think about it,' he suggests, like I'm going to be able to *not* think about the next time I'm going to see him. Like I'm *not* counting down the days. 'You will be at home, yes?'

'I thought we weren't thinking about it.' I will not be able to think about anything else all week. 'I shouldn't be wishing your holiday away.'

'William—'

'Sorry.'

'It's—it's fine,' he says, still laughing. *Ugh.* 'It's fine. I miss you too.'

I sink further under my duvet, eyes closed tight against what promises to be a cracking headache. 'You do?'

'I keep phoning you.'

'I guess.'

He leaves me sitting in silence for a moment. Have I upset him? I still feel a little bit floaty from hearing him say he *misses* me, and I definitely need a glass of water or two.

'I am enjoying my time here.' He sounds so impossibly close for someone on the other side of the world. 'But—' oh, *God* '—I miss you. I think I should have asked you to come with me.'

Somehow, through the haze and throbbing in my brain, I manage to be sensible. 'I wouldn't have been able to come. Too much coursework.'

'I know. But the thought is nice.'

Oh, *God.* Does that mean he's thinking about me? Does that mean he imagines I'm there? I don't know—I don't know what to think or what to say and it's half eleven at night for him.

I need to be sensible. 'I'm going to be less pathetic this week,' I say, making us both laugh. 'Hey! I am. I'll go to all of my lectures and get these assignments handed in and—'

'And see Lilley again on Friday?'

'Does that matter?' I hope it *does.*

'No.' Unfortunately, he sounds completely honest.

I purse my lips, disappointed.

'I'm not sure I can wait another whole week before speaking to you again, though. Can I speak to you on Thursday?'

My stomach flips and I don't bother to point out that it was only five days. 'Of course.'

'I'll phone you again.'

'Thank you.'
Another laugh, and I try to keep it replaying in my head all day. 'It is not for you.'

Forty-Four

Talking to Dan on Thursday is a blessing. Peter and Cas have asked me to come with them to the SU on Friday, and I guess I can't say no. Not after going last week.

But I hesitate when I tell Dan about it.

'What's wrong?'

'I dunno,' I mutter, wrapped up in my duvet again. I have left my bed this week, honest. It's just sensible for Dan to call me right at the end of his day, which happens to be right at the start of mine. 'I just guess I—I don't know.' Pathetic. I scrub my hands through my hair. 'Is it okay?'

'William,' he hisses. 'You do *not* need my permission to go out. You don't need my permission to do *anything*. Go out and get drunk and kiss people—have a good time, please.'

I close my eyes. How does he always guess so close to the truth?

'Just be careful.'

I make a vague attempt at a laugh.

'I think I understand,' he says. 'We have done everything together for weeks. But that doesn't mean you can't do things without me.'

I speak into the duvet. 'I know. I'm just being an idiot.'

'You are.' He says it gently, so it doesn't hurt, but I wrap my free arm around my chest. 'Have a good night. I'll phone you again on Saturday.'

'You're sure it's okay?'

The noise he makes is *incredible*. It's a groan—a frustrated, *please believe me* groan—and it scratches through me.

'Have fun. Relax. Please—I want you to have a nice time. You deserve it.'

I whimper and he thinks he's upset me. I am far from upset.

'Relax, William. Relax. It's okay.'

'I'll try.' I stretch my neck and sigh. 'Sorry, Dan. It's just *weird*.'

'I know. Don't worry about it—and don't get upset.'

It would be so easy to beg him to come home. I chew the inside of my cheek and groan, instead. 'I'll do my best. You never know—you might get a drunk phone call from me.'

He laughs. 'I cannot imagine you drunk.'

We laugh at each other for a little bit longer before I let him go to sleep. It's past midnight for him, and I would think long phone calls annoy him if it weren't always him who starts them in the first place.

God, I miss him.

Forty-Five

Cas turns up at my block on her own, carrying a tote bag which makes suspicious clunking noises each time she moves, and says Peter's meeting us there.

I fully fail to hide my disappointment.

'You can't judge him,' she mutters, shuffling past me in the corridor and leading the way to my bedroom. 'You've spent all your damn time this semester with Daniel.'

Oh, God.

I follow her in silence until we reach my room, and then I miss my opportunity to argue. She stops still as soon as the door opens, mouth in an *o*.

'What?'

'What the fuck has happened to you?' She sweeps into the room, making a big show of stepping over the little molehills I haven't quite cleaned up. I guess I could have washed my plates. '*You* do not live in this room. I don't believe it.'

I pull a face and sit on the edge of my bed. I've made it, at least. 'I've been busy.'

'But you're a tidy person.'

I shrug.

'I *knew* something was wrong.'

'What do you mean?'

'Since Dan went away—'

'I've been busy, Cas!'

Instead of responding, she takes the bottles out of her bag. Rum and vodka. *Brilliant*. I stare at the vodka for a moment too long, the feel of Lilley's lips on mine still overwhelmingly vivid.

'Promise you'll make an effort tonight.'

I blink quickly and bring my thoughts back into the room in time to see her splashing vodka into a glass.

'What do you mean?'

215

'At least *act* like you still love Peter—'

'What the hell are you on about?'

She hands me the glass with one eyebrow raised and iron in her eyes. 'When was the last time you messaged him first?'

Oh. A lead weight crashes through me, pinning me to the ground. I have a feeling I haven't been the one to text him first all semester, and she knows.

'I—I don't know.'

'Exactly. I thought I should give you a heads up, so you can be on your best behaviour tonight.' She sits beside me and knocks our arms together. 'Hey, it's alright.'

'I'm sorry, Cas.'

'I'm not the one you need to apologise to.'

I sigh and let myself lean into her. I should probably take this moment to confess what happened with Lilley last week, but a much more dangerous question slips from me, instead.

'Be honest with me, alright? Why doesn't Peter like Dan?'

The pause between my question and her answer is so long that I don't doubt, even for a moment, that she's telling me the truth. Especially as she takes a sip of her rum before speaking.

'He's jealous. He's convinced you two are in a relationship and he hates that you don't trust him enough to tell him and—and he's jealous.'

I rub my forehead and sink forward, curled over my glass. 'What's he jealous of? He has Anthony. You know, the first time I met him, they both completely blanked me.'

That little injustice doesn't quite weigh up against me ignoring my best friend for a whole semester, and we both know it. Cassie finishes the splash of alcohol left in her glass and shrugs, eyes on the carpet as she speaks.

'Think about it.'

'That doesn't help.'

'I don't think I should say.'

Fine. Even though she guilted me into telling her basically everything about Daniel, I can respect her ability to shut her mouth. I groan, mumble another apology, and drain my glass.

Neat vodka has an uncanny way of making me stop caring for a few moments. For the first few shots, the apathy only lasts while the vodka makes its way down my throat. After a while, though, the hazy fire which burns in my chest is enough to make me forget how awful I've been to Peter. It's enough to make me forget how much I regretted kissing Lilley last week, and it's almost enough to make me forget how much I need Daniel's arms.

Almost.

Forty-Six

There is a massive queue to get in by the time we reach the SU and I instantly regret not picking up a jacket. It is *freezing*. I cuddle Cas to my chest for as long as I can, trying to keep some heat between her skin and ridiculously small dress, but we're both turning blue by the time we reach the doors. A lot of the carelessness brought to me by the alcohol has left, now, chased away by the goose bumps on my arms.

A hug from Dan would really help.

He's the other side of the fucking world.

Peter finds us near the bar, Anthony in-tow. I've never spoken to the guy and, now that I'm considering the impossible volume of rock between Dan and I, I can't bring myself to even look at him.

Cas forces a little plastic shot glass of something that smells of mouthwash into my hand, and I look up.

'Drink this, then be lovely,' she mutters, lips at my ear. 'Come on. Sulking won't bring him back.'

I would love to be the sort of person who could throw the alcohol on the floor and storm out. Instead, I nod and swallow the drink in one and try to smile. It's a grimace.

'I'll do my best.'

She steps back, takes her shot, and promptly orders four more. I realise, now, that I have my back to Peter and Anthony. Who do I think I am? Wiping my hand across my face in an attempt to brush away the crippling emptiness, I turn to them and smile.

Another shot later, Cassie makes us dance. The wooden dancefloor is already soaked, even though it's early in the night, and I stumble and slide with each step. I'm not the only one: every few moments, someone's arms windmill as they try desperately to catch themselves on something—or someone.

Fortunately for me, I'm being towed along by Cas. I don't

218

really need to lift my feet—she's just dragging me forward.

Fortunately for Lilley, I'm not *too* drunk and haven't quite dulled my reflexes. I catch her as she slips, and I'm not quite sure what I'm expecting from her when she looks up and recognises me.

She hugs me. It's *weird*.

'You smell really nice,' I mumble, apparently forgetting *everything*. Ugh. I frown, letting go of her slowly in case one of us falls. 'I thought you were going home.'

She shrugs and lets her hand linger on my waist. 'I came back yesterday.'

'Just for today?'

She nods, and I don't really get chance to ask anything else because Cas takes over. I don't get to ask who she's come with, or to wonder where Kieran is. I just get swept up by my friends and I'm *trying* to dance. Or, at the very least, I'm trying to not look uncomfortable.

Those last two shots hit me at about the same time and make the room spin. Cas is clinging to Lilley's arm, shouting about something, so I call for a break.

We stumble back through the crowds, past the bars, and into the smoking area. I thought it would help to get out into the open air but Dan should be here, and the smell of cigarettes mixed with the absence of him is enough to make me forget where I am. I hide my face in my hands, trying to steady myself.

'What's wrong with you?' Lilley asks, poking me in the ribs. The pain of it makes me gasp and I nearly double over, glaring at her.

'He misses Daniel,' Peter says, uncharacteristically coldly. It freezes me.

And, of course, Lilley knows. She knows more than Peter and Cas put together and she's the last person, really, who I would expect to defend me. But she does it.

'He's alright, isn't he?' she asks me, putting a hand on my arm. I nod, and she turns sharply to face Peter, where he's standing with his hand in Anthony's back pocket. 'Leave him alone about it.'

He bristles. I think it's the alcohol, or the shock at being told off, and I don't like it. 'Why are you yelling at me? He's been a dick!'

'Oh, Peter, you have *no* idea,' Lilley snaps. She takes a step towards him. 'You don't have a clue.'

'And you *do*?' Peter glares between us, cheeks burning red. 'I don't know about you, Lil, but Will's hardly spoken to me this year.'

I groan and step forward. There wasn't really the chance to apologise inside, and now it looks like I've left it too late. 'I'm sorry, Peter—'

'Fuck off.'

I recoil, like he slapped me.

'You don't give a shit how I feel.'

'You know that isn't—'

He shakes his head and I have never seen him look this angry. 'You don't. You don't care.'

'How can you say that?' I step past Lilley, away from Cassie, and reach for Peter. It's not a surprise that he shrugs away from me, but it hurts. 'I've been distracted, I know. But I'm—'

'Distracted? You think *distracted* covers it?'

'Peter, let it go,' Cassie breathes, appearing right beside him. Anthony, bless him, is as useful as a square tyre and hangs back. 'Talk about this when you're sober.'

Peter shakes his head. 'I never get chance to talk to him. I may as well say it now.'

Between us, Cassie and Lilley share a look.

'Tell me what I can do to fix this,' I suggest, moving closer to Peter. He closes his eyes, like he's in pain, and my stomach flips. 'Shit. I'm so sorry—'

'I can't believe you ditched me for him.' It comes out in a rush, like a barrier in him burst. 'I can't believe you didn't see how much it hurt.'

I pull a face and glance at Cassie but she's keeping a carefully neutral expression. It's impressive, given how much alcohol she's had. 'What do you mean?'

'Are you in a relationship with him?'

Jesus Christ. 'No.'

'Do you *want* to be?'

'Does it matter?'

'Yes!'

'Why?'

'Because if you can't even trust me enough to tell me you're gay—'

'I'm not gay.' I'm glad Lilley's behind me, so I can't see the look on her face. 'Don't pretend this is about relationships. This is about you and me.'

Peter lets out a sharp breath and looks at me, eyelids red. He's going to cry, and the whole world has just turned to ice.

Oh, *shit*.

'Peter—'

'I hope you're as happy with him as I am with Anthony,' he whispers, stepping back. 'But he's not good enough for you.'

If I'd had one or two fewer shots of alcohol, I might be able to let that go. As it is, I erupt. I split right through each of those fissures and fractures which have been forming for the last *five years* and I spill across the floor.

'What the fuck is your problem?' I move towards him again. 'You don't know anything about him!'

'I know enough!' Peter's hands are shaking. 'I know he's a junkie—'

'Don't talk about him like that!' I swear, I've never been so angry in all of my life. And then an awful, awful thought registers and I stare at Peter, like he's just ripped his own arm off. 'How do you know?'

'It's *obvious*—'

'No, it's not.' My voice trembles. 'Peter, who have you been talking to?'

The world stands still while Peter and Anthony share a glance, working out whether they should tell me.

Anthony surprises me by speaking. 'His ex is a guy called Matthew, right?'

Dumb, I nod.

'He's on the football team with me. We're friends.'

Before I can scream about how dangerous this is, Peter talks. 'And he's told us—'

'What the fuck has he told you?'

'Daniel's a manipulative dick and made him—'

'Are you stupid? You do realise that when I first met Dan *he* was the one with the fucking broken ribs, don't you?'

Peter looks like I've slapped him.

'I can't believe you could see how ill he's been and still believe—'

'I've barely seen him though, have I?' He's backtracking. I'd almost feel a sense of achievement, but— 'I haven't seen either of you because you spend all your free time sneaking around and fucking—'

'We're not in a relationship!'

'Then stop acting like it!'

This isn't me. This isn't something I do. But neither is skipping lectures—neither is leaving washing up on my bedroom floor.

I spin and grab Lilley by the shoulders. We make eye-contact for half a moment. I don't think she's drinking—I haven't seen her with a glass—and she understands far more than I do when I lean into her and press our lips together.

She saves me a bit of embarrassment by kissing me back. Still, it's the worst thing I've ever done and I can feel the world splashing around me like I'm on a boat.

I turn back to Peter, trembling all over. 'I wouldn't do that if I was in a fucking relationship.' I hate that we're arguing and it's made much worse when Lilley slips her arms around me. 'I wouldn't do that to him and you fucking know it.'

Peter chews his lip and, for a moment, I think he's going to step towards me. Instead, he shakes his head and backs away, finding Anthony's hand.

'He's messed you up, Will.'

I can't leave it like that. I can't have *anyone* thinking Dan is bad.

'Don't blame Dan for *anything*.' I try to step forward but Lilley's arms tighten around my waist. 'If I haven't told you everything that's down to me—that's nothing to do with him.

222

And you don't know, Peter, you don't know half of—'

'Because you don't fucking talk to me!'

I can feel the whole world hold its breath. What is he expecting me to say? He shakes his head and mumbles something, walking away with Anthony's arm around his back.

I feel sick. Sick enough to lie down on the soggy, cigarette-butt covered floor.

'I'll go after him,' Cassie whispers, stopping to press a gentle kiss to my cheek. Shit. 'I love you, Will. It's okay. Talk to him tomorrow.'

I wish I could smile at her, but I can't move.

'It's okay. I'll find you in a bit. Text me if you go home.'

She and Lilley share another look, and then I'm left there with my ex-girlfriend. And Lilley is dangerously good at reading me.

'He's really jealous,' she says, like I couldn't work that out for myself. 'Why don't you just tell him you fancy the guy?'

I manage a tiny, tiny shrug before tears splutter from me. Wonderful.

For once, she's being sensitive. Maybe friendship is good for us, because this is a softer side to Lilley I rarely saw when she was my girlfriend. She stands in front of me, tilting her head so I have to look at her. 'Will, it's okay.'

'I'm not—I'm not in a fucking relationship—'

'Okay, okay.' She wipes my face for me, using the palms of her hands. Ugh. She smells lovely. 'I know. Do you love him?'

She asks it so gently, and so plainly, that I don't really get chance to think to deny it. All I can do is nod.

'Peter doesn't understand it's difficult for some people.' God, I needed to hear someone else say that. 'You don't need to come out, Will. You don't have to explain anything. Is Dan okay? Have you heard from him?'

Breathing feels a lot easier than it did a minute ago. 'He's okay. We spoke yesterday.'

'Alright. You know you can trust me with anything, right? If you want to talk about this, or if you want to scream about how worried you are or how pissed with Peter you are, you can

223

talk to me. Okay?'

I laugh. It comes out sort of bubbly, like I'm nervous about sounding too happy while there are still tears on my face, and she kisses my cheek. It's a bit like how Cassie did it, but it feels…

Warm.

Forty-Seven

I t's *weird.*

Lilley and I keep catching hold of each other. We touch hands when we're dancing. When Cassie finds us to say Peter's left with Anthony, she leans into me. I loop my arms around her. I rest my head against hers and then my hands are on her waist. On her hips. Shit.

That kiss was a mistake.

Which kiss? The one to prove to Peter that I'm not in a relationship, or the one last week? I haven't asked about Kieran, but I know Lilley well enough to not press that button again. If it were something she wanted to care about, she'd have mentioned him. So I guess this means they've broken up.

So I guess it's okay when I find myself with my hands in her glossy hair, breathing across her skin and moving towards her like we didn't break up so many months ago.

I need to make some things *entirely* clear before we go any further.

Firstly, I'm still not quite out. Not properly to Dan, and definitely not at all to Cassie and Peter. Lilley knows. I think she always knew.

Secondly, I am *not* in a relationship with Lilley. A handful of kisses and this one night don't mean anything. I'm not falling in love with her. I'm not going to text her over the weekend, begging her to come and visit me during Christmas.

This isn't serious and taking her hand to walk across campus to my room doesn't mean I'm any less in love with Daniel. I think she understands. I think she knows I just want to be close to someone. I think it's what she wants too.

Going to my room is a mistake, but we kiss again as I'm trying to open the door and stumble down the corridor. We fall into my room, just about remember to lock the door, and start removing each other's clothes while sliding into my bed. It's

225

almost like we never broke up.

Almost.

The difference is she falls asleep almost straight away and I sit there for a long time, staring through the darkness and desperately trying to keep breathing.

Forty-Eight

Do you remember what I said about people when they're sleeping?

Lilley looks very human. She's pretty—obviously, I think she's pretty—but some of the delicateness is lost when her face relaxes into sleep. His dark hair is tangled above her, on the pillow, and she looks like she's fallen.

Daniel asleep is perfection.

He'll be wide awake. I can't remember what he said he was doing today and I *suck*. All I can think is that none of last night would have happened if he were here.

Daylight starts creeping around the blinds and I blink at it, shocked. Did I stay awake? I feel dry and horrible, so it's quite possible. Lilley has hardly moved all night.

It's morning. Dan *must* phone me soon.

I can't tell him what happened.

As soon as the thought crosses my mind I brush it away. How could I *not* tell him? He trusts me. He's going to ask me what happened, and I can't *lie* to him.

Not anymore.

Lilley wakes up. Asks how I am.

I hum.

She moves around the room, finding last night's clothes and trying to talk to me. God, I feel sick. I can hardly keep my head up. It's like someone's filled it with lead.

Lilley leaves the room, saying something about the toilet. Fine. Cool. Whatever. The door clicks shut and I topple over, lying across the bed with my knees half pulled to my chest. I put my phone down some time ago, but my hand still feels like it's holding onto something. I'm still waiting for it to ring.

The door opens again, and I don't realise at first that Lilley isn't alone.

'Will?' It's Peter, and I can't believe we argued. I can't

227

believe he's here. I can't believe he really hates Dan so much that the thought of us being in a relationship turned him so vile.

Oh, shit, I can't believe he knows Matthew.

'Hey, I'm sorry about last night. I'm an arse. Can we talk?' It doesn't look like I have much of a choice, because he sits down, near my head, and keeps going. 'I thought you knew.'

Confused, my face defrosts enough to frown at him. He's pink around the edges, burned with embarrassment, but his eyebrows are pulled together. If I didn't feel so sick, I'd sit up.

'Will—' his voice catches and he flinches, like coughing hurt him. 'I've had a big, stinking crush on you since I met you.'

Lilley moves to the window, trying to look like she isn't listening, and I push myself up on shaky arms.

'Why didn't you tell me?' I sound almost as bad as I feel.

Peter blinks quickly and looks away, lips quivering. 'Thought you were straight.'

Oh, no.

I finish sitting up and throw my arms around him, not sure which one of us I'm supporting. His hands are gentle on my bare waist, like he's afraid of upsetting me, so I hold him tighter. He doesn't smell like Daniel. He doesn't feel anywhere near similar in my arms but, when his chest shakes with a deep breath, I realise this isn't necessarily a bad thing.

'I'm so sorry,' I whisper, chin on his shoulder.

'Is it just him?'

I wish I could say *yeah*. Instead, I shake my head and hold him as tight as I dare.

'I'm sorry for what I said about him.'

I groan and sit up, ears ringing. I definitely need a glass of water. 'Just promise me you're going to stay away from Matthew. He's *dangerous*—'

'Yeah, he's Anthony's friend, not mine.' He says it very quickly and I squint at him. 'Don't worry. I trust you way more than him.'

'You didn't, though—'

'I was jealous as fuck.' Peter's eyes are huge, swallowing a

228

good half of his round face. I chew my cheek. 'I kinda hated Dan already for stealing you away from me,' his face burns like a traffic light, 'and Matthew gave me an excuse to hate him even more.'

I shake my head. 'What have you actually said to him?'

He shrugs, glances over at Lilley, and speaks without looking at me. 'That my best friend dumped me for his new boyfriend who works in the café at the SU.'

I groan and close my eyes. 'Did you tell him my name?'

'I—yeah.'

There's no point in getting angry or upset. I take a slow breath through my teeth and hold it, thinking this through. 'I won't tell Dan until I see him. He'll just worry and there's nothing he can do in New Zealand.' I look back at Peter and there are tears on his cheeks, so I try a smile. 'Don't worry. Just stay away from him.'

Peter nods, wipes his cheeks on the back of his hands, and I think he's going to say something else when my phone rings. I'd almost forgotten about it.

Almost.

I stretch back and snatch it up from my desk, heart thundering. There's so much I need to say but, when I press *answer*, my voice leaves me.

'William? Are you there?'

'Yeah—yeah. Hi.' I thought I'd beaten the tears this morning but, at the sound of my favourite voice in the world, I've crumbled. I slip away from Peter and lie back down on the duvet. 'How are you?'

'Better than you sound.'

I half laugh and curl up, trying to hide my face. I can't begin to process what Peter's told me. I can't think of anything except how much the miles separating me from Dan ache.

'How are you? Did you go out last night?'

Oh, screw last night. Lilley notices I'm crying and breathes my name, crossing the room to sit with us. Peter puts his hand in my hair.

On the other side of the world, Dan hears my sniffing. It's nothing new for me to cry when I'm talking to him, but he panics.

'What happened? Are you okay? Did someone get hurt?'

I gasp and just about manage to speak. 'I'm okay. I—I'm okay. It's fine.'

He thinks for a moment. There's no way he's letting me get away without telling him, and another wave of tears spills from my closed eyes.

'Tell me, William. Please just tell me.'

'I can't.'

'Why not?'

I cough a few times and take a deep breath. 'Because I feel shit about it and I want you *here*.' I ignore my friends. I ignore how nice it feels to have someone stroking my hair, because Peter really should stop. It's going to hurt him. Oh my God, he knows Matthew. 'It can wait.'

'Is it why you're crying?'

'Mostly.' Regret of sleeping with Lilley is mixing with how bad I feel for Peter and how worried I am about Matthew and how sick I feel from missing Dan, and it's making it difficult to tell the four apart.

'Please tell me,' he whispers. Once again, it's like the distance between us is nothing. 'Oh, William. I'm so worried about you.'

I lick my lips. 'Don't be.'

'I *am*.'

'I just can't—I can't—'

'You can tell me anything.'

Well, shit. I know I should be able to. I should be able to say *Dan, I love you more than the sun* but I can't.

Telling him about Lilley is comparatively easy.

'I had sex with Lilley.' It comes out in a rush, blurring together. Did he hear? There's a pause, which makes me worry I need to say it again, and Peter strokes my hair again.

'Okay.'

Is that it? Is that all he can say about it? A pulse of tears pushes through me and I blub, wishing so desperately to see him.

He tries to calm me down with whispers. 'William, it's

okay. It's okay. I'm not upset. Did you think I would be?'

Honesty slips from me. 'I think I hoped you would be.'

He hums. 'Okay. What if I tell you I thought this would happen?'

'I don't know. I don't know why I'm so upset. I don't know why I did it or why it fucking matters—'

'It doesn't matter.' I want to believe him. 'It doesn't matter—it doesn't change how I feel about you.' What? 'Did you think it would?'

Forgetting how to breathe is a regular occurrence for me now, but this time it feels serious. I bite my cheek so hard my teeth cut through. 'I can't do this while I can't see you.'

'Okay, okay—'

'Just tell me we're okay.'

He manages a little chuckle. 'We're okay—of course we're okay. There are only eight more days until I come home.'

I sit up. Peter pulls me into his arms and my absolute lack of attraction to him slaps me in the face. Isn't this exactly what I'm dreading happening with Dan? Oh, damn. 'I can't wait.'

I make him tell me about where he is. What the air tastes like. What the sea looks like. What the streets are like. He talks to me for maybe half an hour, coaxing me gently back out of the darkness I'd trapped myself in, and I don't want to say goodbye.

'Speak soon?' My eyes are closed again. They've been closed for a while.

'I'll phone you tomorrow. William, talk with Peter.' Oh, if only he knew. Poor Peter. 'Talk to Lilley. You aren't in a relationship with her now, are you?'

Oh, God.

'No,' I breathe. 'No.'

'Good.'

'What?'

He clears his throat and I'm dangling over the edge, holding on by my fingertips. I'm going to fall. I don't know what's at the bottom.

'We'll talk about it when I'm home,' he whispers. 'But I'm glad.'

I slip. I'm falling and I *think* he's there to catch me.

'You're glad?'

'If nothing else, it means I don't have to give you up on Sunday nights.'

Forty-Nine

Peter and Lilley stay with me all day. They don't make me explain what Dan and I talked about, even though they must have questions, and Lilley is sure to make it absolutely clear that one night does *not* mean we're in a relationship.

I wonder, now, why I made such a fuss.

'Wait,' Peter mutters, sometime into the early afternoon. We're all sprawled together across my bed. 'Lil, aren't you dating Kieran?'

She shakes her head firmly and the little drop of panic I'd felt dissolves. 'Not as of Monday morning.'

'Oh, Lil—'

'No, it's fine. I think we all know it wasn't working out very well.' She gives me a tiny smile. I'm not sure how I'm meant to feel. Relieved? Sad for her? Guilty? 'Don't worry about it. I'm happier now.'

'I didn't think to ask.'

She shrugs. 'Not your job to make sure I don't cheat on people. But I wish it hadn't upset you so much.' We're back on *this*. Great. 'Did you sleep at all?'

'I didn't, no.' I can't quite look at either of them. 'I dunno. I just realised it was irresponsible and—'

'And you felt like you were betraying Dan,' Peter whispers.

I speak quickly. 'Only like I'd have felt if I'd fucked someone without you and Cas knowing.' It's almost true. It might have convinced them a few weeks ago. 'It's just weird. And we—we mean a lot to each other.'

Okay, that *might* have worked. Because Peter's good and doesn't say anything else. He doesn't make a fuss when Lilley asks about what Dan's doing in New Zealand, and when it becomes breathtakingly obvious I adore him.

Lilley's the first to leave. She kisses my cheek, tells me to

Louise Willingham

talk to her soon and leaves in the dress and shoes she wore last night. Which means Peter and I are alone together and I can't look at him.

'Will?'

I sigh and peer at him through my eyelashes. I still haven't put my glasses on, but he's close enough to not quite be a blur.

'We're alright, yeah?'

'Of course.'

'It's not—it's not *weird*—'

I shake my head sharply and catch his hands. 'Not at all. Are you okay?'

He shrugs. 'Embarrassed enough to die.'

That's a feeling I'm familiar with. 'Yeah, but are you happy with Anthony?'

'Oh, yeah.' He brightens, like the sun coming out from behind a cloud. 'He's great. It's just been a weird few months for me.'

'For me, too.'

I think we've fixed it. He looks less like an injured animal, now, and it's taken me this long to realise he's wearing the same clothes as last night. I guess this means he stayed at Anthony's, but I realise now I have no idea *where* Anthony lives.

I feel the weight of our argument slip from my shoulders. 'I had no idea.'

'No, I know. You can be a bit stupid.'

'Hey!'

He laughs and shoves me softly, dimples positively glowing. 'You're stupid if you think Dan doesn't adore you.'

I pout.

'Stop that. It's sickening how he looks at you.'

'Peter—'

'Are you seeing him over Christmas?'

I shoot him a glare that could cut glass. 'He's in New Zealand.'

'I know, but when he comes back.'

I shake my head. 'No. It'll be New Year and I'll be at home.'

234

He hums, rubbing his thumb into the back of my hand. 'That's a shame. When are you going back?'

I look at the time. 'Soon.'

'You're going home today?'

'Yep.' I shrug, looking around us. There's quite a lot of tidying to do. 'I don't see any reason to stay another night.'

'Well,' he says, getting to his feet, 'tell me when you get home. And talk to me while you're away.'

'Of course.' I flash a grin. I am *exhausted* but it's so nice to smile at him again. 'Thank you for coming and seeing me. Are you okay?'

He nods, pokes my cheek with a fingertip, and steps towards the door. 'I'm alright. Glad I got it off my chest.'

I stand up so I can hug him. 'Love you. Stay safe, alright?'

He laughs and turns to the door, throwing me a wink. 'Yeah. Love you too.'

Fifty

Being home is *weird*. Turning up on the doorstep at half ten at night is a highlight, even with Kirst shrieking in my ear that I was supposed to let her know when I was getting to the train station.

It doesn't matter. Paying for the taxi is worth it for the flood of hugs I get.

And, for this evening, I'm too tired to worry about missing Dan. I'm too tired to worry about Peter and I'm too tired to be stressed that I haven't done any work since Thursday.

I don't have time to be tired: the decorations are up and the house smells of Christmas. I'm allowed a few days off.

And Dan will be home in just over a week. Even if I don't get to see him straight away, it makes a difference. It's exciting.

Being around my family, who don't even know Dan exists, is oddly refreshing. It's a bit strange but they just ask about Cas and Peter. We talk about my course, my upcoming placement, my exams. No mention of Lilley, and it makes a nice change.

No mention of Dan. So, largely, I don't think about him —except every time I close my eyes, every night, and every morning. Every time I catch the scent of coffee. No one in my family smokes, and I miss the smell of cigarettes.

And then Christmas Day hits us.

We wake up early. It's six in the morning—five in the evening for Dan—and I feel *awful*. It's like I have a hangover, but I didn't drink last night. My head is full, woolly, and there's a sharp pain somewhere behind my eyes.

I want to slink off back to bed, but there are presents to open. Food to prepare. My cousins on Mum's side of the family are coming over and that's great but I need time *alone*.

I want to be left alone to sulk.

Why am I being such an arse? Even if Dan were in the country, I wouldn't be seeing him today. I almost definitely wouldn't be seeing him.

I'm helping Mum with breakfast when my phone rings and we're both so surprised that I almost don't answer it. It's eight o'clock.

Nine for Dan.

I grab my phone and scurry out of the kitchen, mumbling a sort of apology. I don't think Mum saw the name, so I guess she must think it's Peter or Cas, and no one tries to follow me.

I answer as I'm running up the stairs.

'Hi—Dan—hi—'

'Happy Christmas,' he laughs, and I collapse onto my bed. I am *grinning*. It's not like we haven't spoken since I got home, but this one's special. It's *Christmas*. 'How are you?'

'I'm good—happy Christmas, Dan.' I curl around my pillow, pretending it feels like him. 'Have you had a nice day?'

'It was lovely. I thought I'd give you chance to wake up before I phone you, but I couldn't wait any longer.'

Oh, God. I feel that drill through my chest.

'We woke up at six,' I admit. 'Christmas is a *thing* here. Mum's family are coming over for lunch. There's going to be a bunch of us, and we're cooking dinner—'

'Did I interrupt?'

'Only breakfast, and that doesn't matter.'

He hums. 'Have you told your parents about me?'

Shit. 'I don't really know what to say. They'll ask loads of questions.'

'You'll have to introduce me one day. Would they mind me?'

I think I just left my body. 'Dan, who the hell could *mind* you?'

'You know what I mean.' I really don't. He has to explain. 'Would they mind that I'm gay?'

I bloody hope not.

'Not at all,' I breathe. 'They'd probably go *oh, okay* and that would be it.'

'You're sure?'

237

'I'm sure.'

'Okay. I'm sorry—'

Hearing him say sorry is my least favourite thing in the world. 'Hey, no. Don't apologise for asking. I understand. It's fucking terrifying.'

'It is. How are you?'

I've already told him I'm fine. Is this him trying to revisit the whole me-half-coming-out thing? Or is he hinting at my night with Lilley? God, I haven't even mentioned the thing with Peter, yet. Whatever; I guess the answer is *firmly pretending nothing matters*.

'I'm okay, Dan,' I say. 'I'm really happy to hear from you.'

A little chuckle. I bury my face in the pillow I'm crushing. 'I'm glad you answered. I thought you might be too busy—'

'Never too busy for you.'

'Thank you. Have you spoken to Lilley?'

Well, there you go. He is very good at not letting me avoid things.

'Yeah, she's fine. We're friends.'

'Friends?'

'Yeah.'

'Good.' Why does it matter, Dan? Just tell me. 'Peter?'

Oh, bloody hell. 'Peter's okay.' I say it too slowly and it's clear I'm hiding something. 'Dan, don't tell him I told you—'

'Of course not.'

'He told me he has a crush on me.'

The silence from New Zealand makes me instantly regret telling him.

'But nothing—nothing's there—'

'No, you said you didn't like him like that,' he breathes. 'Is he okay?'

'Yeah, we talked about it on Saturday. Lilley made him come over because I—I was a bit of a mess.'

'I know. I wish I was there.'

'So do I.' It comes out too quickly, and there's a silence that I can't bring myself to break. A stupid, dreamy part of me is imagining him saying *screw it, I'm coming home*.

After an age, he sighs. 'Are you okay?'

'Yeah, Dan. I'm fine—'

'Are you okay knowing Peter likes you?'

I frown at the room. 'Why wouldn't I be? He's still my best friend.'

He lets out a sigh that sounds like he's relieved. 'Good. What do you eat for Christmas dinner?'

The change of topic is blinding, but I stick with it. I tell him about the people coming over and how long they'll be with us, and time flies like it always does with Dan. It's almost ten by the time we hang up.

I run back down stairs, blushing a ridiculous amount. Dad's reaction is predictable, honestly, but it *hurts*.

'Who was that?' And then, before I can answer, 'a new girlfriend you haven't told us about?'

'No,' I say, teeth tight together as I make a beeline for the kitchen. 'A friend.'

'They okay, hon?' Mum asks, popping my breakfast in the microwave and raising an eyebrow at me. 'Is it someone we know?'

'They're okay,' I say. 'I met him this year—he works in the SU and he's on holiday in New Zealand.'

'Oh, wow,' she mutters. 'Does he have family there?'

'No, just wanted to visit.'

'What's his name?'

'Daniel.'

'And he's alright?'

I roll my eyes. 'Yes, Mum. We talk every few days.'

'For two hours?'

I wrinkle my nose. 'We had a lot to talk about.'

'What like?'

Christ, does it matter? 'Christmas, family, that sort of thing.'

'Why isn't he with his family?'

I am not surprised that she'd ask such a blunt, thoughtless question, but I'm not impressed. 'He doesn't have a family, Mum. He doesn't have many friends.'

She's quiet for a moment. 'You should have invited him here.' *I know.* 'Maybe next year. What course is he doing?'

'Politics,' I mutter, taking my plate out and leaning against the worksurface to eat. 'He's taking a few months off for—for some personal stuff. So he'll be re-sitting January exams in the summer.'

I am *not* going to explain that he's twenty-six. I don't think *I've* accepted he's twenty-six.

I manage to escape any more questions about Dan by throwing myself enthusiastically into helping with lunch preparations. I run around the living room and dining room with the vacuum. I throw some abandoned wrapping paper at Kirst, who retaliates with a broken bauble from the tree, and Dad has to step in before we actually damage something.

It's nice.

Fifty-One

Sunday is an awful day. An awful morning, at least, because I haven't heard from Dan since Wednesday and I don't know what this means. Is he saving his phone battery for the journey? Is he on his way home yet? Is he going straight to his flat? Has there been a delay with his flights?

God, I don't know. I want to spend the day hidden in bed but I've made a really big thing out of my six exams so I need to at least *try* to revise and I drag myself down the stairs at half eleven, looking and feeling like I've got a hangover. Again.

Kirst offers me coffee and I nearly cry.

Instead, I manage a little smile and just ask for water. She reminds me that I need to eat and comes back with a yoghurt, spoon, and glass of water.

'Do you work this hard at uni?' she asks, gesturing to the giant stack of notes I've managed to produce in the last four days.

I shrug.

'Seriously? I thought you went out to the SU every week.'

'Only a few times this semester,' I say, wrinkling my nose at her. 'I'm a really boring person, Kirst. You know that.'

'I know you're a fucking nerd,' she says, right as Mum walks past. She earns herself a hiss of *language!* and rolls her eyes at me, waiting for Mum leave the room before continuing.

'You are, though. Have you made any friends on your course yet?'

I *glare*. 'Yes, Mum. I work with people and I'll be revising with them when I go back but they're not the same as—as Peter,' I say, because I nearly said *Daniel*. I haven't even mentioned him to Kirst yet. 'That doesn't matter, though.'

She purses her lips. 'The best thing about my course was sharing the pain of it with other people.'

'I do that.' I manage a smile. 'Stop worrying. I have

friends.'

This conversation is one we've had almost every year of my academic career, and I don't get it. I've pretty much cut ties with everyone I went to sixth form and high school with; she collects people by the dozen.

At the perfect moment, Peter sends me a text. I show Kirst the notification and stick my tongue out, earning a gentle swipe to my shoulder as she leaves me to it.

10:55 **Peter**: Dan comes home today, yeah?

Why the fuck does he 1) know, 2) care?

10:58 **William**: ... so?

11:03 **Peter**: Are you coming back to uni to see him?

11:04 **William**: ... no...

11:12 **Peter**: Oh

11:13 **William**: What?!

11:21 **Peter**: If you WERE I'd tell you 'I'm going back tonight because I realised I need some books I totally didn't leave in my room and wondered if you wanted to meet up' but if you're staying at home fair enough! How is home?

We talk a bit about Christmas and our families and he talks about Anthony but I am shaken. I can't believe he asked if I was coming back to see Dan and I'm jittery. I'm angsty and irritated and it's late into the afternoon by the time I calm down.

Kirst tells me I need to eat more, and I *know*.

I make a big deal out of helping to cook that evening. Mum and I are both in the kitchen, chopping veg and boiling water, and it's nice. I'm having flashbacks to sixth form, when she would make me help *so you know some recipes for uni!*, and a lot of the tension from my conversation with Peter has gone by the time the doorbell rings.

Dad gets it.

I think nothing of it.

'William?'

It takes me just over ten steps to leave the kitchen and walk far enough into the living room to see him, and I honestly couldn't tell you what I'm thinking as I cross through that space. I'm not expecting any visitors.

I stumble to a stop. I'm very aware that I look awful. I haven't shaved for days and I haven't washed my hair and my glasses are so smudged I *could* be making up what I'm seeing but, no—he's there.

Is that a tan?

I swap my shock for a bemused grin and close the distance between us, grabbing Dan for a hug without thinking what my family are going to say.

Shit, he smells good. Maybe it's a credit to his deodorant, but I've never been so comfortable inhaling someone after they've spent nearly thirty hours travelling. And he's had a cigarette recently. I can almost see the smoke still curling from his jacket.

Maybe I should introduce him.

But I don't know how long he's staying for and, if this is just a fleeting visit, I need to hold onto him for as long as possible. I need to absorb him—to remind my muscles what he feels like.

Dad clears his throat and, shit, I've got to do this. I pull my arms from Dan and take a half step back.

He's blushing. *Oh.*

'Hey,' I manage, voice alarmingly rough. Oops. I swallow and take another step away from him. 'Um, this is Daniel.' I throw one hand into my hair before it grabs him again. 'You just got back?'

'I just got back,' he says, filling the room.

Mum's smiling, Kirst is smirking at me, and Dad just seems confused.

'Sorry for not warning you.'

I can't breathe.

'It's fine. William mentioned you've been away,' Mum says, maintaining that smile. I want to high-five her. 'Come in, sit down. Do you want dinner?'

He clearly hasn't thought about this and glances at me. 'I haven't slept for thirty hours,' he mutters, and I think I know what this means. I hope I know what this means.

'Are you in a rush to get home?' I ask, and he blesses me with the best response I could hope for.

'I just came from home.'

My thoughts whir and land together in one place: Peter.

I am *grinning*. Shit. My cheeks hurt.

'So you want to stay?' I have to be very careful to not put my hands on his waist. 'You can. It's okay. If you're tired you could go to my room and have a nap if—if you want.'

He *smirks* at me, like he knows just how helpless I am. 'Do you mind?'

'Not at all. It's okay, isn't it?' I turn back to Mum in time to see her nod. 'Shall I show you where to go?'

This is ridiculous. This is crazy and I can't breathe and he's right there, following me up the stairs to my bedroom.

'I can't believe you're here,' I manage when it's just us. I flick the light on and cross the room, drawing the curtains.

He *chuckles*.

'Shit. Was it Peter?'

'Hmm?'

'Did he tell you where I live?'

Dan's leaning against my wall, looking exhausted, and nods.

'Fucking knew it.'

'Are you angry?'

'No!' My face is hurting from all this smiling—my glasses aren't quite resting on my nose. 'No, I'm really happy. I'm *really* happy.'

He just smiles at me. 'You look it.'

'I can't believe you've done this.'

'I have done it.' He pushes away from the wall and takes

a deep breath. 'Can I stay the night?'

'*Yes*. Definitely.'

'Will your mother mind?'

I shake my head but, honestly, I'm expecting to be told I have to sleep downstairs. That's something for me to argue with her while he sleeps, though.

'She'll be fine, I'm going to get asked a *load* of questions, though.'

We're close enough together for me to smell him again. *Shit*. I feel like I've been zapped with a shot of caffeine. His eyes are doing that awful hazy thing again and he must be exhausted.

'Good luck with them. Are you sure I can stay here?'

'*Yes*.' I grab his hand for a very short moment, like I'm checking he's there, and flip the duvet back. I clear some stuff from the floor, realising far too late that he's brought a rucksack with him. 'Just make yourself comfortable.'

He catches me from behind like he sometimes does when I'm being too energetic and rests his head against mine. He can definitely feel my pulse—his hands are flat against my chest, my waist—

'Come back to me when you can.' His breath hits my hair. 'I wanted to see you. I need to sleep, but I needed to be near you.'

I swallow down a whimper. Oh, God. 'Are you staying?'

He hums into my ear. 'I would like to stay for a couple of days, if that's okay.'

I slip my fingers between his and hold onto him, like he might drift away. 'It's *definitely* okay. I should talk to Mum.'

A little sigh flutters across my skin, a butterfly dancing over a dandelion. 'I will be here. I promise you.'

I grunt and force myself out of his arms. Still not entirely sure he's there, I turn to face him, hands fidgeting. 'Bathroom is just next door,' I manage, nodding to my right, 'and you can come downstairs whenever you want. If you wake up and I'm not here just come down—don't be scared.'

For a moment, it looks like he's going to pull me into another hug. 'Thank you, William. Where will you sleep?'

Good question. 'Hopefully in here.'

He raises an eyebrow and waits for an explanation.

'Mum might kick up a fuss, but I doubt it.'

'Wake me if you sleep in here.'

'Why?'

'So I can move.'

'Don't be an idiot,' I say, and it comes out a little bit too sharp. He turns his head and looks at me through the corners of his eyes. 'Sorry—I'm sorry. But I can't make you move out of the bed. I'm never going to do that. Either I'll sleep on the floor, or—'

'William? Dinner's ready!'

We both jump at the sound of Dad's voice.

'Down in a sec,' I call back, making Dan jump *again*. 'Shit. Sorry.'

He catches my shoulders in his hands and speaks with his lips in my hair. 'Do not apologise.' I am *warm*. 'Go down and eat. Talk with your family. I will be right here.'

Before I can make an absolute fool out of myself, he releases me. He whispers again that he isn't leaving and watches, smiling, while I walk out.

I have to double back just to make sure he's there. He laughs, tells me to eat, and I carry that laugh with me the whole way down stairs.

Fifty-Two

The mood downstairs is *weird*.

'That's Daniel?' Mum asks, handing me my bowl but not quite letting me take it.

I nod.

'Is he okay?'

'Yeah, I think so,' I mutter. 'Do you mind that he's here?'

'No, no.' That smile again. 'Did you know he was coming?'

'Definitely not. I'd have said—or asked—if I had.'

'Yeah, I know you would,' she sighs, giving me a quick squeeze and surrendering the bowl so we can walk to the table. 'He's the one you spoke to on the phone Christmas Day, yeah?'

Heavens. 'Yeah, he is.'

'Been in New Zealand.'

'Yep.'

'No family.'

God, shoot me. 'Nope.'

'How long is he staying for?'

'I don't know. I hope for a couple of days,' I admit, sitting down opposite Kirst. She is still smirking at me, and it's distracting. 'Is that okay?'

'Yeah, of course it is.'

'How *old* is he?' Kirst asks and, honestly, I want to kick her. My silence is telling and they all look over at me. 'He's clearly older than you.'

'Why does it matter?'

'I want to be sure he's not creeping on my baby brother.'

'He isn't.'

'Are you sure?'

'Fu—Jesus Christ, Kirst,' I hiss. Mum and Dad are just

247

watching us, leaving it to my sister to sort this out. 'He's twenty-six. But I'm *nineteen*—'

'You're still a baby.'

'In four years I'll be a *doctor*.'

'*Still* a baby,' she snaps. 'He's what, six or seven years older than you?'

I shrug.

'Hasn't he got any friends his age?'

'Not really, no.'

'Not really?'

'Kirst, he—' I sigh and rub my eyes. If he's staying with us for a few days, I may as well tell them. 'He's been in a really bad relationship. Like, so fucking bad.'

'William—'

'Really bad.' My voice shakes. 'And I happened to be there while he was trying to escape it and we—we've shared a lot.' I manage to look at my sister for a moment and her mouth is open. 'His ribs were broken, and he didn't exactly have a *good* life before the relationship, and he's been struggling with a load of things but he—he's a really nice guy.'

Kirst breathes out a long sigh. 'Are you sure he's not a danger to you?'

I laugh at the thought of Daniel doing anything to hurt me. It's outrageous to even mumble the idea. 'Definitely not a danger to me.'

'You're sure?'

I nod and Dad starts eating.

'He's very tall.'

I laugh again. 'He is. He wouldn't hurt me—I think we're actually best friends.'

Kirst mock-gasps. 'Do *not* tell Peter that.'

I convince myself to start eating, even though I feel sick. I think it's from excitement. 'I think Peter knows. Dan said Peter gave him our address.'

Kirst slams her cutlery down on the table and groans. 'Okay, *stop*. Is this guy into you?'

'Kirst,' Mum hisses, and I've made eye-contact with my sister for a moment too long. Or maybe it's just the right amount of time. 'Don't joke about that sort of thing.'

'About what, Mum?' Kirst challenges, leaning into the table with her eyebrows raised. 'If Dan's first move after getting back from *New Zealand* was to come and see Will, I'd say that's some good commitment. If they're together—'

'We're not,' I say quickly, cutting in because this is *too* much like every conversation I've had in the last few weeks with Cas and Peter. 'We're—we're not.'

Kirst isn't convinced. Shit. '*But,*' she says, dragging it out, 'if they *were,* it doesn't matter. Does it?'

She has thrown our parents right under the bus and I can't quite breathe.

'Of course not,' Mum mutters, staring down at her dinner. 'Of course it doesn't. It doesn't matter.'

Hmm.

'I guess there's no chance of you getting him pregnant,' Dad says, trying to lift the mood and failing miserably. I feel trapped, like a wild animal surrounded by guns, and I'm ready to have a full argument but Kirst speaks again.

'That's beside the point.' She waves her fork around. 'It doesn't matter *who* Will falls in love with, right?'

Jesus Christ.

Mum looks up at me and shakes her head, lips in a tight line which I'm sure she thinks looks like a smile. Dad isn't much better, and I can see the way he's trying to think of something else mildly amusing to say, so I speak looking at Kirst.

'Yeah, well.' I do a terrible job of not showing my sister how much her support means to me. 'Doesn't matter, but thanks.'

She's smiling quietly to herself. She fucking *knows.*

'Welcome,' Kirst says, before the parents can be awful. 'Is he staying in your room?'

'I guess.'

'There's space for you both, isn't there?' Kirst asks and, Jesus, I can't keep up with her. Does she approve of him?

Mum puts her cutlery down. 'I don't—I don't think—'

'You let Peter stay in his room last summer,' Kirst says

very quickly, speaking over her. She's like a body guard. 'Let him stay with Dan.'

'Why do you care so much?' Dad asks and I'm sort of glad he *did* ask because it's what I want to know, too.

'Peter messaged me this morning telling me he was coming,' Kirst admits. I almost stand up. 'He told me that you two are really close and you miss him.'

Mum and Dad look like they've both just been slapped.

They're all waiting for me to say something, so I shrug. 'I guess, yeah.'

Mum squints at me for a moment. 'Are you comfortable with him?'

I nod.

She gestures to the ceiling. 'Do you want to stay up there with him?'

Enthusiastic nod.

'Fine. Is this what you want?'

I swallow and nod again. 'Definitely.'

Kirst grins. Mum and Dad go back to eating their dinner, occasionally throwing little glances at me. I can see their thoughts whirring—*is our son gay? Is this his boyfriend?*

I'd love to say *yes*.

*

I go upstairs as soon as I can justify it to check on Dan. He is fast asleep. The light is off, and his rucksack is down on the floor by my wardrobe, with his shirt folded carefully just to one side. The duvet—*my* duvet—is pulled right up to his hair, and he's lying on his front, so I wouldn't really know he's topless without spotting that discarded shirt.

I sink down to my knees and stare at him. God, he must have been tired—for him to be so fast asleep and in an unfamiliar place.

He shuffles a bit and I'm expecting him to wake up but he just hooks his arm above his head. His face is pressed right into my pillow, like he *likes* the smell, and I'm struggling to believe what I'm seeing.

He's here, in my room.

Everything he does is perfect, but there's something tranquil about the way he sleeps. I'd watch him all night.

I didn't think I'd see him again this side of the new year. I didn't think he'd tan in the sun, either, but there's a definite line around his neck and arms where he was covered by a t-shirt. It makes his hair look brighter, but that could be an effect of the sun, too.

It's still early in the evening. I can't really justify going to bed, yet.

Slowly, knees creaking, I push up to my feet. It takes a huge amount of strength to turn away and leave the room. I pull the door closed behind me, leaving him in a safe little bubble, and creep back downstairs. It's hours before I can justify going to bed, and each minute scratches against me like a blunt knife.

Fifty-Three

I wake to the sound of Dan timidly asking for coffee and I'm glad, now, that I slept on the floor. Mum's in the doorway, being entirely pleasant to him, and neither of them notice I'm awake until I fumble for my glasses.

Some days, I really hate not being able to see clearly as soon as I open my eyes.

Mum smiles at me. 'Morning, William.'

I mumble a hello and stretch. My bedroom floor is *mildly* more comfortable than my floor at uni, and I guess I'm grateful. 'Are you making drinks?'

She rolls her eyes at me, says something about me being lazy to Daniel, and leaves us.

The air in the room is perfectly still.

'Part of me thought I'd made it up.' I hardly dare to look at him in case I *have* made it up.

'What?'

'You being here,' I say. He's sat up in my bed, with the duvet just covering up to his knees. Shirtless. Tanned. He looks a lot healthier than when he went away. His cheeks are a little bit softer and he looks bright—but the good night's sleep could have helped that.

His hair is a little bit too long. It's flicking up behind his ears.

'I'm here,' he whispers, a moment late.

I smile at him and shuffle around, facing him but putting a little bit more space between us. I don't need to be tempted to join him in bed—not when Mum's about to come back upstairs.

'Is it okay?'

I roll my eyes and pull my knees up to my chin. 'I've missed you.'

'Do you mind that I asked Peter for your address?'

I shake my head.

'Do you mind that I went straight to sleep?'

I laugh and shake my head again. 'Dan, *no*. I don't mind—I don't mind at all because I'm just so glad you're here. You look like New Zealand suited you.'

It works—he smiles and looks down at himself. He stretches out his arms and casts his eyes up, from his fingers to his shoulders. 'I think it did.'

'Meet any cute boys?' *Jesus*. Did I just ask that?

He looks almost as surprised to hear it come from my mouth as I am and shakes his head. 'None who were notable.'

'Oh?'

'None, William.'

I grin at him, so he knows I'm not trying to push him, and shrug. 'You had a nice time though, right?'

'Oh, yeah.' He twists a little bit, so he's facing me, and I want to tell him to be careful. But it's been months—his ribs are fine, now. This doesn't stop me worrying. 'I took photos for you.'

My face lights up. 'You did?'

'Many.'

'You'll have to show me later.'

I'm more excited about seeing the photos than I think either of us expected, and I'm making him talk about them when Mum comes back in. She asks why he went, what he saw, what the flight was like. They're all things I want to ask but I leave it to Mum and, when she eventually leaves us to get up and dressed, I feel like the topic of New Zealand has been exhausted.

The next question he asks me is a thousand miles away from New Zealand.

'What happened with Lilley?'

I guess this is payback for my question about cute boys.

'You know,' I mutter, fiddling with the hem of my clean jumper. He waits. 'We slept together.'

It feels horrible to say. It shouldn't—it was two weeks ago—but it tastes like bleach in my mouth. And now I'm thinking about it, and I haven't thought about it since getting home.

253

'Are you going to again?'

I shake my head very sharply. An attempt to look at him fails, and I look out of the window, instead. The world outside is murky and damp. 'It wasn't like that. It was a spur of the moment sort of thing.'

'I think I'm struggling to understand why.'

He sounds uncomfortable. I'm pretty sure he's frowning at me.

'Peter pissed me off,' I say, and he wasn't expecting that.

He comes to stand beside me and I consider closing my eyes, so I'm not tempted to shoot a glance at him that might get stuck.

'I kissed Lil to—to prove a point and it sort of went from there.'

He's being unusually curious. 'What point?'

'Jesus—' it slips out, and now he thinks I'm annoyed with him. All the irritation is at myself. 'Peter was asking about you, and made it sound like I'm *hiding* something from him—like we're in some secret relationship I don't trust him enough to tell him about—but obviously I *would* tell my friends if I was in a relationship. And I *wouldn't* kiss someone else if I was in a relationship.' I'm not really breathing properly. 'I reacted badly, but it proved my point.'

The silence after my rambling echoes through me. With each reverberation I'm catching my breath, expecting him to say something.

It takes a long time.

'Did Peter get the message?'

'I think so.'

'Good.' He moves so he's leaning against the windowsill, facing me, and I'm definitely being rude by staring out of the window. He can cope with that. 'I'll try to not be too hurt knowing the thought of being in a relationship with me is so upsetting to you.'

What?

My jaw drops open and I spin to say something stupid like *I'd love to be in a relationship with you* when the door swings open and in walks Kirst.

I *glare* at her.

'Am I interrupting?' she asks, one eyebrow raised as she purposefully glances between us and the bed. 'Mum's making a fuss over breakfast so I think you need to get downstairs. Morning, Dan,' she adds, dropping the eyebrow to smile at him. It's lifted again when she fixes her eyes back on me. 'Get moving.'

I roll my eyes but, thankful she's saved me from *that* conversation, take a step to follow her. Dan doesn't copy me and I pause.

'Are you coming?' I try to smile at him but I think I've really upset him. By not answering, by making such a *fuss* over whatever crap Peter had been assuming.

'Yeah. I will go outside—'

'I'll come with you.' I think I've ruined everything. I'm sure I have.

He starts to shake his head and it's been a while since he's done the blunt *no, thank you* thing to me.

'Please?'

Thank heavens, my pathetic attempt at begging him works. He smiles very slightly, picks up his phone and cigarettes, and indicates I should lead the way.

I do, but I check over my shoulder every few steps.

I take him through the house, mumbling a quick *yes, in a minute* to Mum as we cut through the kitchen, and into the back garden.

I should have put shoes on. Or a coat.

He doesn't comment on the soggy patio or the cold air that seems to stick to us, even though it must be horrible after spending weeks in a New Zealand summer, and lights a cigarette. He's not looking at me.

Fine. I guess I'm going to have to just say this.

'Dan, it wasn't because it was *you*.'

His head snaps up to look at me so quickly I almost take a step back.

'You know—you know it's not *that*. It was the way Peter was making assumptions and talking about them as if they were facts and I *hate* people assuming things about me.' Doesn't

255

everyone? 'Are you upset?'

He fixes an entirely fake smile on his face and shakes his head. 'Thank you for explaining.'

'What's wrong?'

'What?'

I catch his free hand and I'm being too pushy, I know I am. 'What else have I done to upset you?'

'You haven't—'

'Dan, come on—'

'I'm *fine*, William,' he whispers, giving me a *not fine* look through wide eyes and chalky skin.

I want to step towards him, but my feet are stuck to the ground.

'Thank you for explaining.'

Whatever it is, he's not going to tell me. I only have myself to blame. I make my way very slowly towards him, creeping up on him while he's concentrating on the cigarette, and he jumps a little bit when I put my hand on his waist.

'I'm sorry for upsetting you.' I watch very closely when he closes his eyes. 'I'm really upset I did it.'

He hums, wrapping his free arm around my back. Thank *God*.

'I shouldn't have slept with Lil.'

'Ah,' he sighs, pressing his face into my hair. He takes a deep breath and his chest moves against mine, almost knocking me backwards. 'It does not matter.'

'I think it does.'

'No.'

I laugh. Because it's so ridiculous that I slept with my ex —because it's so ridiculous that Dan is in my garden, smoking a cigarette—because I don't know what else to do now I know I upset Dan by apparently not wanting to be in a relationship with him.

Does that mean he *wants* a relationship?

I back-step very quickly through my thoughts. It's not that. It's a big thing for Dan to trust someone as much as he trusts me. If even *I* can find things about him that would put me off dating him, how is he going to convince someone he doesn't know yet that he's worth a shot?

I'm thinking this through with my face pressed against his neck. Maybe it isn't giving me the most clarity. Maybe being able to feel the steady thudding of his heart is giving me too much confidence—or making me too desperate.

'Dan, I'm—I'm—'

'Will, I need you to put this away before I can wash up!' Kirst yells, throwing open the back door and releasing a whole flood of demons. I hold a finger up to her and stagger away from Dan, fully aware that she's been watching us and burning up with it. And, shit, I was going to tell him.

Wait. Does Peter know I'm bi, now?

Dan smiles softly at me and kills the cigarette. 'Are you okay?'

I can't think of how to answer, so I hum.

He finds my hand with his. 'What were you going to say?'

No fucking way can I say it now. 'I'm sorry I upset you,' I whisper. He's going to argue, so I close my eyes. 'Don't say I didn't because I did. I know I did. But you're my best friend and I trust you more than *anyone* and I love that we're friends now and it was honestly just that Peter was making assumptions about me. I would have been pissed off if he decided I was with anyone.' I squint at him through one eye. 'Do you understand?'

He sighs and nods, trying a little smile for me. 'I thought I had done something wrong.'

'Nope, never. Not at all.'

The little smile grows. 'Thank you.' We stand there, managing to forget that I'm meant to be tidying and almost forgetting how cold it is. But he waves the cigarette stub and frowns a little bit at me. 'What shall I do with this?'

Fifty-Four

He asks how long he can stay and I quite honestly say 'as long as you want'. So, when he asks when I'm going back to university, I suggest he goes back with me.

He lights up.

'Do you mind?' he asks, glowing face shadowed slightly by a little frown. He's leaning towards me, sat at one end of the settee, and I resist the urge to reach and hold his cheeks and just touch his hand—lightly, subtly, with my fingertips—instead.

'Do I look like I mind?'

We clear it with Mum, of course, and she says something about making sure I do plenty of revision.

'I am used to him revising,' Daniel says, grinning across at me. 'I think I might be able to sit some of these exams, after this.'

Bad idea. I'd never be able to concentrate on an exam if he were in the room with me.

Mum asks him about his course, and they talk for a while. It's perfect. It's heaven. He's sitting with his ankles crossed, face freshly shaved, and a mug of coffee held gently between his hands. She's stretched across the other settee, laughing every now and then and glancing at me occasionally. I reluctantly leave them about an hour after lunch to do a bit of revision because I've definitely fallen behind and it's quite some time before he comes and finds me.

I'm just a room away, but the difference having him so close makes it tangible. I can taste him in the air.

He barely has to speak. He just sits at the table, with his book, and spends time near me. He laughs a few times when I grumble at myself—when I make a mistake, or when I drop a pen lid. He offers to quiz me on the ever-growing pile of flash cards when I'm done and I have missed the sound of him pronouncing Latin names so much I struggle to say 'yes, please'.

I sleep on the floor again. He doesn't question it, and I hope he realises I'm just nervous about Mum. It's not that I don't want to be near him.

And, if I'm honest with myself, I'm still a bit scrambled up from admitting to him that I would date a guy. He hasn't mentioned it. And his reaction to thinking I *wouldn't* date him has hurt, because I've spent the whole day wondering if it's actually what he wants. I dream about it. I think I always dream about it. I dream about kissing him and holding his hand and just being *near* him. Dreaming about even just *seeing* him has featured a lot since he went to New Zealand. But who can blame me? When we spend time together, we sit *together*. I don't think he's noticed what lying with my head on his shoulder does to me.

Maybe it's a good thing that he doesn't notice. Or, maybe, it would all just be easier if I told him.

It would be so much easier if I told him.

But he isn't ready for a relationship—he's told me that. *He's* been honest. And, even though I know he's not ready for it, surely it would be best if I just told him what's going on.

Dan, I think I've fallen in love with you. But it's okay—I'm not going to try to make you my boyfriend because I know you're not ready for that. I just want you to know how I feel.

It should be so simple.

Fifty-Five

We're sitting in silence when Kirst comes in. I think she's going to ask me to do something and I'm prepared to say *in a minute* when she asks, 'is this what you do for fun?', instead.

I glare at her. 'Since when has exam season been a time for fun?'

'Uh, since whenever your boyfriend comes over for New Year's.'

Excuse me?

'We're not—'

'I'm not his boyfriend,' Daniel says, and it hurts like a bone saw stuck in my ribs. He's smiling, not at all pissed off like I am. 'And it upsets him when people think I am.'

'That's not fair,' I say, voice tight. 'You weren't there, Dan—it wasn't like that.'

'What was it like?' Oh, shit. His smile has completely gone and he looks… desperate. The sudden change makes me hold my breath. 'I still do not understand why it makes you so upset.'

Oh, no.

I very much need to tell him about Peter and Matthew, but I've forgotten every word in the English language—and I don't know any of the other languages he knows, and it's getting harder to keep my head up with each beat of my heart.

Kirst tries to help. 'Will, it doesn't matter if—'

'I know it doesn't matter. It's not that it's—it's *you*,' I nod at Dan, who looks like he's made of stone, 'and it's not that Peter thinks I have a *boyfriend* because I—I—'

Because I might one day. I really hope I do.

'Okay, good,' Kirst says, speaking over where my sentence fell flat. I should have said *because I'm bi* but the room is spinning, like I stood up too quickly, and Dan and I are staring at each other. She doesn't seem to notice. 'I'm not going to lie to you, but I *did* worry my little brother was a little homophobe for a few moments there.'

I can't look away from Daniel but I wish, with every bone in my body, that I could get up and leave. I can't feel anything. I can't even find my mouth to move my lips to make a sentence. I just know I look devastated, and I'm glad.

'Obviously not,' Kirst says quickly, leaning towards me. Shit. *Shit.* 'Will, are you gay?'

Technically? No. I shake my head.

'Okay. You know I don't give a shit if you are, right?'

I nod. I need to find my voice.

'You know I love you,' Daniel whispers. 'No matter what.'

Nothing in the history of the universe has ever hurt so much. He is perfect, leaning towards me with his arms on the table, the sleeves of his jumper pushed up to show his tanned, scarred wrists. Shit. I close my eyes for the first time since Kirst started this conversation and I would sell my soul to hear him say that every day.

Instead of having a complete breakdown, I blurt out the rest of mine and Peter's argument. I definitely should have told Dan this a couple of days ago.

'Peter knows Matthew.' It rushes from me and I don't dare open my eyes. 'Anthony's on the same sports team as him and they've spent time together and Matthew's been telling lies about you. They—they know things.' I squint at him, expecting something awful. Instead, he looks tired. 'I didn't want to tell you while you were away but Peter said some—some stupid shit and it really upset me—'

He slips from his chair and comes over to kneel beside me. I hold my breath, keeping the tears in for just a moment more.

'Don't be upset,' he whispers, and that's it. Snotty tears burst from me and, breaking my heart, he laughs. 'Hey, shush. I'm okay. I know he knows. We spoke just before I left New Zealand. I asked for your address, and he told me everything.' His hand finds my cheek, wiping away some tears. 'It's okay. I'm okay. Peter knows the truth about him now and he apologised for what he said about us. Stop crying, William.'

I try. God, I try, but I've felt so tense for so long and Dan just said he loves me. It's like how I say I love Peter, and I can't process how much this hurts.

'Is this why you were so upset with him?'

I sniff away tears and frown.

'Because he was talking about me and Matthew?'

Largely, I guess. I nod, because it's a great way to get out of explaining how crushed I feel every time I imagine having the courage to tell Dan how consumed I am by him, and he stretches up to put his arms around me. He smells amazing.

'I'm okay, now. I'm okay. I'm safe.'

I'd love to never let go, but my sister is gawking at us and I feel like I'm on stage. As soon as Dan sits back, she speaks.

'Who's Matthew?'

Ugh.

Dan keeps one arm around my back and explains. 'My ex. We were together for just over a year but he broke my ribs.' Feeling the way I shiver, he tightens his arm around me. 'William has been an amazing friend, but I think Peter was jealous of all the attention I was getting.'

He throws a smile up at me which would have turned my insides to mush even on a good day. Feeling the way I am, moments after hearing him say *I love you*, it turns to smoke. One breath of wind and I'll be gone.

Kirst, bless her, catches entirely the wrong part of this. Her *concerned big sister* expression switches to a grin and she glances between us. 'You're gay?'

I can't believe this. I'm watching Dan come out to my sister and I can't even breathe the word *bisexual*.

Dan is smiling, proud of himself, and nods. The enormity of it hits me square in the chest. This guy—who killed for a country which wouldn't protect him and who barely escaped his last relationship alive—is *proud* he's gay. It's the most beautiful thing I have ever seen.

And now they're talking. I think they're trying to subtly give me a moment to collect myself, but they're absorbed with each other and Dan's telling her about Matthew and it's too

262

much.

Hoping they don't notice, I sink so my head's on the table.

It's times like this I expect a text from Peter.

I almost pull my phone out and call him, but Dan's arm is still around me and his thumb is resting on the seam of the waistband of my jeans. It's a perfectly natural crinkle in fabric to rest on, but one centimetre and his thumb would be *inside* my clothes. That's quite an alarming thought so I sit up, legs crossed, and try to join the conversation.

Dan doesn't seem too concerned about Matthew knowing so much about us. I think I'm more worried about it than he is. He explains, sitting on the floor beside me, that he's feeling more confident—like he would be able to stand up for himself, now. He's put on some weight since leaving for New Zealand, and I think it's done him some good.

The conversation lulls, and Kirst gets to her feet. 'Do you guys want drinks? I think we deserve alcohol or something after that.'

Dan laughs and stands up, holding his hand out for me. Oh, no. I take it, because I can't ever miss an opportunity to feel his skin, and I'm still holding it when we join Kirst in the kitchen.

'I'm going outside for a moment,' Dan whispers, dropping my hand into the empty air and shooting through the back door before I can even say *okay*. I'm left staring after him, hand prickling and eyes burning from tears.

'That was intense,' Kirst says, voice low and hand resting on the top of a bottle of pop.

I shrug.

'Promise me it's not always like this.'

I snort, dragging my eyes away from Dan. 'Nah. Normally we just sit and I revise and he reads. Or we talk. We do a lot of talking.'

'About what?'

'All sorts.'

'Have you ever met this Matthew?'

'Nope, and I don't want to.'

'Good.'

I look up at her.

'You are happy, aren't you?'

'Incredibly so.'

'Make sure he keeps you that way.'

'Kirst—'

'Friends are meant to make you happy,' she says, raising an eyebrow and giving me a *look*. 'But he smokes.'

I properly laugh at that and glance out of the window at him. 'Yeah. I know.'

'Doesn't that piss you off?'

'Yeah, but he's gone through enough in the last few months. I can't be mad at him.'

She hums and splashes some vodka into a glass, topping it up with the pop she's been teasing open. 'I can tell him off though, right?'

Again, I manage a laugh. 'Yeah, go for it.'

Fifty-Six

I'm spending New Year's Eve with Daniel.

I want to scream about this with someone. I want to talk about how significant this is but, instead, wine soaks through my veins and I grin and lean into him too many times.

We're all sitting in the living room, a few bottles into the night, when Dan crushes us all in Scrabble *again*. Mum mutters something about second languages and I am so proud I might burst.

'English is one of five,' he says, and they don't understand to begin with. There are a few shared glances, but Kirst sees the way I'm beaming and gasps. 'Russian, English, French, Spanish, German. I learned from my mother and while working.'

Kirst is busy gawking at him and I recognise myself in her. Fortunately for my embarrassment, I already know this about him. And, instead over being overwhelmed, I'm just the smuggest thing on Earth.

'French?' Mum asks, leaning forward. Dan nods, and she asks him something and, *oh my God*, he replies in gorgeous, smooth French that sounds so different to his English that I have to stare at him.

I feel light-headed.

Kirst is still watching me, eyes giant saucers above her nose, and I bite on my lip. I am so obvious I may as well be wearing a high-vis jacket, but it doesn't matter with Kirst.

'Wow,' Dad mutters. I'm inclined to agree. 'Doesn't this mean you're smarter than William?'

Dan laughs and blushes. It's beautiful. It's so beautiful. My head is swimming a little bit and I think it's time I swapped wine for water.

'No,' Daniel says, 'just that I know more languages.'

I mean—that's a fact. That's not something anyone could

265

argue with. Dan does this—he's very good at putting the conversation somewhere no one can hurt it or break it.

Dad makes us all stand up for the count-down and it would be far too easy to stretch up and kiss Daniel. He's right beside me. The clock hits midnight and this is it—this is the first thing I'll do this year.

I hug Dan. He hugs me. We'd hold each other forever, I think, but there are three other people around us who I owe hugs to. So I pull myself away from him, knowing just how lucky I am that he's the first person I've touched this year, and turn to Mum. I see Dan and Dad awkwardly exchange hugs and then Kirst flies at me, pulling me away from Mum and almost choking me with her arm around my neck.

'So proud of you,' she whispers. I laugh, trying to keep an eye on Dan as he lets Mum hug him, and pat her hands.

'Thanks.'

'I mean it. He's cute—'

'Kirst—'

She shuts me up with a kiss to my cheek. 'New year, okay? You've got this. You're both going to smash it.'

I give her a squeeze. 'Thanks. You too—you know I'm proud of you.'

She just winks, releases me, and catches Dan. Dad and I share a very quick hug and that's it: the last night of the year is done.

I'm itching to go to my room with Dan.

It takes about an hour. We finish the last bottle of wine and pick at crisps and limp salad until Mum announces she's going to bed and I almost leap to my feet.

I count, instead. Down from ten.

And then I turn to Dan. He's gazing at me, blue eyes hazy from wine, and it breaks my voice. I try again.

'Want to go to bed?'

He nods.

We say goodnight. He follows me upstairs, not breathing a word, and it takes far too long for my feet to hit each step—for my body to move through the air, up to my bedroom. I feel like a record that's been slowed down.

And then we're there. In my room. And it's New Year's Eve.

If we were at uni, there would be no doubt I'd cuddle up to him under the duvet. We'd sleep holding each other and it would be a bit awkward in the morning but we'd just do it without thinking.

But we're in my parents' house and I'm definitely going to sleep on the floor.

As soon as I shut the door he breathes my name and, when I turn to look, he sweeps me into his arms and presses a kiss into my hair.

Oh, shit.

'You made this year bearable,' he whispers. I close my eyes and I'm just about staying on my feet, clinging to the sides of his shirt and putting all of my weight through my toes. 'I could not have done this without you.'

I could try to play it cool—I could *try* to hide just how much I adore him.

'You're the best thing to happen to me in a long time,' I hear myself say. 'I still can't believe you're here.'

A light chuckle, and he releases me. But he kissed me. He kissed my hair. 'I'm here. We should sleep. I think you are a little bit tipsy.'

God. Say tipsy again, *please.*

I just grin at him and, reluctant, let go of his shirt. 'Only a tiny bit.' I sweep my glasses off my face and put them on the side. There—I'm sober enough to understand the risk of treading on them. 'I'm mostly tired, I think.'

He hums and turns the light off. We could almost believe we're entirely alone.

'I'm sorry about Peter.'

I thought we'd got over this. I grunt and pull my shirt off, not looking at him.

'Tell me if I ever upset you like that.'

'You, too.'

He chuckles and the rustling of fabric tells me he's shirtless, too. It would be so nice to sleep next to him. 'Okay. I mean it when I say I'm lucky to have you.'

I sit down on the floor before looking at him. He's standing at the foot of the bed, clearly not sure where he's supposed to go.

I nod to the pillow. 'I mean it when I say I'm lucky to have *you*. I really did think I might lose you.'

He sighs and comes towards me, sitting on the edge of the bed and doing a brilliant job of gazing at me. 'I am only out of that because of you.' There's another little sigh before he lies down, on his front with his arms folded under his head, face towards me. 'I would definitely have gone back to him.'

'Glad you didn't.'

'Me, too.'

For once, our silence is a little bit uncomfortable. I *think* it's because we're staring at each other through the darkness, each of us trapped in the whites of the other's eyes. I feel too far away from him.

He kissed my hair.

'Goodnight, William.'

I lie down and close my eyes and imagine he's closer than he is.

'See you in the morning.'

I hum and turn around, so I can't be tempted to reach for him or anything else stupid. 'Goodnight,' I mumble, and that's it.

It's the end of the night—it's the end of the year. And I got to spend it with Daniel.

Fifty-Seven

On New Year's Day, Mum makes us go for a walk. For some reason, this makes Daniel laugh—and he's still smirking at me when we pile into Dad's car and drive the short distance to one of our favourite patches of heathland.

Dan's not going to explain why he thinks this is funny, even though we hang back from my family and let them walk ahead of us. Even though we're talking about *our stuff*—about my exams and the placement I'm starting soon, about what he's going to do for the rest of the year, about Peter and Cas and Lilley.

'I am worried about Matthew,' he says, when the movement of walking has warmed me up enough to unzip a layer.

I frown up at him and almost trip over.

'Not *about* him—about what is going to happen.'

I nod and let him go first past a tree.

'I think you will be safe. But I *am* more worried about being on campus with you. Especially if he knows Peter.'

I wasn't expecting that. 'Oh.' I kick the ground. It's childish, but I feel like it helps. Somehow. 'That sucks.'

He flashes a smile at me. 'Does it?'

Oh, you know it does.

I glare at him but he keeps smirking. Damn it. 'You know I'd miss you.'

'You know you're always welcome at my apartment.'

I hope that's true. We keep walking, still a way behind my family, and he looks up at the sky. I'm ready to catch him if he stumbles and manage to trip myself up again, instead.

God, how embarrassing.

He catches my arm in his hand and laughs at me, loud enough for Kirst to turn around and look at us. We make eye contact and I blush and it's so bad that I almost trip over again.

269

Which just makes Dan hold me even tighter. Which just make everything worse.

Kirst keeps walking, drawing our parents' attention to something else, and Dan goes one step further and pulls me right into his arms. My feet are awkwardly crossed and I'm definitely going to fall over as soon as he lets go of me but it's nice. It's very nice.

'I'm not putting you in danger,' he whispers, head bowed into my neck. I grunt and close my eyes. 'You understand that he *would* hurt you.'

'I know, I know. But I don't want to only get to see you on weekends.'

He sighs and I feel him press against my neck. Was that another kiss? 'We would still see each other.'

'But only at your house.'

'Does that matter?'

'Yes.'

Standing up, he raises an eyebrow at me.

'As I said. It will *suck*.'

He pulls back. Without him wrapped around me, the air feels *cold*. I zip my coat back up.

'I will still see you,' he promises. 'We will still have Sunday nights but don't make me risk him seeing you with me.'

I pout but accept it and he completely surprises me by taking my hand before we start walking again, fingers slipped through fingers. 'I guess seeing you *once* a week is better than you flying off to New Zealand.'

His laugh makes my chest ache. 'I did miss you.'

'Nowhere *near* as much as I missed you.'

'You had Cassie and Peter and Lilley,' he points out. 'I was on my own.'

I shoot a glare at him. 'You did choose to go on your own, though.'

'You wouldn't have been able to leave because of all your work—you said that yourself.'

'Yeah, but if you'd asked maybe we would have gone away another time. Or we could have just gone somewhere else.'

His hand tightens around mine. I can't believe this—
we're holding hands on our first walk of the new year. I feel
wild, like I might take flight at any moment.

'Maybe we still will.'

I can't physically reply to that without sounding like I'm
choking on something, so I let us walk in silence for a while. If
anyone looks back and sees us holding hands, I don't notice.
I'm not even really paying attention to birdsong—I'm lost in
thought of a plane journey with Dan. A hotel room with him.
Exploring a new, foreign country with him—maybe with him
translating things for me or talking to restaurant staff.

He drops my hand and I look up in time to see Mum
watching us. Ah, crap. I'm too out of it to react and just keep
walking, my hand feeling horribly free and alone as it swings in
the cold between us.

'Will I ruin it if I smoke?' Daniel whispers, and it takes me
a moment to realise he's asking for my permission. I roll my
eyes.

'Your lungs? Yes.'

He sighs and doesn't move to take out a cigarette, like I
thought he would.

'Hey,' I poke him very gently. 'You can smoke, silly. I'm
just being worried about you.'

'I think smoking is much less harmful to me than heroin,'
he mutters, and I think I've upset him. He's not looking
anywhere near me. 'And I don't think I could quit.'

I touch his arm and ask a question I've never thought of
before. 'How long have you smoked for?'

He chews his lip. 'Ten years.'

I swear under my breath and he turns away from me,
hiding. 'You're doing brilliantly with everything else, though.'
I've ruined it. 'Do you still take your prescription?'

He nods, still facing away with his arms crossed around
his waist.

'I'm proud of you.'

He shoots me a glare over his shoulder and I bristle.

'*Hey.* I'm pretty sure this is one of the things we said I'm allowed to be proud about.'

'I suppose so.'

'It is. And I was super proud yesterday,' I say, because I haven't been lovely enough to him recently and he needs to see how much I care. It's been a while since he's curled away like this. 'When you told Kirst you're gay.'

He shrugs. 'It is not a big thing.'

Excuse me? 'It is, because you don't know how people are going to react.'

'She is your sister.'

'Yeah, but you still don't know.'

He sighs and turns to face me.

'Every time you say it, you're opening yourself up to the world and giving everyone a chance to hurt you. But you say it anyway because you're stronger than they are and you *should* be proud of yourself.'

He catches my shoulders in his hands and holds eye-contact with me for a moment too long before responding. Like so many times before, his irises take my breath away. 'We might have to keep reminding ourselves of that,' he whispers, and I'm too surprised that he's included me in this to react when he leans in and kisses my cheek. 'Thank you.'

I can't quite open my eyes. I feel like I've been hit with a blast of something beautifully refreshing *and* beautifully calming. A mix of lemon and lavender. He kissed my cheek.

He *kissed* my cheek.

I think he realises he's destroyed me because he flashes a smirk and fishes out a cigarette. He takes a few steps away from me to light it and glances down the valley, at my family, to remind me we should be walking.

Yeah.

The problem is, I'm not sure I have legs any more. I'm not sure I'm connected to my body because he kissed my cheek and said *we* because he fucking knows I'm bi and he's just waiting for me to say it.

I should say it. I'm watching him breathe through that cigarette and I adore him—I really do—but I can't risk losing whatever this thing is. It's a fragile thing. It's a tense, strained thing that stretches between us and is desperately trying to pull us closer together. What if he doesn't like it? What if I scare him, and he runs away, and this thing snaps under the extra pressure?

I can't do it.

I just smile at him and make sure I remember how it felt to have our fingers together somewhere we weren't alone. I make sure I remember how it felt to have his lips pressed against my cheek.

Fifty-Eight

Time flies with Daniel. There's one more night at my house and then we're on a train back to uni, his rucksack and my suitcase on the floor ahead of us. He has his book on his lap, but he hasn't opened it yet.

He's talking to me.

I half considered spending the journey revising, but these couple of hours with Dan feel important. We haven't discussed who's going where once we reach the station, but from our conversation yesterday I guess he isn't coming back to my room. I'm not sure why he would, but I wish it was going to happen.

'I have another appointment on Monday,' he says, head back against the headrest but looking at me. 'Before work.'

I want to ask about this evening, but he's looking at me as if I've just done something fascinating. I'm smiling without meaning to, waiting for him to explain himself. 'What is it, Dan?'

'Do you want to stay with me on Sunday?'

'Yes, please.'

He chuckles, letting me see a flash of his teeth, and glances around the carriage. 'Good. And then your first exams are Wednesday and Thursday, yes?'

I whimper. 'Don't remind me.'

Another laugh. 'I will leave you alone from Monday.'

'*Hey*,' it comes out a little bit sharply, 'I need to know how your appointment goes.'

He shrugs. 'These are important exams.'

'You're important, too.'

Oops.

Fortunately, he smiles. He looks beautifully relaxed, skin still glowing golden from the New Zealand sun, and doesn't seem to be anticipating danger for once. 'I will still be here in a

274

month. You have one chance at this.'

I pull a face because he's right, but I don't like or accept it. 'I still have time for you. Let's just see how it goes, yeah?'

He hums and lets it go. I'm trying not to think he's just looking for an excuse to stop spending time with me because he literally just invited me to spend the night with him on Sunday. And that means he wants to see me, so I'm not allowed to get stroppy.

The train journey is far too short.

Our station pulls into sight and I almost just *don't* get off. Where would we end up? Somewhere in Wales, I think, but Dan's already standing up, and I have no right to hold him hostage. I grab my suitcase and lead the way to the door.

While we wait for the train to reach a standstill, he puts his arm around my back, hand on my waist. It lasts for moments—seconds, between reaching the door and catching ourselves on handles—but he's holding me.

We call for a taxi and I hope, for a few breathless heartbeats, I hope. Because we're getting *one*.

'The taxi can drop you off first,' he says, taking the opportunity in the car-park for a hasty cigarette. Disappointment hits my gut and I step away from the smoke. He sees. He moves away.

'Okay.'

He's pulled into himself, elbows digging to his ribs and body curled away from mine. I can't bring myself to apologise, because the disappointment is burying me, but I know it's unreasonable.

The taxi turns up and Dan doesn't speak to me. He kills his cigarette and walks around to the other side of the car and there's a chance we've fallen out. The driver asks where we're going and Dan gives my address.

I glare out of the window the whole of the fifteen-minute journey. I feel sick, and I'm blaming the travelling. Why am I being such a brat? Dan came to my house straight after getting home from his holiday. We had New Year's Eve together, so I've had way more time with him than I ever thought I'd get. I've been so lucky.

I think that's the problem. I don't want this luck to run out.

We pull up near my block and I'm about to mumble a thanks to the driver when Daniel reaches forward and pays. He tells the driver to keep the change and doesn't quite look at me before getting out of the taxi, catching his rucksack in his hand.

My *thanks* is lost as I scramble out of the car, dragging my suitcase with me. The door slams shut and I hold my breath.

'Don't say now you left your key at home,' he says, attempting a smile. But it's tight and lacks commitment. 'If you want me to go—'

'No, Dan. I never want you to *go*. That's the fucking problem.'

He throws his hands in the air and steps to nowhere in particular. 'I don't know what you want me to do.'

'Just—just be yourself,' I mutter, unable to come up with anything better. I'm sulking and I hate myself for it. Shit. 'Sorry, Dan.'

'I don't understand.'

God, he sounds upset. His words are heavy and I was trying to dig my key out of my pocket but now I'm staring up at him and I am one hundred percent going to cry. He's frowning, eyebrows pulled right together and lips pressed tight, and I want him to relax. Smile. Smirk. Roll his eyes. *Anything*.

'You should have just gone home if it's what you want to do.' I manage to soften my voice. Good. 'You didn't have to come here. I'm just being a dick.'

'What if I wanted to come here?'

'You made a very good point *against* being here with me.'

'Yeah, well, I did it last semester,' he mutters, hands in his pockets. 'If people see us together then *fuck* it.'

I think I'm going to collapse.

I'm meant to be getting my key. Instead, I'm staring up at him with huge eyes, jaw dropped but lips not quite open and heart drumming against my chest. And I can't decide what's had the biggest effect on me: *what* he's said or how he said *fuck*.

I don't get chance to wonder much longer.

His phone rings, and it's such an unusual occurrence that

neither of us react straight away. When he does realise he should answer it, he raises an eyebrow and half turns away.

I really shouldn't listen.

But who would be calling him? Owen, from the SU café? Peter, for some unimaginable reason? Matthew's number is blocked. That doesn't mean he wouldn't be able to use someone else's phone.

This thought registers at about the same time as the things Dan's saying get through to me and I freeze.

'No, I understand,' he breathes. 'Is he awake? Did he ask for me?' He glances at me, pale as a ghost, and turns away again. 'I will be a few minutes. I'm—I'm at the university. Okay, thank you. Which—which ward? Thank you.'

He hangs up.

'Matthew is in hospital and he asked to see me,' he says, still facing away. 'He overdosed New Year and just woke up.'

Shit. 'Dan—'

'I'm going.'

'No *way*.'

'He nearly died!' he cries, turning to look at me. He looks awful. He looks like he did that first Monday night. 'He nearly died. He could have died—'

'You could have died when he pushed you down the stairs!' I counter, abandoning my suitcase and stepping towards him.

Horribly, heartbreakingly, he backs away from me.

'How can you be sure it was the hospital?'

'It—it was a number I recognise,' he mumbles. 'From making my appointments.'

'Are you sure?'

'Yes.'

'It might be one of his friends—'

'It is the hospital,' he says, voice clipped. He's still holding his phone. 'I'm going to go now.'

'You can't!'

He just looks at me, raising the phone to his ear again. I'm breathless, speechless, and he orders a taxi.

'Five minutes.' He glances at his phone screen before

putting it away. 'He asked for me. I've got to make sure he's okay.'

I flounder for a moment. 'I'll come with you.'

'Absolutely *not*.'

'I can't let you go to him—'

'I can't have him in the same *building* as you, never mind the same room!' His voice rings through the cool air.

I blink quickly. 'And you think the same doesn't apply to you?'

'I need to see—'

'You *don't*, Dan!'

'If he'd died—'

'Then the world would be better off!' It echoes around us and he squints at me. 'Let him go.'

'You are training to be a doctor,' he reminds me, somehow so close that I can smell his skin. 'I hope you have better morals than this in three years' time.'

I'm winded, like he just backhanded me in the stomach. 'I can't let you go to him, Dan.'

'You can't stop me, either.' He steps away. Oh, *God*. I feel something press against my throat and reach for him, taking feeble handfuls of his jacket. He wipes me away. 'William—'

'If you go back to him he will never let you go again!'

He takes another step.

'Dan, I'm gonna lose you—'

He is stone. 'I'm worried about him. I need to see he's okay.'

I shake my head. What would he do if I tried to get in the taxi with him? 'He won't let you come back to me.'

'He doesn't have a choice.'

'You really think you'll be able to just walk out of there if he's nice to you?' I reach for his jacket again but my hand falters. 'You're giving up.'

'Is that what you think?' He slides a hand into his hair, looking like he's about to scream. I might join him. 'After *everything*—'

'After *everything* you're just going straight back to him! You're giving up!'

'William,' he snaps, and I hate him using my name like that, 'I need to see him. I don't expect you to understand.'

'Why wouldn't I understand?'

He shakes his head, walking away again. But he asked the taxi to pick him up from here—I heard the conversation. He can't be planning on going far.

'Why wouldn't I understand, Dan?'

He closes the distance between us in less than a breath. 'You do not know what it's like to have one person in the *world*. You do not know how much I relied on him or how much I owe him or how much I worshipped him.'

I can feel his breath on my face.

'He was everything to me. He was the first person I loved. He was the first person I trusted enough to tell I'm—I'm gay and you wouldn't understand that—of course you wouldn't.'

I'm broken. He's still talking, voice shaking like he's going to cry. I'm not crying. I'm not breathing.

'If he died from an addiction I have recovered from I couldn't live with myself.' Oh, just shoot me. I'm already bleeding. 'He asked for me. He is ill and he asked to see me and I *want* to see him.'

A taxi drives around the corner and parks a few metres away from us, here to take him away in record time. I expect one of us to say something else, but he turns to go.

I catch his arm. He tugs away, and I grab his jacket. His wrist. He frees himself again but I throw my arm around the front of his waist and I think I'm going to say *please don't go* but I do something altogether more desperate.

I kiss him.

I was aiming for his cheek, but my lips definitely grazed his. They're dry. I drop my arm from around him, like I've been burned, and the air between us is freezing. I stagger away, wishing more than anything that he would catch me and press his face into my hair or my neck, but he just stares at me.

I don't say anything. I couldn't. Not even if I was paid.

I grab my keys blindly from my pocket, turn, and stumble towards my block. I almost forget my suitcase. I don't see him get into the taxi, but the soft *thud* of a car door is followed

heartbreakingly quickly by the sound of the engine and I
almost don't make it to my room. The world is full of heavy
smoke and I wish he'd said something. I wish he'd stayed.

Fifty-Nine

There is absolutely no point in me trying to get any work done this afternoon. There is no point in me doing anything except sit by my phone, refreshing and refreshing the screen until a message from Dan comes through.

It takes several long, painful hours.

16:26 **Daniel**: I'm going home. He's okay. I won't see him again.

I wish that was reassuring. I wish I believed him. I wish I could phone him, but I feel like I've had every ounce of strength sucked from me and I don't reply for a long time.

17:03 **William**: Okay. I hope you're safe

17:05 **Daniel**: I am. Did you do some revision?

17:08 **William**: No

17:10 **Daniel**: Oh. Can I come over?

I'm not actually sure I can cope with seeing him, and I'm trying to work out how to reply when my phone rings. I expect it to be Daniel.

It's Lilley.

So I answer it, deciding this stilted conversation with Dan can be put on hold for a few minutes, and sit up a little bit.

'Hey,' I say, voice cracking. I cough.

'Hey, Will, are you back on campus?' Her voice brings some sort of *normal* back into the room and I stretch my neck, feeling like I've come out of hibernation.

'Yeah, why?'

'Are you doing anything tomorrow?'

She's speaking very quickly. I frown at the empty room and shake my head. 'No, just revision.'

'Brilliant. Could I steal you for a few hours in the morning?'

'Sure. What for?'

'I'll tell you when I see you,' she says, trying to laugh, trying to make this sound like it's a good thing. But, honestly, I've heard so much *bad* in the last few hours that I've forgotten what it's like to be optimistic. 'Don't worry. I'll come around to you for nine, alright?'

'Okay. Promise you're okay.'

'I'm okay, Will. How was Christmas?'

Christmas? Bleak. New Year? Bittersweet. I mumble some fluff about having a *great time* and being *so behind on revision now* and she laughs, sounding like she meant this one, and says goodbye.

I guess I should reply to Dan.

17:20 **William**: Yeah, come over.

Like I could ever turn down an opportunity to see him.

He doesn't reply to me. I realise I've abandoned my suitcase and summon the energy to start unpacking it, taking out all the washed clothes and hanging them in my wardrobe. It's mindless, productive movement which doesn't quite take my mind off the afternoon but which helps me to breathe. And I really need to remember to breathe.

My phone buzzes where I left it on the floor and, for a moment, I consider leaving it where it is. But I know it's Dan, and I wake the screen to see he's telling me he's here. Okay. I should let him in.

I kissed him.

We don't quite look at each other when I let him into my block. We don't talk on the short walk down the corridor and I think, when we reach the room, I'm just going to scream.

Instead of screaming, I lock the door and look up at him.

It's a mistake.

He looks even worse than when I last saw him.

He's pale, but I expected that. I expected the strong smell of cigarettes. I didn't expect how red and raw his eyes are, burning from tears, and he's trembling very slightly. If I wasn't so used to being around him, I might not notice the way his muscles keep contracting.

The nausea I've felt all afternoon fades. I hear myself breathe his name but he flinches, turning away from me and striding to the other side of the room.

'He was very ill,' he says, looking out of the window. 'I don't know what they had given him, but he was very talkative. He said I look well.' I wonder if walking towards him would upset him. 'He said he misses me.'

'Dan—'

'I know.'

I glance at his wrists, just about visible under his sleeves, and I'm checking for damage. There's nothing obvious.

'I told him I am glad he is recovering but I do not want to see him again and I—and I don't.'

Somehow, I'm not convinced. I move to stand by the foot of the bed, half way between the door and Daniel.

'Not after the last few weeks.'

I didn't expect that, and I sink to perch on the very edge of my mattress. 'New Zealand was good for you.'

'So were the last few days with you.' He says it so quietly, and to the glass of the window, that I almost can't hear.

A silence threatens to choke us, but I'm pretty sure I need to keep him talking. 'I missed you so much. Thank you for coming to mine. I don't think anyone could ever do anything more wonderful.'

Finally, he faces me. And there's a tiny, pleased smile on his lips. Those dry lips. 'I'm glad it was okay.'

'Okay? More like best thing *ever*.'

We've made eye contact, and I think we're stuck. I think one of us is going to mention the kiss, but he just comes over to sit beside me.

'When do you want me to leave?'

'Never,' I say, too quickly. A tiny blush brightens his cheek and, honestly, it's a relief to see his heart is still working. 'I'm seeing Lilley at nine tomorrow morning.'

He nods. 'How is she?'

I shuffle. 'I'm not sure. I think—I guess I'll find out tomorrow.'

A tiny, tiny laugh. It's precious.

'How long do you want to stay?'

He looks up at the ceiling, stretching his neck. 'I never want to go. I think you thought I had enough of you earlier.'

'I worried.'

He does it. He does the most perfect, most natural thing in the world and puts his arm around my back. He twists, pulling me towards his chest, and pushes his face into my hair like he has done so many times before.

'I'll be gone before you see Lilley. Is she coming here?'

The scent of his neck stuns me. I barely manage a nod.

'I'll be out of the way.'

I wish I had the confidence to kiss the skin so close to my lips I can taste it. Instead, I rip myself away from him and move, sliding further onto the mattress. He follows me, keeping his arm around my back, and I wish he was never going to leave.

'Talk to me about something,' I hear myself say.

He hums into my hair, asking for an explanation.

'Something nice. Anything. I like hearing your voice.'

He chuckles at that and I can feel it vibrate through his chest. 'Okay. What do you want to eat tonight?'

I groan. I have no food in the kitchen.

'Shall we buy something?'

'Yeah, but it's still early. Unless you're hungry—'

'No.'

'Okay.' I sigh, admitting defeat, and peel myself away from him so I can sit back against the headboard.

He realises what I'm doing and takes his shoes off before joining me.

'Talk.'

His soft chuckle fills me again and I sit with my head on

284

his shoulder, eyes closed. Before speaking, he presses another one of those kisses to my hair—an innocent, tender, protective kiss—and I would sob if I had any energy left in me.

He talks about his family. He explains, in the quiet of my room, how he's a student with enough money to fly to New Zealand for three weeks.

'My mother was from Spain,' he whispers. I guess this helps explain how beautifully he tanned while he was away. 'She left home to marry my father when she was eighteen. Her father had owned hotels. I met him twice and I have no other family so he left his money to me.'

I nod, letting him know I understand but I'm not going to ask for more details, and he kisses my hair again. If this is a thing we do, now, I'm more than happy about it.

Sixty

I wake up with his arm still around me and the reflection of my room in the window against the evening sky. Is it a surprise that I fell asleep with him? Is it a surprise that I've missed most of the evening?

'William?' he breathes, noticing I'm waking up. 'Are you okay?'

My glasses have pressed into the one side of my face and it feels like I might have a bruise but, apart from that, I feel okay. So I smile for him and stretch, rubbing the side of my nose.

'You fell asleep about an hour ago.' He keeps his voice soft, like he thinks I might just roll over and carry on sleeping.

'Sorry.' He gives me a look—a *don't be silly* look—and I blush. 'Did you want to get food?'

We order pizza. After weeks of cooking with Mum it feels heavy and greasy but I'm too tired and too comfortable with the idea of only seeing Dan for the rest of the night to venture into the kitchen. Oh, I'm exhausted. Despite my nap on Dan's shoulder, I'm ready to go to bed by half nine. And he notices. Of course he does.

'I'm tired, too,' he says, catching me yawning for the fifth time. 'I think we should go to bed.'

'Basically there already,' I point out, standing up to take my shirt off. Keeping my back to him, I swap my jeans for pyjamas. It's absolutely ridiculous to be embarrassed about this after all the nights we've spent together, but I still catch myself blushing. 'Take the bed.'

I thought he'd argue, but he laughs. And it's a good, strong laugh which makes me turn around.

'The last time I stayed here we shared. I understand you were worried about your mother at your house, but don't think I was happy about making you sleep on the floor.'

I chew my lip.

'If I am in the way—'

'You're never in the way.' I go back to the bed, a little too eagerly. 'I just didn't want you thinking you had to sleep on the floor.'

He raises an eyebrow at me before pulling his shirt over his head, folding it up and letting it fall to the floor. Oh, wow. 'No, I know you will always volunteer to do that. Even though my ribs are fine, now.'

'Still not worth the risk.'

He sighs, very slightly irritated, and we sit beside each other. Under the duvet. Even if I weren't already exhausted, the warmth from his body would totally send me to sleep.

I thought we might talk some more, but he seems to have settled down for the night. He lies on his front, face turned towards me, and it's impossible for us to not touch. So I go for it. I lie my arm over his back, hand on the shoulder furthest away from me, and I think I see his shoulders relax. I'm sure I hear him sigh.

'Goodnight,' I whisper around another yawn. He smiles, eyes closed, and I am so incredibly close to leaning in and kissing his forehead.

He opens one eye to squint at me. 'I missed having you close to me.'

Well, shit.

I could do with taking my arm away from him and maybe just rolling out of the bed to be in some air that doesn't taste of him but I manage a smile, instead. I wriggle, like I'm trying to get comfortable, and move an inch away from him. I wish I were moving closer.

'It sucked. But you're here, now.'

He nods, face rubbing against the pillow. 'I'm not going away again.'

It slips from me and I really wish I could stop doubting him. 'You might.'

'Not without you.'

287

Sixty-One

I know I need to get a grip and smile and say *bye!* when he leaves but it feels impossible. He's right next to me when I wake up, and he should always be here.

Somehow, I manage it. He stays with me until quarter to nine before giving me a *look* and standing up.

'I should go.'

'Maybe.'

'I *should*. Lilley will be here soon,' he points out, turning away from me to pull his shoes on. I take the moment to breathe and prepare myself for a goodbye.

'I'll speak to you later.' I try to smile for when he looks back at me. 'Promise me you won't see him again.'

His shoulders slip, like he lost the little bit of energy it takes to hold them back. 'I promise.' He stares at the corner of the bed. 'I will tell you if they contact me again.'

'Thank you. I was so worried about you yesterday.' I may as well be honest. I may as well remind him how much he means to me. 'I don't think I could cope if you went back to him and we lost our Sundays.'

Fortunately, he smiles. I stand up and he grabs me straight away, pulling us together and crushing me quite firmly in his arms. I love it. My glasses have been knocked sideways but I don't need to be able to see at the moment—I just close my eyes and breathe.

'Come over this weekend and stay with me.' Ah. I probably won't see him tonight. A little drop of disappointment hits my skin. 'And I'll come to you after your exam on Thursday.'

My head snaps up. 'Sure?'

'Sure.' There's not even a sparkle of doubt and we're so close together I can feel the line of every one of his muscles.

I hold him as tight as I dare. 'I can't wait. See you

Sunday.'

I should expect the little kisses by now. But the last one was such a disaster and this one makes me stagger. He leans in to press his lips to my cheek, just below the arm of my glasses, and lingers there. His hands are on either side of my waist, keeping me still.

I close my eyes. 'Dan, I'm sorry about yesterday.'

'What do you mean?' He isn't letting go of me. He's barely moved his lips from my skin.

'The—uh. The kiss.'

He freezes, stuck holding me too close. 'I assumed it was a mistake.'

'It was!' He tries to move back, so I push my forehead into his shoulder. I'm hiding. 'I was aiming for your cheek and if I upset you at all I'm sorry.'

'I thought so. It is okay.'

I hope he means that. But I let it go and, more importantly, I let him go. I pull myself away from him, making sure he can see me smiling, and he touches my chin with his fingertip.

'Sunday,' he says, like he's willing it to come sooner. I am. Days without him, after days with him, feel like torture.

But I let him go. I follow him to the door of the block, taking every second available to me, and he presses another little kiss to my hair before leaving.

Louise Willingham

Sixty-Two

People coming to my room and looking like an absolute mess is becoming quite a theme. Lilley looks the worst I've ever seen her, and she pulls a face like she knows it.

'I've called a taxi to fetch us from here,' she says, stepping into the building and rubbing her forehead. Her dark hair is pulled back in a sleepy ponytail, loose wisps floating across her eyes, and she's wearing jogging bottoms. I think I only saw her like this three times while we were dating.

I follow her to my room. 'Where are we going?'

She's carrying a little backpack that doesn't look like it could hold much more than an A5 notebook. I'm going to need my shoes. And a coat—Lilley's coat looks almost big enough for both of us. 'Lil?'

'Day trip,' she says, smiling and not at all reassuring me.

I raise an eyebrow and perch on the edge of my bed, so close to where Dan had been sat, to tie my shoes.

'How was Christmas?'

'Day trip to *where*?'

'Town. Did you get to see Dan?'

I narrow my eyes at her. 'Yes, I saw Dan. Christmas was fine and he is fine and he had a great time in New Zealand. *Where* are we going?'

She sighs and sits down on the floor, knees up to her chin. 'Promise me you won't freak out.' My first thought is she's getting a tattoo. But why would she want me there for that? 'Will, promise.'

I stare at her. 'I promise. Tell me what's going on.'

She squints at me and speaks very quickly. 'I visited the family planning clinic yesterday and had the first pill to induce an abortion. You're keeping me company while I go back today and take the second one to finish it off.'

I am glad I am sitting down.

290

'To—to do *what*?'

She's hiding in her knees, curled up and looking so small on my carpet. 'Abortion, Will. Don't worry.'

'Lilley—'

'I'm pretty sure it's Kieran's,' she says, turning huge, terrified eyes up to me. Pretty sure? 'But there's no way I'm—I know what I'm doing. I just need you to be there with me.'

Pretty sure? She's *pretty sure*, but not certain? Half of my mind runs away with this doubt, spinning out of control and almost choking me. The other half stays in the room with us and recognises how important it is that I stay calm.

I can't remember much about that Friday night and I'm worried that, if I think too hard, troubling details will come back to me. I don't need to know.

I slip to the floor, kneeling in front of her. 'Thank you for trusting me,' I whisper, making her splutter a nervous laugh. 'I'm—shit. Does anyone else know?'

She shakes her head.

'Shit. Okay. How do you feel?'

'Terrified.' She pushes some loose strands of hair out of her eyes. 'Absolutely terrified. I only found out two days ago.'

'Oh, shit, Lil—'

'I haven't told my parents and I'm not going to. They don't need to know. No one—no one needs to know but I realised I wanted someone with me today.'

I take one of her hands from where it's wrapped around her leg and do my best to look reassuring. 'I understand. When's the taxi getting here?'

'Any minute now.' She takes her phone out of her coat pocket and puts it on the floor between us, screen up. 'I knew you'd help.'

'Well, of course.' I rub my thumb into the back of her hand. 'Like I could ever make you go through this on your own.'

She smiles and pushes those same strands back again. 'Yeah, well. You're a nice guy. Dan's lucky.'

I freeze.

'I don't mean like that,' she snaps. 'But he *is*. He's lucky

291

that he's found you after everything.'

I shrug. 'I guess.'

'Don't be dense.'

I stare at her fingernails. 'I don't want to talk about him. All I do is talk about him.'

'You are a bit obsessed, you're right.' She squeezes my fingers, like it's *me* who needs comforting. 'It's okay. I found his Facebook profile, and he *is* cute.'

I shake my head. 'He never uses the damn thing.'

My heart is still thundering. *Abortion.* I didn't expect this.

She laughs, and it's so nice to hear. 'I could tell. Used it enough to meet you, though.'

I groan and she laughs again and, okay, I guess I don't mind talking about this. It's distracting her. 'Has Cassie been telling you about me?'

'She told me this when it happened. Don't worry.' Her phone screen wakes up with a text: the taxi's here. 'Are you ready?'

I nod, standing up and pulling her with me. I grab my phone, my key, and my coat, and we leave my room.

We don't talk in the taxi. What would we talk about? Babies?

We find our way through the hospital—a place I'm going to get very familiar with over the next few months—and she gives her name at reception. We take seats in the waiting room and we've got twenty minutes. The smell of antiseptic in the air is reassuring, and I sit right back in the plastic chair.

'They might try to not let you in,' Lilley warns. 'So I need you to be a tough guy and just elbow your way into the room.'

I laugh. 'Tough guy? Me? Lil, I'm *pathetic*.'

'Okay, you are—cry at them or something until they let you in. Just do *not* leave me.' She kicks my foot very softly. 'Otherwise there's no point you being here.'

'I'm not going to leave you, don't worry. But I'm sure they'll let me in. They'll probably think I'm the—the.'

I can't say it because, shit, I guess I might be. I'm purposefully not doing the maths, because the less I know the better.

'Yeah, probably. I'll explain if they give me chance.'

'Thanks.'

'No problem. Have you ever thought about having kids?'

I look at her, incredulous. This is a waiting room full of people in our situation—or very similar situations, at least. And she wants to talk about *having* kids, rather than doing everything in our power to avoid that.

'Um, not—not really.'

'Neither had I.' There's a funny look in her eye, like she's trying to see something that isn't quite there. 'If you *do* ever have kids though, I have to be aunty.'

'I think Kirst will have that job.'

'Yeah, but you can have as many aunties as you like—and you *know* you'd want me to influence any kid of yours,' she says, eyebrow raised. She's focusing on the room again, now, and hits me with a *look*. 'I'm *brilliant*.'

'Oh, you are.' I'm close to laughing again. Why? Is it nerves? 'But I don't—no. I don't think I'll be having kids.'

'Really? Don't you dare now tell me that I'm the only girl you'll ever love.'

I snort and hide my face in my hands. 'You're the only girl I've loved so far, is that okay?'

She sniffs. 'Fine. Do not expect me to say it back.'

'Well, no—I'm not a girl.'

She backhands me in the stomach and we shouldn't be laughing so much. We shouldn't be having such a good time. But I've missed her.

A name gets called, but it's not us.

'Lil, I do love you,' I say.

I've surprised her and she turns wide eyes onto me.

'Not like—not like I thought I did last year. You're right, you're like a sister. If I ever do magically have kids, you *have* to be an aunty.'

She grins and leans into me, bumping our shoulders together. 'You're like a sister, too.'

I laugh and give her an awkward, one armed hug, and then her name gets called. It makes us both jump and she picks up the little backpack in one hand, taking my hand with the other.

'If you leave me, I'll scream.'

Sixty-Three

Once we're in the room, the nurse tells us to get comfortable and leaves us for a moment. I think it's so Lil can have a few more moments of thought but she spends the time tying up her hair again and adjusting her bra.

'Should I take it off?'

'Hey?'

'I don't want to be more uncomfortable than necessary.'

'Jesus Lil, if it's making you uncomfortable take it off,' I say, glancing at her backpack. 'No one will care.'

'Sure?'

'Lil, it's *your boobs*.'

I drop my eyes to the floor while she reaches up under the back of her hoodie and unhooks her bra. She stuffs it in her backpack, stretches, and flashes a grin at me.

'I'd have done that even if you'd said it was a bad idea.'

'Oh, I know.'

The nurse comes back and, as Lil said, there's another pill to take. I haven't dared to ask about the first one, but the way the nurse is talking makes it sound like we're just waiting for the twenty-four hours to pass before she takes this next one. And then, as Lilley hoped, we get to sit around in her hospital room for an hour or so. Just to make sure everything's *clear*.

God, this is horrible.

The small, unassuming white tablet disappears with a sip of water and the nurse suggests Lilley walks around for a bit. There's no way she's going to risk going back out to the ward, so she does laps of the little room we've been given.

She sits down every few loops and chatters constantly for just over half an hour.

And then something clearly happens, because she turns pale and grabs my hand, dragging me through to the bathroom that's just for her. I ask if we should call the nurse, but she shakes her head. She pulls down those tracksuit trousers and sits straight down, clearly trying to hide something from me. But there's no point. I know, and she knows I know, what's happening. She knows I don't care.

I kneel down in front of her and take one of her hands. 'Does it hurt?' I ask, and she just shakes her head. 'Lil, it's okay—'

'It's more *uncomfortable*,' she hisses, leaning forward over her knees. Our hands are tight together. 'Ah, shit.'

'Sure you don't want the nurse?'

'She'll come in soon anyway. Just talk to me—jabber about something.'

My mind goes blank. What do you talk about in this situation?

'I kissed him,' I blurt, because it's the only thing I've been able to think about since it happened. It's there, in the background of every thought. 'By accident. But it was a kiss.'

'How do you *accidentally* kiss someone?' She sounds tight, like she isn't breathing. I don't think I am, either.

'I was going for his cheek.'

'Is that something you two do?'

I nod, then shrug. 'It's something he does. But he—he saw Matthew last night.'

'The ex?'

'Yup.'

'I bet that was intense.'

'I think so.' I shuffle, so I'm more comfortable, and speak looking at her knees. 'The hospital phoned Dan to say he'd overdosed but wanted to see him.'

'Overdosed?'

I groan. 'Heroin.'

'*Shit*.'

'So Dan was super upset, of course, and we argued but when he left I just—I just wanted him to know I care.'

She squints at me.

'He sometimes—sometimes—' something's stuck in my throat, like a half-swallowed sweet, 'kisses my hair or whatever. So I wanted him to know I care.'

Lilley hums, not convinced, and rubs her free hand over her forehead. 'So you kissed him.'

'It wasn't a real kiss.'

'Did it *feel* like a real kiss?'

I can't answer that.

'Will, when are you going to tell him?'

'Tell him *what*?'

'That you're…' She trails off, eyebrows raised and pulled together. I'm trapped, locked staring at her, and it's suddenly so easy. It comes out in one breath.

'I'm bisexual.'

She flickers a smile. 'Well, yeah. There's that. But what about the other thing?'

Excuse me?

I'm flustered, suddenly too hot and too cold, and I almost drop her hand. I almost shake myself free and leave the room, but I stay there, rooted, and gawk at her. What more does she want from me? Doesn't she realise what I've just done?

'Will, you need to tell him you love him. Let him know how important he is to you.'

I close my eyes and shrug. 'One thing at a time. He doesn't have a clue.'

'I bet he does.'

If I'm honest with myself, I bet he does, too. And I bet he'll just smile when I tell him I'm bi. I bet he'll touch my cheek and ask if I'm okay, and then he'll ask me to stop crying because he wants to be happy for me.

So why haven't I told him yet?

The nurse comes in and I stick a smile on my face, reaching up with my free hand to brush some hair back for Lilley. She winks at me, leaning into my hand, and accepts the offer of a hot water bottle.

A *hot water bottle*, in the middle of all this, feels hilariously benign.

Eventually, the pain of it is too much for even Lilley to hide and she shoves me roughly to one side. The nurse seems to know what to expect but I'm almost too slow and have to leap out of the way when Lilley jolts forward, throwing up all over the floor.

I don't hesitate.

'I'm on it,' I say, letting go of her sweaty hand to tiptoe around the bathroom to the main room.

The nurse tries to call me back, but, damn, I need to do *something*. Having a pool of vomit on the floor really isn't going to help Lilley, and it's much better to use the nurse to help her manage the pain, so I skip out into the ward and find someone who will help mop up.

They come straight to the room with me, smiling sympathetically at Lilley and making beautiful small talk, like you might get in a hairdressers. I let them carry on and give Lilley my hand again.

It's a long time until she feels like she can stand up and, even then, I'm nervous. She looks like she's been suffering from a flu. I help her to her feet while the nurse helps pull up her jogging bottoms and we guide her back to the main room, where she can lie on the bed and catch her breath.

'When do you need us to leave?' I ask, sitting on the edge of the bed and looking up at the nurse. She shrugs, refilling a plastic cup for Lilley to drink from.

'Whenever you're ready. Get your stomach settled before you try travelling far from a loo, though,' she says, fixing Lilley with a sudden warning glance. 'Don't leave until you're ready.'

I'll admit to being surprised. It must be a quiet day, otherwise I'm sure she'd want us out as soon as Lilley felt like she could stand up. We share a look as the nurse leaves.

'Might stay a week or two,' Lilley mutters, winking and moving so one hand is under the pillow. I'm still holding the other. 'Are you alright?'

I nod and try smiling. 'Feel shit for you.'

'Don't worry about it.'

'You know it's what I do best.'

'True.' She closes her eyes. 'Hey, you know what you could do.'

'What?'

'Run and find me a bag of crisps.' I laugh but she squints at me. 'I'm serious.'

'You want crisps?'

'They might just help everything settle. And I'm starving.'

I can't help but agree with her and get to my feet. 'Any particular sort?'

'Plain, if you can. If you get me anything with cheese I'll throw up again and I won't push you out of the way this time.'

'How ungrateful.' I lean in to kiss her hair without thinking about it. When I pull back, she's looking at me with a raised eyebrow. 'Don't go anywhere.'

'Don't take forever.'

I leave, planning on going down to the café we passed by the front door. It shouldn't take me too long but I get the feeling Lilley wanted space—just a moment or two—and I walk slowly, taking the time to read the names of other wards.

I wish I knew where Matthew was.

I purse my lips and keep walking, head down and eyes fixed on my feet. What would it matter if I did know where he was? Would I go? Would I try to sneak a look at him? How would I ever explain that to Dan?

Someone bumps me sideways, running around a corner, and I don't have to look up to know who it is. I don't have to ask because I can taste him in the air.

Sixty-Four

Everything happens far too quickly.

Daniel catches me, hands on my shoulders to stop me from toppling over. My ears are ringing. Part of my mind is still fixed on *crisps, plain, not cheese* but this is far more important.

'What the hell are you doing here?' This is it. I know *exactly* what he's doing here, and he just stares at me with saucer eyes. There's something on his eyebrow but I can't process it. 'You came to see him?'

He looks like he just saw me walk through a wall. 'William—'

'You promised you wouldn't!' I can't look at him. I don't want to argue but finding him here is too close to a nightmare. 'Were you going to tell me?' The air is thick, and he doesn't speak. 'Dan—'

'I tried.'

Well, I don't like that.

I squint at him but here it is. The next factor in this moment that feels like it's stretching out endlessly into the future. I see his wrists.

Fresh, glistening red lines peer out from under his jacket sleeves. Never mind Lilley being sick; I feel something leave my stomach and slam my hand over my mouth.

'He phoned me this morning.' Dan sounds awful, like he's been screaming for hours. 'He phoned me and I was—I was bad but you were with Lilley so I did not want to interrupt.' He takes a breath that makes him cough and I reach for him, stumbling over my feet. 'I sent you a text.'

Shit. I haven't looked at my phone since Lilley got to my room—actually, I don't think it's made any noise at all.

'I had to come. Because I—because I didn't know what to do, but—'

'Danny!'

300

As if I've been trained, I grab Dan's hand. I don't give him chance to argue and drag him back up the corridor I just came down, reasoning that I can't leave the hospital without at least explaining myself to Lilley but there's no way I'm letting us talk to Matthew, either. Because who else would call him *Danny*? Who else would be here and would recognise him?

When it's clear we aren't being followed, he stumbles to a stop and leans heavily against the corridor wall. His breathing sounds awful, like none of the breaths are filling his lungs. I wait, barely able to look at him and still convinced I'm going to throw up. His eyes are closed and his eyebrow...

'Dan, has he touched you again?'

He whimpers, slipping and threatening to collapse to the floor. I catch him, pulling him into my arms with too much force and almost making us fall over anyway. It doesn't matter. I've got him.

'Dan, this is what's gonna happen,' I whisper, free hand pushing up underneath his jacket. The back of his jumper is wet. 'We're going upstairs to tell Lilley what's happening. Either she'll get a taxi with us, we'll sit and wait for her, or we'll leave. And then we're going to your flat, you're phoning your therapist, and I'm not letting you out of my sight until I'm sure you're not going to—going to—' I shake my head rather than say it, but he understands. 'We're getting you a new phone number.'

He laughs once and it's cold and tired but it's a *laugh*. I hold him even tighter. 'I think we should have done that earlier.'

I groan and kiss whatever I can reach—his shoulder. 'I think so, too. Are you okay?'

'I will be.'

I don't think I like that. Even so, I let go of him, except for one hand, and look at his face for the first time in far too long. The skin of his left eyebrow is torn and bleeding and I stare at it, breath caught in my chest.

'Yeah,' I say, 'you will. Let's go.'

We don't talk on the way back to Lilley's room. I just concentrate on feeling the warmth of his hand, and he sounds like he's concentrating on keeping his breathing steady.

I open the door and we walk into Lilley's room, hands locked together and carrying a huge thundercloud with us. Understandably, she hasn't got a clue how to react and just sits up, mouth open, and waits for one of us to give her an explanation.

I can't.

And it becomes clear pretty quickly that I can't.

'Well, I'm ready to make a move,' she says brightly, picking up her little rucksack and swaddling herself in her coat. 'Come on. Let's sign me out and get a taxi.'

We follow her, numb and clinging to each other, to the desk. Lilley and I sign out. She thanks the nurses for their help before taking my free hand and steering us down the corridors —back to where we've just been. And, as we pass the point where I'm pretty sure Matthew saw us, Daniel stumbles and we come to a stop.

'Lilley, keep him here,' I croak, passing Dan's hand into Lilley's. Or, trying to. He clings to me, shaking his head. 'Just a minute.'

'Do not go to him. We should just leave,' Dan whispers, like he's scared someone's going to hear us. Of course he is, Matthew is meters away. 'I can't let you go to him.'

I want to argue. I want to tear myself away from Dan and face Matthew—I want to do something with this furious energy that spikes each time I look at the cut on Dan's eyebrow or the scratches on his wrist.

He shakes his head, hand still crushing mine. And, just when I think he's going to say something else, he kisses my forehead.

It's more than anything he could ever say.

And I accept it. Right now, there's nothing I can do to help other than take him somewhere safe.

So we leave the hospital.

Being faced with the possibility of me hunting down Matthew seems to have done something to Dan. He won't let go of my hand, but he's standing taller. He's more alert when we step out into the carpark than I've seen him since we

302

returned to uni, and he pulls his phone out, calling for a taxi.

'We're going to take you home,' he says, nodding at Lilley. She's staring, wide-eyed. 'You can have William for as long as you need but, when you are better, I need him.'

Despite everything, a grin cracks over my face. His accent is filling me.

'Just drop me off,' she says, letting go of my hand. I hadn't realised she was still holding it. 'I'm okay, now.'

My eyelids flutter and I try to find some energy. The day isn't over, yet. 'I don't want you to be left alone.'

'I'm fine. I'll talk to you this evening.'

I groan, well aware I'm not going to win this one, and tip my face up to the sky. 'Do you promise you'll phone me if you need anything?'

'Promise.'

It will have to do. I stand there with my eyes closed until the taxi gets here, and we all bundle into the back. I realise, a minute or so into the journey, that we should have made Lilley sit in the front. Her eyes are fixed on the little bit of windscreen she can see past the driver, face cold with concentration as she fights away nausea.

Despite what she said, I tumble out of the taxi with her when we reach her building. Behind me, I hear Daniel ask the driver to wait.

'Let me make sure you're comfortable,' I say, almost catching Lilley's hands.

She raises an eyebrow.

'Please, Lil. I want to help.'

'You have helped,' she says, keys out. 'I'm okay. I feel much better than I did two hours ago.' I grimace, making her sigh. 'Will, I'm okay. Go and look after him. I'll talk to you later.'

I droop, running out of energy like it's sand in an hourglass, and she gives me a hug.

'Tell me if anything happens,' I mumble, letting her go and accepting that, maybe, she doesn't need me now. She needs to go to bed and sleep for a few hours, and she can do that without me worrying around her.

She unlocks the door. 'Go and look after him,' she repeats, slipping into the building and disappearing from view. I take a breath.

When I turn back to the taxi, Dan's doing a remarkable job of looking okay. Yeah, his eyebrow is swollen and cut, but he's smiling. He's waiting patiently for me to say what I want to do next.

'Can we nip to my block?' I ask, sitting behind the driver. 'I need to fetch my work.'

Dan nods, takes my hand to hold on the seat between us, and gives the driver my address. The two of them make very light small-talk and I spend the whole journey concentrating on breathing.

Lilley is okay. Her bad day is over, and, if she'd wanted me to stay with her, she'd have said. I have to concentrate on Daniel, now—and that's something I've become very good at over the last few months.

Sixty-Five

By the time we reach Dan's flat, it's nearly three in the afternoon and I realise I haven't eaten all day. He pays before we clamber out of the taxi, carrying my laptop, revision notes, and overnight bag between us, and we don't say anything until we're in his room.

I thought he'd stop outside for a cigarette.

'First thing's first,' I mutter, taking my things through to his room before heading straight to his little kitchen, 'where's your first aid kit?'

'Hmm?'

'For your eyebrow and—and wrists.' I'm erratic, opening cupboards at random.

He goes into the bathroom and comes back with a bag of plasters, wipes, and dressings.

'Thanks.'

'I can do it,' he says, but it's feeble and lacks any real conviction. So it doesn't take much for me to convince him to sit on the settee and let me help; a sideways glance and a raised eyebrow while I wash my hands.

'Tell me what happened.' I kneel in front of him. I see to his eyebrow first, wiping it and using some strips to keep it pulled together. It is going to leave him with a massive bruise —maybe even another scar.

He sighs, and his breath hits my face. 'He phoned me using the patient phone at about half nine this morning. Said he needed to see me because he—' he coughs, closing his eyes and leaning over his knees, towards me. 'He missed me and wanted to talk about *us*. I tried to say no but he said he misses me and wants me back. I hung up and it was a difficult few minutes.'

'What did you do?' I ask, even though I know the answer is under his sleeves, just between us.

305

He squints at me.

'How bad is it?'

'Not bad.' Oh, God. 'But I was upset.'

I reach up to push my forehead against his, sure one of us is going to start screaming. 'I'm sorry I wasn't here.'

'It isn't your fault. You had to help Lilley.'

I groan and sink back down, looking up at him for a moment before starting on his wrists. 'You should take your jumper off.' I move back so he can tug it over his head, leaving him in short sleeves. 'I'll tell you about her in a minute. Keep talking.'

I see this next sigh leave his chest. 'I decided to go to him just before eleven. He has been moved into his own room so we were alone and he—and he lost his temper very quickly when I said I am not coming back. There was an empty glass on his bedside table.'

He doesn't have to say anything else. I clean his wrists, even though it looks like he's already done that, and wrap gentle bandages around them. Now the terror of finding him so close to Matthew has worn off, they don't look so bad. Just scratches. I just don't want to risk knocking them and making them worse.

I also don't want to risk catching a glimpse of them and being reminded of how very delicate he is and of how easy it is for me to not be there for him.

'I walked out and found you.'

'Did he try to follow you?'

'I think so, yes.'

I can't hide this shiver and get to my feet to wash my hands again.

'You understand why I could not let you look for him.'

Oh, I do. I nod, coming over to sit beside him on the settee, and close my eyes. He puts his arm around me, holding me like he so often does, and there are a few minutes where neither of us have to say or do anything. We're just *together*, and it's enough.

'Lilley had an abortion.'

He reacts far more than I'd expected and sits up straight,

turning me so I have to look at him. His eyes look like they're glowing. 'Was it yours?'

For a tiny moment, the thought of having a child with Lilley settles in me, and it's ridiculous.

'William?'

'I don't think so.'

'What?' He touches my jaw with the tips of his thumbs. 'What do you mean?'

'She isn't sure and it doesn't matter, anyway. It doesn't matter.'

He takes a trembling breath and leans in to kiss my forehead, like he did at the hospital. Like he's done so many times. 'Is she okay?'

'I think so, yeah.'

'Are you okay?'

'I will be once you've spoken to your therapist and changed your phone number.'

He laughs, pushing his face into my hair and sliding his hands down my arms from my shoulders. 'You are amazing.' He rubs his thumbs into my knuckles. 'I will do all of that soon. Just promise me you're okay.'

'Promise me *you* are.'

Another kiss. I'm not sure how many more of these I can take. 'I am okay, William. Thank you.'

'I can't believe I didn't get your messages.' I twist so I can pull my phone out. And there's the answer: the damn thing has run out of battery. Frustrated, I drop it to the floor and hide my face in his shoulder.

'Never mind,' he breathes.

'Never mind?'

'It doesn't matter.'

'But if I'd spoken to you—'

'I might still have gone to see him,' he admits, making me go queasy again. 'I needed to tell him it is over.'

'But you might not have got hurt.'

He shrugs, moving his hands to rub my back. One waits at my neck, holding me in his shoulder. 'Maybe. I am so lucky I found you.'

I nod and we sit there, breathing together, for a long time. I would just curl up with him and fall asleep, but I'm very aware that he needs to speak to a *professional* about his day. He's also probably gasping for a cigarette, and I am *not* letting him go outside without me there with him. No way. Forget it.

'Phone your therapist,' I whisper, lips against the bare skin of his neck. 'Do you want me with you?'

He hums.

'Dan?'

'I will go to my room.' He rubs his thumb into my neck. 'But in a moment. I don't want to let go of you.'

I close my eyes and let him hold me, listening to each breath and revelling in the way his chest hits against mine. I haven't done enough breathing today. I don't think Dan has, either. Lilley definitely hasn't, but I tell myself she's in fresh air, now.

Oh, I really need to put my phone on to charge.

I groan and sit up, ripping myself away from Dan like I'm tearing a page from a book. Only it's not so permanent. He seems to understand *it's not over yet* and cups my cheek very briefly with the hand that's been resting on my neck before standing up, leaving me on the settee, and taking his phone out.

'I don't know how long I'll be,' he warns, hesitating by his bedroom door. I find a smile for him.

'Doesn't matter. I'll be right here.'

'If Lilley needs you—'

'I doubt she will, but I'll knock and interrupt.' I throw in a wink. I'm not sure why. But it makes him smile and he stares at me for another heartbeat.

I would stare at him forever.

He clears his throat and goes into his room, shutting the door very softly between us. And, finally, it catches up with me.

This would be the prime moment for Peter to text me. Or maybe he'd phone me. As it is, my phone is currently resembling a building brick and I haven't got the energy to stand up and put it on charge.

I sink forward, into the settee where Dan was just sitting, and close my eyes. They leak but it's not violent sobs like I'd feared: I cry like my eyes are just making too many tears. I'm overflowing. My breathing hitches but I catch myself, hand pushing through the back of my hair. I could do this for hours.

I twist, so I'm lying on my back, and take my glasses off. They're filthy. The movement has woken me up somewhat and I realise, a few minutes too late, that my phone charger is in my bag. In Dan's room.

I groan and close my eyes again.

I'd leave it, but I told Lilley to phone me if she needs help. What if she's sick again, or the bleeding gets worse, and her call goes straight to answerphone? In the other room, I can hear Dan talking to his therapist. I was determined to just leave him to it but he could be speaking to them for hours.

Shit.

I'm not sure I can cope with anything else going wrong today. I stand up, grinding my teeth, and cross the carpet to his door. Oh, God. He's going to think I'm coming in to tell him I'm leaving.

I'll have to speak quickly.

I stick a smile on my face and knock softly, pushing the handle at the same time. There's the sound of movement and I creep in, knowing I'm blushing and knowing he's going to panic.

'Just need my charger,' I breathe, blinking quickly and regretting leaving my glasses on the floor.

Dan raises his hand to swipe at something sitting on his cheeks and it doesn't take a genius to realise he's crying. 'Are you okay?'

I nod, reaching my bag and fumbling for the zip. It would be so much easier to take the whole thing out with me, but he would definitely worry I'm leaving.

'Is Lilley okay?'

'I assume so.' I look up to smile at him just as my hand finds the wire. 'I'm okay. Keep talking. I'm not going anywhere.'

He's frozen, like he can't quite believe it, and I overreact.

309

I should smile, repeat that I'm okay and I'm staying, and go back to the settee. Instead, I find myself standing up and walking over to his bed. If I sit down, I will never leave. And he needs to continue with this conversation. So, like he has done so many times to me, I kiss his forehead.

Before he can catch me—before I can start crying again and before I can convince myself it's easier to just never break skin-contact—I leave. I make sure he sees me smiling before I shut the door.

This feels impossible.

I stretch my neck and go to the socket closest to the settee and sit on the floor, cradling my phone while it comes back to life. It's remarkably soothing. As soon as there's enough battery percentage, I wake it up and wait for everything to load.

I have no idea what time it died, but there are a lot of messages for it to catch up with. There's something from Cassie about revision for next week's exam, but I ignore it. I hold my breath, watching the rest of the notifications fly in, and feel it like a sting each time Dan's name flashes over the screen.

No point in lingering on them. I open our conversation and read over what he sent, giving myself *just five minutes* to absorb this pain. It's in the past. However he was feeling when he sent me these—when he made the decision to go back to Matthew *again*—is over and buried and I've done everything I can.

I tell myself this, but the five minutes slip by alarmingly quickly and I'm crying again by the time I look at the other conversations.

As always, there's a message from Peter.

12:45 **Peter**: How are you?

It's direct, to the point, and remembering he knows Matthew makes my stomach flip again. It's amazing, really, that I haven't actually been sick over the last two days.

16:04 **William**: Alright thanks. Do you
know anything that's happened to
Matthew this week?

I expect a long text message but my phone rings instead.
It's a relief.

'Hey,' I say, tipping my head back and closing my eyes. 'I
guess this means you *do*.'

'I do.' He sounds very grey. 'So, I warned Anthony about
him.'

'Good.'

'Yeah. And he was really cool with it and that was all fine.
What *wasn't* fine was he phoned me yesterday to say Matthew
had text him some gibberish and, after a phone call, we worked
out he'd overdosed and was in hospital.'

I hum, like I'm telling him he's correct, and rub my eyes.

'Shit. Yeah, so Anthony was worried and wanted to go
and see him but we argued a bit. I repeated what you and Dan
have told me and we ended up not going.'

That's a relief. 'Thank fuck.'

'Yeah.'

'Has Anthony spoken to him again?'

'Nope. I think Matthew was offended he didn't go and see
him.'

'Well, I'm glad you didn't go.'

There's a pause, where Peter picks up on everything I
haven't quite said. 'Shit,' he breathes. 'Did Dan go?'

'Twice.' It hurts, a knife in my stomach, and I push my
hand into my hair. 'Yesterday and today. Today he—he got
hurt.'

'What?'

I shiver and say it very quickly, trying to get it out of me.
'They argued and Matthew threw a glass at him which cut his
eyebrow. He's talking with his therapist now.'

'Oh, shit.'

'I know.'

'What are you doing?'

'Sitting in his living room.'

311

'No, I mean about Matthew.'

I groan and look over at the bedroom door. 'We'll get Dan a new phone number.' I'm annoyed we didn't think to do this sooner. 'And I guess he's going to have a lot of appointments over the next few weeks.'

Peter hums. 'Sounds good. I'll let you know if we find out anything else but promise me you're not going to do anything stupid.'

'Like what?'

'Like find Matthew and try to hurt him.'

I frown at the room. Has Peter been following me? I can't admit I've been to the hospital, though—I can't mention Lilley. 'I think I'm the last person likely to do that. When have I ever hurt anyone?'

'Never, but this Matthew *has* hurt the guy you're obsessed with.'

I sigh but, for once, I can't fight it. 'I'm not going to try to hurt him,' I promise. 'I'm just going to look after Dan and concentrate on my exams.'

Peter hums. 'Promise we'll meet up soon.'

'Definitely.'

'I understand if you bring him with you.'

I sigh loudly, dropping my hand from my hair. 'He's not a pet, Peter.'

'No, I know. I'm just saying it's okay.'

The steady talking that's been coming from Dan's room stops and I sit up, expecting him to appear. 'Yeah, thanks. I'll talk to you soon.'

'Promise?'

'Promise.'

I hang up, drop my phone to the floor and reclaim my glasses, and get to my feet. I hold my breath, trying to hear *anything* from Dan, and creep towards the door.

He swears. I'm past the settee when the door opens and Dan comes out, wearing a very rough smile.

'Did you speak to Lilley?' He goes straight to the kitchen and fills the kettle.

I drift towards him. 'Just Peter.'

'Does Anthony know about Matthew?'

Wow, that was to the point. I swallow something and hover near the end of the work surface, studying him. He's moving too quickly. 'He does.' It's impossible not to notice how the mug he's holding trembles. 'He was going to visit him but Peter talked him out of it.'

He coughs. 'Good.' I'm expecting this next bit, and I wish I'd kept my shoes on. 'Will you come outside with me?'

'Absolutely.' I'm torn, for a moment, between grabbing my shoes and not moving away from him. I'm considering going out in my socks.

Fortunately, he's in the same situation as I am. We sit in silence on the settee, pulling on our shoes, and he grabs his keys.

I really don't know what to say. I stand outside with him, not quite touching arms, and let the cigarette smoke swirl around us. He's almost finished his second one before we speak.

'I don't know what would have happened if you were not there today,' he says, staring down the road at nothing in particular. 'I still have an appointment on Monday.'

I touch his arm. 'And then you're going to work?'

He shrugs and reaches to kill the cigarette. 'Yes.'

'Maybe you should just not go in.'

He laughs, looking up at me. 'Why not? Matthew will not be on campus.' It's a very good point. 'I will be able to keep busy, at least.'

I sigh, accepting it, and glance at his lips. 'I guess.'

'Let's go inside.' He takes my hand again, leading me to the door. 'Have you eaten today?'

Ah, shit. I don't have to respond.

'I am not surprised.' He lets go of my fingers to put a hand on the small of my back to guide me back up the stairs. 'What do you want? After you've eaten you can have a nap.' *Not* the moment to think how lovely that sounds in his voice. 'You look tired.'

'I'm fine.'

He laughs, flicking on the kettle again and opening the

313

fridge. He's still fluttering around, like a moth by a lamp. It's exhausting to watch.

'Okay. We should do some revision tomorrow, too.'

I grunt and give in. The distance between us has been too great for too long and I stand behind him, hands on his waist. God, it's tender. He leans straight into me, letting out a little sigh as he relaxes. It makes getting drinks and food difficult, but neither of us think to suggest I let go of him. Why would I do that to us? Why would I ever choose to move away from him?

'Breathe,' I remind him when we're sat on the settee together. We've had soup, and our bowls are on the floor.

He turns a raised eyebrow at me.

'You're really tense and I think you need another cigarette but it's cold out there.'

He chuckles, sounding like he's surprised I could make him laugh on such a day, and twists to put a hand on the side of my face. I should be used to this by now.

'You can stay here.'

'No way.'

Again, it's an easy battle to win. He rolls his eyes and stands up, hand out for mine. We don't talk at all this time and we don't need to. Once we're outside and the cigarette is lit I just stand there, arm around the front of his waist, and listen to each and every breath.

Sixty-Six

We run the risk of falling asleep on the settee again. Time flies past us, and we've barely said anything to each other all evening but that's okay. In his flat, where nobody can touch him, we're safe. The TV is talking gently to us, giving our thoughts something harmless to focus on, and I'm sandwiched between him and the back of the settee. Part of me is expecting another call from the hospital, but it doesn't come.

Instead, my phone buzzes. It's still on the floor, where I can't reach, and I do *not* want to move. I do *not* want to think about anyone other than Dan.

He realises and chuckles, using the arm around me to give me a gentle squeeze. 'Are you going to look?'

'No.'

'It might be Lilley.'

I groan.

'Do you want me to see who it is?'

'Go for it.'

With another chuckle, he reaches down with his free hand and unlocks my phone. I have no idea when we learned each other's passwords, but, at this point, I'm surprised if I *don't* know something about him.

'Lilley.'

I close my eyes for a moment, preparing for the worst. My shoes aren't far away, and a taxi would only take a couple of minutes to get to us. I'll have to take Dan with me—no way am I leaving him on his own.

'What's she said?' I stretch my neck and try to psych myself up to leave the warmth of his arm.

There's a pause, where I think he's just finding the message. But then it keeps going.

'Dan?'

'She—she says she's okay.' He isn't breathing. 'I

315

shouldn't have looked.'

'What?'

He passes me the phone and lies back again, head against the arm of the settee with his eyes shut and chin tipped to the ceiling. I don't have to look at the screen to know what he's read, but I do it anyway.

> 20:12 **Lilley**: I'm okay, don't freak out. Have you told Dan you're bi yet? He needs to know how you feel about him and he looked like he needed some good news

I let my phone fall back onto the floor and sit up sharply, covering my face with sweaty hands. Oh, *God*.

'Are you okay?' He sounds miles away.

I glance over at him and he hasn't moved.

'I am not upset.'

'You look it.' I'm torn between leaping to my feet and leaving and sinking down to lie on the floor. My heart is thundering. 'I should have told you.'

'Hmm?'

'I should—I should have told you I'm bi.' I've said it twice in one day and Dan's still staring at the ceiling, expression hidden under a neutral mask. I've told him. He knows. 'If it helps, I only really told Lilley today.'

He shakes his head—the first movement since I sat up. The air around me feels stale. 'I don't care when you told her.' I wish I could believe that. 'Why couldn't you tell me?'

'What?'

'Why were you scared to tell me?'

I think it's pretty obvious, and just sit there for a moment. Maybe he'll guess it out-loud and I'll be able to just shrug and nod my head.

'What could I have done to help?'

I close my eyes again and try to take a breath. I'm impressed I'm not crying. 'It wasn't *you*. It was me. It's all me.'

'I don't understand.'

'What? What is there to *not* understand?'

I'm getting ratty, and the anger is all at me. I'm not sure he knows this, and I'm about to apologise when he sits up and catches my cheeks between his hands. They're warm.

'I tried to let you know you were safe to tell me,' he says, piercing me with his shining blue eyes. There's a redness to them and I can't believe he's going to cry before me. 'I knew. I hoped I knew. And I hoped I was someone you could trust—'

'Dan, shit—'

'—Because I don't care,' he continues, fingers slipping back into my hair. His wrists are too close to me and I can see the bandages around scratches left by something I can't begin to think about. My lip trembles. 'You know I don't care who you like.'

'But I like *you*.'

There it is.

For less than a heartbeat, we're frozen. The ground beneath my feet has crumbled and I'm slipping, plummeting towards some sort of conclusion. I might not survive this. He looks like he's thinking the same.

He leans forward to push his forehead against mine. It's enough to make my tears overflow and I close my eyes, dreading whatever apology he's about to whisper.

'I understand why you were scared,' he breathes, 'but it is okay. I like you too.' He doesn't understand. I'm about to push away from him and scream but he's perfect and holds me there, hands meeting behind my neck. 'I would not have been brave enough a month ago.'

What?

I squint at him, spilling more tears, and wait. We make eye contact and it must scare him, because he reaches up to kiss my forehead. It's slow, like he thinks it's going to be the last time.

He whispers to the air above me, begging some higher power to make this hurt less. 'You *did* say you would date a man. As soon as you said that I regretted going away. And then you slept with Lilley, and you were so upset with Peter. I was so worried. Peter knows.'

I blink. 'Peter knows what?' Mercifully, I don't sound

quite as feeble as I feel.

He shakes his head.

'Dan?'

'He knows I love you,' he sighs, like he's been keeping it a secret all his life. 'He knows I adore you but I was too scared to say anything. I told him while I was away.'

'You—what?'

He isn't breathing. I don't think I am. 'I've been saying that I could not have a relationship yet. I could if it were with you.'

I shake my head and sit back, breaking out of his hands. He's looking at the ceiling, trying desperately to keep the tears in his eyes, and I don't think. I don't think about next week's exams, or the mountain I still have to climb to finish my degree. I don't think about his past, or the nightmares he still has, or the conversation I'm going to have to have with my family.

I kiss him.

This time, it's on the lips. This time, it's on purpose.

Monday

'Are you ready?'

Definitely not. We've told my friends to meet us upstairs at tonight's LGBT social, and I'm ninety-percent certain they know what we want to tell them. Somehow, knowing they'll guess what's happening is making everything more difficult.

Dan drops his hand from my bedroom door-handle and tries again. 'We could just message them.'

'No,' I say, putting my stack of flashcards down again on my desk. 'I need to tell them properly. I owe it to them.'

'You don't owe anything to anyone.'

I look up at him, wishing I could believe that.

Dan frowns even deeper, restless hands pulling at the cuffs of his jacket. I'm not the only nervous one. 'I'm not letting you do this unless you want to.'

'I want to do it,' I say, more to myself than to him. I stand up, discover with some great relief that my legs are still capable of bearing my weight, and stagger across my room to stand beside him. 'I think having the whole day to think about it has made me more nervous than I need to be.'

'Lilley already knows,' Dan reminds me, touching my chin with his thumb. 'Peter knows how I feel and will have guessed about us.'

'But I haven't actually told any of them about *us*.'

Dan sighs and leans down to kiss the tip of my nose. My eyelids flutter, as if he hasn't done this several times since Friday, and I grin.

'Let's go and tell my friends.'

*

For once, I think the walk from my block to the SU could do

with being longer. We take our time over each step, walking hand in hand with cigarette smoke swirling around us, and my thoughts keep drifting from *what am I going to say* and through the last three days.

At first, it was like nothing changed.

We went to bed together on Friday night like we always do: oblivious to the idea of *personal space* and finding it far too easy to wrap around each other. This time, though, I rested my arm across his shoulders without any guilt. This time, I kissed him before falling asleep.

It wasn't until Saturday morning that I realised I hadn't actually told him I love him. So, naturally, I blurted it as soon as the thought crossed my mind—which was the instant I opened my eyes.

Dan's been looking at me with the same stunned expression ever since.

We hesitate outside the SU while he finishes this latest cigarette and my nervousness must be getting to me because I fail to hide the way I sneer at the stub.

'I know,' he sighs, releasing a final lungful of smoke into the evening air. 'I'll quit.'

I blanch. 'What?'

'It will be difficult, but—'

'You'll quit smoking?'

With a little grimace, he nods.

I didn't dare let myself hope for this. We talked about it on New Year's Day, but I thought that was the end of the conversation; he's been addicted for too long. Maybe I underestimated him.

While I'm staring up at him, wondering how to react, Dan makes a decision. The hand I'm not clinging to slides into his pocket, grabs the silver box of cigarettes, and tosses it swiftly into the bin.

I leap at him.

I throw my arm around his neck, stretching up on my tiptoes to reach, and hold him so tightly one of us might stop breathing. He barely stumbles under my weight and frees his hand from mine, so he can wrap both arms around my back.

'I'm so proud of you,' I say, voice heavy with the threat of tears. 'I know it's gonna be hard, but you've already done so well—'

'I haven't started yet,' he points out.

'I mean with everything else.'

Dan kisses my hair. Like every time before, it sends a flutter of butterflies through my stomach and I squeeze my eyes shut, wanting this feeling to last forever.

'I love you,' he whispers, like saying it too loudly is dangerous. 'I don't want to keep doing it around you, and I don't want to get ill. I know you worry.'

'I do,' I admit, taking a deep breath through his jumper. Is this the last time he'll smell of smoke? 'Thank you. I—I love you.'

Even though he's known for months, I feel a rush of embarrassment every time I admit to having more than friendly feelings towards him. Even though we've spent eight nights in a row together since he got back from New Zealand. Even though we're about to tell my friends we're in a relationship.

I slide down from his shoulder and tip my head back so I can gaze up at him. He's wearing that patiently bemused expression again, eyes soft and dry lips in a little smile.

It would be easy to keep stalling. For instance, I could stretch up again to kiss him. I could start talking about nicotine replacement therapies. I could start crying because I'm just so damn proud of him.

Fortunately, or unfortunately, he sees all these possibilities cross my mind and beats me to it. He kisses me, grazing his lips across mine for the briefest moment, and takes my hand again.

'Let's go inside.'

Walking into the Students' Union has never been so difficult. By the time we're through the sliding doors, my hand's sweating in Dan's and he makes us stop again.

'Are you sure you're ready?' he whispers, glancing around us to make sure no one's listening. There are a couple of people eating late, but no one we recognise. No one's going to look at us twice. 'You don't have to tell anyone.'

I nod, resolute. 'I can't go another day without telling them you're my boyfriend.'

Boyfriend.

He looks like he likes the sound of that. He squeezes my hand and lets me lead us through the ground floor of the SU, to the stairs. I've never realised how steep they are before now. I climb one, two, three steps before tripping over my feet and nearly crashing onto my face.

Dan's reflexes are so sharp he catches me before I've even had chance to gasp in fear.

'Do not fall now,' he mutters, keeping his arms around me until we reach the safe flat surface of the first-floor landing. 'Oh, God.'

I think he's picked that up from me.

I smile up at him, even though there's a fifty-fifty chance I'm going to throw up from nerves, and lead us through the heavy doors into the social. It's quieter than usual, because so many people are busy with exam revision, and I wonder if we could have possibly chosen a less subtle way of doing this.

I see Peter straight away and my blushing cheeks must be like hazard lights because he's on his feet before Daniel's even though the door. Sitting opposite him and Anthony at one of the booths are Cassie and Lilley, and time pauses for a few heartbeats while I register the way Lilley's arm is thrown casually across Cassie's shoulders. I notice the way they're angled towards each other, almost on each other's laps, and I feel a hot rush of pride fill my chest.

The room falls silent.

I think the world is about to change.

Doing my best to pretend I haven't noticed the twenty pairs of eyes burning into mine and Dan's joined hands, I dodge puddles of spilled drinks and cross the wooden floor to my friends. There are two chairs waiting for us and by the time we've sat in them the room's gone back to a gentle hum.

I think Cassie and I are blushing as badly as each other. Anthony tugs Peter's shirt, reminding him to sit back down.

'So,' Lilley says, smirking at me past Cassie. 'Why are we all here?'

'Have a guess,' I laugh, glancing at Dan through the corner of my eye. I worried he'd be tense—bowing his head, holding his breath—but he's doing everything in his power to stop himself from grinning. His ankles are crossed and he's relaxed, twisted a little so he can cradle my hand between both of his. His confidence gives me a zap of energy, like a spoon of honey, and I blurt it out. 'Dan and I are dating.'

Cassie looks like she's about to cheer, but Peter beats her to it.

'About time,' he mutters, kicking me sideways under the table. I think I expected shouting, or fireworks, but my friends just grin at me. 'Since when?'

That's a fair question.

'Friday,' Dan says, giving my hand a squeeze before letting go. He drapes his left arm across my shoulders, like we so often sit when it's just us, and his confidence after everything makes it difficult to hold back tears.

I catch Cassie's eye and we both grin, aware we match.

'Dan,' Anthony says from the corner, 'I'm so sorry about everything.'

Some of the softness leaves Dan's face as he shakes his head. 'Don't worry,' he says. 'We are all okay now.'

I'm inclined to agree.

I settle down under Dan's arm with my head on his shoulder and keep grinning at Cassie, waiting for her to explain the bright lipstick mark I've just noticed on the side of her neck.

She blushes so much I'm sure Lilley feels the temperature change.

'We hung out Friday evening,' Cassie whispers, doe eyes huge. 'So now I'm dating your ex. Is that okay?'

I laugh and stretch across Dan to lightly bump her arm with my fist. 'Of course it's okay, stupid. You be nice to her though, Lil. Alright?'

Lilley winks at me and kisses the back of Cassie's hair. They suit each other: Lilley in her standard all-black and Cassie in pastel pinks and blues. They're like complimentary seasons. Seeing them like this after the tension of last semester makes

323

something like peace fall across my chest, and I glance up at Dan to make sure he's happy, too.

Quick as a flash, he winks and kisses me.

I lean into him, stretching up to keep our lips together when he first pulls back, and catch handfuls of his shirt. He tastes of smoke. Peter whistles, embarrassing me enough to make me stop, but Dan is all I can see. Even when we pull away from each other. Even when I sit back in my seat, pulse thundering in my ears and lips tingling with electricity.

I think we suit each other, too.

This book has been written and rewritten more times than I can count. I've spent the last seven years with Will and Dan, trying their voices in different settings and working out exactly what their story is. It was always about recovery and it was always a love-letter to someone who believed they were unworthy of love. Sometimes, I wrote from Dan's perspective. Sometimes, Will and Lilley had a child. Sometimes, Dan was an internationally feared assassin and Will was the exasperated nurse—or doctor—or IT guy who had to keep him out of danger.

Always, I was lucky to have the most supportive friends and family. The friendships I made way back in school have stuck with me through puberty and into adulthood, while we've stumbled over words like bisexual and queer and graduate.

There are too many of you to thank by name.

   -The friends I've known and loved since primary school. You are like sisters to me, but you know that already.

   -The friends I've known and loved since high school and sixth form. I think back to those days sat in the quad, or beneath the sixth form centre, and I can't help but smile. We've grown so far.

-*The friends I've known and loved since university. Studying Geology and Physical Geography at Keele quite obviously changed my life, and my time there was what it was because of you lot. As we blunder forward through adulthood, I think back to those evenings in the Sneyd and I miss you all so much. The friends I met at Southampton, too, who watched over their coffees and hot chocolate as I frantically typed up edits between lectures.*

-*The Keele University LGBT+ Society Committee, 2016-2017. With you was the safest and boldest I've ever felt. I treasure every meeting—especially the ones where I was trying to write up my dissertation but refused to miss a social. Your encouragement and support gave me the push I needed to write Not Quite Out. Will could do with a committee like you. We all could.*

-*The Writing Community on Twitter, who gave me the confidence to share my writing with the world and have shown genuine excitement for Will and Dan since I started tweeting about them in 2018. You're a bunch of legends.*

-*SRL Publishing, for liking my pitch during a #pitmad event, loving Not Quite Out (typos and all), and enthusiastically working with me on this—even during the worrying early days of lockdown. It's a difficult time to bring a book into the world, and I'm so grateful to be working with you.*

-*My partner, who has given me unwavering support since the word go. Your patience with me while I ramble my way through plot-holes, and encouragement when I talk myself into nearly giving*

-up, has kept this book alive. I'm proud of you for everything you do.

-A whole legacy of pets, but specifically Dot and Bella for all their typing advice.

-My family, who have filled my world with books and notebooks since before I could read. I think loving books is genetic, because not one of you ever questioned the ever-growing mound of books in my room, or the hours and hours I spent hunched over my laptop.

Finally, I'd like to leave a quick note to you, the reader. *Not Quite Out* exists because the whole concept of coming out is weird and messy and painful and, honestly, it's a different experience for everyone. That's okay. Give yourself time.

This book would not exist without all of you.

ABOUT THE AUTHOR

Louise Willingham is an environmental scientist and writer whose interests vary from Pre-Raphaelite art to going to rock and metal concerts. While studying for her BSc at Keele University, she was a regular at the village pub quiz and a vocal member of the LGBT+ society committee. *Not Quite Out* is her debut novel.

Stay up to date with her writing news on her Twitter account (lw_writes), Instagram (lw.writes) and website (louisewillingham.wordpress.com).

CPSIA information can be obtained
at www.ICGtesting.com
Printed in the USA
LVHW041742260121
677549LV00015B/2853